# Sarti

Ivana L. Truglio is a book lover. She always has been! Ivana made up her mind to be a writer when she was six years old and never looked back.

Through the years of learning to fly, studying archaeology and ancient history, and finally working in office jobs, she never stopped reading and writing. For 11 years, she worked for multinational publishing companies in the tax team (don't hold that against her!) and learned all the tricks of the trade to start her own publishing company.

Contact Ivana
linktr.ee/ivanaltruglioauthor
Facebook: @ivanatruglio
Instagram: @ivanaltruglioauthor

Also by Ivana L. Truglio

The Paradise Series
*Rilla*
*Illaria*
*Crystal Dragons*
*Child of Paradise*

*Kora's Choice*

The Guild Series
*Inventrici*

# Sarti

## Guild Series

## Ivana L. Truglio

JONQUIL
PRESS

First published in Australia in 2023
by Jonquil Press
ABN: 99871403756

A catalogue record for this
book is available from the
National Library of Australia

NATIONAL
LIBRARY
OF AUSTRALIA

ISBN: 978-0-6483416-6-6 (paperback)

Cover illustration by Jane Green

Typeset in Adobe Garamond Pro 10pt/11.5pt

*For all the seamstresses in my life.*

# ACKNOWLEDGEMENTS

Writing acknowledgements is difficult! There are so many people that help in various ways. My readers, of course, inspire me to keep writing with their constant enthusiasm for my books.

The amazing writing community on Discord, most notably Zola Hobbit, HyperCaz, Dom The Wicked Captain, Tori J. and Jane Bennet. From beta-reading to providing wise (and sometimes unwise) suggestions and encouragement, I cannot thank you enough.

Thank you to my brilliant editor, Anicee Dowling. Without her sharp eyes and crafty ways, this book would have a myriad of inconsistencies. Thankfully, she didn't want to throttle the characters in this book nearly so much as the previous one!

A special shout out to the wonderful women who tried (and failed) to teach me the ways of a seamstress – Aurelia Pirillo, Marisa Truglio, Grazia Balzarano, Connie Ferlazzo. All of you left your mark on this book, whether you physically helped me with a section of it or not.

As always, thank you to my family. I spent a great deal of the dreaded lockdown writing this book. You gave me space to do it and didn't complain when I hid myself away from you for hours at a time.

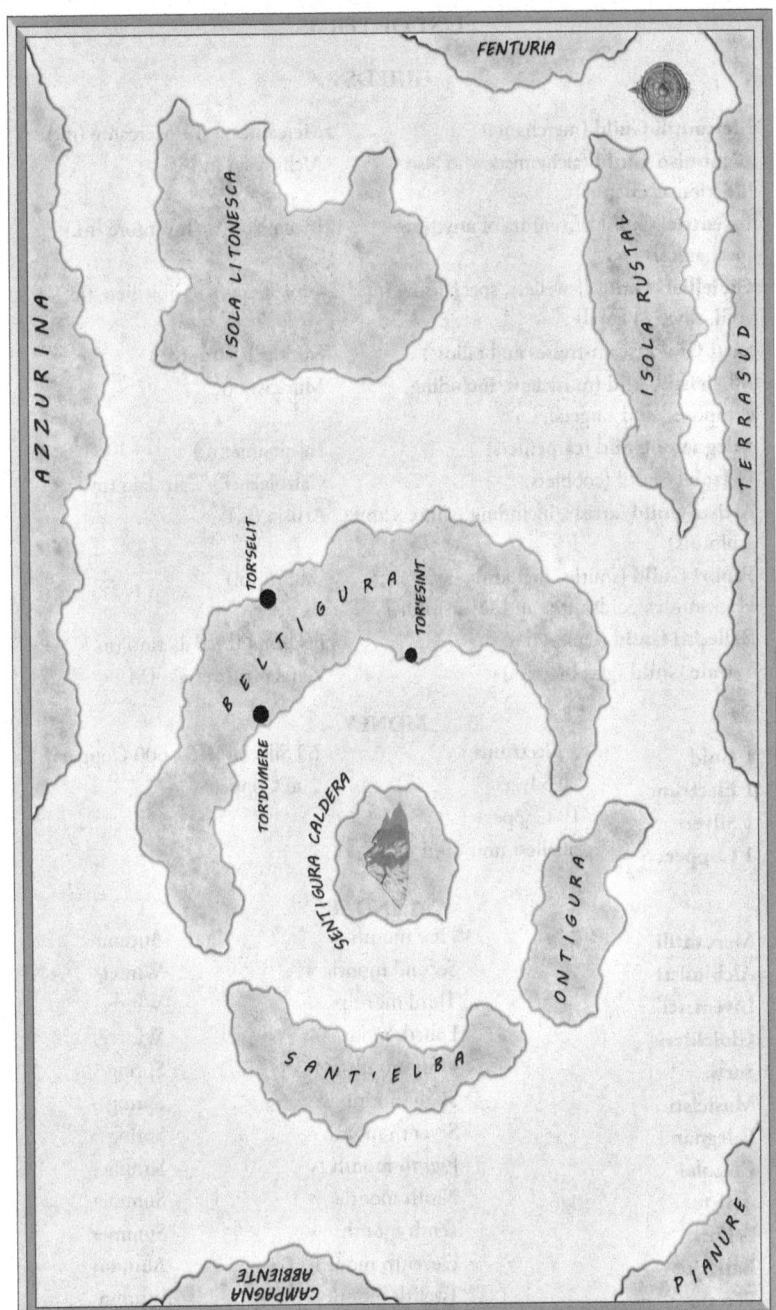

# LIST OF TERMS

## GUILDS

**Mercantili Guild** (merchants) — Mercantessa (f.)/Mercante (m.)

**Alchimisti Guild** (alchemists who also function as doctors) — Alchimista (n.)

**Inventrici Guild** (inventors of anything mechanical) — Inventrice (f.)/Inventore (m.)

**Gioiellieri Guild** (jewellers, specialising in gold, silver or coral) — Gioielliera (f.)/Gioielliere (m.)

**Sarti Guild** (seamstresses and tailors) — Sarta (f.)/Sarto (m.)

**Musicisti Guild** (musicians, including composers and singers) — Musicista (n.)

**Falegnami Guild** (carpenters) — Falegname (n.)

**Calzolai Guild** (cobblers) — Calzolaia (f.)/Calzolaio (m.)

**Artiste Guild** (artists, including painters and sculptors) — Artista (n.)

**Fabbri Guild** (smiths, including blacksmiths, goldsmiths and silversmiths) — Fabbro (n.)

**Ballerini Guild** (dancers) — Ballerina (f.)/Ballerino (m.)

**Vetraie Guild** (glassblowers) — Vetraia (f.)/Vetraio (M.)

## MONEY

| | | | |
|---|---|---|---|
| **1 Gold** | 3 Electrums | 60 Silvers | 600 Coppers |
| **1 Electrum** | 20 Silvers | 200 Coppers | |
| **1 Silver** | 10 Coppers | | |
| **1 Copper** | smallest unit of money | | |

## CALENDAR

| | | |
|---|---|---|
| **Mercantili** | First month | Autumn |
| **Alchimisti** | Second month | Winter |
| **Inventrici** | Third month | Winter |
| **Gioiellieri** | Fourth month | Winter |
| **Sarti** | Fifth month | Spring |
| **Musicisti** | Sixth month | Spring |
| **Falegnami** | Seventh month | Spring |
| **Calzolai** | Eighth month | Summer |
| **Artiste** | Ninth month | Summer |
| **Fabbri** | Tenth month | Summer |
| **Ballerini** | Eleventh month | Autumn |
| **Vetraie** | Twelfth month | Autumn |

## DAYS OF THE WEEK

| | |
|---|---|
| **Gildadi** | Trading Day (Guild Day) |
| **Ramedi** | Trading Day (Copper Day) |
| **Argentodi** | Trading Day (Silver Day) |
| **Legaramedi** | Trading Day (Electrum Day) |
| **Orodi** | Trading Day (Gold Day) |
| **Mercatodi** | Market day, every second week for Guilds, every other week for regular vendors |
| **Riposidi** | Rest day |

## GLOSSARY

| | |
|---|---|
| **Amministratore (m.)/Amministratrice (f.)/ Amministratori (pl.)** | administrators |
| **Amore** | love |
| **Companion** | life partners who have had a commitment ceremony |
| **Coppola** | flat hat |
| **Corallo** | coral |
| **Corso** | course |
| **Funicolare** | cablecar |
| **Limoncello** | lemon liqueur |
| **Maestra (f.)/Maestro (m.)** | Guild Mistress/Master |
| **Mamma** | mum |
| **Marinaia (f.)/Marinaio (m.)/Marinai (pl.)** | sailors |
| **Miglio/Miglia** | mile/miles |
| **Nipotina** | granddaughter |
| **Nonna (f.)/Nonno (m.)** | grandmother/grandfather |
| **Panettiere** | baker |
| **Pasticceria/Pasticcerie** | pastry shop/s |
| **Papà** | dad |
| **Piazza** | square |
| **Piede/Piedi** | foot/feet |
| **Pollice/Pollici** | inch/inches |
| **Ristorante** | restaurant |
| **Signora/Signore** | miss/mister |
| **Tesoro** | treasure |
| **Trinzale and lenza** | decorative headwear |
| **Vecchietta (f.)/Vecchietto (m.)/Vecchietti (pl.)** | old people |
| **Via** | street |
| **Zona** | zone |

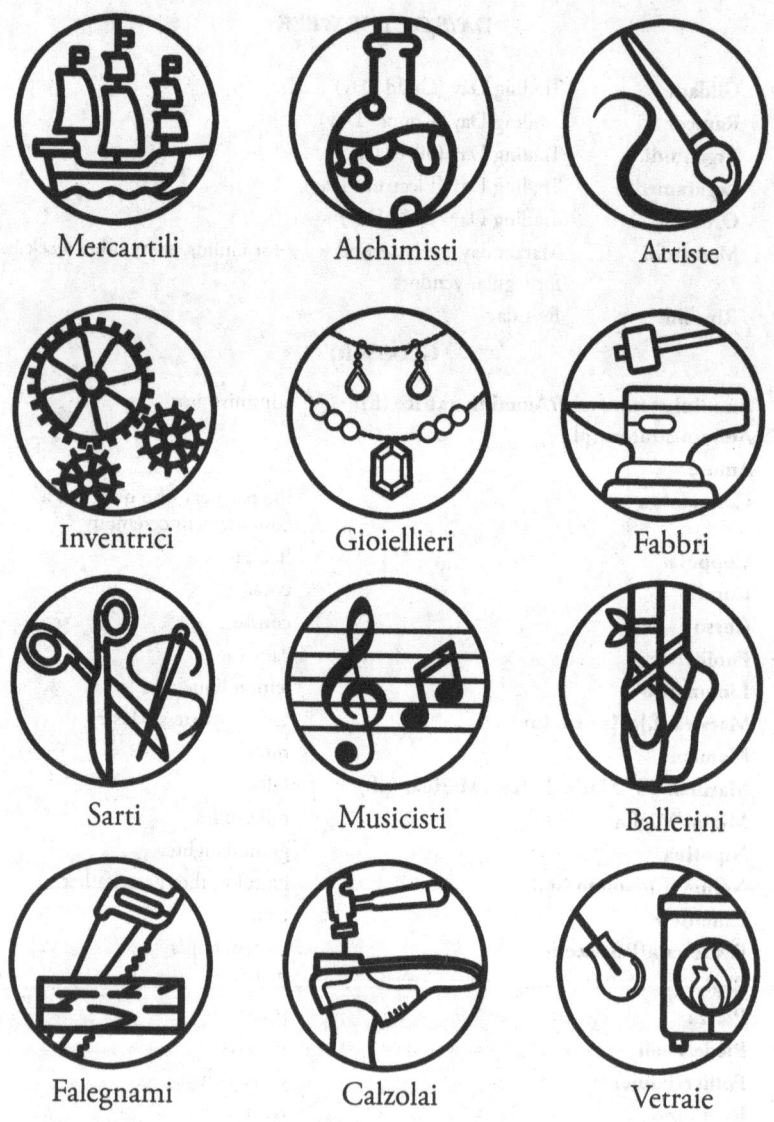

Mercantili

Alchimisti

Artiste

Inventrici

Gioiellieri

Fabbri

Sarti

Musicisti

Ballerini

Falegnami

Calzolai

Vetraie

Author's note: For the sake of having a single version for each Guild name, I alternated between the feminine and masculine for those that weren't gender neutral, completely understanding that this is not how the Italian language works.

# Chapter 1 – Orodi 20 Alchimisti 230 Years After Implosion

Greta clasped her hands together, resisting the urge to smooth down her work dress and reveal her frustration.

"Signora Loyola, you must understand that the type of material you have requested is not readily available in Tor'Esint. Had you given me more notice, I could have sourced it for you. As it is, I'll find you the next best thing."

"I've given you all the notice I had." Signora Loyola drew herself up to her full height. It wasn't that she was particularly tall, but the elegance with which she carried herself made her appear to tower over others. Greta hated it when people did that. She knew it was intended to intimidate and, if it was done in connection with anything other than her work as a Sarta, it might have affected her.

"Be that as it may, I simply cannot source such a fine blue silk and still have time to sew your dress in less than three weeks. You will either need to make do with the material I have in stock or give me time to find something more to your liking somewhere in Tor'Esint."

Signora Loyola narrowed her dark brown eyes. "At that point, I may as well take my business to whoever has the finest material today."

Greta clenched her hands tighter and returned a brief, insincere smile to the arrogant woman. "You *could* do that, Signora, but had you wanted a substandard Sarta, you wouldn't have come to me in the first place. You know I am the finest Sarta in Tor'Esint."

Signora Loyola hesitated. Her lips twitched as she looked around the workshop trying to gauge if Greta really was as good as she claimed.

"Three weeks, then. That's plenty of time for you to source material and sew my dress. I want a shimmering blue, but nothing ostentatious. You could use that new material I've heard so much about – the one I heard Ranieri Sarto's using these days. Something to make my guests envious and adoring at the same time. I shall, of course, direct them all to you for their new gowns if they are suitably impressed."

"Of course, Signora," Greta replied smoothly.

Word of mouth was how she came by most of her business. A recommendation from Signora Loyola would ensure she had orders right up until the annual Guild Ball. On the other hand, if her client was less than impressed, she would make certain that Greta's business dried up almost overnight. Of course, she would still have her regular, less wealthy clients, but she could not survive on those alone. There were too many Sarti on a lower Guild Mark who would charge customers a cheaper price than Greta was willing to.

"I will find a striking material for you. Now if you'll please step this way, I'll take your measurements."

As Signora Loyola stepped behind the curtain of the dressing room, Greta signalled to Sofia, her youngest apprentice, to look after the shop. Sofia dutifully walked around the shopfront, tidying away thread-cards and material samples as she went.

Greta waited until Signora Loyola started tapping her foot impatiently before walking behind the curtain with a measuring tape, pencil and her order pad.

"Is this the corset you'll be wearing with the dress?"

Signora Loyola shrugged. "I haven't decided yet."

Greta sighed. If only her customers could have some forethought before coming in to order a dress. Taking her measurements twice, once with the corset tightened and one with it loosened, Greta wrote them down against the outline of a mannequin on her order pad.

"Now, as to the cost," Greta said as her client redressed herself.

"Three electrums."

"That may do for the material, yes," Greta agreed, struggling to keep the irritation from her tone. "I require another eight electrums for my services."

"Eleven electrums! Are you quite mad? Six Electrums, that's my final offer." Signora Loyola tilted her chin up sharply.

Greta raised an eyebrow. "If Signora would care to remember that there is a *Gold* Guild Mark on the door, it would go some way to explain the price. *One* gold for my speedy services to ensure you have a magnificent evening gown is quite reasonable. Another *two* for the trouble and expense it will take to purchase your particularly luxurious choice of materials is the least you should be affording me."

"Three gold then," Signora Loyola said through gritted teeth. "But this had better be the most amazing gown anyone in Tor'Esint has ever seen."

Greta smiled. "Of course, Signora. That's why you came to me. I *only* create amazing gowns. Come back on Gildadi for a fitting. If you could wear the corset you intend to use with this dress, that would help. Or bring a selection along so we can see which works best."

The pompous signora lifted her chin, turned on her heels and left the workshop, setting her feathered hat on her head with a flourish. Greta waited until she had disappeared from view before letting out a long breath. She put her notebook on a table with a sigh and flexed her fingers before smoothing down her dress.

"Sofia, be a dear and fetch Annika and Marta for me."

Greta almost missed the flicker of annoyance on Sofia's face – almost. She'd have to do something about the infighting among her apprentices. It was becoming more overt. She would need to deal with it before it disrupted her business.

It was her own fault for taking on too many apprentices too quickly – she had heard the whispered comments behind her back. But the excitement of quickly rising through her Guild Marks and being allowed *three* apprentices had been too great at the time.

Annika had just barely been with her a year before Marta came along. And then later that same year, Sofia had joined them. Greta couldn't honestly say that she regretted her decision taking them all on, but she regretted the way she'd made Marta, and then Sofia stay behind at the store on every client visit she made. Things needed to change but Greta had an important commission to begin straight away.

"You asked for me?" Annika asked haughtily as she shouldered her way past Sofia and Marta. Greta caught Sofia's eye roll and shook her head in admonishment.

"I'm going out, possibly for the entire afternoon, to source some material. You're in charge while I'm gone. Don't take any commissions for completion this week. Signora Loyola's gown will take all my attention. If any repairs come in, you can begin on them yourself – give the easier ones to Sofia. Marta will help you when we return."

"Yes, Maestra." Annika nodded.

"Very well, then. Marta, you're coming with me." Greta turned to go but looked back at her apprentices. "Girls, I expect you not to embarrass me while I'm out."

It was, possibly, a cruel thing to say. The girls never purposely did anything to embarrass her but leaving Annika in charge never sat right with Greta. Annika was the oldest apprentice, but she revelled in the position and would likely make Sofia do more than her fair share when Greta wasn't around. Much as Greta wished to, she couldn't very well leave a third-year apprentice in charge of a fifth-year.

A brisk stroll around Zona Sarti with Marta in tow confirmed that the kind of material Signora Loyola had requested simply wasn't available, but Greta had to at least have looked before resorting to other measures.

It was unfortunate that Signora Loyola was so firm on her decision. *Shimmering* blue meant it would have to be satin or silk. The silk shipments had been few and far between lately. Not everyone was happy to broker deals through the Mercantili Guild, which made it difficult to find the variety of cloth the Sarti Guild had been accustomed to before the Trading Edict.

Greta had her own contacts in Tor'Selit who could sometimes be of assistance. They didn't have any bans there, but the Guilds in other cities were finding it increasingly difficult to trade directly with Guilds in Tor'Esint. The main advantage other cities on Beltigura had was that they could still trade freely with Isola Litonesca and Isola Rustal.

Isola Rustal was known for its roaring silk trade. Greta had made a contact there years ago, but it had been too dangerous to import anything directly since the Trading Ban. The Mercantili Guild had set guards up and down the docks, checking all incoming and outgoing boats to make sure they had the correct paperwork. More recently, they'd created a blockade around Tor'Esint. Any privately imported goods were confiscated by the Mercantili Guild and kept until a tariff was paid. Any outgoing goods were not confiscated but the private ships were charged an exorbitant fee by the Mercantili Guild before being allowed to leave the docks.

It wasn't much better trading inland, but at least if you had a blazermobile, you wouldn't be checked going in and out of the city – there simply weren't enough Amministratori to police every route. People travelling via the funicolare were not so fortunate.

Greta didn't own a blazermobile herself. Even though she had her Gold Guild Mark, it was still prohibitively expensive to purchase one. She knew her friend, Aveline Inventrice, had only managed to afford the conversion because she worked closely with the Alchimisti. *Used to work* closely with them, Greta reminded herself. The Amministratori were getting more efficient at finding people who were breaking the ban. Every action was scrutinised.

Walking back along Via Mercato without any success finding the material she needed, Greta knew she'd have to take Marta with her all the way to the other side of town to her fabric warehouse. Even there she mightn't find the material she was after in the specific colour Signora Loyola required.

The wind blew furiously, whipping her skirts around her legs. Even with a hatpin, Greta had to hold onto her hat to keep it from blowing away. Poor Marta's loose hair was getting terribly knotted as it flew across her face.

"I'm *not* walking across town in this weather," Greta muttered under her breath.

Struggling through Piazza Mercantile, she led Marta to Aveline's workshop. It had been more than two weeks since the Inventrice had returned from her sudden trip, but Greta hadn't managed to see her yet. If she didn't know better, she'd have thought Aveline avoiding her. Well, Greta wasn't going to let that hold her back.

She walked up the stairs to Aveline's workshop and pushed the door open. A sudden gust of wind snatched the door out of her hand and flung it violently against the wall. Aveline's apprentice – was his name Nevio? – rushed to close the door.

"Good morning, Signora Sarta," he greeted her with a smile that grew even bigger when he saw her apprentice. "Good morning, Marta."

Greta returned the smile warily, watching Marta's coy glance. She had more than an inkling that Nevio had a crush on her middle apprentice and didn't want to encourage the boy. They were both still quite young and years away from finishing their apprenticeships.

"Good morning, Nevio," she replied, smoothing down her dress and removing her hat. "Is Aveline around? I need to beg a favour."

"Upstairs, Greta."

Greta looked around until she saw a metal funnel hanging over Nevio's workbench. Aveline's voice floated out of it.

"I suppose I'll just go upstairs then," she said to the apprentice who nodded, his eyes never leaving Marta. Greta saw the young girl blush at his obvious attention to her. "Marta, stay here and try not to distract Nevio."

"Yes, Maestra," Marta replied, without taking her eyes off Nevio.

Greta sighed and showed herself through the curtain concealing the rest of the ground level. She'd been here often enough to know the stairs were just beyond it. Why Aveline was asking her upstairs at this time of day was beyond her. The Inventrice should have been hard at work in her workshop by now.

Greta lifted her skirts to ascend the narrow staircase. Like most of the Guild houses in Tor'Esint, Aveline's house was a two-storey building with the living quarters above the workshop. It worked well in such a Guild-centric town, but Greta hated all the narrow stairs.

Out on the landing, Greta looked from side to side, trying to find Aveline. "Where are you?" she called out.

Aveline did not answer, but Greta heard retching and hurried to the water closet.

"Aveline? Are you ill?" she called through the closed door.

Aveline whimpered. Greta waited in concern. There was the sound of running water. The door opened and a pale faced Aveline stepped into the hall. Greta peered at her closely.

"You don't look at all well."

"I'm fine," Aveline answered weakly.

Greta crossed her arms. "People who are *fine* do not heave up the contents of their stomach. What in Caldera's smoke is wrong with you?"

"I didn't vomit." Aveline grimaced. "I tried, but nothing came out. I've not been feeling well lately."

Greta stared at her long and hard. "Did you catch something on the Caldera?"

"No. *This*," she said, gesturing to herself, "is more recent."

"Have you told your Alchimista?" Greta persisted. "Do you use Lucrezia?"

Aveline shook her head. "I haven't had time."

Greta frowned. "You haven't had time for a *lot* of things since your return."

"Reta, really, I don't have the energy for this," Aveline said in an oddly subdued voice. "What do you need?"

"Uh..." Greta faltered. Aveline was not usually so quiet, or irritable. "I wanted to borrow your blazermobile. But this may not be the best time for you."

Aveline headed to the stairs. "It's fine. You can drive it this time. I'd come with you, but I'm going to start falling behind with my work if I spend any more time out of the workshop. What with the extra..."

Greta waited for her to continue, but Aveline shook her head.

"Just make sure you return it in one piece. I'll be needing it later this afternoon."

"Yes, of course. I'll only need it for an hour or two and will take good care of it."

Aveline forced a smile and nodded. Greta wished she had time to stay with her today, but Signora Loyola's dress was complicated and would require all of her attention. But she'd need to make time for her friend – at the very least to make sure Aveline saw an Alchimista.

*** 

"Iiiaaahh!"

"Marta, for Caldera's sake, be quiet!"

Marta squealed as the blazermobile swung around every corner. It was grating on Greta's nerves. She'd never have brought the girl along if she could carry the cloth by herself. But those bolts of fabric were heavy!

Eventually, they arrived in the warehouse district and Greta pulled up in front of the one she rented from the Sarti Guild. All Guilds had warehouses on the outskirts of town. They rented them out to Guild members whose workshops could not house all the items they needed. She, along with other Guild members, trusted their Guilds to be discreet about the contents stored in the warehouses. If the Mercantili Guild were to find out about all the trade going on behind their backs, it would cause a big smoking mess.

By the time Greta had unlocked the door to her warehouse, Marta was just getting out of the blazermobile on shaky legs.

"Hurry along, Marta. I don't have all day!"

She could see Marta doing her best to walk, though the girl was unsteady on her feet.

"Sorry, Maestra," Marta mumbled. "I'm not used to these blazermobiles. They scare the smoke out of me."

Greta raised an eyebrow at the expletive but said nothing as she ushered the girl into her warehouse. She closed the door quickly behind them, not wanting watchful eyes to glimpse what she had in storage.

Grappling in the dark, she found the rope on the side of the door and pulled down. The blinds covering the high windows rose to flood the warehouse with sunlight.

"There's even more here than last time," Marta gasped, hands covering her mouth.

Greta nodded with a satisfied smile. The bans had made things more difficult but, so far, Greta was still managing to conduct covert negotiations with her own sources. It meant she could charge exorbitant fees for material that she was stockpiling more cheaply in large quantities. Of course, she couldn't use it on every order or sell it to others in the Sarti Guild or questions would be asked. But this dress was an exception.

Signora Loyola was extremely influential. Though not a Guild member herself, her parents had made quite a handsome living in the Gioielliere Guild. She was now one of the major landholders in Tor'Esint and would never have to work a day in her life.

For a recommendation from a person like that, Greta would bend her own rules. Usually, she would feign more extreme difficulties in getting the material – invent trading delays and expenses – giving herself more time to complete an order. But not this time.

"The silk, Maestra?"

Greta shook her head. "No. That will raise too many questions. I think a fine satin will do nicely. Search those bolts for a nice blue. I need to see if I have any organza left."

Greta always met her suppliers here. It was easier to be discreet if you were the only party involved. It had the added advantage that she could organise the unpacking of crates so that her materials stayed in order.

Her cottons and wools were along shelves in the middle of the room, blocking the view to the more expensive satins and silks along the back wall. There was a section with sheer fabrics, mostly tulle and organza. The tulle was stiff enough for petticoats and dancers' tutus. The organza was a soft and smooth type of silk for more elegant ware. There were ribbons in bulk, a section with specific materials set aside for corsets, and hoops in assorted sizes for wide skirts.

Sorting through the sheer materials, Greta's caught sight of a gorgeous pale blue organza. She pulled out the half-sized bolt and sighed at the feel of it – so luxuriously soft!

"Have you found anything?" Greta called out to Marta.

"I think so," Marta replied from behind a shelf. "But it's too heavy for me to lift."

Greta navigated her way around to the satins. Marta had her hand on a tall navy bolt. It wasn't the colour Greta had in mind, but it would go quite nicely with her lighter shade of blue. She put the organza up against it and smiled. It was a perfect combination.

Marta looked at her in confusion.

"How are you going to use the two of these together?"

"Just wait and see!" Greta grinned at her. "Now help me bring it over to the cutting table."

Together, they struggled to lift the navy satin bolt from its place. Careful not to let it drag across the floor, Greta directed Marta's movements until they'd reached the long wooden cutting table. It was identical to the one in her workshop. On the long edge was a measuring stick so she could measure out the material before cutting it and on the short edge was a groove for her scissors to glide down.

Greta measured out seventeen piedi of the satin and cut it carefully. It was likely to be an excessive amount, but it would afford extra strips for the laces she would need. Her regular laces would not do for this.

Next, she measured out nine piedi of the organza. She wouldn't need as much and it was the more rare and expensive material. Technically, she shouldn't have any available to her. It had hardly been seen in Tor'Esint before the Trading Ban and was now too expensive to get through the Mercantili Guild. The organza would set this dress apart from all others at the dinner party. As would the style, Greta thought to herself in satisfaction. Ideas were already churning in her mind. All she had to do now was get back to her workshop and draw.

Perhaps if she had enough organza left, she could make a light shawl – not that Signora Loyola deserved it with her haughty manner.

They returned the bolts of material to their places, Marta grunting from the effort. From under the cutting table, Greta pulled out a large sheet of brown butcher's paper. She carefully folded her material and wrapped it in the paper. There was no need to let curious eyes see what they had retrieved from the warehouse.

*** 

Back at home, Greta secluded herself away in the back of her workshop, hidden from view of any customers. She got to work with her pattern book to figure out the best way to use both materials together. Minutes, or perhaps, hours passed. Sofia came in with a cup of tea, but when Greta finally reached out to drink it, the tea was cold.

"Urgh!" she swallowed the sip with a grimace. "Sofia, another cup of tea please!"

She heard Annika's tittering as Sofia walked through to the back of the workshop red-cheeked to take the cold cup away. Greta determined to do something about Annika's inflated opinion of herself as oldest apprentice – Annika would be made to do housework and Greta would finally take Sofia under her wing for a project.

By the time Sofia returned with a hot cup of tea, Greta already had the thin brown pattern paper ready on both cutting tables with a pencil on each. She noticed Sofia's longing glance and smiled.

"It's about time I show you how to do this. I want you to take my measurements and create an identical pattern to this one for me."

Sofia stared at her open-mouthed but did not move. Greta swallowed the rising guilt. She should have been a better Maestra to her apprentices.

"Unless you'd prefer I ask Annika or Marta do it instead?"

Greta hid a smiled as her comment prompted immediate action. Sofia found the order pad, took the measuring tape from her work dress pocket and began her first task.

It was clear that Sofia was less practiced at this than Annika and Marta. Greta had to correct her with every single measurement.

"The length of the arm should be from the tip of the shoulder, not from the neck," Greta corrected Sofia, pointing out the right location.

When she noticed Sofia's cheeks redden while measuring her bust, Greta instructed her again. "Don't be afraid to measure the chest correctly. Every signora would rather the slightest touch of the tape on her breasts with correct measurements than no touch at all and incorrect bust measurements."

Sofia nodded firmly and got on with her measurements in a more confident manner. When she was finally done, Greta compared her measurement sheet for Signora Loyola to her final sketch and wrote down the figures for each part of it. She would make a cotton dress from the pattern and tack it together for the first fitting before she began cutting the actual material. It would avoid great expense should she make any mistakes, especially given that the corset could change the measurements.

It was the way her own Maestro had taught her. Of course, she'd tried things differently when she earned her Copper Guild Mark, but a few costly errors had brought her back to Maestro Ranieri's techniques with burning anger and shame.

Thinking of him brought a sudden well of emotions. Living with him for so long had made him feel like a second father to her. She hadn't visited him properly in months, only managing a wave from across the piazza every week or so on her way to the haberdashery for her latest project. Greta planned on a long visit with him once this dress was finished.

"Now Sofia, I should have taught you this last year. I'm sorry I never seem to have time, but this dress will make the wait worthwhile. If you can manage such a fine evening gown, there's nothing you won't be able to do."

Sofia smiled broadly and walked over to see the sketch Greta held out to her. She took it reverently and looked at it admiringly. But Greta could see the hesitation. By this point in her apprenticeship, Sofia should at least be able to make simple dresses from a pattern. Greta was ashamed to admit she didn't know if the girl was capable of that yet.

"I don't expect you to be able to do it as quickly as me. I've had *years* of practice."

Sofia shook her head. "That's not what I was worried about. Will Signora Loyola wear something so ... revealing?"

Greta's stomach dropped. She held out her hand for the sketch and looked at it again.

"It's not really revealing – the organza will only give it the *appearance* of being revealing."

Sofia shrugged, seemingly unsure of herself. "I just remember what she was wearing yesterday. There wasn't a bare patch of skin aside from her face and hands. Perhaps her arms are horribly disfigured."

Greta stared at Sofia mutely. It was true. She'd never seen Signora Loyola in anything other than very conservative clothing – but while she was pleased Sofia had noticed, it wouldn't change her mind.

"Perhaps I can add sleeves if she complains. I may need more organza for that though. And it certainly won't look as good as this." Greta shook her head determinedly. "No. No sleeves. This is a *magnificent* evening dress the likes of which Tor'Esint has never seen. We'll start a new fashion with Signora Loyola."

Greta refused to acknowledge Sofia's nervous smile. She was confident in her design and her skills to make it work. Signora Loyola hadn't made any request other than "something to make my guests envious and adoring at the same time" and this dress would certainly do that.

# Chapter 2 – Mercatodi 21 Alchimisti 230 Years After Implosion

Greta rubbed her gritty eyes. She'd barely slept. Things hadn't gone as well with Sofia's patternwork as she'd hoped, and Greta had been forced to suspend the girl's work on the dress. She was a third-year apprentice who should have possessed more skill than she currently did. The fault was Greta's alone and she knew it – she was suddenly thankful she hadn't seen Ranieri in a while – she couldn't bear the shame of admitting it to him. Poor Sofia had to settle for watching Greta and fetching things for her the entire afternoon.

There was the sound of shuffling feet at the side of the workshop. Sofia appeared, rugged up in a woollen dressing gown over her nightgown. She stopped in her tracks when Greta sat up.

"I'm sorry, Maestra Greta," she whispered. "I didn't mean to wake you."

Greta shook her head. "No matter. This dress won't make itself and Signora Loyola will be coming in two days for an initial fitting."

"I'm sorry you wasted so much time on me."

The girl hung back near the stairway, eyes to the ground.

Greta sighed. "Sofia, do stop apologising. It's not *your* fault that I didn't teach you well enough in your first few years. When this dress is further along, I'll take the time I should have before to teach you how to draw and cut a pattern. That was remiss of me. But for now, could you fetch me some breakfast? I'm famished. And wake Annika and Marta. They'll need to set up and tend the Mercatodi stall today."

Sofia managed a small smile as she bobbed back towards the kitchen. She returned ten minutes later to fetch Greta.

"I'm not bringing your breakfast out here. I'm too scared we'll ruin your work."

Greta looked at the cut paper pattern and array of materials over her workbench and swallowed her protest. Sofia was right. If she hadn't been so tired, she wouldn't have suggested it herself. She followed Sofia to the kitchen where she was greeted with the sight of thickly sliced bread, boiled eggs, and a strong pot of black tea. Greta noted that Sofia had set out four places, even though Annika and Marta had still not arrived downstairs. She took a slice of the lightly toasted bread and crushed an egg onto it.

"You're getting the hang of the toasting rod," she said between mouthfuls.

Sofia smiled. "I still don't know how twisting the handle a few times makes it so hot, but I'm not going to complain if it means warm bread every day."

Greta watched Sofia as the girl sat across from her and began eating. She wasn't a conventionally pretty girl like Marta who had an oval face, delicate

11

features, and petite bone structure. Sofia had a rather plain, heart-shaped face but she had an infectious dimpled smile. Greta had even seen it work on a doleful Marta when Annika had been teasing her. A broad smile from Sofia would make Marta stop crying long enough to give a short smile back.

But the feature that Greta admired the most was Sofia's thick hair. It was a light brown, streaked through with bright gold. Greta had never seen hair like it before. It truly was striking. Everyone else in the household had chestnut brown hair, just like Greta herself. It was the most common hair colour in the south of Beltigura. Only northerners had lighter hair.

"Sofia, where's your family from?"

Her sudden question startled the girl.

"I can't remember, Maestra. I know I came to Tor'Esint when I was very little because I remember a long, long trip before going to the orphanage."

Greta frowned; she hadn't realised Sofia was an orphan. It wasn't right to know so little about her apprentices. She should have asked everything about them in their first months with her.

"What happened to your parents?"

Sofia stared into her teacup. "They didn't come to Tor'Esint."

"So ... they passed on in your hometown and there wasn't an orphanage there?"

"No, Maestra," Sofia replied in an unusually soft voice. "My parents aren't dead. At least they weren't when I last saw them. The orphanage in Tor'Esint was the only one that would take me while my parents were still alive – that's why they sent me here."

Greta froze with her egg-smeared bread halfway to her mouth.

"Why in Caldera's smoke would they send you away?"

Sofia shrugged. Greta wanted to ask so many more questions, but Sofia's continued silence stopped her. Ranieri had known so much more about her, her family's past. Greta needed that here. She would do better.

"Well, for what it's worth, you're part of *my* family now and I would never send you away."

Sofia nodded but continued to stare mutely into her teacup. Greta took the hint and ate the rest of her breakfast in silence. Annika and Marta arrived as she was finishing and helped themselves to a warm breakfast. Sofia took her own and Greta's dishes to the sink and rolled up her sleeves.

Greta walked over and lay a hand on the girl's shoulder. "Let the others do the dishes today. You and I have work to do. Get dressed and meet me in the workshop."

There was a stifled gasp from Annika, which Greta pointedly ignored. Before Sofia could protest, Greta ushered the girl to the stairs and turned back to Annika and Marta.

"Once you're done here, set up the Mercatodi stall." She held up a hand, forestalling Annika's protests. "Sofia needs her turn to work with me too.

Take repairs that you can manage yourselves. Any orders will only be started after this dress is done."

She followed her own advice to Sofia and headed upstairs to get make herself presentable for the day.

\*\*\*

"Now *this* you can help me with," Greta said, picking up a cut-out piece of the pattern. "We're going to pin it all around the mannequin to make sure it's right before we start to cut."

Sofia regained some of her usual enthusiasm as they worked together on the mannequin. Signora Loyola had larger proportions than the last outfit Greta had made, so she showed Sofia how to expand the mannequin with the turn of some handles until they had the correct measurements. Together, they pinned the brown paper around the mannequin. Greta stepped back when they'd finished and smiled in satisfaction.

"That should do quite nicely."

"It's ... erm ... very brown," Sofia ventured carefully.

Greta laughed. "Oh Sofia, use your imagination! Look at the material over there and picture it here instead of the brown pattern paper. Can't you see it?"

Sofia tilted her head from side to side with a frown. "No."

"Well, I can, and you will too after a bit of practice," Greta reassured her. "Help me undo it now so I can start cutting the material. I'll use cotton for the satin and linen for the organza."

Greta was used to working with Annika and Marta. They knew how she moved around the workshop and when to duck or step back. Things weren't quite so easy with Sofia. It only served to further remind Greta she'd not taken as much care of this apprentice as she should have.

When they were finished, Greta double checked which sections of the pattern should be satin and which should be organza. She carefully placed the pattern pieces on the cotton and linen and set herself up to start cutting.

Once she'd cut the first piece, she handed the pattern paper to Sofia. "You can draw in my dimensions on here or you can keep watching me. It's up to you. I won't mind if you make mistakes."

Sofia hesitantly took the proffered paper and stared at it. Greta turned back to her work once more. She knew from experience with Annika and Marta that apprentices did not like working with their mentors looking over their shoulders. Nervous apprentices made for very bad workers.

By one o'clock, Greta had finished cutting all the material. She peeked over her shoulder to where Sofia sat, head in hands, staring at the paper with pencil marks rubbed out all over it. Greta let out a silent sigh. She wished Sofia felt more comfortable asking for help.

"If you want a break, I'm going out for a walk. The Mercatodi stalls always intrigue me."

Sofia jumped up at the chance and practically ran to the front door. Greta smoothed down her work dress, adjusted her Gold Sarti Guild Mark brooch and joined Sofia, picking up a small basket on the way. She locked the door behind them and walked down the three steps to the street where Annika and Marta were tending the stall just in front of her shop. No one ever dared try to take her spot. It had been hard-won over years of setting up early, so no one else could try to claim it. It was a fortunate position, located along the northern edge of Piazza Mercantile.

"Annika, mind the key to the shop. Sofia and I are going for a walk. If you're lucky, we might even bring the two of you something back."

The look of undisguised disbelief that crossed Annika's face made Greta smile slightly. It was about time she was knocked down a peg or two. Greta took Sofia's arm in her own and guided the girl down towards Aveline's stall. The surprising trend of allowing a fellow Inventore to set up a stall right beside hers two months ago had continued. Greta certainly wouldn't want another Sarta stall beside her own, but then again, Aveline and Telchide specialised in different inventions and likely wouldn't steal business from each other.

At this time of day, Aveline's stall, like many of the Guild stalls, was quiet. However, Greta knew the coffee bars would be bustling. She'd never acquired the taste herself – coffee was too bitter – but it wasn't the only thing they served. Caffè Eleonora had garnered a reputation for the best sfogliatelle in Tor'Esint.

"Aveline, we're going to Caffè Eleonora. Can I bring you back anything?"

Aveline looked up tiredly. Greta noticed Telchide glance at Aveline with a pained expression, but he remained silent and kept working on the pocket watch in front of him.

"Maestra, why don't you take a break? I'll mind the stall for you," Nevio suggested quietly.

"Oh Aveline, *please* can I come with you?" Telchide's young daughter begged, jumping up from the stairs.

"Teresina, what have I told you about imposing yourself on others?" Telchide asked her sternly.

The girl contritely held her hands behind her back and looked up at him, her head lowered.

"I'm sorry, papà, but it's *Aveline*. She won't mind, will you?"

Greta exchanged glances with Sofia. This was most unbecoming behaviour even if Teresina was just a child.

"It's alright Telchide. I don't mind," Aveline replied listlessly. Greta bit her tongue to prevent herself saying how exhausted her friend looked. "Resi, you know the way to Caffè Eleonora. Why don't you walk ahead with Sofia? Choose something nice for everyone and we can sit down to eat if you find a spot."

Sofia looked questioningly at Greta, but all she could do was shrug. The situation had been taken out of their control. Teresina took Sofia's arm without ceremony and began walking down Via dell'Oro before Aveline had taken Greta's arm.

Greta allowed Aveline to set their pace – she was looking decidedly unwell. It was not long before Sofia and Teresina were lost from view.

"Veli, have you been to see your Alchimista?" Greta asked after a block of silence.

Aveline shook her head. "Reta, really I haven't had time since yesterday. Besides, at least I'm not feeling any worse."

Greta raised an eyebrow. "That's not as reassuring as you seem to think."

Aveline smiled weakly and patted her hand. "I'm sure there's nothing terribly wrong. I'll visit Lucrezia when I have time."

"Very well," Greta sighed. "Tell me about your trip, then. Did you *really* go to Sentigura Caldera?"

"I did indeed," Aveline said proudly, a touch of her usual fire showing through her exhaustion. "Lucrezia and Telchide came with me."

"What's it like then?" Greta asked curiously. The Caldera was visible from Tor'Esint, but only as a smudge of black and green.

"You'd never believe it, but there's a jungle inside it filled with so many palm trees we practically lived on coconuts. Hot streams run all the way through it." Aveline sighed heavily. "It was so *luxurious* to bathe in them. But that's the only thing I miss from the Caldera."

She suddenly went quiet. Greta didn't know what to make of it.

"Erm, did you find what you were looking for?"

Aveline nodded absently then looked at her sharply. "Who said I was looking for something?"

Greta pulled away from her in exasperation. "Veli, why else would you traipse into the Caldera? I can't imagine it was an easy expedition and it would have taken some great expense to get there in the first place."

Aveline's lips tightened into a thin line. An uncomfortable twinge in Greta's stomach forced her to take a deep breath as she retook Aveline's arm. She hated confrontations.

"I'm sorry, Veli. We all have our secrets. I just didn't realise this was such a big one for you. I can't be the only one who knows you went to the Caldera."

"Actually, you're one of the very few, and only because I needed you to make our leather gloves," Aveline admitted. "I'd say only our households, Kesida and a handful of our fellow Inventrici and Alchimisti know."

"Oh." There was nothing else Greta could say to that. It made her wonder if Aveline would have told her at all if she hadn't ordered the gloves.

"Maestra, over here!" Sofia waved a hand at them as they approached Caffè Eleonora.

As Greta expected, there were no tables available, but Sofia and Teresina had found room enough for the four of them at the bar.

"My treat today," Greta said as Aveline began to fish in her coin pouch. She raised a hand at her friend's attempt to disagree. "Does Telchide take coffee or tea?"

"Papà loves coffee, but Serenita refuses to make it for him. She doesn't like the smell and won't have it in her kitchen."

Aveline started at that. "I had no idea. He never asked for coffee when we worked together."

Teresina raised her eyebrows. "Papà's too polite to ask and you probably bring him tea without asking, don't you?"

"Indeed," Aveline said, growing quiet again. "Well then, one coffee for Telchide and a peppermint tea for me."

"Girls, a hot chocolate each?" Greta asked.

Sofia and Teresina nodded eagerly. Greta signalled for a server and pulled out an electrum coin in expectation of the cost. "A peppermint tea, a jasmine tea and two hot chocolates to have at the bar please. Then one coffee and three small boxes of mixed sfogliatelle and cannoli to go."

She took the tall ceramic cups from her last visit here out of the basket and placed them on the counter for a discounted price.

"Very good, Signora Sarta," the server said before repeating the order back to her and taking the cups.

Greta and Aveline took a seat to enjoy the break in their busy day, but their conversation didn't continue. Telchide's young daughter monopolised the conversation asking a hundred questions of everyone seemingly about everything she could think of. It was exhausting!

Eventually, Aveline placed a hand on the girl's shoulder. The effect was immediate – Teresina closed her mouth and smiled politely. When their boxes of pastries, and Telchide's coffee were ready, they left with the girls walking ahead again. Sofia had the boxes of pastries, but Aveline declined to allow Teresina to hold her papà's coffee.

"I'd say Telchide's trained his daughter well, but she seems to behave better for you than for him," Greta ventured, when the girls were far enough ahead.

She detected the hint of a smile on Aveline's lips.

"Teresina got used to my company when Telchide and I worked together the weeks leading up to our expedition," Aveline explained. "Now that we aren't working together so much in our workshops, she's taken to visiting me every other day. The condition is that she can only visit me on trading days if she is quiet and polite in front of customers. The hand on her shoulder has become a signal that she needs to be very quiet."

Greta tried not to be judgemental, but she couldn't help it.

"Are you certain it's wise to allow another man's child to grow so close to you? You aren't her mamma. What if Sebetine returns and discovers her daughter is fonder of an Inventrice than her own mother?"

Aveline's step faltered. Her grip on Greta's arm tightened suddenly as coffee almost spilt out of the tall cup.

"She won't," Aveline said in a hushed voice. "There were ... new developments."

"New developments?" Greta asked in just as hushed a voice. "What are you talking about?"

They were nearing Piazza Mercantile, and the stalls were starting to bustle again.

"It was in the newssheets a week or so ago. I'll explain another day, Reta. Thank you for the tea and pastries."

Aveline walked behind her stall and handed Telchide his coffee. The Inventore nodded his thanks to Greta without moving from his seat. They were already sharing out the pastries Greta had bought for them, though she noticed that Sofia was protectively cradling the last box of delicacies.

"Another day, Veli. I'll hold you to that," Greta said in a cheerful tone, not wanting the others to realise something was amiss. "Good day, Telchide. You have a lovely daughter in Teresina."

Telchide glowed with pride and pulled his daughter in for an embrace. She did not seem to mind at all and hugged him back tightly and kissed his cheek.

Greta swallowed the sudden lump in her throat. Her father had been just as affectionate with her when she was growing up. She tried not to think about how much she missed him and her sister. At least she still had Ranieri when she ever had the chance to see him.

Before her feelings had a chance to overwhelm her, Greta waved farewell, took Sofia's arm and walked back to her store and her waiting work.

# Chapter 3 – Riposidi 22 Alchimisti 230 Years After Implosion

"I'm going to tack together the dress now," Greta called out, looking at the cotton and linen on her workbench. She heard a pencil clatter to the other workbench moments before Sofia appeared at her side.

"Tell me why we do this," Greta said, threading her needle.

Sofia stood to attention and looked up as though the answer was written on the ceiling. "So that we can put it together quickly and take it apart easily if there's a problem."

"Correct. If we're using the final material, it also makes fewer holes in the fabric in case we need to take it in or out for width."

"Yes, Maestra," Sofia said seriously.

"How are you going with your pattern?" Greta asked as she began to tack the bodice together.

The bodice would take the most concentration. There were four cotton sections and one linen for the front and another two cotton sections for the back, as well as the cotton insert to go behind the lacing and the linen neck piece.

"I've drawn in your measurements as best I could, but I'm not confident I've done it correctly, Maestra," Sofia said, twirling a strand of her long golden-streaked tresses around her finger.

"Very well. I'll take a look when my fingers need a break," Greta promised.

She lightly stitched together the bodice with Sofia hovering over her shoulder, finally feeling comfortable enough to ask questions. The girl was a sponge. This one dress alone might make up for the time Greta had neglected to teach her more advanced techniques.

"Are you breaking for lunch today, Maestra, or working straight through?" Marta asked, popping her head into the workshop from the kitchen.

Greta frowned and listened to the Guild Halls chiming a half past the hour. If Marta was checking with her, it must be past midday now. She stretched her neck all around and looked down at the bodice. She'd managed most of the front. There was only one panel left.

"Just this panel, then I'll come in. Sofia, you don't have to stay if you're hungry."

Sofia shook her head. "No, I want to watch. Besides, if I don't stay to make you take a break after this, I know you'll skip lunch again."

Greta kept her eyes firmly fixed on her work. There was no point in arguing – Sofia was right. She couldn't count the number of times she'd missed meals in the past because of the latest order she'd been working on.

It took her another half hour to finish the front of the bodice at which point Sofia placed her hand over the rest of the material and looked pointedly at her. Greta rolled her eyes at Sofia but obligingly put down her needle and thread.

Together they made their way to the kitchen where Marta and Annika were sitting and talking.

"Maestra, can I make myself another dress with Marta's help?" Annika asked as soon as she walked in. "I'm growing out of mine. Marta can have them instead and Sofia can have her old ones. We'll just have to adjust the busts accordingly, unless Marta's happy to pad out her corset."

Marta coloured brightly at that statement. Annika did indeed have a fuller bust, but that was only to be expected from an eighteen-year-old! Poor Marta had not yet grown into a larger corset and though Sofia was a year her junior, the younger apprentice was close to overtaking her.

Greta tried to ignore the comment entirely, but Annika watched her expectantly. She drew in a short breath and did a mental calculation – three practical and fashionable work dresses, a nicer version of the work dresses for the Mercatodi stall, and a regular dress for cleaning duties.

"Annika, when you can show me that all the repairs and adjustments are done to my satisfaction, you can turn your attention to your dresses. If you're growing out of them, you can take out the bust and lengthen the skirts – that's why we put the extra material there in the first place. Then, and only then, may you devote your time to making another dress.

"Now, if you don't mind, I'd like to enjoy a quiet lunch before getting back to work. Signora Loyola will be back first thing tomorrow morning and I will not leave her waiting, no matter how arrogant she is. You might do well to remember that dresses like hers pay for the roof over your head."

Greta sat down at the table and cut herself a thick slice of bread, spread a generous layer of pesto on it and covered it with a thin slice of cheese. Sofia sat beside her and did likewise. Annika narrowed her eyes and twirled her chestnut brown waves around a finger.

"When *I* become a Sarta, I won't let anyone treat me the way Signora Loyola tried to treat you," Annika stated firmly. "I'll demand their respect or refuse their business."

Greta hid a smile behind her bread. She knew other Sarti who had felt the same way during their apprentice years.

"You may change your mind when you realise there are plenty of Sarti in Tor'Esint. Certainly, more than enough for customers to pick and choose to whom they bring their business.

"Remember, I'm a *Gold* Sarta. If I were a Copper Sarta, I would have grovelled to retain business from such an influential customer. In fact, had I been a Copper Sarta, she would never have deigned to set foot in my workshop in the first place."

Annika set to plaiting her hair as Greta spoke.

"Now, Annika, you're in your fifth year and your apprenticeship will soon be over. Have you given any thought to what you might like to submit for your first Great Work? Remember it needs to be good enough to earn your Copper Guild Mark. Most Sarti submit a pattern."

"Lucky it's nothing to do with her stitch-work," Sofia mumbled to Marta just loud enough for Greta to hear.

Greta carefully kept her eyes averted from the two of them but as Marta tittered into her hand, Annika turned a deep shade of red. What was she missing here?

"I haven't really thought about it," Annika replied defensively, her nose lifted high in the air. "What did *you* submit for your first Great Work?"

"I modified one of Maestro Ranieri's coat patterns and submitted that. Mind, I had his permission to do so. I would never have modified another Sarto's pattern without their permission."

Annika paused her plaiting and glanced at Greta. "Could I modify one of your dress designs then?"

Greta choked suddenly on her bread. Sofia patted her back until she stopped coughing.

"I guess that answers *that* question," Annika said bitterly. "Don't worry. I'll figure something out myself."

"Let me think about it," Greta said, trying to placate her. "I hadn't realised you would want to modify one of my patterns. When you have some spare time, why don't you sketch a few different ideas and we can look at them together."

Annika nodded slowly, wound her plait into a bun and stuck two long hairpins to keep it in place.

"Will you buy me my first pattern book then?" Annika finally asked.

Greta saw the spark of excitement in her eyes. She'd been a fifth-year apprentice herself when her very first pattern book had been given to her by Ranieri. The difference was, she hadn't had to ask him. He'd clearly known what an apprentice wanted and needed by the time he took her in.

"I'll see what I can do," Greta replied evasively. Her regular bookbinder might not be available and if she was going to order one pattern book, she might as well order three. That way when Marta and Sofia needed one, she'd have them ready. "Well, that dress won't tack itself. Ready Sofia?"

Sofia stared at her with big eyes, a small bite of bread in her mouth and the slice not even half gone. Greta sighed.

"I suppose I could do with a cup of tea first."

Annika jumped up. "I'll do that, Maestra. But you've inspired me. Could you spare a sheet of paper for me to draw a few sketches while I make you tea?"

Greta only paused a moment before nodding. She'd never seen Annika so eager to work. Was it the slightest bit of positive attention or the thought that it would help earn her Copper Guild Mark that made the difference?

A few minutes later, she returned with two sheets torn off her order pad and two pencils. She placed them on the table, one in front of Marta, the other for Annika, and sat down to await her tea. Marta instantly began sketching while Annika finished the tea preparation. The teapot and four cups were placed on the kitchen table before Annika sat down to her own paper and pencil.

Greta tried not to be obvious about watching them, but she couldn't help it. Marta had turned the page over to the blank side and sketched out two designs before Annika drew her first line. The older apprentice paused, pencil held high and stared at the page.

"I can't do this with everyone watching," Annika muttered under her breath.

She poured herself a cup of tea and took her things upstairs. Greta watched her go uneasily. It had never occurred to her that any of the girls might not be able to produce their own designs on the spur of the moment. When Signora Loyola had ordered her new dress, Greta had thought of and discarded at least a dozen ideas by the time she and Marta had arrived at the warehouse district. A Sarta who couldn't design was a Sarta who would never progress very far. But there was little she could do about that. Either the girls had it in them or they didn't. It would mean the difference between gaining their Gold Guild Mark one day, or forever remaining on Silver or Electrum.

Greta poured three cups of tea, left one for Marta and put the other two, along with the teapot, on a tray.

"I'm going back to work. Sofia, come along when you're done."

She left her two younger apprentices in the kitchen and returned to her workshop to continue with Signora Loyola's dress.

# Chapter 4 – Gildadi 23 Alchimisti 230 Years After Implosion

The bell on the front door jangled loudly to announce Signora Loyola's arrival. Greta looked up at the wall clock startled – she was early! She still had the back laces to attach. It would have to do. They were largely for decoration anyway.

She rose from her chair and carefully smoothed down her dress.

"Sofia, get the pins and come with me but for Caldera's sake be silent. This customer is difficult enough to deal with without any extra complications."

To her credit, Sofia showed no sign of irritation at that comment.

Greta draped the lightly tacked dress over her arm and waited patiently until Marta came through the curtains to announce Signora Loyola's arrival. It would never do for any customer to think they were so very important that Greta would rush out to meet them.

Marta held the curtain open as Greta walked through into the shopfront.

"Signora Loyola, how lovely to see you again. If you'll step behind the curtain, I'll help you with the dress."

The imposing woman tilted her head up and sniffed loudly. "I may be wealthy enough to have all the maids I desire, but I am still capable of dressing myself."

Greta gave her a brittle smile. "Of course, Signora, but the dress has only been lightly pieced together to allow for the fitting. Any of the threads might easily come loose without my assistance."

Signora Loyola raised an eyebrow but, thankfully, did not protest any further. She walked into the dressing room behind the curtain. Greta waited until she heard a huff of impatience before announcing her entrance, Sofia only one step behind her.

Greta quickly scanned the signora's arms to ensure Sofia's thought that they were disfigured was merely an unjustified concern. There were no blemishes at all, but the skin which should have been a lovely, rich bronze was a much paler shade. It was obvious Signora Loyola preferred covering her arms. Greta hoped she hadn't made a mistake with the style of her dress. She helped Signora Loyola slip the dress on over her head without pulling loose any of the thread holding it together.

"Will you be wearing this corset with the dress?" Greta asked, hoping she wouldn't need to make further adjustments.

"Yes. This is the one that works best with my evening gowns," Signora Loyola confirmed.

Greta nodded, satisfied. She motioned Sofia closer, took a small handful of pins from the pincushion, put a few between her lips and began taking the dress in around the waist and letting it out around the bust. The neckline was also a little too tight for comfort, so she cut a slit in the front to make it wider.

Greta stood back to admire her work and replaced the final pin in Sofia's pincushion. As every customer did at this stage, Signora Loyola looked down at the cotton dress. Greta bit her lip in anticipation.

"Do you have a mirror?" Signora Loyola asked. "Bring it in here. I want to see what you're planning on making before you bother continuing."

Greta suppressed a sigh. Signora Loyola was reputedly one of the most difficult people to work with. Greta had not worked with the signora yet herself but had heard frequent mention of her from other Sarti Guild members.

Sofia moved calmly, but swiftly, to do her bidding. Marta helped her carry in a full-length mirror and placed it at just the right angle for Signora Loyola to examine herself in her dress. Greta resisted the urge to ask what she thought. It would soon be evident enough.

Signora Loyola looked in the mirror and turned herself this way and that, trying to see every angle. Eventually, she stopped fussing and looked Greta in the eye. Greta held her hands tightly behind her back, so the pompous signora would not see how white her knuckles were.

"It appears a rather plain dress, but I've been mistaken before," she added magnanimously. "What material are you planning on using?"

Greta answered in a steady voice. "I think I may be able to source some fine satin in the colour you've requested. The organza will be more difficult to find, but I've a few places left to look. The combination of the fabrics would make quite a stunning dress, no matter how plain the design."

"Organza?" Signora Loyola asked, feigning disinterest.

Greta smiled and leaned in conspiratorially. "It's a new type of chiffon that is so fine and soft to the touch that you can barely feel it's there. It's sheer, but elegant. A fine light blue matched with a navy satin would be absolutely breath-taking."

Signora Loyola turned her head this way and that again, trying to imagine it. Greta explained the cotton represented the satin and the linen marked the placement of the organza. She didn't say that she'd already found the material. Knowing Signora Loyola, she would then expect the dress in under three weeks and Greta would need every available moment to complete the order.

"Will there be any beading? Or embroidery?" Signora Loyola asked.

Greta bit her lip, stood back and studied the cotton and linen dress. "Sofia, be a dear and fetch my pattern book."

Sofia, thankfully, did not actually run to do her bidding but turned and walked with purpose. She returned in a short time with the pattern book and a pencil. She handed both over. Greta opened the pattern book to the page with Signora Loyola's dress and considered it thoughtfully for a few moments. She drew in a few beads along the neckline and down the middle of the bodice along the organza section.

"Yes, I believe we can include some beading. However, that will add more time. At least another week."

"No." Signora Loyola shook her head. "Impossible."

Greta drew a deep breath.

"Signora, forgive my bluntness, but I happen to know that your music box will not be ready for another month, and I *know* you won't have your dinner party planned for that very day. You've given me only three weeks to complete a newly designed dress with extremely rare fabrics to source. Another week is needed for the beading, which as you must understand is quite time consuming, and will bring it to four weeks. It will still be ready before your dinner party."

Signora Loyola went very still and looked at Greta suspiciously.

"How do you know that?" she asked quietly. "About the music box."

Greta smiled as nicely as she could. "Telchide Inventore is acquainted with my good friend Aveline Inventrice. She mentioned the immensely intricate music box Telchide is creating and how much care he is taking with every note to ensure that you have only the finest of his creations.

"Please, allow me the time to do the same for you with this dress. You don't need it in three weeks, so don't force me to work quickly and sacrifice quality because, quite frankly, neither of us will be happy with the result if you do."

It was possible she'd gone too far, that she'd said too much and was about to lose an extremely important customer. Greta tried not to hold her breath as she waited for Signora Loyola to say something. Anything. The signora's features softened.

"I must say, it's nice to hear that he's taking so much pride in his work. I knew I was right to go to him. My friends told me I was taking too much of a risk using such an awkward man, but I've seen what he can do.

"Very well. I will give you the time you request. Four weeks. But I don't want word of this getting out. I don't want any other Sarti Guild members knowing that I can be reasonable."

She winked at Greta and smiled broadly. Greta huffed in surprise and started laughing. "Of course not, Signora. I will ensure your *reputation* stays intact. I could even go to great lengths to complain about how difficult it was working with you, if you think it will help."

Signora Loyola nodded and reined in her smile. "You'd be surprised the lengths people will go to, to please you, if they think you're difficult to begin with. There are only a few, like yourself and Telchide Inventore, who have the tenacity to stand up to me. Though, in this case, you're lucky you knew when the music box is to be completed, or I really would have insisted on the shorter timeframe."

Greta returned her smile and replied, "And I would have refused the beading to ensure your dress was completed on time. It would not have been anywhere near as marvellous."

Signora Loyola smiled broadly. "I like you. You're feisty. If this dress really is as stunning as you say it will be, every one of my friends, and their friends, will be knocking down your door for months to come for new designs. Just ensure you make them wait a full four weeks before giving them their dresses. Agreed?"

"Agreed."

Greta gave her pattern book to Sofia and proceeded to help the now friendly customer out of the dress. It was but a moment's work. Greta was so used to doing it that she didn't really need Sofia holding her pincushion, but thought it was important for the girl to be involved in every stage of this dress. Even the tedious parts.

When Signora Loyola left the workshop, Greta disappeared into her workshop and called Sofia to follow her.

"Now tell me, what did you learn?"

Sofia blanched at the impromptu question. "Erm, not to give the customer what they want?"

Greta laughed. "Is that how it looked? How in Caldera's smoke do you think I'd ever get repeat customers if they weren't getting what they wanted?"

Sofia frowned and chewed her lip. "To ... stand up for yourself."

Greta smiled. "Exactly! Never let the customer boss you around. Well, not on your Gold Guild Mark anyway. You may need to every now and then on a Copper or Silver but, even then, you should be setting a certain standard. People will come to understand that you refuse to compromise your work for their fickle whims.

"Signora Loyola was playing a game, but she didn't know I had background knowledge. It's helpful to know the movements and interests of important people. This time it was pure luck. If Aveline hadn't mentioned the music box in passing, I would likely have bent to the three weeks with no beading. I would have made a wonderful dress, but this will set it over the edge."

Sofia put the pincushion down and handed the pattern book back to Greta.

"Is that why you didn't tell her you already have stores of satin and organza – because you were playing a game?"

Greta laughed lightly. "Yes, indeed. Playing games with our clients is almost as important as being a good Sarta. If you don't play games with them, they begin to think that they can walk all over you and pay you less."

She lowered her voice and leaned in close to Sofia. "Don't ever tell her I said this, but that's why Aveline got her Electrum Guild Mark before Telchide and always has plenty of money to spend. It's not because she's a better Inventrice than he is – she isn't – it's because she knows how to play the game better than he does. I mean, just look at the perfect little music box he traded me for Teresina's sleeves."

Sofia's eyebrows shot up in surprise. Greta put her finger to her lips and her apprentice nodded solemnly.

"Now, to find the perfect beading. Why don't we leave Annika and Marta to watch the shop while you come out with me?"

"Oh really, Maestra?" Sofia gushed in excitement. Greta looked at her oddly and Sofia lowered her eyes. "You may not have noticed, but I've never come shopping with you."

"Never?" asked Greta in surprise.

"Never." Sofia shook her head, still looking down.

Greta lifted the girl's chin and looked her straight in the eyes. "That's all about to change. We shall pretend you're my first apprentice for the entirety of this dress and see if we can't right the wrongs of the past three years."

Sofia's large smile spread all the way to her sparkling, green-flecked eyes. She nodded enthusiastically, a small tear escaping down her cheek, rolling into her dimple. Greta wiped it away and patted her cheek.

"Let's go."

Sofia walked out into the workshop, more confident than Greta had ever seen her. Even when Annika turned her contemptuous smile on the girl, she did not falter.

"You forgot the dishes," Annika sneered.

Greta tilted her chin up to look down on her oldest apprentice. "No, she didn't actually. I told her to leave them for you."

Annika's face fell. She stared in horror at Greta, then at Sofia, who showed only the slightest hint of smugness. Greta rubbed her forehead, trying to find the right words.

"Annika, Marta, Sofia ... I realise things have not been going well with everyone's apprenticeship and that's my fault for taking on too many of you too quickly. I plan on fixing that problem. From now onwards, you will each shadow me for an entire project. Sofia will be shadowing me with this one. Annika and Marta, you've had more training. You can manage the shopfront, mend any simpler repairs and, of course, do the cooking, cleaning and laundry. When this project is done, it will be Marta's turn, then Annika's."

"But..." Annika started.

Greta put her hand up. "My word is final Annika, unless you'd prefer to relinquish your position with me and put your name back on the apprentice list. I hear it grows longer every week because of the troubles with the Inter-Guild Edict."

"No, Maestra," Annika replied through clenched teeth.

Greta nodded and looked over to Marta, who had remained silent the entire exchange. "What about you?"

"I think it's a wonderful idea, Maestra," Marta replied easily. "I'll volunteer for the mending over the cooking and cleaning, if you don't mind."

Greta smiled and nodded. Marta had played that hand rather well. "I don't mind at all. It's about time Annika got her hands dirty. Annika, I want to see that kitchen sparkling by the time Sofia and I return. And don't forget to prepare a light lunch for everyone while Marta keeps the shop."

Before Annika could argue, Greta ushered Sofia out of the door. She winked at Marta as she passed the smiling girl. Marta grinned back at her. Apparently, they'd been waiting for Greta to bring Annika down a peg or two. Hopefully it would make her easier to work with. Greta was not averse to sending the girl back to the Guild for a new Maestra if her attitude did not change. And soon. Unhappy apprentices were not productive or good learners.

Out on the street, Sofia turned and hugged Greta. Greta froze from the sudden public familiarity but recovered quickly, patting the girl on the back before disentangling herself.

"Maestra, you'll never know what it means to me that you did that!" Sofia gushed. "I won't let you down. I'll listen and I'll learn and..."

"You'll not say another word about it," Greta said, taking a purposeful step back. "Now, let's see about those beads. My favourite shop is a few blocks from here. Why don't we pick up a few olive rolls on our way?"

Sofia nodded enthusiastically and fell into step beside Greta. They walked past Aveline's workshop on the way through Piazza Mercantile. Greta paused and looked up the stairs.

"Do you know that Inventrice?" Sofia asked, stopping alongside her.

"Well, of course," Greta replied in surprise. "That's Aveline's workshop. Have you never been in?"

Sofia shrugged. "I've rarely been out with you. My only outings are to the market when we need more food and sometimes down to the dock on Riposidi."

"Right, well I'll show you her workshop now. Come on."

"But the beads!" Sofia protested.

Greta laughed and pulled her arm. "We have all day to source the beads. This will only take a few minutes."

They walked up the stairs and into the workshop. Nevio looked up at their arrival, but Aveline was nowhere to be seen. Again.

"Nevio, where is she this time?"

Nevio shifted uncomfortably. "Out. She'll be out most of the day. Is there something you need?"

Greta frowned. Something had definitely changed since her return from the Caldera, but Aveline was being very quiet about it.

"Tell her I'm inviting myself for tea this evening, after closing."

Nevio shook his head. "I'm sorry Signora Sarta, but she'll be at … she has a prior engagement."

Greta narrowed her eyes. Nevio knew something he wasn't telling her. Greta was not used to being denied information. She found she did not enjoy the experience.

"Very well, then ask her to call on me or send a message as to when I can call on her."

"Yes, Signora Sarta."

Greta sniffed and turned. In her annoyance, she had forgotten the girl was there. "Oh, Nevio, this is Sofia. She's my youngest apprentice. Sofia, this is Nevio, Aveline's apprentice."

Sofia heartily shook the proffered hand. She was not as delicate a girl as Marta. Certainly nothing to tempt Nevio, which was a blessing. If his attentions ran to *two* of her apprentices, she would never hear the end of the bickering.

"Let's go, Sofia, or we won't find any olive rolls at the markets."

Sofia allowed herself to be ushered out of the workshop and onto the street with no complaint. Greta was thankful that she wasn't as strong-willed and opinionated as Annika. She really could not handle more than *one* Annika in her life.

***

By the time they reached the bead shop, Greta was putting the final bite of her rosemary roll in her mouth. They had indeed run out of olive rolls by the time Greta and Sofia ordered.

Sofia had timidly picked out cinnamon buns instead. Greta settled for her third favourite roll – the herb rolls had sold out too. If they'd also been out of rosemary, she would really have been put out. But thankfully they had two left. Greta had bought both – one for her afternoon tea. The girls could share the cinnamon buns. She didn't like their chances of getting anything edible from Annika's first attempt at cooking and refused to go completely hungry because of it.

Greta carefully wiped the crumbs from her hands and smoothed down her dress. She noticed, with some amusement, Sofia mimicking her actions with one hand, the other holding the paper-wrapped bundle of precious pastries.

They entered the bead shop and were greeted by an assistant.

"I'm looking for blue beads today – navy if you have them," Greta told her.

"Of course, Signora Sarta," replied the shop assistant. "Any style in particular?"

Greta was well-known in this particular shop, but even if she hadn't been, the Gold Sarti Guild Mark pinned to her bodice would have instantly given her status away. Greta took great pains to pin it on every day in such a fashion that it looked like she had taken care with the placement but wasn't trying to flaunt her status. It was a delicate balance.

"I need something that sparkles or glitters, but not for a child. It must be elegant, understated."

The shop assistant nodded, wide eyes darting around the shop. Her shoulders relaxed as her eyes stopped on a particular display.

"This way, Signora Sarta."

Greta followed her, motioning Sofia to walk beside her. The shop assistant held out a large card for Greta to examine. It had a variety of different beads stitched to the canvas front. Greta examined the beads before her and passed the canvas card to Sofia.

"What do you think?" she asked. "Think of the material we're using, the colours, the textures. And think of the pattern of the dress. Imagine it all in your head and picture these beads on it. Which do you think would work best?"

Sofia took the card hesitantly and studied it. Greta watched her carefully. Sofia's choice now was going to tell her a lot about the girl. In this one decision, she would know if the girl had any taste or imagination whatsoever. She clenched her fingers tightly behind her back so her apprentice wouldn't notice her nerves.

Sofia pointed to a rounded bead with flattened edges, like a hexagonal prism. Greta raised an eyebrow. It wouldn't have been her first choice, but it wasn't terrible.

"I'd mix some of these with some of those," Sofia said, pointing to a longer, smoother bead.

Greta scrunched up the canvas to bring the two beads together.

"That actually might work, if we add in some of these as well." She pointed out a smaller, round navy bead. It had a sheen to it, without being overtly shiny, just like the longer bead. "I think you've got the right idea with this hexagonal one, but it might look better in a shade of silver. Do you have any of those?"

She turned to the shop assistant, who had remained silent during their discussion. The assistant looked at the chosen bead and nodded.

"Wait here a moment, I'll get you that board."

She walked to the other side of the store. Greta knew the silver beads were on that wall. The way the store was set out by colour rather than shape was one of the things Greta liked about it the most. It was easier for her to match a colour to her material and the look at the shapes available rather than find the right shape first only to realise it didn't come in the colour she needed.

"Here you go, Signora Sarta," the shop assistant said, handing her the card. "Is this what you're after?"

Greta took the card and examined it, making sure that Sofia could see it at the same time. She held different silver beads next to her two chosen navy beads.

"Yes, I think this one will do nicely." Greta pointed out a small silver bead that looked like a piece of cut glass. It provided exactly the right effect.

"I'll need two dozen of these silver ones, one hundred of the long navy and three hundred of the round navy."

The shop assistant didn't bat an eyelid at the request, but Sofia gasped loudly.

"Do we really need so many?" Sofia whispered.

Greta glanced at her in confusion.

"We do," she replied evenly. "How else do you think we'll be able to create this pattern?"

She tapped the pocket where her pattern book was safely ensconced. Not that she didn't trust her apprentices, but she would never leave her pattern book unattended. If it fell into the wrong hands, well, her entire livelihood as a Sarta could be over. Other Sarti could use her non-patented designs and pass them off as their own, bringing in the profits that Greta herself deserved. It did not bear thinking of.

The shop assistant left them talking and went to prepare the order. Greta took the opportunity to explain a few key points to Sofia.

"I know you haven't spent any time with me outside the workshop, but don't ever question me in public. It would not have done when I had my Silver Guild Mark, and it certainly won't do now that I have my *Gold* Guild Mark."

She pointed to the pin on her bodice to emphasise her point.

"Secondly, do not draw particular attention to what we are creating, nor who it's for. There are many people who would be very happy indeed to try to steal our customers out from under our noses or take up as much of our required materials and accessories as possible so we have little to nothing to work with. Do you understand?"

Sofia hung her head. "Yes, Maestra Greta. I understand."

"Good. Now let's collect our order before any other Sarti start snooping around it." Greta smiled to take the edge off of Sofia's unease, but she could see that it didn't work. Poor Sofia. She really deserved a better apprenticeship.

They walked together to the counter and awaited the shop assistant, who had disappeared out the back to find the packets she needed to fulfil the order. It didn't take very long, which was another reason why Greta liked this store. They had their beads in pre-made packets of one hundred to make it easier for Sarti needing larger orders.

"Shall I put it on your monthly invoice, Signora Sarta, or are you paying for these today?"

"I'll pay for them today, thank you." Greta smiled sweetly. She knew if it went on her invoice, others would pay to look at what she had bought and possibly try to make something with the same beads. The competition between Sarti was rife in Tor'Esint – whoever said otherwise was deluding themselves.

She paid ten silvers for the beads, took the brown paper package and left the store with Sofia in tow. They took a more direct route back to Greta's workshop. She didn't like to dally when carrying important items for an order.

As they approached the workshop, Greta heard screaming. She exchanged worried glances with Sofia and broke into a run up the stairs. Greta looked around and realised the shopfront was abandoned. She would not let Marta get away with that.

Another scream from the kitchen made her leave the distressingly empty shopfront. Sofia pushed the door open and stopped dead, forcing Greta to bump into her.

There was water everywhere. Greta stared at a soaking wet and ash-covered Annika.

"What in Caldera's smoke is going on here?" she yelled, her usual calm demeanour gone. "Annika, clean up that water before it leaks into the shop or *my workshop*! Marta, get back in the shop. Sofia, come with me."

She didn't wait to see if the girls were following her orders – they always did. But she would demand an explanation later. Annika would not be allowed to get away with this, just because she was the oldest apprentice. She had no right to make such a mess in the kitchen and cause such a ruckus that it could be heard from the street. The indignity!

Greta strode into her workshop and looked around. Her cut pattern was still where she had left it and nothing else looked like it had been touched. At least it appeared the girls had followed her instructions to stay out of the workshop. She placed the brown paper package on the table and smoothed down her dress. Somehow that motion always served to calm her.

"Maestra, would you like me to make you a cup of tea?" Sofia asked timidly. "It will help calm your nerves."

Greta shook her head. "Ask Annika to do it."

"But ... Annika doesn't know how to make tea."

Greta turned and looked at Sophia in disbelief. "What do you mean she doesn't know how to make tea? All she needs to do is boil water and pour it over tea leaves. Besides, she made a pot of tea yesterday."

Sofia shrugged. "Yes, but she doesn't know how to light the stove. She always makes me or Marta do it. That's why she waited until you were out of the room before doing anything yesterday."

Greta rolled her eyes. "That girl is incompetent at almost everything but sneering. Fine, you are permitted to teach her how to light the stove, but she's doing the rest herself and you're coming straight back here. Understand?"

Sofia smiled that big, infectious smile of hers and Greta couldn't help but return it, even in her annoyance. That girl would go far with such a sweet, hardworking nature and her smile. Greta knew she shouldn't have favourites, but Sofia had been hers almost from the moment she joined the household. Annika was too snide, always ready to take people down. Marta was nice enough, and competent, but too timid. She let Annika walk all over her and did nothing to stand up for poor Sofia who bore the brunt of Annika's wrath.

But Sofia ... she took Annika's ire when she had no choice, but that did not mean she allowed the older apprentice to walk all over her. She made sure to give Annika her fair share of trouble when she could. She stood up for Marta or tried to make Marta stand up for herself. And she kept her head down and worked hard. The most amazing thing about Sofia was that she was still willing to help Annika even though she had an inflated view of herself.

Greta was glad she'd decided to change how the apprentices worked. Not only would it put Annika in her place, but it would give Sofia the time and attention she needed to thrive. It was about time all her apprentices had that.

While she waited for Sofia to return from the kitchen, Greta opened her package and carefully stored the new beads in the little cabinet she'd had commissioned specifically for those small items. It had been an expensive order, but one she was grateful for.

For every item she made with glass, metal or wooden beads, she kept all her extras in this cupboard. It meant that if anyone came in for repairs, she would likely have the items she needed without needing to go out to the bead shops. The bonus was that if she just needed a little something to add flair to an order, she had a variety of items to choose from.

It was something her own Maestro had taught her to do during her apprenticeship, and though she had her own workshop now and had found different ways of doing many things, there were still others she did exactly the way he'd taught her because she'd never found a better way to do it.

"I miss Ranieri," she sighed. It had been such a long time since she had last seen him.

"Ranieri Sarto?" asked Sofia, walking back into the workroom. "Did you use to work with him?"

Greta smiled. "He was *my* Maestro. A talented man and a good teacher. He was the best I could have hoped for."

"Has he left Tor'Esint then?" Sofia asked.

"No," Greta replied quickly. "Of course he's not. I simply haven't seen him in a long time. We're always both so busy. We hardly even get to speak at the Sarti Guild meetings."

Greta blinked herself out of wishing for things that she couldn't change.

"Right, well, let's get started then," Greta said as Sofia sat by her side. "Have I shown you how to stitch on beading?"

Sofia shook her head.

"You can practice that then. We're going to have to sew hundreds of beads onto this gown, and I could certainly use your help with it if your hand is steady enough. Fetch that off-cut over there and get a thin needle and thread."

Sofia promptly did as she was told. Greta showed her the little cabinet of beads and selected the cheapest ones she had. Not that the beads would remain on the off-cut, but if any fell and were lost, she didn't want them to be the beads for the signora's dress.

"I know it's tedious doing this over and over, but the more you do it, the better you become. If your stitches are smooth enough by the time we're up to that section of the dress, you can help me with the new beads we bought today."

Sofia nodded good-naturedly and watched Greta as she sewed a bead on. Greta passed the off-cut to Sofia and watched as the girl tried her hardest to thread her needle.

"We'll need to make the stitching as fine as possible, so thread the needle with both ends of the thread. You may need to wet the tips between your lips to make them fine enough to go through the eye. There you go, that's it. Now bring the needle up from the back. Good girl. And now put the needle through the bead and back through the material. Wonderful! Now before the thread goes all the way through, pass the needle through the loop at the end there to keep the thread from slipping."

It wasn't wonderful – this was a very basic skill, but she had so neglected poor Sofia that she hadn't even mastered some of the first-year apprentice skills. Greta felt a gnawing in her stomach that would not go away. It was all she could to do keep a positive look on her face as Sofia struggled with the simple task.

"That's the way, Sofia. Now, what I want you to do is get my pencil, draw a design on the material and sew beads around that design. Can you do that for me?"

Sofia put down the needle and material and took the pencil from Greta. "What design?"

"Oh, anything will do," Greta answered breezily. "A flower, a bird, a boat. Whatever takes your fancy."

Sofia stared at the material, pencil in hand and froze. Greta frowned. "You can draw, can't you?"

"Not *very* well," admitted Sofia.

"Just a circle, then. Draw a circle and do the beading along the line."

Sofia nodded and drew a circle. Her tongue stuck out the side of her mouth as she did so. It was something that would have looked endearing on a child but was slightly ridiculous on an adolescent.

She left Sofia to her beading and turned her attention to the brown paper pattern. There were some minor adjustments to be made from the fitting that morning. Greta set about making those changes before getting everything ready to cut the actual material for the bodice.

As she did every time she began a new project, she cleared her workstation of all unnecessary items. Everything that she used often was placed in the shallow drawer under the workstation, everything else was put away in its proper place. She could just as easily have asked Marta or Annika to clear the table for her, but she found a particular sense of calm from performing that ritual herself.

Before long, the workstation was clear. Greta laid out the navy satin on the workstation, dull side facing up, and placed the brown paper patterns for the bodice on top of it facing downwards, moving them around to find the optimal position where she would waste the least amount of material. With white chalk, she dot-traced the pattern on the material. It made it easier to cut and could easily be washed or rubbed away when the dress was finished, though Greta took extra care by chalk marking the inside of the dress.

When all the bodice pieces were traced, she found her sharpest scissors and carefully cut the satin along the dotted chalk lines. She loved the sound the scissors made as they cut clean crisp lines through the material. It was a sound she'd never heard replicated anywhere but in a Sarta workshop. She wondered if any of her customers had heard the sound before. It was so unique, she doubted she could describe it to them.

Greta lost track of time. She noticed when Annika came into the room with a tea tray, but only because Sofia harshly reprimanded her for coming into the workshop with soaking clothes.

"You're not my Maestra," Annika sneered. "I'll dry myself when I feel like it."

"You'll kindly remove yourself from my workshop with those wet clothes,"

Greta said sharply. "How dare you endanger our livelihood so cavalierly. If you haven't done so, finish cleaning the kitchen and change into a dry set of clothes before even *thinking* of setting foot back in here or the shopfront."

Annika had the hide to glare at her. Greta returned her gaze evenly. She would not be cowed by a lowly apprentice.

"Yes, Maestra," she said venomously.

Greta was almost expecting her to upturn the tea tray out of spite as she walked away. But she didn't. She placed it on the small tea table far from all the patternwork. Greta let out a breath she hadn't realised she was holding.

"Would you have said that even if she hadn't been mean to me?" Sofia asked, pouring the tea.

It was an odd question. Greta thought about it while blowing to cool her tea.

"Probably not, but only because I hadn't noticed her until you mentioned her wet clothes," Greta answered truthfully. "I meant what I said. Annika should have thought about what she was doing. She was too busy trying to regain the upper hand with you that she paid no attention to the consequences of her actions.

"She shouldn't have come in here with wet clothes. I have expensive materials, accessories and patterns all over the place, any of which could be damaged or destroyed by water. She knows that. She was simply too angry, or tired, or frustrated to care."

Greta wondered, not for the first time, whether Annika would ever purposely jeopardise her. It was uncommon, but not unheard of for arguments between Maestri and apprentices to go awry. With the Trading and Inter-Guild Edicts, any falling out could have catastrophic consequences for the mentors.

She sipped her tea until it was all finished and placed it carefully back on the tray. She had learned to enjoy her tea all in one go, rather than sip it over long minutes. It was not advisable to keep a tea tray in the workshop indefinitely. Sofia did the same herself and took the tea tray back to the kitchen. She was gone longer than Greta expected.

"What took you so long?" she asked when Sofia finally returned. "Surely you didn't get into another argument with Annika, did you?"

"No," Sofia replied with a grin. "I asked Marta what happened to flood the kitchen and cover Annika in ash."

Greta raised her eyebrows. "And?"

"And ... it seems Annika tried to light the stove herself just before we arrived and set her clothes alight instead. Marta heard her scream and ran to the kitchen, which is why the shopfront was unattended. She saw the fire and grabbed the bucket of water Annika had used to rinse the dishes and threw it at her to douse the flames."

Greta laughed. "Well, that's one way to do it."

Sofia smiled broadly. "Marta said she wasn't trying to get Annika in trouble with the water, but it was the only way she could think to put the fire out quickly."

The thought sobered Greta. A fire in her workshop was no laughing matter. If it had been anywhere other than the kitchen, it could have caused real damage. Fires were a potentially catastrophic problem in Tor'Esint. Though much of the town was built with stone, enough of it was wooden that if one building caught alight, it wouldn't be long before the entire city was in flames.

"That was quick thinking. Remind me to praise her for it," Greta said. She almost added "in front of Annika", but she didn't want to let Sofia know how much the older apprentice was grating on her nerves.

"Now, show me those beads. How are they coming along?"

Greta stood up and went to Sofia's workstation. There was plenty of light in the workroom. Rather than have wall windows, like a regular room, Greta had insisted they be bricked up and a large skylight created in the ceiling, making use of the sunlight for more of the day. She refused to allow candles in her workshop and the friction lights were only good for a few minutes at a time. The inconvenience of using them was too great for an extended period. She wished there was another source of light, other than flames or friction. Surely someone in the Inventrici Guild must have thought up something by now. Why wasn't it on the market?

Sofia held up her handiwork for Greta to see. Greta leaned in close to examine it in detail.

"You have a very precise hand," she remarked. "I expected to see more mistakes."

Sofia tilted her head and examined the piece of material herself. "How can you tell I didn't make many?"

"I pointed out that off-cut for a reason. With this material, there would be visible holes for every one of your mistakes. I can see one, two, three, four." She pointed to each of them with a needle as she counted them out. "And you have over thirty beads I would guess."

"Thirty-two," Sofia corrected her.

"Well, four mistakes from thirty-two beads, especially when it's your first time beading, is quite impressive."

Sofia blushed brightly. "It's similar enough skill to darning stockings and edging, really. And I've been doing that for three years now."

Greta didn't comment. The gnawing sense of guilt had returned. But Sofia was correct. All that edging she'd been forced to do had certainly given her lots of practice. It was possible that Sofia had an even finer hand than Annika.

"Sofia, be a dear and fetch three stockings that need to be mended from Marta and ask the girls to come in here for a moment."

Sofia frowned but went to do as she was requested. Greta was surprised she hadn't thought to try this experiment earlier. It was high time she found out which of her apprentices was quickest and which had the finest hand. It ought to be Annika, but she had a sneaking suspicion it wouldn't be. Greta checked her thoughts. She shouldn't be so harsh to Annika. It wasn't the girl's fault that her nature was so ... well, horrid. There was no other way to accurately describe her. But she might be talented too. Greta would soon find out.

It wasn't long before Sofia returned with Marta and Annika, now in a fresh set of clothes.

She was holding three stockings that all had small holes and tears in them.

"Girls, I'd like you to take a stocking each, select your needle and thread, and mend your stocking. I want it done properly and in a timely manner. When you are finished, bring it to my workbench."

Sofia immediately went to find the correct needle and matched up the right colour thread to her stocking. Marta matched the right colour thread and took her work back to the shopfront – it could not be left unattended. Annika was the only one who didn't move.

"A stocking?" she asked indignantly. "You want me to mend a *stocking*?"

"Yes," Greta replied, without looking up from her work.

"But, *why*?" she whined. "I'm a fifth-year apprentice! I should be helping you with *that* dress."

Greta answered easily. "Because I am your Maestra, and I've asked you to. Go away now. You can keep Marta company in the shop."

She didn't look up but paid attention to the sounds as Annika looked through the needles to find one she wanted and clattered through the thread to find one that matched her stocking. At least, that's what Greta hoped she was doing. A stocking could not possibly be mended properly with the wrong colour thread.

The workshop was quiet and peaceful while the girls tended to their task. Greta cut the last satin section of the bodice and moved onto the organza.

When she was done, she turned to find the first stocking was on her workbench. Neither Annika nor Marta had entered the room. Greta glanced over to Sofia, who was painstakingly continuing her efforts with the beading project. Trying not to be obvious about it, she sat back down at the workbench, took up the stocking and examined it closely. She could barely see the stitching it was so fine. And the thread matched the colour so perfectly that had Greta not known it was damaged in the first place, she wouldn't have been able to tell that it had been repaired.

"Do you work so quickly on all your repairs, or was it just this one?"

"All of them," Sofia replied without looking up. "I've done a lot of them. Annika used to thread a needle for me and give me her share to do until I started to refuse. Now she gives them to Marta. Sometimes I feel sorry for Marta and help out, but usually I tell her she shouldn't let Annika boss her around so."

Greta frowned, though at least it explained Sofia's earlier difficulty threading and why her beading was conversely decent. "When does she do that?"

Sofia looked up. "Every day, Maestra."

"What?"

Sofia shrugged. "Did you think she was so very fast to be done so much quicker than the two of us?"

Greta didn't answer. Seeing Annika's reaction to darning a stocking and the fact that Sofia had finished hers first made Greta revisit her assumptions.

Marta walked into the workshop and placed her stocking on the workbench.

"Thank you, Marta," Greta said with a smile. "Please continue your mending and don't let Annika cow you into darning her stocking."

A bright blush bloomed over Marta's cheeks as though Greta had caught her out at a plan. The girl nodded and returned to the shop.

Sofia laughed quietly in her corner. "Did you know she was planning on helping her or was that a guess?"

Greta raised an eyebrow at her cheeky apprentice. "It was an *educated* guess. After you're done with that beading, I want you to find the cheap, white cotton and cut out the bodice to my measurements that you took yesterday."

Sofia's eyes lit up. "Really?"

Greta nodded nonchalantly.

"Smoking Caldera! My first dress!"

Greta smoothed down her skirt. There was no point dwelling on what she hadn't taught Sofia.

Annika didn't bring in her stocking until Sofia had already traced her bodice pieces. Greta was clearing a space amongst all her old equipment to set up the extra mannequin for Sofia's dress when her older apprentice threw the stocking on her workbench.

"Thank you, Annika. Now, I want you to ask Marta what she needs help with in the shopfront."

"Yes, Maestra," Annika said through clenched teeth.

"Oh, and Annika, dear, you do exactly as she tells you. I will check up on you both soon."

Greta didn't bother looking up as Annika stormed out into the shopfront. She would deal with her later.

"Sofia, help me pull this out," she grunted as she tried, yet again, to lift the mannequin over the piles of cloth.

Sofia willingly obliged and soon they had a second mannequin standing next to the first. Greta wiped her brow and looked at the mess on the floor. Some of the cloth was so old she didn't even remember purchasing it. She bundled it back into the corner and vowed to deal with it when this dress was done.

"Maestra?" Marta walked into the workshop in the early hours of the afternoon. "There's a woman here to see you."

"Marta, I told you, we can't take any new orders right now," Greta replied in annoyance.

Marta nodded. "I know. I told her so, but she still insists on seeing you."

Greta sighed. "Very well, tell her I'll be there in a moment."

Marta nodded and left the workshop. Greta turned to Sofia.

"Pin your bodice to the mannequin, then meet me in the shop if I'm not back when you're done. Understood?"

"Yes, Maestra," Sofia replied.

Greta nodded. "Good. Right."

She turned, fighting the urge to smooth her dress down again. It did not need smoothing. Out in the shopfront, a young signora was waiting patiently for her. Greta took in the woman with one glance. She had dark brown hair, almost black, and eyes to match. She was petite in every sense of the word, but not as young as Greta had first thought. The woman must have been well into her fourth decade.

"Can I help you?" Greta asked as the woman's eyes settled on her.

"I hope so," the woman replied. "My name is Letizia di Bibiana. I work for the Tor'Esint Amministratori. You are Greta Sarta, are you not?"

"I am," Greta replied, her palms began to sweat as she thought of all her illicit activities.

Letizia nodded. "You were apprenticed to Ranieri Sarto, were you not?"

"Yes, a number of years ago now," replied Greta frowning.

The woman smiled. It was a kind smile, but Greta did not want to trust her.

"I need you to come with me."

Greta stayed where she was. "Why?"

The woman glanced at her, then at the two apprentices watching them.

"You're not in any trouble, Signora Sarta. I simply need your help for a short time. You'll be back before end of trading, I promise."

Greta straightened her spine. Well, that was one good thing at least. She nodded and poked her head into the workshop.

"Sofia, I'm going out for a while. You're in charge while I'm gone."

Sofia looked at Greta in confusion. "Sorry?"

"You're in charge. You know I've asked Annika to help Marta, so make sure she does. When you're done with your current task in the workshop, begin on edging my material. Anyone else who runs out of things to do can help you with the edging. Then teach Annika how to cook dinner."

Annika scowled at the last comment just as Sofia grinned. Greta acknowledged neither of them. It was not for her to show favour for one apprentice in front of the others.

"I'm ready," she told the Amministratrice.

Letizia nodded and walked out of the shop. Out on the street, she spoke again.

"I'm taking you to the Tor'Esint morgue."

Greta stopped walking, forcing Letizia to turn and come back to her.

The signora spread her hands out apologetically. "I'm sorry, Signora, but I need you to identify Ranieri's body."

"What?" she whispered.

"A body was found at the docks this morning," Letizia explained. "We believe it may be Ranieri. He has no family, and we cannot find his current apprentice. You're the first name that came to everyone's mind to identify him. Seems as though he spoke of you often."

"How..." Greta swallowed. "How did he die?"

Letizia shrugged. "We're not certain yet. The investigation will proceed once you've identified him."

Greta nodded. She didn't know what else to do. The Amministratrice patted her on the back, then continued down the street. Greta followed her to a blazermobile parked on Via Mercato just off Piazza Mercantile. She got in wordlessly and stared numbly through the window on the way to the morgue. She'd never been there before. She'd never seen a dead body before. She didn't want Ranieri's to be the first.

Letizia led her into a featureless, stone building. It was cold inside, much colder than outside, but that was always the way with stone buildings. They stopped in front of a wooden door and Letizia motioned for Greta to go in. Greta smoothed down her dress nervously and took a deep breath before opening the door.

A body was laid out on a large stone slab. She couldn't tell without getting closer if it really was him. Some part of her believed that if she just didn't look, he wouldn't be dead. Another part of her knew that it wouldn't make a difference if she looked or not. *Someone* was dead and she had to see if it was Ranieri. *Her* Ranieri – the man who had become as much a father to her as her own. The man she had just been saying she wanted to see again. How cruel fate was! This was *not* how she wanted to see him.

"Signora Sarta?" Letizia called out. "You need to go in."

Greta nodded, mostly to herself, and walked in. As she got closer, she tensed. The man's face was green-tinged and bloated. She couldn't tell if it was Ranieri. Not from his face. She looked at his hands. His fingertips were tinged green. Dried green foam crusted the corners of his mouth. His open eyes were green where they should have been white.

"Is it him?" a man in a red apron asked her without emotion.

"Why is everything green?" she asked, not answering him.

The man shrugged. "It's not the first case we've seen, but all the others were women."

Greta felt a rising panic. "Was he murdered? Were they all murdered?"

"We won't know until we complete our investigation," he told her dispassionately. "Now, can you please identify him so we can get on with our jobs?"

Though she was already almost certain it was Ranieri, the green tinge in his eyes, around his mouth and on his fingernails made her just that little bit hesitant to identify him.

"Is it safe to touch him?" she asked. "I need to see his arm, here."

She pointed to the underside of her left forearm. The man undid the button on the dead man's sleeve and rolled it up. The tattoo of the Sarti Guild Mark removed all doubt from her mind. When the Trading and Inter-Guild Edicts had come into effect and the first people had been stripped of their Guild Marks, Ranieri had insisted on being tattooed with his Guild Mark so it could never really be taken away from him.

"It's him."

She confirmed the death of her Maestro with a sense of detachment. Like she was watching someone else from a distance. It made her feel less like vomiting.

"Will you let me know the results of your investigation?" she asked. "I'm the closest thing he had to a family."

Letizia stepped in at this point. "Of course, Signora Sarta. I shall inform you personally."

Greta nodded her thanks.

\*\*\*

On the blazermobile ride back to her shop, Greta tried to find out more about the deaths.

"Did all the women have the same green features as Ranieri?"

Letizia nodded. "Some weren't quite as bad, others were worse but, yes, they were all green."

Greta shook her head. "Is it a poison then?"

Letizia risked a sideways glance at her while she was driving on a straight road. "It could be. But we can't find a common link between any of them. Unless they were murdered."

"But who would want to murder Ranieri Sarto? He was the kindest person I've known."

The Amministratrice shrugged. "It doesn't matter how kind someone was. Perhaps it was a lover's spat, or a deal gone wrong. He could have accidentally angered the wrong people. But it might not be murder at all. It could just be a coincidence."

Greta nodded to herself. She thought of Ranieri and the workshop that had been her home for so many years. He still took on apprentices, but usually only one or two at a time. She smiled to herself – had he made the same mistake she had when he was younger and learned not to have too many apprentices at the same time?

"What will happen with his workshop and his apprentice now?" she asked before she could stop herself. "I don't mean that I want them, I just wonder what will happen."

"Don't worry. You don't strike me as the avaricious kind." Letizia huffed out a laugh.

"There should be a Final Testament. Somewhere. Most Guild members keep theirs with their Guild just in case something happens in their workshop. I'll ask there first."

"When?" asked Greta. Usually, she wouldn't be so inquisitive and play her hands so openly. Her nerves were getting the better of her.

"We can pass by there now if you have time," Letizia offered. "I'll need to inform the Sarti Guild anyway."

"Please, if you don't mind," Greta replied with a short nod. "I'd like to be there when you tell them. In case they have questions. As you said, he has no family."

Letizia said nothing but turned the blazermobile towards Corso Delle Gilde. It was the street which ran along the bay. Every Guild had its hall there so that none could claim they had a better position than others, though in truth some were still better placed than others. The Mercantili, Inventrici and Alchimisti Guilds were at the centre intersection of Via dell'Oro, closer to the docks. They were among the oldest Guilds. Presumably, the docks had been meant to stretch out all the way along the street, but Tor'Esint had never grown that large.

The blazermobile stopped in front of the Sarti Guild Hall and they got out. Greta hesitated at the steps. Letizia looked pityingly at her.

"It will be no worse than identifying him and you managed that just fine."

Greta took small comfort in that. She disliked people saying how well she handled things. If things needed to be done, she did them no matter how unpleasant, and then got on with her life. It wasn't that she was happy to do those things or that carrying on was easy – it was simply what needed to be done. What use was there in falling apart?

She walked up the stairs and into the Sarti Guild Hall. Letizia followed her. Without sparing a glance for the Great Works on display, Greta walked purposefully to the administration desk.

Ludovico Sarto looked up at her approach. He smiled, until he saw the Amministratrice.

"What's happened?" he asked, looking from one to the other.

Letizia raised an eyebrow at her. Greta shook her head. It was not her responsibility to tell the Guild. Letizia squared her shoulders and faced Ludovico.

"Signore Ranieri Sarto was found dead this morning. He has been formally identified by Signora Greta Sarta. We are here to inform the Sarti Guild and request they hand over his Final Testament if indeed he has one here."

Ludovico Sarto blanched. "What happened?"

"We're not certain," Letizia replied unhelpfully.

Greta frowned but said nothing. It was technically true but there were suspicions. Why had Letizia told her but wasn't telling Ludovico? Was it only because they couldn't hide the state of Ranieri's body from her.

"Can you search for the paperwork?" Letizia asked again, rather more forcefully.

Ludovico Sarto rang a bell on his desk. Another Sarta Amministratrice came down a side passage – Greta did not recognise this one.

"Watch the desk for me. I need to search for some records." The Amministratrice stood behind the desk, trying to look purposeful and failing. Ludovico turned his attention back to Letizia. "I may be some time."

"We'll wait," she replied.

Greta forced a smile when Ludovico glanced at her. This was not the way she'd expected to spend her afternoon and she was certain the same was true for the Sarti Amministratore.

After a few minutes, Letizia began pacing the room. Greta did not join her. Instead, she sat on one of the long benches provided along the wall. It put her directly across from some of the earliest Sarti Great Works. She marvelled at what had been considered a great work back when the Guild was first established. There were needles of all sizes, thimbles, spools, buttons of all different materials. They must have been amongst the first Great Works that the Inventrici Guild had started to poke their sticky fingers into.

Greta knew it was a jealous thought, spurred from bitterness at how powerful the Inventrici Guild had grown. She herself had collaborated with Aveline Inventrice to create the zipper before the Inter-Guild Edict had come into effect.

Aveline could have insisted on keeping the invention for herself, as she was the one who had truly created it. Instead, she had given Greta the second prototype to lodge as her own Great Work with the Sarti Guild in conjunction with Aveline's Great Work with the Inventrici Guild.

They had both benefitted from that. Greta had earned her Gold Guild Mark and Aveline her Electrum Guild Mark. Guild rules dictated that no other Inventrici or Sarti could now create or sell a zipper without paying a small patent fee to them. The fee was a pittance, really. Only a copper per zipper, but they were such popular items that Greta's own profits had doubled in the first year. She knew Aveline came from money, but it still must have made quite a difference to the Inventrice.

She wondered if people outside the Guilds knew how important Great Works were and that even seemingly insignificant ones could completely change the fortune of the creators. If they were popular or useful enough, of course.

The downside was that you could only ever submit four Great Works in your life. So, it was worth taking great care which ones were submitted. Few Maestri told their apprentices about that before their first Great Work was submitted. It made most of them waste that first chance of gaining ongoing patent fees.

Her own first Great Work had been a coat. It was nothing so very special but was considered adequate to earn her a Copper Guild Mark. Many Sarti apprentices earned their Copper Guild Mark by creating a variation of something which already existed. They really only needed to prove that they could create a pattern from scratch, which was what almost every customer would want from them the rest of their career.

She learned about the copper patent fee at that point because a few other Sarti Guild members had requested permission to use her design. She'd been proud of her coat at the time, but it really wasn't such a wonderful creation that everyone would want one.

With her second Great Work, she'd taken more care. Maestro Ranieri had encouraged her with the coat, though he must have known it would never have earned her much in its own right. He tried to convince her to submit another Great Work soon after, but she'd staunchly refused. She'd thought it more important to take the time to create something worthwhile. In fact, she remembered how angry she'd been with him when she realised that he'd known about the patent fees and encouraged her to submit something as worthless as a modified coat.

Her throat felt tight suddenly. That was the first time she'd stopped talking to him. It hadn't really been intentional, but she had been so angry that she hadn't taken the time to visit him, and he was too busy to visit her. Just like she herself was now. She knew she was going to pay for this delay later with late nights. But this was important. She still couldn't wrap her head around the fact that he was gone. It didn't seem real.

When she'd first met Aveline, things had changed dramatically and quickly. It had been years ago. Aveline was still on her Copper Guild Mark then, and Greta on her Silver Guild Mark. Aveline had come in looking to purchase a work dress. Something that she could comfortably wear in her workshop but was practical enough for her work.

Together, they'd come up with the idea of pockets for dresses. It wasn't such a stretch of the imagination and Greta couldn't understand why no Sarta had yet to do it. It wasn't really something that should have been considered for a Great Work, but she'd submitted it anyway.

It hadn't been accepted, as pockets in themselves weren't new, but it had made her very popular among the fashionable signore of Tor'Esint. Her clientele doubled almost overnight. The pocketed dress may as well have been a Great Work for all the business it brought her.

Her Electrum Guild Mark was earned soon after the pocketed dress submission for an outer corset made of leather with pouches built in for workbooks or pattern books and loops for alchemical vials or tools. She'd simply taken the pocket idea one step further.

By this point, she'd changed her mind and agreed with Maestro Ranieri that she should have concentrated on working her way up the Guild ladder as quickly as possible. Now she could start charging more to her already extensive client list.

She'd reunited with him and apologised profusely for being so stubborn. He'd smiled that calm and knowing smile that always put her at ease, no matter how badly she felt, and everything had gone back to normal. They had both made a consistent effort to see one another at least once a fortnight.

Once she earned her Gold Guild Mark for the zipper in collaboration with Aveline, there had been even less time. Their meetings went from fortnightly, to monthly, to just a few times a year.

Greta clasped her fingers tightly. That was what she regretted most of all. The fact that he was her favourite person in Tor'Esint, and she barely got to see him. Was being successful really so important as to lose touch with close friends?

"I have it here," Ludovico said, walking back into the room, waving a piece of paper in the air.

Greta looked up, startled. She'd been so lost in thought that she hadn't heard him return. Letizia halted her pacing and walked purposefully towards him. Greta, curious despite herself, stood up and joined them.

"What does it say?" asked Greta. It earned her a sharp look from Letizia, but she didn't care. She had just as much right to find out as anyone else.

"It's addressed to you."

Ludovico held out the sealed paper to her. Greta stared at it.

"Well, open it!" Letizia snapped.

Greta stared at her until she apologised. Ludovico continued to hold out the Final Testament to her. Greta smoothed her dress and took it. With extreme care, she pulled the wax off one part of the paper. The brittle wax broke into tiny pieces in her hand. It must have been written a long time ago.

Trying not to breathe too quickly, Greta opened the paper. It was dated twelve years ago – her final year as an apprentice. That was an awfully long time for Ranieri not to have changed his mind about anything.

*Gildadi, First day of Sarti*
*Two hundred and eighteenth year After Implosion*
*The Final Testament of Ranieri Sarto*

*To my apprentice, Greta Sarta (for I know you will soon become one of us), I leave everything – my wealth, my workshop, everything within my workshop and my own personal stores within my warehouse. In addition to this, I give you the ongoing patent fees to all my Great Works.*

*I am certain we will argue about your own Great Works, so I hope by now you understand why I encouraged you to rise quickly rather than focus too much on the brilliance of each Great Work. I had always planned to look after you. You were my brightest apprentice, and my favourite.*

*If we are still at odds, I forgive you as I hope you can forgive me. If we are speaking but have no time for each other, know that I understood. It's always difficult for two such talented people to remain as close as I'm certain we did.*

*For my last piece of advice, choose an apprentice you like, their character and their work – it can be one of your first or one of your last – give them the rights to your work when you die so that they may thrive and have every opportunity you ever wished for them. I am helping you to change your world. You can help your chosen apprentice do the same thing.*

*Together we can do great things!*
*Forever your Maestro and friend,*
*Ranieri Sarto*

*Post Script*
*To the Sarti Guild, I give the gift of a workshop of Greta Sarta's choosing (assuming she currently has one of her own). I wish for this workshop to be given, or sold if you think it necessary, to a worthy Sarti Guild member.*
*Ranieri Sarto*

Greta read it through twice. Her fingers were trembling, and she had to re-read lines over and over to decipher his script. Tears stung her eyes moments before they fell down her flushed cheeks.

"Well, what does it say?" Letizia asked, annoyed.

Greta looked up at the impatient face, the emotionless eyes.

"Nothing you need concern yourself with. It's for me and the Sarti Guild. No one else."

"Rubbish!" Letizia said, holding out her hand for the paper. "There will be all sorts of legalities to sort out."

Greta shook her head. "No, there won't. He left everything to me. *Everything*."

Ludovico drew in a sharp breath. Greta knew he had understood what she was not saying. The Amministratrice likely had no idea about patent fees. There would be nothing like that in her line of work. Greta was not going to be the one to spill the secret.

"If it makes you feel better, Ludovico can read the testament, but it is a Guild matter, and I will not allow this document to pass to anyone outside the Sarti Guild."

Greta handed the letter to Ludovico who took it and immediately began to read it.

"This is preposterous!" huffed Letizia. "I am a Tor'Esint Amministratrice. Guild matter or not, you *must* show me the letter. It could prove pertinent to the case at hand."

Ludovico quickly scanned the letter and looked up with a harsh expression.

"You have no authority within these walls unless you have an accusation against a Sarti Guild member about breaking the Trading Edict or the Inter-Guild Edict. You will, of course, need proof to back up any accusation, so I suggest you choose your next words wisely."

Letizia's face turned an unhealthy shade of red as she stood there, hands clenched into tight fists. Greta felt afraid of her for the first time that day. Could she really be so angry over this? What did the Amministratori want with a Sarto's Final Testament in the first place?

"In that case, I must ask you to leave, Signora Amministratrice. Greta Sarta will make her own way home after the matter of the Final Testament is settled."

Letizia glared at him with fire in her eyes, then spun on her heel and stormed down the hall of Great Works, slamming the Guild Hall doors shut behind her.

Ludovico waited a few moments, then took Greta by the arm and led her into the inner chambers of the Guild Hall. Greta infrequently had cause to walk past the administration desk, except to the large hall where the Guild meetings and the annual Guild Ball were held, on the rare occasion they won the bidding war for the ball.

However, Ludovico did not take her to that room. He took her down a long corridor, lined with wooden doors. They passed so many, she didn't know how he was keeping track of which one he wanted. He chose one, seemingly at random, and ushered her inside. He locked the door behind her and waved the paper in front of her face.

"We have a problem," he told her. "No one has ever tried to pass on their patent fees to someone else. Technically, I don't even know if it's allowed."

"Well," Greta laughed mirthlessly, "Ranieri was never one to play by the rules. What do we do now?"

Ludovico read the testament again. Greta waited patiently. She knew it was a wasted work afternoon – there was no point in getting upset about it.

Eventually, Ludovico looked up again. "Do you know what he has in his warehouse, or is it better not to ask?"

Greta shook her head. "Not specifically, but I can imagine he wouldn't want the Amministratori poking around in there. Much like most Guild members, I should think."

"I thought as much," replied Ludovico, chewing on his lip. "What about in his workshop?"

"No, he would never keep anything there that he shouldn't have."

"I suppose we start there, then." Ludovico ran his fingers through his thick mop of hair. "This is a mess. I don't know how we're going to sort it out. We'll need the Maestri's approval to pass on the patent fees to you. And we'll have to sort out the workshop situation. You'll need to decide which one to keep. Same for the warehouse presumably."

Greta's mind slowly ticked over the situation. Ludovico had hit on an important point. The last time she'd seen Ranieri's workshop was over three months ago, but even then, it looked the same as when she'd been apprenticed with him.

She smiled at the memory of his bolts of cloth surrounding the walls on every side, his mannequins taking up the entire street window. There was barely any definition between his workshop and his shopfront. Only his living quarters were completely separate.

It was cosy, comforting – more like home than her own workshop ever felt, but she knew there was no point in having two workshops much as she might love both of them.

"What will happen with his apprentice?" Greta asked. "I'm not even certain I've met this one."

Ludovico shrugged. "Teodoro has just begun his second year. I suppose we'll ask around if anyone wants to take him right away, otherwise he'll go to the top of the apprentice list." He gave Greta an appraising look. "I don't suppose *you'd* consider taking him?"

"What? No!" Greta replied before she could stop herself. "I already have three apprentices and I'm struggling with them as it is. I can't imagine taking on another one, even if the Guild allowed me to."

Ludovico sighed. "No, I don't suppose they would. I really don't think anyone else is in a position to take on a second-year apprentice right now though. It's always difficult to take over teaching from someone else. I just thought, you knew Ranieri's style the best. You'd probably be able to teach the boy the same way."

Greta paused. There had been such a big gap between earning her Copper and Silver Guild mark that she'd taken on each apprentice straight after earning her Silver, Electrum and Gold Guild Marks, without any thought for their development. She barely had time to teach them as it was. Greta had never known Ranieri to have three apprentices at once. She was certain he would have warned her off doing so if he'd had the chance, but she hadn't asked him before applying for Marta, and then Sofia.

She knew she wasn't teaching them the way Ranieri had taught her. This week, saying that she would take one apprentice and show them the entire process of making a dress from start to finish, was the first time she'd started to feel like she was in control of the situation, like she was finally doing things the way Ranieri had with her.

It all clicked into place.

Every time she had rebelled against the way she'd been taught – things had gone badly for her. Every time she'd done as Ranieri had taught her, even if it were different to what other Sarti would have done, things went better.

So, she found herself thinking, what would Ranieri do in her position?

"Dovi, do you know offhand how much Ranieri's Great Works bring in per month?"

Ludovico shook his head. "No, but I know it's a handsome amount. He always collaborated heavily with the Inventrici Guild. His Copper Great Work was the self-tying cravat. Then there's the adjustable fabric wall mount, I believe it's used more in haberdasheries and Sarti warehouses than actual workshops. I'm sure you know the one – where you turn a handle to rotate it until your desired bolt is in front of you? Then there were the magnifying glasses. Those are quite expensive, so not as common. His Gold Great Work was the retractable measuring tape. Just the tape on its own would bring in a hefty price. Why do you ask?"

"If no one will take him, does Ranieri's apprentice *have* to just go back on the list? Could he, for example, live with me and my apprentices but take care of Ranieri's workshop for me? He could take small orders for repairs that he could easily do himself to keep his skills up. Then when I'm done with my older apprentice, I could take him on. We could use Ranieri's patent fees to help pay for the boy's upkeep if it's enough."

Ludovico laughed. "It's enough, by far. But do you think it would work?"

Greta shrugged. "I honestly have no idea. What I can tell you is that I can't deal with four apprentices in my workshop right now. I'd like to be able to teach one my skills, let another tend my shop and mend clothes and send the other to keep the boy company in Ranieri's workshop. I could alternate them for every new project, so they all get a turn, and they'll learn independence by keeping shop without me."

"It could work, if you trust your girls."

Greta narrowed her eyes at him. "I trust my girls. They wouldn't do anything stupid in a workshop. I can only assume neither would Ranieri's boy."

"Fine, fine." Ludovico held up his hands. "Why don't you head home. I'll see if I can find the boy and bring him to you until things are decided. If you have time tomorrow, I'll take you to Ranieri's workshop and warehouse so we can figure out how to deal with everything."

"And the patent fees?" Greta asked. This wasn't something she was going to let slide just because it was a difficult problem to solve.

"I'll ... talk to the Maestri. They may need to consult other Guild Maestri to see if this has come up before. It may take some time before the matter is resolved."

"Very well," Greta said, smoothing down her skirt. "Just ensure the patent fees are tallied up during that time so I'm not left short when the matter is resolved."

Ludovico shook his head at her. "You presume too much. Don't get your hopes up Greta. You'll be lucky enough if the Maestri agree to your unconventional apprentice solution."

"I know," Greta shrugged. "I'll expect to see you later with the boy."

Ludovico nodded and opened the door for her. Greta wasted no time in leaving the Guild Hall.

\*\*\*

When she returned home, it was to the sound of utter calm. Marta was happily edging navy satin in the shop. Sofia and Annika were nowhere to be seen.

"Maestra, we expected you much earlier. Is anything the matter?"

Greta didn't even know how to begin answering that.

"Where are the others?" she asked instead.

Marta frowned. "Annika's cooking dinner and Sofia's in the workshop edging the organza. Seems Annika wanted as little help as possible in the kitchen."

Greta closed her eyes and breathed deeply, wondering if she could trade Annika for Ranieri's boy. She shook her head. It was a cruel thought brought on by tiredness and stress. Annika's character needed shaping, that was all.

"Ask them to come in here, please. We have things to discuss."

Marta immediately left to do her bidding. She was a sweet girl, very obedient, but with little backbone. Greta would need to do something about that. The only one of her apprentices she didn't want to change at all was Sofia.

Could Sofia be the one she chose to favour, as Ranieri had chosen her? It was probably too soon to tell. She still had years to get to know Sofia before making that decision.

The girls entered the workshop, whispering amongst themselves. They would get no answers from Marta, as she had none to give. Greta silenced them all by raising her hand.

"My old Maestro, Ranieri Sarto, has died. He has left everything to me. We will deal with all the legalities of it in time. The most immediate change will be with his apprentice. As you are aware, I cannot take on more apprentices, but it is likely that no one else will want to take on the boy.

"I have proposed an arrangement to the Sarti Guild. I will spare you the details. For now, all you need to know is that the boy, when he is located, will be brought here to stay with us. It may be a permanent situation; it may be a temporary one. We won't know until the Guild decides on several issues surrounding Ranieri's death."

Greta eyed her apprentices. Marta and Sofia looked apprehensive, but Annika was absolutely furious.

"Questions?" Greta asked.

"Where will this *boy* sleep?" Annika asked, not bothering to hide her anger. "We've barely enough room as it is, and I won't be giving up *my* bed for him."

Greta smiled a thin, tight smile. "No, I don't suppose you would *ever* dream to suggest that for yourself. However, as we don't have any beds to spare, you may find yourself sharing with Marta or Sofia, while *their* bed is given to the boy."

"What?!" Annika shrieked. "No! Absolutely not!"

"I'll give you a choice, Annika," Greta replied coldly. "You share your bed with a fellow apprentice, or you sleep on the floor. Am I understood?"

"I won't do it!" Annika yelled. "It isn't fair."

Greta took a heartless pleasure in the pain she was causing Annika after years of letting the girl get her way with everything.

"Thank you for making the decision so easy for me," Greta said with a smile. "Ranieri's apprentice will take *your* bed. You can sleep on the floor."

"No," Annika sulked. "I'll sleep in Marta's bed."

Marta frowned at the proclamation. "No, you won't. Maestra said you can sleep on the floor. I'm not sharing my bed with you when you're being horrid."

Well, good for her, Greta thought to herself. Marta had finally found her spine. It had probably been helped along all day with Greta and Sofia refusing to take any nonsense from the older apprentice, but at least she had finally gotten there herself.

"She didn't mean it," Annika said in a sickly-sweet voice. "Of *course* I'll share with you."

"No, you won't," Greta reaffirmed. She did not trust Marta to assert herself twice in a minute. "Now, go back to the kitchen and prepare enough food for another person."

Annika stared at her, wide-mouthed. She had never been treated like this in Greta's workshop and Greta knew it was her own fault. She should never have allowed Annika to act so superior to her fellow apprentices when they began. She should have kept a closer eye on who was doing what with the mending. Which reminded her.

"Sofia, be a dear and bring out everyone's stocking to me. Annika, stay a moment before finishing dinner."

Annika crossed her arms with quiet fury. Sofia went into the workshop and returned shortly after with three mended stockings.

"This is mine," she said, handing Greta the stocking which she had inspected earlier that morning. "And this is Marta's and this one's Annika's."

Greta examined the stockings carefully. Sofia's was the best by far. She could hardly tell where it had been mended. The thread was a perfect match, and the stitching was so fine that it was hard to see.

Marta's was only marginally worse. She'd chosen the correct thread, but her stitching wasn't quite as fine as Sofia's. However, it was still good enough that no customer would have cause for complaint.

Finally, Greta examined Annika's one. She was appalled by the workmanship. The stitching was woeful – worse than a first-year apprentice. And the thread was completely the wrong colour.

"Sofia, Marta, you've both done a lovely job on your stockings. I'm impressed. It's clear that you've both taken pride in your work all the years you've been here."

Annika huffed as the girls exchanged broad smiles with each other.

"Annika. What can I say?" Greta inadvertently scrunched the problematic stocking in her hand. "Your darning is appalling. I will not have any customers of mine complaining because of your poor sewing. When you've finished making dinner, you will re-mend this stocking until I am satisfied with the quality.

"Tomorrow, *you* shall be the one mending all the clothes. Marta may help you if we're running behind on orders, but otherwise, I'll need her to continue edging the satin."

Annika yelled wordlessly and threw her arms down before turning towards the kitchen. Greta let her go. There was nothing else to say to the girl. When she was certain Annika was out of earshot, she gathered Sofia and Marta closer to her.

"Things are going to change from now onwards. I know I haven't been the best Maestra I could be up until this point, and I want to do better. Annika, for all her *wonderful* qualities has suffered just as much as the two of you from this, only in a different way.

"I meant what I said earlier. I will keep each of you with me for one project at a time while the other two tend the shop and mend any simple repairs and edge material. If there is time to spare between those duties, there are many skills I should be teaching you and I apologise I haven't already.

"The most important thing you can do for me is to not let Annika get away with her usual nonsense. That will go for me as well. She's not to order you around and force you to do her share of the work. You are to come to me if you notice her slacking off. You're also to come to me if you notice she is trying to pass of sub-standard work like *this*."

She shook Annika's stocking in front of them. They both looked closely at Annika's handiwork. Marta gasped at the atrocity, but Sofia laughed long and loud. Greta couldn't help but join in.

"It's no laughing matter," she said between giggles. "We need to fix this problem."

"You just called Annika a *problem*," Sofia said and even Marta joined in the laughing.

\*\*\*

Much later that evening, there was a knock at the door. Trading had been over for hours. Annika was cleaning the dishes from her just edible cooking. Greta, Sofia and Marta were gathered around the kitchen table having a nice cup of tea and a chat about nothing significant.

Greta rose to answer it. Ludovico stood on the street with a boy no older than fifteen, roughly Marta's age. The boy was rubbing his arms, eyes downcast. Ludovico's hand rested on his shoulder.

"Come in out of the cold," Greta urged them.

Ludovico gently pushed the boy inside and followed him in. It didn't look like he was happy to be there but, Greta reflected, he must be upset with his change in circumstance as well as the death of Ranieri. She wondered what would happen to her apprentices if she died suddenly or was taken to prison or stripped of her Gold Guild Mark. It did not bear thinking about.

"Greta, this is Teodoro di Pierluigi. Teodoro, this is the signora I told you about – Ranieri's old apprentice, Greta Sarta."

Teodoro nodded and offered up his hand to her. Greta shook it firmly as did he. She intensely disliked people with limp handshakes – they were either weak or they thought *she* was weak and didn't want to injure her.

"Teodoro, there's food for you in the kitchen, just through that door."

Greta pointed the way, and the boy obediently left the room. She turned her attention back to Ludovico.

"What news?"

Ludovico looked behind her to check the boy had gone in.

"We found him in Ranieri's workshop, huddled away behind bolts of cloth. He wasn't surprised to hear Ranieri had been found dead – it was almost like he'd been expecting it. I asked him what he knew, but he feigns ignorance. If you can get anything out of him, let me know."

Greta nodded. This raised more questions than answers. She needed answers.

"Did you talk to the Sarti Maestri?" she asked him.

Ludovico spread his hands wide. "I showed them the testament. They said to leave the matter with them. That they would discuss it."

Greta sighed loudly. She hadn't really expected an answer so soon, but it certainly would have helped her make plans.

"What of Teodoro?"

"As you suggested, they agreed he can stay with you for now. He can finish current repairs that he would have done anyway and accept the payment for them himself if you wish. Beyond that, again, they need to discuss it. They were happy enough for one of your apprentices to accompany him in Ranieri's workshop until the matter is sorted."

"Well, that's one small blessing," Greta replied. "Have you explained the situation to Teodoro?"

Ludovico shook his head. "I only told him he'd be spending the night here."

Greta rolled her eyes. "Give the boy a little stability, Dovi! Let's tell him now. My girls know about everything but the *extra* matter."

She didn't need to say what she meant; Ludovico knew. And until *that* matter was resolved, it would be safer to say nothing.

Greta ushered Ludovico into her kitchen. She realised that he had never, in fact, set foot inside her shop so late in the evening, let alone the domestic side of her house. Well, there was nothing for it. Decorum went out the window when there were stray apprentices to care for.

She found Teodoro sitting at the kitchen table, quietly eating a bowl of pasta. Annika had done a passable job of it, even though it was a little bland. Sofia and Marta were sipping their tea and watching him with an almost scientific interest.

"Girls, this is Teodoro. He'll be staying with us for a while. Teodoro, these are my apprentices, Annika, Marta and Sofia."

Teodoro nodded but kept eating.

"We've set aside a bed for you, but there aren't many rooms in the house, so you'll be in with the girls. The Sarti Guild has agreed you can stay here until other arrangements can be made. Does that suit you?"

Teodoro looked at her from behind blank eyes. He shrugged. Greta supposed it was the most he was capable of right now. She herself felt like curling up on her bed with a blanket and having a long cry. It wouldn't help Ranieri, and it certainly wouldn't help her own situation, but it might make her feel that little bit better.

A world without Ranieri in it was just ... unfathomable. She didn't want to think about it. For the moment, she would pretend that it was one of their long absences between seeing one another, that he wasn't really dead. But that couldn't last. She knew the sadness would come tumbling down on top of her at some point. She only hoped it would stay bottled up at least until her charges had gone to sleep.

"Teodoro, I'm going now," Ludovico called out to the boy. "If you need anything, ask Greta and she will help you. If you need me, you can find me at the Sarti Guild Hall. Understand?"

Teodoro looked up and nodded. He didn't get up to farewell Ludovico. Greta showed the Guild Amministratore to the door. When she returned to the kitchen, Teodoro had risen to bring his plate to Annika.

"You can clean that yourself," she told him.

Teodoro shrugged and was about to do so when Greta stepped in.

"Annika, I thought I made it clear that you'll be doing domestic chores today. That includes Teodoro's. Now, Teodoro, come with me and I'll show you the house."

The boy left his plate on the bench for Annika. She scowled at him, even after Greta shot her a warning glance.

Greta pointed Teodoro towards the workshop and watched her girls. They all looked at him with varying degrees of interest and friendliness. It was certainly going to be an interesting few days until things got settled.

She started her short tour of the house. "This is my workshop. Through that door is the shopfront where you first came in. Over here are the stairs to go up. Let me show you the bedrooms."

Teodoro followed her up the stairs. They were narrow and dark. She wished there was a permanent solution to light the way without fire. Instead, she pulled out one of a set of three friction lights that Aveline had made for her in exchange for a new coat and wound it up.

The small light was only bright enough to light the area directly around them. Greta pointed out the bedrooms and the water closet to Teodoro.

"I'm sorry there isn't much room here. But you can have Annika's bed for tonight and we'll sort out a more permanent solution later."

Teodoro looked around the rooms in silence. He nodded when she told him about his bed, but still said nothing. Greta was beginning to wonder if the boy was mute.

"Teodoro, I'm sorry about Ranieri. I loved him too. At least now you're here, we can remember him together."

The boy gave her an odd look. "I didn't love him. Not like he loved you and I s'pose you loved him. He spoke about you all the time."

"Oh." Greta didn't know how to answer him. She'd assumed any apprentice of Ranieri's would adore him as she had. "Well, I'm sorry your apprenticeship ended so abruptly. Ludovico and I are doing everything we can to fix that problem."

Teodoro shrugged. It made Greta wonder if he cared about his apprenticeship at all or if he were one of those children who had put his name down on every Apprentice List in Tor'Esint in the hopes that at least one of them would choose him. She'd heard of children like that before. It was mostly orphans or children whose parents needed to get rid of them because they were getting too expensive to feed.

"Right, well, I've got work to do. You can go to sleep now or get to know the girls. The choice is yours."

She left the boy in the room and returned to the kitchen. Annika had finished the dishes by the time she arrived and was having a cup of tea with the others.

"Annika, did you have time to re-darn your stocking this afternoon?"

Annika nodded.

"Go and fetch it for me, please."

Greta waited patiently for Annika to return with her stocking and held out her hand for it. She examined it closely.

"You made quite a mess of this when unpicking it. I'm certain the tear wasn't so large earlier today. But at least you've chosen the right colour thread this time. The stitching still needs work, but it's passable. I'll expect better from you tomorrow."

Annika took the stocking, her face flushed brightly. She wasn't used to Greta saying anything about her work. Clearly, this entire day had not gone as Annika would have expected, but Greta had no sympathy for her.

"Sofia, come show me your progress in the workshop."

Sofia led the way with a glass lantern into the workshop. It was the only way Greta allowed a flame in here. She still felt it was a great risk, but there was little other choice when she had to work past sunset.

"I finished tacking my bodice, just like you did with the cotton and linen. And I finished the beading on the circle design, but I haven't done much of the edging on the organza."

She showed her work proudly to Greta. The beading was perfect. The bodice left much to be desired, but Greta had expected that. She spent time explaining to Sofia how to fix it, how to pin it in place so that she knew where to take it in or let it out. Sofia listened intently and insisted on fixing it there and then. Greta was impressed with how quickly she picked up the skills now that she was being paid enough attention.

Greta looked at the time. It was well past nine in the evening.

"That's good work for today, Sofia. Off you go to bed and we'll continue this in the morning."

Greta lit another lantern before she left, causing Sofia to turn with a frown.

"Aren't you going to bed now too?" she asked.

Greta smiled and shook her head. "Not just yet. There are some things I want to do first."

Sofia stood there for a moment, looking as awkward as Greta had ever seen her.

"I ... I'm sorry about Maestro Ranieri. I know you were already missing him yesterday. I can't imagine how you must feel now. I just want you to know that ... you'd be missed too, if you died."

Before Greta could reply, Sofia left the room. Greta smiled through her tears. Yes, Sofia would be her special one. She was the only one who noticed anything about her and who took in everything she had to say like it was written on a golden leaf.

# Chapter 6 – Argentodi 25 Alchimisti 230 Years After Implosion

Ludovico came early to bring Greta to Ranieri's workshop. She'd been up half the night, tossing and turning, playing out her memories of Ranieri, berating herself for not following his example as a good Maestro, agonising over all the time she should have spent with him – he was family to her. He knew it would happen too. He'd said as much in his will. So why couldn't she forgive herself?

His death was too raw. She didn't want to dwell on it and by going to his workshop, she wouldn't be able to avoid it.

"I'm sorry, Dovi, I don't have time. I lost half a day of work yesterday and with an extra mouth to feed, I cannot afford to fall behind."

Ludovico gave her an odd look. "You needn't worry about that."

"You don't know," Greta replied firmly. "Not until the Maestri have made their decision on the matter."

"But..." Ludovico paused. "Then, you didn't know?"

Greta looked questioningly at him. Ludovico glanced around the room, clearly not wanting to be overheard.

"Even if the Maestri don't agree to ... the other matter, Ranieri had a fortune stashed away. He saved like a miser, right from the beginning. And he left *everything* to you. Everything. You could choose not to lift a finger the rest of your days and still not starve."

Greta heard him, but the words weren't sinking in. It was impossible for her fortunes to change so completely. She couldn't understand how her maestro had managed to save such a sum.

"You must be mistaken, Dovi. Ranieri always bought the latest inventions and spared no expense for the finest materials he could find. I constantly worried he would lose everything."

Ludovico smiled in a knowing way. "That's true, but those inventions and fine materials only brought him more money. Ranieri was the richest Sarto in the Guild. And now, as his heir, you are. I've already made the transfer to your vault as there was no question about *that* side of things."

Greta's legs felt suddenly weak, her head heavy. Before she could fall, she took a seat at her workbench.

"How much are we talking about? Do you even know?"

Ludovico dragged another chair over and sat in front of her.

"Greta, you now have well over five thousand gold coins in your Guild vault."

Greta's ears started ringing as her pulse raced. She found the wastebasket just in time to heave up her breakfast into it.

Sofia came running into the room. "Maestra, is everything alright?"

"Water, girl. She needs water." Ludovico instructed her.

Greta was thankful for that. She didn't think she could talk. Her entire world had just changed.

Sofia returned shortly with a glass of water. She stood by Greta, helping her drink it and refused to leave when Ludovico tried to shoo her away.

"She can stay," Greta said in a hoarse voice. "Sofia is my little rock."

That earned a smile from the girl, which in turn made Greta smile. She managed to muster up some strength and let herself think of what Ludovico had told her. Five thousand gold pieces was beyond imagining. She wondered if even Aveline had that much money at her disposal. She would be able to buy anything, even from the Mercantili Guild, and not feel the pinch. Though she wouldn't want to. Not if she could help it. But she might be able to help other Sarti Guild members, to raise their fortunes so that eventually they could overthrow the Mercantili Guild and their ridiculous Edicts.

"I thank you for the information, but it doesn't change my position right at this moment. I have a dress to finish, commissioned by Signora Loyola. It must be perfect, and it must not be late. Permit me to deal with this other matter later?"

Ludovico hesitated, clearly reluctant to talk about patent fees in front of an apprentice, but then he nodded. "Will you still be sending Teodoro to finish the mending jobs at Ranieri's?"

Greta thought about it for a moment. She was not entirely certain about the boy. It might be better to keep a close eye on him.

"Actually, no. Could you bring all Ranieri's unfinished jobs here and place a sign in his window directing people to my workshop to pick them up?"

Ludovico shrugged. "Yes, that would be possible. I'll take the boy with me so he can help me find all the orders. What if there are large jobs?"

Greta nodded. "Bring those too. Though I might have to write to those customers to explain the inevitable delay."

"Very well." Ludovico stood and held out his hand to her. Greta shook it but did not stand. She wasn't certain her legs could carry her yet. Ludovico noticed and turned to Sofia. "Take care of her, girl. She's had quite a shock."

Greta saw Sofia's worried glance, but the girl nodded and forced the glass of water back into her hand. Ludovico showed himself out and took Teodoro with him as he passed through the showroom. Greta barely noticed. It felt like the world was moving past her. She just wanted it to slow down and stop so she could catch her breath. She closed her eyes and breathed quickly. Her head was spinning. Her stomach churned uncomfortably, and she heaved again.

Sofia had anticipated her, and Greta opened her eyes to see the wastebasket was in front of her face, still full of vomit. Which made her vomit again. She closed her eyes and pushed the basket away.

"Water," she whispered.

Sofia held the glass to Greta's lips and helped her take a sip, and then another. Slowly, she opened her eyes. Sofia was watching her closely. The poor girl – she had no idea what had caused this, but she was willing to do all she could to help Greta anyway.

What had she ever done to deserve such dedication from the young girl? If anything, Sofia should resent Greta for her neglect over the past three years. It seemed implausible that she didn't.

"Are you feeling better?" Sofia asked after a quiet moment.

Greta nodded. She had been so lost in thought she hadn't noticed that Sofia had taken the waste basket out of the room and, with it, the stench of vomit. It was one thing she could not abide. The smell, sight, or sound of it only made her feel worse. Greta forced herself not to think of it as bile seeped into her mouth. She swallowed it back down and took another sip of water.

"Thank you, Sofia. Please ask Marta to continue edging the satin and have Annika tend the shop and continue her mending chores. Then we can return to our work back here."

She tried to smile at her apprentice, but she couldn't muster the strength. It had been a trying few days.

\*\*\*

Greta spent the morning helping Marta and Sofia with the edging. It was something she usually left for the girls to do alone, but this dress was causing her no small amount of stress and she needed to focus on something simple right now.

The bodice was going to take the bulk of her time, and the promised beading would only add to that. However, Greta was fast coming to the conclusion that Sofia would be able to help with it. The beading could only be tackled once the bodice was finished. Organza was so fine and flexible a material that if they did the beading beforehand and then stitched it into the satin, it might stretch in ungainly ways, making the beading look wrong.

She used the finest needle she had to edge such a delicate material, her thumb protected by a copper thimble. It made Greta recall the one at the Sarti Guild Hall. That had been one of the first Great Works. If that patent fee had been inherited, the current Sarta would still be earning a fortune. Every Sarta in Tor'Fsint used copper thimbles, as did every apprentice. It was hard to think of doing a full day's work without one.

If Ranieri's plan to pass his patent fees on to her worked, it would set an important precedent, not only for the Sarti Guild, but for every Guild in

Tor'Esint. Potentially, Guild members could pass on their patent fees to their non-Guild family members, distributing wealth further than it had ever been.

Greta smiled to herself. Ranieri had not just planned to change *her* life, but the entire town's. If it worked.

"No!"

The shout brought Greta back to her workshop.

"I'm done with this. I won't do any more!"

Greta gently put down the satin and walked into the shop. Annika was standing, fists clenched, red in the face, glaring at Marta. The younger apprentice had her hands on her hips, returning the glare. Ranieri's boy stood between them with a bundle of clothes. The door was open behind him.

"What in Caldera's smoke is going on?" Greta demanded in a low tone. "Raised voices are *never* allowed in my workshop. Imagine what passersby will think!"

No one answered her. Greta turned her attention to Annika. She was certain her oldest apprentice was the one to blame.

"This *boy* has returned from Ranieri's workshop with a whole bundle of repairs and *Marta* is under the impression that I'm to help him with that as well as do our repairs."

Greta straightened her spine and took a calming breath.

"Marta is correct. Your needlework is appalling – the only way to improve it is to do more of it. If that means mountains of repairs, then that is what you'll do."

"No," repeated Annika in a softer voice, though no less venomous. "I don't see why I should have to help with Ranieri's repairs. They aren't *our* responsibility."

It dawned on Greta that perhaps she had not explained everything to her apprentices. Perhaps it was time to do so now.

"Teodoro, close the door please."

He shook his head almost imperceptibly. "But Ludovico is still coming with the larger orders. I was meant to go and help him when ... *this* happened. I only need to know where to put the clothes. That's all."

Greta drew in another breath and held it. She pointed to an empty basket.

"Put them in there for now. We'll sort it all out in a moment. Marta, go and help Teodoro bring in the rest of the orders with Ludovico."

To her credit, Marta obeyed without question. Greta should have asked Annika to do it, but she was not prepared to endure an outburst from the girl when she was certain to have yet another in just a few more minutes. The prospect of trading Annika for Teodoro was becoming more enticing the more she thought of it.

Sofia joined them in the shopfront as Teodoro, Marta and Ludovico entered with armloads of material and patterns. Greta's eyes bulged at the sight of it all. She didn't have space in her workshop for so many extra projects.

"Where do you want them, Maestra?" Marta asked from behind a bundle of unnaturally bright green material.

Greta had never seen the likes of it before. She pinched the skin between her eyes where a headache was beginning to manifest.

"The kitchen table. Put it all on the kitchen table until I find some space. Dovi, you could have told me how much there was before bringing it all here."

"Sorry, Greta," Ludovico replied in an unapologetic tone. "I don't have so much time to be running your errands back and forth, checking how many orders there were for you. I brought it all in one trip, so you don't need to worry about it later."

Greta sighed. "Very well. Thank you for running my *errands*."

The three of them disappeared into the kitchen and reappeared quickly. Marta went back to her usual spot behind the counter, Teodoro shadowing her. Ludovico tipped his hat to Greta.

"I'll let you know as soon as I hear about the other matter. In the meantime, you're going to need to think about the workshop situation and what you intend to do about it. And Greta," he leaned in closer so only she could hear him, "I'm sorry about Ranieri, I really am. Watch yourself in case the same thing happens to you."

Greta leaned back to look him in the eye. "Was it murder then?"

He shrugged. "It's not the first case of this *green death* we've seen. Be careful, Greta. We can't afford to lose you too."

Ludovico's whispered breath on her ear suddenly made Greta feel uncomfortable. She and Ludovico had once been intimate and they were as close to friends as a Guild member and an Amministratore could be, but that was all. That was as much as she wanted or needed in her life.

Greta pointedly took a step back from him. She saw the confused, then pained expression flicker in his eyes. She cursed herself for having misread the situation so badly. He hadn't wanted that either. And now she had made things awkward between them. Hopefully, not for too long.

She closed the door behind Ludovico and locked it, turning back to face the room full of apprentices, not all of which were hers, but all of whom were now her responsibility.

"I have some important decisions to make in the coming days, mainly due to Ranieri Sarto's death. These decisions will affect each of you in some way, but I'm certain that I have not foreseen everything, so you must forgive me if other things arise which I do not mention today."

Greta looked at each of them in turn. Annika was the only one who was already angry. Sofia smiled encouragingly, as though she were the oldest apprentice in this situation. Greta adored her for that. Marta waited patiently as ever but Teodoro appeared almost bored. Greta couldn't understand the boy.

He'd already told her that he did not love Ranieri – a thought which she found unfathomable. He also didn't seem to care about his apprenticeship at all, nor had he expressed any sort of gratitude to Greta for taking him in. She wondered if it had been a wise decision, but it was done now and there was nothing to do about it for the time being.

"You may have understood by now that Ranieri left everything to me, including everything in his workshop. For this reason, we've brought all his unfinished orders here so that we can complete them for his customers. The repairs shouldn't be a problem. For the larger orders, I'll send the customers a letter to enquire whether they want me to complete the orders for them. I have little doubt that most of them will still want their orders.

"At some point, I'll need to decide whether to remain in this workshop or move to Ranieri's workshop. It's not a decision I will take lightly as it will affect all of us. I will also need to make an arrangement with the Sarti Guild regarding Teodoro."

At the mention of his name, Teodoro looked up.

"What sort of arrangement?" he asked sharply.

Greta was put off by his accusatory tone. She smoothed down her skirt before she could stop herself. It was a habit she wished she could break.

"For one thing, how your apprenticeship will continue. There may be other Sarti out there who are willing to take on a second-year apprentice, but we won't know until the Amministratori ask them. For another, whether you should live with us until such time as your apprenticeship is sorted out. This will only become a long-term arrangement if no other Sarta will take you. Then you would need to wait for one of my own apprentices to achieve their Copper Guild Mark before you could officially become one of my apprentices."

Teodoro crossed his arms, frowning. "And what if I don't want to continue my apprenticeship? Or if I don't want to stay here?"

Greta blinked. And then blinked again, trying to make sense of the boy.

"Well, is that the case? Do you wish to discontinue your apprenticeship?"

The boy shrugged. "Don't know. But I don't want *you* or anyone else making that decision for me. I signed up with the old coot just to get out of the orphanage. Sarti have one of the shortest apprenticeships, so I thought I'd be out on my own in a few years."

"*Old coot?*" Greta repeated coldly. "You will speak of Ranieri Sarto with the respect he deserves. He was one of the most well-renowned Sarti in

Tor'Esint, possibly even Beltigura. I remember people coming all the way from Tor'Dumere and Tor'Selit in the hopes of obtaining a commission from him."

"I don't care," Teodoro said. "He was a boring old coot who never let me have any fun. He made me stitch things all day long and asked me question after question about all his orders. Like I cared! If they find a new Maestro for me, then I *might* consider staying in the Guild. Otherwise, I'll be a shop boy. Anything to get out on my own."

Marta moved ever so slightly away from Teodoro, towards Sofia. From the corner of her eye, Greta noticed the two girls holding hands tightly. Even Annika was looking at the boy wide-eyed. This sort of behaviour was not to be borne. How dare he speak of Ranieri and the Sarti Guild so dismissively?

"I see," Greta said coldly. "Unfortunately, Ludovico has placed you in my care until such time as he can find you a new Maestro. If this arrangement is not acceptable to you, then you are free to walk to the Sarti Guild this instant to make other arrangements."

Teodoro appeared to consider his options. Greta knew from her own experience that he wouldn't have any money saved up. Apprentices didn't earn anything. If Ludovico couldn't find anywhere else for Teodoro to stay, he would have to come back here with his tail between his legs and beg for her forgiveness and charity. She was not certain she would give it to him.

"I'll stay until the mending's done anyhow. I overheard you say that you could pay me for it. Right?"

"That is correct," Greta said through gritted teeth. "But if you accept that payment, then I expect the work to be flawless."

Teodoro shrugged. "It will be. That's all I've been doing for two years, is sewing. I'm bored to death of it."

Greta gritted her teeth further. This was not at all what she had been expecting when she invited Teodoro into her house.

She wondered if Ranieri had understood this boy's character. Had he known the ungrateful whelp was as bad as this? Perhaps he had. Perhaps *that* was the reason he had only had one apprentice – because he couldn't stomach the thought of a second apprentice's learning being tainted by this one. Greta found herself hoping that Ludovico found some alternative to get the boy out of her house as soon as possible.

Well, she wasn't going to let this boy disrupt her routine any more than necessary.

"Sofia, you'll stay in the workshop with me. We need to edge that material. Marta, mind the shop and see if you can't sort through Ranieri's larger orders to see which are more urgent. I'll need to send letters to those customers to see if they're happy to wait for me to finish my current orders first or if they wish to take their order to another Sarta."

Greta waited for the two girls to leave the room before turning her attention to Teodoro and Annika. She did not want the others to hear this.

"The two of you have shown extraordinarily bad attitudes these past few days. Teodoro, from what you've said, I can only assume your attitude has always been this negative towards the Sarti Guild. I don't want you poisoning my girls' minds so keep your head down and your mouth shut. If you happen to finish your mending before Ludovico produces another option for you, we'll figure out what to do then.

"Annika, as you can see, there are few Sarti apprentice positions available and not everyone who has one deserves it. I would hate to have to send you away in exchange for an apprentice who will appreciate the skills I can teach them.

"You're still on mending and meal duties until your attitude and your stitching improves, though I wish you could help with the edging. Make a pot of tea for me and bring it into the workshop, then continue with your mending. I want to see every item from both of you before it's deemed ready for collection. Understood?"

They both nodded. Quietly. Greta was thankful that neither of them now seemed in the mood to give her any lip. She was not in the frame of mind to take it well.

She nodded curtly and turned to enter her workshop. Sofia was already edging one of the satin sections. Greta took the organza to her workbench and began working on that. It would take them the rest of the day to edge the entire bodice. She wished Annika had not neglected her skills so badly. She would have appreciated an extra pair of hands today.

\*\*\*

When Annika came in a quarter of an hour later with a pot of tea, Greta was pleased to see she'd brought two cups with her. There were no snide comments or sneers towards Sofia. Perhaps her reprimand had had an effect. Greta hoped it would last.

"Thank you, Annika," she said courteously. "Once Marta has sorted through Ranieri's orders, please send her in here to help with the edging. If we finish early, she can help you with the mending if the shop is quiet today."

Annika's face broke into a tentative smile, her shoulders falling from their hunch.

"Thank you, Maestra. I'd appreciate that. We have quite a backlog to get through." She looked down for a moment. "I know a lot of that is *my* fault. I'm sorry."

Greta stopped mid-stitch and looked up at Annika in surprise.

"I appreciate your candour, Annika. I'm certain if you work hard, you'll soon catch up to where you should be. I know you have it in you."

Annika drew in a deep breath and nodded. She smiled faintly and returned to the shop. Greta stared after her, deep in thought.

"What did you say to her?" Sofia whispered when Annika was well out of sight.

Greta considered her words carefully.

"Oh, nothing really," Greta replied nonchalantly. "We had a brief discussion about the virtues of learning a trade well."

Sofia eyed her suspiciously, but Greta refused to elaborate. She motioned for Sofia to pour the tea and got on with her work.

\*\*\*

By the time Marta had sorted through the orders, it was well past lunch time. She'd had to take the orders upstairs and lay them out on their beds to see what was what. Greta followed her up later that afternoon to see for herself what the girl had discovered.

There were three suits of varying designs and materials as well as two dresses, both a violent green, but cut in such ways and with varying materials that they would not look the same. Greta had not seen this exact colour before. It looked like one of the newer hues, brought on by alchemically induced reactions.

She didn't trust them herself. Who was to say how long the alchemical colour would last, or if it was safe? Perhaps she was old fashioned, but she preferred natural dyes to alchemical ones. It meant she was more limited in her choice of colours than other Sarti, but with her Gold Guild Mark, she could afford to be picky about which orders she agreed to take. If her customers didn't like her preferences, they were welcome to find another Sarta to create their abomination.

"Were the order forms with them?" Greta asked. "Do you know when they are due?"

Marta pointed to the pages beside each order. It looked as though they had been torn from a bound book.

"I've placed them in order of urgency. This suit is due next week, most of the others a few weeks after, with the dresses due in a month. I can't understand why Maestro Ranieri would work like this, a little from each without finishing any."

Greta smiled sadly as she remembered wondering the very same thing herself when her apprenticeship had begun.

"Ranieri's mind never stopped working, neither did his fingers. But he got bored easily, especially if he had the same items to work on for a prolonged period. He would stop and start as the mood took him for each order. A dress for a morning, a dinner jacket for an afternoon, then trousers the next morning and perhaps back to the dress or a shirt the next afternoon.

"He said it kept him on his toes. He always gave his customers a longer due date than he required just so he could move around between his projects. They would agree to the longer timeframe because, well, he was Ranieri Sarto."

She chuffed out a laugh in memory of it.

"That's like you," Marta pointed out. "You did it with Signora Loyola. I've seen you do it for almost every order, especially lately. Only difference is you don't work on lots of projects at once."

Greta tilted her head sideways as she studied Marta. "You're a smart girl, Marta. Don't let the customers in on our little secret though."

She tapped the side of her nose. Marta smiled mischievously back at her.

"Now, run along and get the brown paper. I want these wrapped up in parcels with their order attached to the outside before trading ends. You can bring them down to the workshop and then help us finish the edging."

*** 

When Marta came into the workshop to deposit the parcels of clothes, Greta noticed her hands were red, almost blistered.

"Marta, what have you been doing?"

Marta turned her hands over and looked at them herself. "I don't know, Maestra. They started itching this morning and have only gotten worse. I thought if I washed them, they'd be fine, but it doesn't seem to have made a difference."

Greta felt queasy at the sight of them.

"Run down to Lucrezia's store and see if she has a cream to help. You can't work with hands like that, and we'll need all the help we can get in the next few weeks. Tell her she can send the invoice with you, and I'll fix her up at the end of the month."

Marta hurriedly put the parcels in a corner of the workshop and left after quickly showing Sofia her hands.

"What could have happened to her?" asked Sofia.

Greta shook her head. Marta had been sorting through Ranieri's orders. They were the only thing the girl had touched that no one else had. Perhaps except Teodoro. Greta put down her work and walked into the shopfront. Annika and Teodoro looked up at her sudden entrance.

"Show me your hands," she ordered them both.

Not bothering to acknowledge their stunned expressions, she studied first Annika's, then Teodoro's hands. Annika's were fine, smooth, and not nearly as calloused as they should have been, but that would soon change.

Teodoro's were not red like Marta's but had signs of healing wounds.

"What's this from?" she asked, pointing to the sores without touching them.

Teodoro shrugged. "Sores I got a week or so back."

"How did you get them?" Greta persisted.

"Don't know. Ranieri got them too. He worked with gloves sometimes. Said the material was starting to hurt his hands, maybe a new allergy or something."

Greta shook her head. "I've never heard of such a thing. It would be common knowledge if Sarti began to develop allergies to certain materials later in their career. Had he been using materials out of the ordinary lately?"

The boy shrugged. "He always used the newest things he could find. He'd been buying alchemically-dyed materials lately. Some green, some purple – whatever he could find. They were all really bright. Hurt my eyes to look at them, some of them did. Mebbe it was those that did it, but mebbe not. None of the haberdasheries we went to had sores on their hands."

Greta knew she was biased against alchemically-dyed materials, but this sounded too dangerous not to be well-known. She scribbled a note on a piece of paper and handed it to Annika.

"Run this down to Ludovico. Tell him it's urgent. I want a meeting tomorrow night, with as many Sarti as possible."

Annika took the note and left the workshop without bothering with a coat. It was unlike her not to take every care with her appearance. She must have understood how important the request was.

"Did any of Ranieri's customers ever complain about similar sores?" she asked Teodoro. "Did any of them die?"

The boy stared at her incredulously. "Course not!"

"Of course not," Greta mumbled to herself. "They wouldn't have connected their sores with the outfits. Why would they?" She shook herself free from her thoughts. "Back to work, Teodoro."

\*\*\*

When Marta returned a short while later, Greta called her into the workshop.

"What did Lucrezia say?" she asked.

Marta handed Greta the jar of white salve. "I need to put this on morning and night, and not touch anything I think might have caused it."

Greta huffed in frustration. "Didn't *she* have any idea what might have caused it?"

"No." Marta shook her head. "I told her everything I touched. She said it might be an allergic reaction to one of the materials, but that it was odd for it to come on so many years after I'd started my apprenticeship."

At that moment, Annika returned. She came straight into the workshop.

"Ludovico said he'll attempt to organise an emergency Sarti meeting for tomorrow night, but he can't promise a large attendance." Annika looked down at Marta's hands and the salve Greta handed back to her. "What's happening?"

"I'm not certain," Greta told her truthfully. "I have a feeling this was caused by some of Ranieri's material, but I won't know more until I can get someone to test it."

"Which material?" Sofia asked from behind her.

"The only ones that looked suspicious were those bright green dresses," Greta replied hesitantly. "I suspect they were alchemically-dyed."

"Couldn't you ask Lucrezia Alchimista to test them somehow?" Marta asked.

Greta bit her lip. It would be better to lose sewing time today and potentially have the test results by tomorrow's meeting. She would just have to work later tonight if the edging weren't finished. Again. She really needed more time. Or another fully trained Sarta. She could certainly afford to hire one now if any were available, but her workshop was already too full for her liking. How had Ranieri ever managed on his own with just an apprentice or two?

"Marta, pass me the parcels containing the green dresses. I'll take them to Lucrezia myself. I need to get to the bottom of this."

Marta went to the parcels and started sorting through them until she found the two she was looking for. They were too large together for Greta to take by herself. She rolled her eyes at the blasted inconvenience of it all.

"Marta, come with me. The rest of you, back to your duties. We're running far enough behind as it is."

Greta took one of the parcels from Marta and carried it awkwardly under her arm. It was at times like this that she wished she had her own blazermobile like Aveline. But it was barely worth the bother of asking to borrow hers right now. By the time she got the keys, she'd have walked to Lucrezia's shop.

\*\*\*

The door to Lucrezia's shop was adorned with a polished Gold Alchimisti Guild Mark. Every Guild member displayed their Guild Mark on their door. Most wore pins or brooches on their person as well. It was a mark of honour, a matter of pride, for even a Copper Guild Mark was an achievement to be celebrated.

The shop was a bustle of activity when they walked in. Greta huffed at the delay she felt sure was in store for her, but an apprentice came to attend her almost immediately.

"May I help you, Signora Sarta?"

Greta turned a stern expression on the boy. "I need to speak with Lucrezia Alchimista. In her workshop, if possible."

The apprentice glanced about the shop and chewed on his lip.

"Momentarily, Signora Sarta. I'll ask if she is available."

"Tell her Greta Sarta said it's a matter of some urgency."

It may have been a lie, but Greta was taking no chances and needed to see Lucrezia as soon as possible.

"Of course, Signora Sarta, of course. Please wait here."

He motioned for Greta and Marta to stand to one side, away from the other customers. They were not left waiting for long. The apprentice soon ushered them past the front counter and into the workshop.

Greta had never been in an Alchimista workshop before. There were glass jars and metal cauldrons of various potions brewing all over the place. Along the walls were shelves full of ingredients, labelled with pictures rather than words in many cases. The smell was pungent – it made her eyes water just standing near the cauldrons.

"Greta, what's this urgent matter?" Lucrezia said, looking up from her experiment. "I already gave your girl the salve to fix her hands."

Greta counted five Alchimisti in the workshop, including Lucrezia. "I'd appreciate a little discretion, if you don't mind."

Lucrezia followed her gaze to the other Alchimisti. She rolled her eyes in annoyance.

"Right, you lot, finish what you're doing and go serve some customers until I call you back."

Greta nodded her thanks and patiently waited until the last person had left the room. She found an empty corner of a workbench to place her parcel and motioned for Marta to do the same.

"I think *this* might have been the cause of Marta's injuries."

"Greta, listen, I appreciate how much you care for your apprentices, but I promise you that salve will clear up her injuries in no time."

Greta clutched her fingers tightly to stop from smoothing her dress. Now was not the time to show her weaknesses.

"I trust you, Lucrezia, but I have a bad feeling about this," Greta persisted. "You've heard about Ranieri, yes? Well, these came from his workshop. His apprentice has healing sores all over his hands and Ranieri had apparently taken to wearing gloves for all the sores he was getting. And there's another thing."

She glanced at Marta, hesitatingly.

"When I identified Ranieri's body, he was green. Everywhere. I thought it might have been poison. The morgue attendant likened his condition to several other deaths in recent months.

"These dresses are bright green and Marta's sores only appeared today, after she'd been handling them. I've called an emergency Sarti Guild Meeting for tomorrow night. I'd appreciate it if you could test the material before then. The more information I have about it by then, the better.

"I don't have to tell you this could spell disaster for any Alchimisti or Sarti who have been dealing with these materials. Both for themselves and for their customers. Your discretion would be appreciated."

Lucrezia rubbed her forehead with the heel of her hand. "This is just what we need. As if the Inter-Guild Edict wasn't bad enough already. I'll do what I can. Do something about your girl."

Greta turned in confusion. Marta was staring wide-eyed at her outstretched hands. She screamed when Greta touched her arm.

"Fix them!" she screamed. "Fix them now! I don't want to die!"

Greta looked at her in alarm. "Marta, dear, you're not going to die. You're going to be fine."

She tried to take Marta by the arm, but the girl jerked away from her, upsetting a cauldron behind her. The solution sizzled into the wood of the workbench. Greta smelled burning hair at the same time as Marta screamed again. Lucrezia took no notice of Marta but found a red cloth to soak up the solution, which instantly stopped sizzling.

Only after that did she turn her attention to Marta. Greta was still trying to soothe the hysterical girl when Lucrezia slapped her across the face. It shocked Greta as much as it did Marta. The poor girl stared at Lucrezia and fell into a sobbing heap. Lucrezia sighed and awkwardly patted the girl on the back, trying unsuccessfully to pass her on to Greta.

"Tell your girl she's going to be fine. Even if it's poison, that salve will leech it out of her system at the same time as soothing her sores. Take her home and give her a dose of this."

She handed Greta a bottle of yellow liquid. Greta looked at it suspiciously.

"It's a chamomile extract. It will calm her – nothing else. Go now before you scare away all my customers."

Greta took Marta by the shoulders and led her out of Lucrezia's shop. A few of the customers stared at them in open curiosity. Greta smiled sweetly at them and simply kept walking. She led Marta all the way back to her workshop. Her apprentice was in shock but there was nothing she could do about it until they were home.

\*\*\*

Back at her shop, Greta sat Marta down on a bench in the kitchen, wiped down the table where the material had been laid out that morning, and gave her a teaspoon of the yellow liquid. It had a strong odour, but it was not unpleasant. Instead of leaving the girl in her shop, where she could disturb potential customers, or leaving her alone in the kitchen, Greta brought her into the workshop.

"What did Lucrezia say?" asked Sofia as they walked in. She blanched at the sight of the older apprentice. "What happened to Marta?"

Greta sat Marta down on a spare seat to trim the singed sections of her hair. "She had a bit of a shock is all. She'll be fine soon."

In fact, soon turned out to be quite a long time. It was well past trading before Marta fell out of her chamomile-induced stupor. They were seated at the kitchen table – Annika had prepared a fairly decent meal without a single complaint.

"What happened to Marta's hands?" Annika asked.

It was the first time Greta recalled her expressing any sort of concern for her fellow apprentice though she couldn't shift the suspicion that Annika was asking so it wouldn't happen to her.

"Lucrezia thinks it may be an allergic reaction to some of the material from Ranieri's shop. She's testing it now to see what it contains to cause such sores. We should change your bed linen to be on the safe side."

Teodoro raised an eyebrow. "It ain't nothing to worry about. The sores go away. Eventually."

Greta held her hands together tightly under the table. "I take the health of my apprentices very seriously, Teodoro. Sores on their hands are painful and unnecessary. Not to mention it will stop them from working and potentially drive away customers."

"And itchy," Marta said quietly.

Greta turned at the sound of her voice. "Let's use the salve. It may help with the itch."

She opened the jar and handed it to Marta. For all Lucrezia's assurances, Greta didn't want to touch Marta's skin herself and risk contracting the same reaction. Marta gave her a brittle smile. She dipped her fingers into the salve and spread it over her hands.

Greta wasn't the only one to avert her eyes from the procedure. She tried to tell herself that it wasn't because she was disgusted by the sight of the sores, but she knew it was a lie. The rapidity with which they had appeared scared her. What could have been so toxic in the material to cause such a reaction? And how had no one else either noticed or cared that it happened?

"I'm going up to bed," Marta announced.

Greta immediately felt guilty. It wasn't the girl's fault that her hands were covered in sores, but she was treating her like a leper all the same. It wasn't fair.

"It goes away," Teodoro reassured her. "It's just one of those things. It's part of being in the Sarti Guild."

"No!" Greta retorted instantly. "*This* is not part of the Sarti Guild. The first occurrence of it should have been reported and all other instances should have been followed up to see if there was a connection. The Sarti Guild is one of the oldest in Tor'Esint. We value our members and should never have let things get this far."

Teodoro stared at her in surprise. Greta reflected that she'd probably spoken a little louder than intended, but he had insulted her Guild. *Her* Guild. It was not for an upstart apprentice who didn't even appreciate his Maestro to badmouth her Guild. How dare he?

"Teodoro, I don't know what passed for acceptable behaviour between you and Maestro Ranieri, but in *this* household, you will not insult the Sarti Guild or you will find yourself out on the streets before you can blink. Is that understood?"

The boy had the good sense to close his mouth. His frown told her that he may not have realised the insult he had dealt the Sarti Guild, nor just how devoted she was to her Guild. Perhaps now he would learn to watch his mouth. Greta did not need him to scare her apprentices or turn them against the Sarti Guild with his thoughtless words.

She felt her cheeks grow hot with anger. It was a useless emotion at this moment – it could not help her.

"Very well. It has been another long day for everyone. All of you off to bed. Annika, you can share Sofia's bed tonight if you don't think it beneath you."

Annika looked at Sofia who nodded in agreement. She smiled her thanks at the younger apprentice. It startled Greta to see such a complete change in the girl. For all of Teodoro's faults, his arrival in their household had made an impression on Annika. In fact, all her apprentices seemed to be benefitting from his uncouth behaviour. They were drawing closer together and standing firm behind the Sarti Guild. It was heartening.

Annika, Marta, and Teodoro left the kitchen one after the other, but Sofia stayed behind. Ah, Sofia. Greta hoped it wasn't reckless to have so completely given her heart to this girl. Something told her it wasn't.

"Maestra, will Marta really be fine?" she asked quietly. "Even if it's poison?"

Greta nodded, then paused. "Who said anything about poison?"

Sofia shrugged. "I just assumed. I mean, I heard Teodoro say he and Maestro Ranieri both got sores from the green material. I just thought, if they're connected, they might have been poisoned."

Greta got up and walked around the table to sit by Sofia's side. She put a hesitant arm around her apprentice's shoulders – she wasn't generally a tactile person.

"Lucrezia assured us that the salve will heal her sores as well as leech out any poison that might be in her. She really will be fine."

Sofia leaned in against Greta's shoulder. "I was so scared for her. Marta's the closest thing to a sister I can ever remember having."

Greta squeezed the girl's shoulder. It was quite telling that she didn't include Annika in her sister comparison.

"So will you tell the Tor'Esint Amministratrice from yesterday what you suspect?"

The question caught Greta off guard. She found herself shaking her head before she had time to think about it.

"Letizia di Bibiana does *not* need to know about this. If I'm correct in my assumption, then the Sarti Guild could be in a lot of trouble. The less the Amministratori know, the better. They would likely expose the truth in the worst possible way for the Sarti Guild and we can ill afford any further problems what with the Trading and Inter-Guild Edicts. We'll be beggared if the Mercantili have anything to do with it.

"It's very important we don't let them know. That's one of the reasons why I've called an emergency Sarti meeting. We need to put a stop to these injuries and deaths as soon as possible, with the minimum information getting out.

"Now, off to bed with you. We've had too many long days lately."

Sofia leaned into Greta for a moment longer before getting up and going to bed. Greta stared after her for a while. She'd never wanted a family – to find a companion and have children. To be honest, she thought she lacked the maternal instinct necessary to make her any good at it.

She was thirty-one years old, and Sofia was fifteen. If Greta had been like some of the girls she'd grown up with, she could easily have a daughter Sofia's age by now. Greta shook her head. Having apprentices was not quite the same thing, but with perhaps one or two of them in her life, she might be lucky enough to have a very good relationship. Sofia could be like her daughter, without the inconvenience of finding a companion, enduring pregnancy, surviving childbirth and then being a slave to the child in its formative years. Yes, this arrangement suited her just fine. Why anyone would go through all of that to have what she was finding with Sofia, or what she'd had with Ranieri, was beyond her.

There was a sound at her door. Greta stepped into her workshop warily. It was late. Trading was well over, and most people should be heading off to bed by now. At the second soft knock, Greta unlocked the door and peeked out. It was Aveline. She looked beyond exhausted, fit to fall on the doorstep.

"I'm sorry it's so late, Reta. But I'll have that cup of tea now if you've got time."

Greta bustled her in. "Of course, I have time! But Veli what are you doing here?"

"Tea first?" she pleaded, unbuttoning her coat. Greta held her tongue and nodded. She went to light the stove, leaving the kitchen door open for Aveline to follow in her own time.

When Aveline finally appeared, she said nothing, but immediately sat. Greta found her favourite teapot and pulled out a selection of teas. It was one of her greatest vices and she indulged herself in it probably more than she should.

"What tea would you like? Perhaps some chamomile?"

Aveline gagged. Greta instinctively pulled back from her. "Veli, are you quite well?"

"A mint tea perhaps? Or ginger?"

"Mint?" Greta asked in surprise. "Veli, you *loathe* mint teas, and this is the second one I've seen you have in only a few days. What's the matter with you?"

Aveline bit her lip. She looked at Greta with frightened eyes.

"I think I might be ... that is to say, I *could* be..." She paused and took a deep breath. "I'm *late*."

Greta rolled her eyes and pulled out the chamomile box in an effort to find the mint behind it. "Yes, it's past nine o'clock already. I know you're late."

Aveline shook her head. "No, you misunderstand. I think I'm ... pregnant."

Greta dropped the box of chamomile tea. It clattered to the wooden floorboards so loudly she thought her apprentices would come down to see what the noise was. Aveline's eyes welled up with tears which soon flooded down her face. Greta stared at her dumbly.

"Well, say something," Aveline said through her tears.

"How?"

It was the first thing that came to her mind and popped out before she could stop herself. She recovered her wits as the kettle whistled.

"I'm mean to say, who is the father?"

She collected the fallen box and searched around for mint. Though it was one of her least favourites, she always had some handy in case others were fond of it. She busied herself making the tea as she waited for Aveline to reply.

"Chide. Telchide. Inventore."

Greta turned sharply. "There's only *one* Telchide, Aveline. I know which one you mean. How did this happen?"

Aveline glared at her as she dried her eyes. "How do you think it had happened? The *usual* way."

The sharp edge to her voice bit into Greta. Aveline was one of her closest friends. She didn't want to continue their conversation like this.

"Fine, fine," she replied placatingly. She finished preparing the tea and brought two cups with her to the table. She sat across from Aveline and took her hand. "You *do* realise he's committed, don't you?"

Aveline took a deep breath and took her hand back. "He's not," she said through gritted teeth. "Not anymore."

"What? How?" Greta asked curiously. "Did they find his companion?"

Aveline hesitated. "No. It's ... a long story. But we believe Sebetine is dead and has been for some time now. Chide approached the Amministratori to have her declared dead. It was in the newssheets a week or so ago."

Greta didn't know what to say. It was all too sudden for her. "You know he has a daughter, and his companion's mamma living with him. I doubt they'll take too kindly to this news."

Aveline's eyes brimmed with tears again. She dabbed at them before they could fall. Greta watched her carefully.

"Veli, have you told Telchide yet?"

Aveline dropped her head down into her arms on the table and shook violently. Greta moved to sit beside Aveline and placed an arm around her friend's shoulder. She held her close, whispering soothing sounds until Aveline stopped crying.

Aveline sniffed and raised her head. "He wants to court me, to be my companion."

"I see." Greta shifted slightly away from Aveline, withdrawing her arm. "Don't make up your mind too quickly. Things like this deserve to be considered properly. You don't commit yourself to someone just because you fall pregnant to them."

"I said no," Aveline told her quietly.

Greta paused. "Well then, that's settled. Lucrezia can give you something to be rid of the child." She tilted her head at the thought. "Or you could keep it by yourself. There are plenty of single mothers in Tor'Esint. No one will care."

Aveline frowned at her. "Most single mothers are not Electrum Guild members with a workshop to run. How can I possibly do that on my own? I *had* thought perhaps I won't keep it."

Greta hesitated. "Veli, you didn't answer. Does Telchide know?"

"No," she whispered. "No one knows. I'm afraid to tell Chide. He already asked me to live with them when we came back from the Caldera. Imagine what he'll do if he finds out. He'll rearrange his entire life to accommodate me."

Greta didn't know what to say. It sounded like most people's ideal vision of commitment and family life. But Aveline sounded sad.

Instead of answering immediately, she moved Aveline's tea closer to her and held her own with both hands to draw some warmth into her.

"Why did you say no?" she asked.

Aveline cupped her hands around the tea and stared into it. "Could you live with the mamma of a previous companion? I can't picture it. And I can't ask him to send Serenita away. But every time I work with him, it becomes more painful to only talk about our experiments. It's more difficult to say goodbye. I don't know what to do, Reta. Tell me what to do."

She looked up at Greta, her hazel eyes showing her pain.

"I don't know, Veli," Greta answered truthfully. "I'm always careful not to get myself into that situation. I refuse to entertain relationships past a certain point. I will *not* fall in love."

Aveline laughed through her trembling. "You think I *wanted* to fall in love with a committed man? You think I *wanted* to fall pregnant to him? Reta, no one would choose this. It just happened."

"You want to keep the child, don't you?" Greta asked carefully. "You want to keep it and live with Chide, committing to him or not."

Aveline didn't answer but Greta knew her friend well enough to understand what she wasn't saying.

"You know, you could always keep the child and hire a nursemaid. You've more than enough money. Then you could continue your work, if that's what you want."

"Of course I want to keep working!" Aveline cried out emphatically. "I've worked so hard to get where I am and Chide and I are so close to a..."

Greta leaned in closer. "Close to a what?"

"Erm, nothing. It's nothing. But, no, I won't be leaving the Inventrici Guild if I decide to keep the child. Chide didn't, and neither do a lot of other Guild members. I don't see why I would have to."

Greta knew Aveline was hiding something, but she didn't pry. Aveline was a private person. She gave out very little information about her life and Greta respected that. After all, with the Trading and Inter-Guild Edicts, everyone had something to hide these days.

Even the most obedient Guild members could not survive if they continued to deal with the Mercantili Guild for every trade. Nor would they thrive if they kept to their own Guild and refused to interact with any other. It was a ridiculous set of rules made more ridiculous by the fact that the Mercantili Guild was exempt from the Inter-Guild Edict. By virtue of their trade, they were forced to deal with every Guild in Tor'Esint. The irony of that appeared to be lost on them, but not on anyone else.

They sat together in silence, drinking their tea, both lost in their own thoughts. Greta wished she had a better solution for Aveline, but there was no easy option.

"Don't take too long to make up your mind. If you're going to be rid of the child, the sooner the better. If not, tell the father. The poor man has a right to know."

Aveline nodded. "I know. I just need time to decide. I can't help thinking I'm being selfish refusing him. His daughter adores me, as I do her. Our apprentices get along famously well and even Serenita ... well she encouraged the relationship, but I want nothing to do with her. Not after all the trouble she's caused."

Greta leaned forward. "I'm sorry, you'll have to repeat that. Did you just imply Serenita *knows* about you and Chide, and she wants you to spend more time with him?"

Aveline nodded, a single tear falling down her cheek. "I think she'd be happy to have me live with them if it meant she could stay too. But I can't do that ... I *can't*."

The silence gaped between them. Greta refilled their teacups. There was nothing she could do to make this decision easier for Aveline.

"Well, on the more practical side of things, if you need help taking out your clothes to fit around your belly, be sure to knock on my door. I'm certain I could come up with a thing or two to suit your shape but still be as practical as you require for your trade."

Aveline smiled. It was the first time she'd truly smiled all evening and Greta was pleased to see it.

"Nevio tells me you've been rather busy lately," Greta said. "I confess, I've attempted to call on you a number of times since your return, but I rarely find you in your workshop."

"Yes, I'm sorry about that," Aveline replied cagily. "My expedition has forced me to hire another workshop to continue with that work. Chide and I are juggling our workloads to fulfil our current orders as well as working on the new project. It's been rather time consuming."

"But you won't tell me what this project is," Greta said hopefully.

Aveline shook her head. "I'm sorry, Reta. But the fewer who know about it, the better. I'm sure you understand."

Greta thought of her own troubles at the moment and nodded her agreement. If anyone outside the Sarti Guild discovered her suspicions to do with the alchemically-dyed green material and its effects, it could be potentially disastrous for the entire Guild, not just for those who traded in those commodities.

"What about your other projects? How are they coming along? I know Telchide's music box must be a priority for him. Signora Loyola was in here only the other day to order a new dress for her dinner party to show it off."

Aveline clapped her hands in delight. "Oh Reta, that's wonderful news! If she shows off your dress to all her friends, you'll have orders right up until the Guild Ball!"

Greta bit her lip through a smile. "I know!" she squealed excitedly. "Can you imagine all the wonderful gowns I'll be asked to create if this works?

I'm so excited!"

"May I see the design?" Aveline asked, just as excited.

Greta nodded and immediately got up to find her pattern book. Aveline was one of the few people she trusted enough to discuss a new design with. Not only was she a dear friend, but she wasn't a Sarti Guild member. That was a definite point in her favour.

Aveline rose to join her. Well, that would work too – then she could show Aveline the material and her ideas for the entire project.

She adjusted the lamp, secured the glass container, and led the way to the workshop. Aveline followed her closely.

"Won't it be nice when we can have fireless lights?" Greta asked absently. "And I don't mean friction ones, though they work well for short spans of time. I'm always terrified these lamps will spill their fire and burn down my entire workshop. I suppose at least at the moment I have another workshop in case that happens."

She set the lantern down on her workbench and went to find the pattern book, but Aveline caught her arm.

"Another workshop?"

Greta paused, her throat suddenly thick with emotion. "I've missed you, Veli. More than you can imagine. So many things have happened and I just ... needed you to talk to."

"Well, tell me now. What's happened?" Aveline moved her grip from Greta's arm to her hand instead and clutched it tightly. "Tell me everything."

Greta fought her tears and lost. She found herself in Aveline's warm embrace, who seemed to know just exactly what Greta needed without being told. She clung on tightly and cried into Aveline's shoulder.

When she'd cried herself out, Greta stepped back from Aveline and dried her eyes. She attempted to dry Aveline's dress, but the Inventrice gently pushed her kerchief away.

"It's Ranieri," Greta said in a trembling voice. "He's ... passed on. And he left me everything. And I mean *everything*."

"His workshop and his fortune?" Aveline confirmed. "That just goes to show he loved you more than you realised."

Greta forced a smile. "Oh, I knew he did. But I didn't know how much until now. I don't just mean his workshop and his current fortune. I mean ... his *ongoing* fortune."

Aveline froze. "You don't mean *his patent fees*," she whispered.

Greta nodded.

"Can he do that?" Aveline asked in hushed tones. "Can anyone?"

Greta shrugged. "The Maestri are deliberating the matter. It will certainly change things if they agree to it. It's a Guild matter after all. So, the Amministratori shouldn't have a say."

Aveline sat on the closest chair. Greta pulled up another chair to join her. They sat in silence for a minute, lost in thought. It really would change every Guild but the Mercantili Guild. That was the only Guild that didn't use Great Works for Guild rankings. After all, how could anyone in that Guild create a Great Work? All they did was broker deals between Guilds and cities. They would have the most to lose from this turn of events should it come to pass.

"He could single-handedly end the stranglehold the Mercantili Guild has on us all," Aveline said after a time. "Even if they start to kill us off, they'll only make the remaining ones stronger."

Greta nodded. The same thought had occurred to her.

"Do you think the Mercantili Guild even knows about patent fees?" she asked Aveline. "After all, none of us ever knew until we submitted our first Great Work, and only then if we earned something from it."

Aveline bit her lip. Greta unconsciously mimicked her. The implications were not lost on either of them. If the Sarti Guild made this decision without consulting other Guilds, they could potentially all follow suit without the Mercantili Guild being any wiser.

"I don't know," Aveline replied quietly. "They have spies everywhere. Perhaps they've found out over the years. It wouldn't surprise me."

Greta didn't reply. Spies. It had crossed her mind that perhaps Teodoro was a spy sent to pry into Ranieri's dealings. It would explain why he wasn't attached to the Sarti Guild, and why he wasn't saddened by Ranieri's passing. Had she been wrong to say so much about the green material in his presence?

"Greta, is something else the matter?"

Aveline's hand was on her arm. Greta hadn't noticed. She laid her own hand over the Inventrice's and patted it.

"No. I'll go fetch my pattern book and show you the material."

They shared ideas about the dress as only friends – not rival Sarti – could. How she had missed her friend these past many weeks!

As the Guild Hall clocks struck ten o'clock around the town, Greta realised her chance to catch up on any work tonight was gone. If she didn't go to bed soon, tomorrow morning would be wasted as well.

"Veli, both of us need sleep, you more than me. Go home and try to rest. I'm here for you, whatever you decide with the child, whatever you need. We'll talk again soon."

She saw Aveline off, then closed the door and leaned with her back against it for long minutes. Aveline was in an impossible situation. Greta didn't know how anything she said or did could possibly help. It would be difficult no matter what she decided to do. Greta was only glad she wasn't the one who had to make that decision.

Greta kept Marta on light duties. Lucrezia's salve had worked wonders on her hands, but Greta refused to risk things any further. When Marta complained that she felt useless, Greta sent her to call on Ranieri's customers with a note explaining about his death and the subsequent delay in their orders. She only sent her apprentice to those customers with larger orders, excluding the two bright green dresses, feeling confident enough that the repairs would not be too delayed if Teodoro put his head down and worked.

Marta was still out when Lucrezia came into the shop. Annika hurried into to the workshop with a mumbled apology.

"Lucrezia Alchimista is here to see you. She insists you drop what you're doing and attend to her immediately." At the look on Greta's face, she added as an afterthought. "*Her* words, not mine."

Greta forced a smiled, carefully placed Signora Loyola's bodice on her workbench and followed Annika into the shop.

"Lucrezia, what a pleasant surprise," she said with forced pleasantry. "I did not expect you to call on me in person. I thought we agreed I should pass by after trading."

Lucrezia waved a piece of paper in the air. "Caldera's smoke! I need to talk to you *now*. Privately."

Greta wished the Alchimista had more discretion. At least there were no customers in her shop.

"This way."

She led the Alchimista into her workshop and dismissed Sofia to the shopfront. Her youngest apprentice quickly removed herself, leaving the pair alone.

"What's the matter?" she asked quietly, closing the curtain behind Sofia.

"*This* is the matter," she said, passing the paper to Greta.

Greta read the words on the paper and frowned. "What's arsenic?"

Lucrezia stared at her as though she'd asked what water was. "You're not serious!"

"I'm a Sarta, not an Alchimista. If I wanted to dabble with such things, I would've chosen *your* Guild."

Lucrezia recovered herself and gestured for Greta to sit as she took a seat herself.

"Although arsenic has many uses, it can be quite deadly. The dress you gave me, the green material, it's laced with arsenic. It was almost certainly the cause of your apprentice's sores. I'm only surprised that's all that happened to the poor girl."

Greta did not say a word. She let Lucrezia's words sink in as her mind whirled with a hundred thoughts.

"Tell me, if I describe certain symptoms to you, could tell me if they are the result of arsenic poisoning?"

Lucrezia shrugged. "Probably. But it'd be better if I could see them for myself."

"That ... wouldn't be advisable," Greta replied. She could only imagine how much worse their current scenario would become if Letizia di Bibiana found out about this. "Green tinged eyeballs, where the whites should be, you understand. Green fingernails. Green froth around the mouth, as though there had been green vomit. Could any of these symptoms be inflicted by arsenic?"

Lucrezia arched an eyebrow. "Resulting in death?"

Greta nodded.

"Yes. I'd say so. Have you seen such a case?"

Greta nodded again. "And heard of another four. They haven't been connected yet, other than the apparent symptoms of their death. I only know that one, for certain, was exposed to arsenic."

Lucrezia drew in a sharp breath. "Does your Guild know about this?"

"Not yet," Greta admitted, "I've called a meeting for tonight. I wanted your report as confirmation. I don't even know where people are getting this material. I'd never seen such bright green cloth until yesterday. Teodoro indicated Ranieri had been using it quite a bit lately, that he'd had taken to wearing gloves to protect himself from the sores. How could he have been so careless?"

"Careless and stupid," Lucrezia remarked. "Unless he got it from a haberdashery, then he's been working with the Alchimisti Guild to alchemically dye his own materials. The Mercantili Guild is going to have a field day with this."

Greta shook her head. "No, they won't. We're going to keep it hushed. Only you and I know about it right now. I'll insist my Guild puts a ban on using alchemically-dyed material – at least the green ones – at our meeting tonight. If you can make some discreet enquiries on your end, perhaps you can convince your fellow Alchimisti to stop providing their alchemical dyes without further testing."

Lucrezia rose to her feet. "I'm not telling you how to deal with *your* Guild. Don't tell me how to deal with *mine*."

"Oh, do sit down and stop being ridiculous," Greta told her sharply. "We need to get on top of this before the Mercantili Guild finds out. It'd be in your interest to call a meeting for your own Guild. It's only practical."

"We'll never be able to keep this from the Amministratori," Lucrezia pointed out. "They're bound to start asking questions about the deaths if they haven't already."

Greta shrugged. "True, but there have already been five deaths from it and they're none the wiser. They aren't even certain it's poison, whether intentional or not."

"Then they're imbeciles. And we're lucky they are." Lucrezia huffed out a laugh. "Fine, you tell your Guild tonight. I'll call a meeting for mine as soon as practicable. What are you going to do about Ranieri's orders?"

Greta chewed her lip. "I'll tell them the orders were lost in transition. I still have the patterns. I can offer to make them from scratch using different material. It won't be a lie when I tell them I don't know where Ranieri got his vivid green material from – if they even knew he was going to use it for them. It's not such a common colour that they would both have requested it specifically."

"Good," replied Lucrezia, as though Greta was her apprentice. "Now all you need to do is keep Ranieri's apprentice silent. He must know about it. I saw the scars all over his hands out there."

Greta only nodded in reply. She had more questions than was helpful in her current relationship with the boy. Why in Caldera's smoke had she been so keen to take in Ranieri's apprentice? She should've known that not all his apprentices were going to be like her. Not all of them were going to belong to the Sarti Guild with their whole heart and live for Ranieri's praise as she had. It had been a mistake. One that she was certain she was going to pay for, in more than the injury to Marta's hands.

*** 

Greta closed the shop at exactly four o'clock and called everyone into the shopfront.

"I'm going to the Sarti Guild Hall. I expect all of you to stay here in my absence. Do not open the door to anyone. Do not leave the house. Am I understood?"

"Yes, Maestra," the girls chorused.

Teodoro arched an eyebrow. "I don't like staying in every evening. I want to go down to the Sarti tavern. My friends'll be missing me by now. They'll want to know what happened to Ranieri."

Greta clenched her hands tightly. "You will kindly keep all information about Ranieri and the circumstances of his death to yourself. There are certain realities of life that you're blissfully unaware of, but should you speak of things you know so little about, your naivety will disappear."

"Yer just worried people'll think he was murdered," Teodoro retorted.

"That's not it at all," Greta replied through clenched teeth. "I need to go now. Teodoro, if I find that you've disobeyed me upon my return, you'll wish you'd never set foot in this house."

Greta locked the door to her shop after her in the hopes that if Teodoro didn't have the key, it would deter him from leaving. Of course, he could still climb out a window or go through the back door and around her neighbour's yard. She shook her head. She didn't have time to worry about him right now. There were more important things for her to focus on.

The Sarti Guild was one of the smaller Guilds. Not everyone in Tor'Esint could afford Sarta clothing and even fewer could afford Gold Sarta clothing, so it was a good thing there were so few people at her level. She knew it was different in other Guilds, but in the Sarti Guild there were currently only five Gold Sarti. *Four* Gold Sarti, she corrected herself. Ranieri's death brought them down to four.

Being one of the highest ranking Sarti, she made a point of keeping an eye on her potential competition. She knew there were eight Electrum Sarti, fourteen Silver Sarti and, at her latest count, twenty-three Copper Sarti. The Copper guild Marks were handed out fairly freely in her Guild. All you needed to prove was that you could create a design from scratch with a pattern of your own making. There was no point being a Sarta if you couldn't do that. That brought her Guild close to fifty members. It was a good number.

Other towns in Beltigura did things differently to Tor'Esint. She knew that Tor'Dumere regulated their numbers more strictly. They wouldn't allow people to earn their next Guild Mark if there wasn't a suitable workshop for them to take over. It made the competition for Guild positions much tenser. Greta wasn't certain it was a good system.

In Tor'Esint, the Sarti Guild members were like one big family, helping each other if necessary, though that didn't mean a certain amount of snooping might occur. She doubted the Sarti worked so well together in Tor'Dumere.

Her thoughts scattered as a blast of cold air blew in off the sea. It was not unusual at this time of year, but Greta didn't spend much time on Corso Delle Gilde, and it took her by surprise. She pulled her coat tighter around her shoulders and flipped the collar up to protect her against the wind.

"Greta! Greta Sarta!"

Greta turned at the sound of her name. A floppy haired young man jogged up to greet her. She smiled in recognition.

"Good evening, Domizio. What a pleasure to see you!"

Domizio always made her smile – his floppy hair, his lopsided grin, his constant happiness. The *almost* constant happiness. His face fell momentarily.

"I'm sorry about Ranieri. I know how close the two of you were."

Greta swallowed the lump in her throat and nodded her thanks. Ranieri wasn't the first Sarto she knew who'd died, but he was the first who she cared for so deeply, and everyone knew it.

Domizio's condolences wouldn't be the last that evening. It wasn't that she wished Ranieri's death would go unremarked, but she wished people wouldn't try to condole with her. She'd never been comfortable with it. She never knew what to say, what they expected of her. Sometimes, it was easier just to smile sadly and nod.

As they drew closer to the Sarti Guild Hall, Greta saw a dribble of Sarti making their way up the stairs. Even if only half their members came, it would be better than none. She only hoped all the Gold and Electrum Sarti would come. They were probably the only ones who could afford alchemically-dyed material and would need to heed her warning.

"May I offer to walk you home after the meeting?" Domizio asked. Greta knew it was an innocent question. He, as most others, would have noticed that Ranieri often walked her home after their Guild meetings. Without her former Maestro around, she might require an alternate escort at that time of night.

"Thank you." She cleared her throat as the words stuck. "That would be greatly appreciated."

That was one of the only reasons it would be convenient to have a companion – as a constant escort where people didn't question your safety or your gossip about your romantic entanglements. Tor'Esint was not a prudish town. There was no expectation for people to be committed before having children.

In fact, with the way the Guilds worked, it was often easier for people *not* to have a commitment ceremony, especially if they were from different Guilds. The children were still raised by both parents but often lived with whoever had the most time or money to spare for them.

The virtue of this system meant that people like Greta, who didn't want any permanent attachments in their life, could bed anyone of their choosing without disparaging comments from the greater populace. Most of the time.

The biggest downside of living in Tor'Esint was its notorious late-night rapists. One would think that, in a civilised place such as this, rapists would be dealt with swiftly, but the newssheets reported at least one attack per week and fewer arrests. Though Greta herself had never been assaulted before, she knew others who had. It would be irresponsible to ignore the potential danger in favour of complete independence, much as she desired it.

They entered the Sarti Guild together and followed the growing crowd towards the Meeting Hall. It was large enough to accommodate a five-hundred-person ball. This year was the Gioiellieri Guild's turn. They had a challenging task ahead of them.

The Alchimisti Guild had hosted last year's Guild Ball. They'd had all sorts of concoctions for people to eat and drink with parting gifts of uniquely scented candles. That was always a crowd pleaser and brought them a good deal of business in following months.

The Mercantili Guild had put in a bid for next year. Their balls were the worst. Not because they spared any expense – they didn't – but because their lavishness often made everyone else feel uncomfortable. No one liked the richest Guild to flaunt their wealth, but the Mercantili Guild didn't seem to care. And why should they? With the Trading and Inter-Guild Edicts in place, they could afford to make enemies.

Greta caught Ludovico's eye at the front of the hall and excused herself from Domizio with a promise to meet him later. He flashed his lopsided smile at her and went to find a seat among the benches which had been set up for the meeting. Greta wove her way through the other Sarti members, nodding politely to those who expressed their sadness at Ranieri's passing, all the while gritting her teeth at the situation.

Under normal circumstances, she'd have locked herself away in her house until such time as people thought they did not need to mention his death to her. But these were not normal circumstances, and she had an important task to perform.

Ludovico took her hand as she approached him. Really, the public familiarity between them was becoming quite unseemly. They'd bedded twice in the past, but that had been months ago, and she hoped that anyone watching would assume it was simply another expression of condolence.

"Did you make any discoveries?" he asked her in hushed tones.

Greta nodded, withdrawing her hand from his. "It's worse than I feared. Did you manage to get a hold of everyone?"

"Almost. All the Gold and Electrum Sarti and most of the Silver – some are out of town. Some of the Copper Sarti said they were too busy and couldn't afford to lose a night of work, but I think I persuaded at least a few of them that it'd be worth their while."

It was a better turnout than Greta had expected, she only hoped that Lucrezia could manage a similar result herself. If the Alchimisti Guild didn't stop providing the arsenic alchemical dye, there would be no way to force the Sarti Guild to stop using it.

The Guild Hall clock struck five times. It was time to begin. An hour after trading was more than enough time for all Sarti in the town to reach the Guild Hall. If they weren't here now, then they weren't coming.

Ludovico walked to the podium at the front of the hall and held up his hands. Raised voices became hushed whispers which died into complete silence. Greta marvelled that people were so attentive to him. After all, he wasn't a Sarto himself, just an Amministratore, but she'd learned that the Amministratori often wielded a great deal of power within the Guilds. If he ever stopped being their Amministratore, he would lose the honorific last name.

"Thank you all for coming at such short notice. If you didn't sign your name as you entered, I'll ask you to sign before you leave. It's imperative that all Sarti in Tor'Esint are aware of this high alert situation. I will now cede the floor to Greta Sarta. Please give her your full attention and keep your questions to a minimum."

Ludovico made way for her to step up to the podium. Greta tried not to smooth down her skirt as she stood in front of all those people, but she couldn't help it.

"Thank you, Ludovico." She turned her attention to the seated Sarti. She recognised less than half of them and knew fewer of their names. She really needed to engage more actively with her fellow Guild members.

"As I'm sure most of you know by now, Ranieri Sarto was found dead two days ago near the docks. The circumstances surrounding his death required me to formally identify him. If that hadn't been necessary, I doubt we'd have this information at our fingertips. I've made discreet enquiries and can now tell you that Ranieri likely died from arsenic poisoning."

There was a loud murmuring in the crowd. Greta paused until it died down.

"His death has been likened to another four deaths in recent months, though the Amministratori are yet to establish a link. I don't know how much longer it will take them, but we need to be prepared when they do.

"I'm not certain how many Sarti use alchemically-dyed material, but I urge you all to stop now. I had the bright green material from Ranieri's workshop tested after I noticed sores on one of my apprentice's hands. It was laced with arsenic – enough to poison hundreds of people. I can only assume it was this same material that caused Ranieri's death along with the other similar deaths."

A hand shot up in the air. It was one of the Electrum Sarti. Greta nodded in her direction.

"Are you suggesting that members of the Sarti Guild have becoming embroiled in assassination?"

Greta gritted her teeth angrily. "Of course not! I'm certain the fatal side effects of the alchemically-dyed material were unknown until now. However, as it didn't take you long to draw that incorrect conclusion, I doubt it will take the Amministratori long to reach it either.

"That's why I must stress the importance of this. If anyone here has stores of alchemically-dyed material, especially the green one, you must dispose of it immediately. It's unsafe for yourselves and anyone who comes into contact with it."

A Gold Sarta stood up. Greta tried not to roll her eyes. Agata was a great Sarta, there was no doubt about that, but she and Greta had never seen eye to eye on anything.

"I paid good money for my alchemically-dyed materials and cannot afford to simply dispose of them. I already have a dozen orders specifically requesting those colours. If I were to do as you suggest, I'd lose on the material and the business. Not all of us are so financially fortunate as you to take such a massive loss in our stride."

It was a fair point. Not everyone could cover their losses if they were embroiled in the alchemically-dyed material market, but it was literally a matter of life and death.

"Of course, if it is merely a suggestion, then you don't need to oblige me," Greta told them. "However, my hope is that the Sarti Guild issues an edict expressly forbidding any Sarti from using or trading in alchemically-dyed materials until each colour has been poison tested by the Alchimisti Guild.

"If word of this gets out, it could do irreparable damage to the Sarti Guild. Not only will you lose more than a few clients and some bolts of toxic material, but the Mercantili Guild will suspect inter-Guild collaboration or assume that you're trading illegally. I don't want the Sarti Guild to lose half its members to the Mercantili Guild's stranglehold, or to their own stupidity."

Greta discreetly motioned for Ludovico to take over once more. His scowl was obvious, but Greta wasn't certain if it was for her or for the reaction she was getting from the Sarti Guild. She looked for a seat in the crowd and couldn't find one anywhere near the front. Instead, she stood up against the wall, in case she was called upon to speak again.

"This is all news to the Sarti Guild," Ludovico lied smoothly.

Greta stared at him in shock. She'd told him the reason for the emergency meeting. He knew what had happened to Ranieri. Why in Caldera's smoke was he lying about it?

"The Maestri will take Greta Sarta's cautionary words under advisement and conduct tests of their own on the supposed toxic material. Until that time, you are welcome to take whatever precautions you feel are necessary, but you are by no means forbidden from trading in or using alchemically-dyed material until further notice."

Greta heard loud huffs of relief amongst the not-so-quiet sniggering. But there were still murmurs. At least that was a good sign. People were discussing the matter amongst themselves. Domizio raised his hand. The murmuring around him quietened and Ludovico pointed to him.

"If we continue to use these materials and it turns out Greta was correct, will the Guild reimburse us for any damages we suffer?"

It was a clever question. Greta smiled. Domizio had effectively asked the Sarti Guild for a guarantee that the materials were safe enough to use and she knew they could not provide it.

"Of course not," Ludovico answered in annoyance. "The Guild has never reimbursed any Sarti for using a material that caused damage to themselves or their clients."

"So, you're admitting that the alchemically-dyed material can cause damage?" Domizio persisted.

Ludovico growled. Only briefly, but long enough for Greta and everyone else to hear it.

"Until we have irrefutable proof, the Sarti Guild will not comment on the matter one way or the other," Ludovico said firmly.

Greta took that as her cue – she doubted Ludovico would give her the floor again if she asked for it, so she would just have to take it.

"I have here *irrefutable proof* that the green, alchemically-dyed material is toxic." Greta waved Lucrezia's report up high. "Lucrezia Alchimista carried out extensive tests on it yesterday and today. She has deemed the material poisonous to anyone who comes into contact with it."

Ludovico took the report from her and read it quickly. The colour drained from his face.

"Very well. An edict shall be passed down tomorrow morning. All Sarti are hereby forbidden from using the green alchemically-dyed material and are ordered to bring in all their current stores to the Sarti Guild."

Greta saw Domizio grin at her. Together, they had managed to force the Guild into action.

"What if we refuse?" Agata asked angrily, standing with hands on hips. "I have too much money tied up in this endeavour to simply *give* you all my stores."

Ludovico stared her back down into her seat. "If you refuse, we'll come into your workshop and take it, by force if necessary. And don't try hiding it in your spare warehouse – we'll check those as well if need be."

"I demand that you reimburse us for any material we hand in. This commodity isn't cheap!"

Greta noticed Ludovico look over her shoulder at one of the Maestri standing against the wall. He shook his head almost imperceptibly. Ludovico sighed.

"The Sarti Guild will not reimburse you for your purchases. We have never done so before, nor we will not start now. You're free to approach the Alchimisti or Mercantili you purchased the material from and request a reimbursement from them, but that may lead to questions you don't want to answer."

Agata stood up again. "You're going to financially cripple us."

Ludovico was unsympathetic to her plight. "If Greta recognised the damage to her apprentice in one day, you can't have missed it either. It's your own fault for continuing to deal with this material. The Sarti Guild cannot take responsibility for your reckless actions."

A Copper Sarta stood up and threw a thimble at Ludovico. There was a hushed silence for a moment before almost every Guild member in the room found something to throw at the Sarti Amministratore. His lack of empathy was unexpected and horrifying. Greta stood well clear of the pelting in case anyone decided she deserved it for forcing the unpopular edict.

"Stop that! Stop that this instant!" Ludovico shouted for all the good it did him. He was pelted with anything the Sarti could find. They only stopped when their pockets were empty. "You will all desist. The meeting is now over! You're to return to your workshops and warehouses to prepare your alchemically-dyed material to be collected for disposal. Sarti Guild Amministratori will visit each and every one of you over the next week to confiscate these items. If it's deemed necessary, your warehouses will be searched as well.

"Furthermore, tests will be ordered for all colours of alchemically-dyed material to ensure safety for use. Until that time, you are cautioned against using those fabrics, but we won't force the issue against other colours until we have proof one way or the other."

Ludovico didn't wait for their reply, or for anyone to find an extra something to throw at him. He left the podium and headed straight for Greta. She straightened her back and stood as tall as she could. He would not cow her when she was in the right.

"Come with me," he growled at her.

He grabbed her arm in a painfully tight grip, forced her out into the already crowded walkway and through into an empty room. Greta tried to jerk her arm free, but he was holding her too tight.

"Unhand me now," she said in a dangerously low voice, "or I will request your immediate removal from the Guild."

He growled at her, held tighter for a moment, then released her suddenly, throwing her back against the wall. Greta's head slammed painfully against the stone. White sparks danced across her vision.

"What were you thinking?" he shouted. "You've caused widespread panic and caused the Guild a massive financial blow."

"What was *I* thinking?" she asked incredulously. "What were *they* thinking? What were *you* thinking?" She was shouting now, and she didn't care. "*I'm* not the one who killed four customers by using toxic material. *I'm* not the one who sold toxic material. But apparently, I'm the only one with sense enough to have it tested! I'm the only one who realised the damage it could do to this Guild if left unchecked!"

Ludovico trembled with rage. His fists were clenched tightly by his side. Greta had never seen him so livid before.

"Domizio will be waiting to escort me home," she said in an unnaturally calm voice. "I shall be on my way."

She moved to open the door. Ludovico took a step towards her, and she paused, heart thundering in her ears. She'd never felt so afraid in all her life. She had never been the object of an anger as hot and violent as lava.

Greta swallowed her fear and felt behind her for the door handle. She turned it and opened the door, bringing her a step closer to Ludovico. His eyes bore into her, but he didn't move. Greta manoeuvred herself around the door and pulled it shut behind her. She gave herself a moment to breathe then walked, as quickly as was decorous, into the hall of Great Works.

Domizio was waiting for her by the door. He flashed a lopsided smile at her – it froze on his face.

"What happened?" he asked.

Greta shook her head. She didn't want to talk about it. She only wanted to leave the Guild Hall. It had always been her sanctuary, and this was the first time it had felt unsafe to her. She wondered if she'd ever feel safe within these walls while Ludovico was still here.

Out on the street, Greta took Domizio's arm and tried to walk briskly, but he kept to a fastidiously casual pace.

"Whatever happened, you're only going to draw attention to yourself by moving quickly," he told her calmly. "You're safe with me. I'll escort you home or anywhere else you wish to go, but we will walk there calmly and, if you feel you can trust me, you'll tell me what happened."

Greta took in a long shuddering breath and forced herself to slow down. Domizio walked silently by her side, not forcing her to talk. She appreciated that, but she wished he'd agree to walk just that little bit faster. The more distance she could put between herself and Ludovico, the better.

"That was a brave thing you did," Domizio told her. "Many others would've been too scared to force their Guild into such drastic action."

Greta nodded, though she didn't feel brave now.

"I bought three piedi of the stuff a few weeks ago," he continued. "Haven't had a chance to use it yet. Was waiting for the right opportunity."

"Did it hurt you?" Greta asked, her voice still trembling.

Domizio shook his head. "I never actually touched it. But the haberdasher I bought it off had sores on her arms. So did a lot of the others in the store. I wonder if they'd figured it out too and just hadn't said anything."

Greta frowned. "I doubt it. They would've had too many materials to narrow down which were causing the outbreaks."

"So why did you think the Sarti should've figured it out?" he asked her curiously.

Greta shrugged. "Sarti generally use one or two materials at a time for orders. It would be highly improbable that they didn't notice any skin irritation when they switched to a new material."

Domizio didn't reply. Greta didn't know if he agreed with her or not, but it hardly mattered. She'd made the connection and was trying to save her Guild from ruin. They should all be thankful to her, not trying to hurt her.

Angry tears coursed down her face. How dare Ludovico try to harm her? How dare he threaten her for doing what was right? How *dare* he?

Greta felt Domizio pat her hand. It was as close to an embrace as was decorous in public. Liberal-minded Tor'Esint might be, but that was behind closed doors – not out in public. She covered his hand with her other one and squeezed it gently for a moment.

They walked towards her workshop in companionable silence. Greta appreciated that. When her head was such a whirl, she couldn't carry on a conversation, couldn't work, couldn't do anything. She froze. And that was not acceptable to her, so she forced her thoughts to quieten so she could focus on her life.

"Greta?" Domizio said tentatively.

"Mmm?" she murmured.

"Do you need help?"

Greta slowed her pace and turned to look at him inquisitively. Domizio pushed his floppy hair out of his eyes.

"I assume you took on Ranieri's orders. Do you need help with them?"

"Well, I, uh," Greta stumbled over herself. "Surely, you're too busy to help."

That wasn't what she'd intended to say. She'd wanted to ask for help, to have a qualified Sarto working with her on projects that she had no time for, but she didn't know how Domizio worked. Or even how they could come to an arrangement.

"Never too busy to help a friend," he grinned lopsidedly. "If you're concerned about payment, I'm perfectly content to take a small cut of the client's fee, not an hourly wage."

Greta smoothed her dress and lowered her eyes as an excuse to find Domizio's Sarti Guild Mark. She spied a copper pin on his lapel and frowned. How long had he been a Copper Sarta for? Surely he should have moved up to Silver by now.

"Are you trying to check my qualifications without asking?" he laughed. "Greta, I really do just want to help you. If you need material cut or patterns drawn up – any part of the process – I'm happy to lend a hand. You don't have to do this all on your own and teach three apprentices besides!"

"Is it so obvious that I'm floundering?" she asked quietly.

Domizio took both her hands and held them gently. Greta felt her skin tingle under his touch but didn't pull back.

"No," he affirmed. "It's *not* obvious, but I know you better than you think

I do. Anyone would struggle under such circumstances, and you've gone one step further and taken in Ranieri's boy for now. I can only imagine how your household of five is faring. Let me help you."

"It's extraordinarily kind of you to offer, Mizi, but you must have orders of your own to work on."

Domizio nodded. "But I can come over after trading and work a few hours with you on Ranieri's orders."

Greta hesitated. "You *could*," she said slowly. "It would be ... most appreciated."

"It's agreed then. I'll come over tomorrow evening after trading and you can show me what you want me to do. Or even just point out the orders and let me find my way if you have no time for anything else."

He pressed her fingers lightly and let them go. Greta almost reached out to hold his hands again but stopped herself in time. This was no time for romantic entanglements, or even just bedding someone for fun. She'd done that with Ludovico and was now regretting it, though it had been months ago.

No. She almost shook her head. She wouldn't let herself think about him now. She was safely away from him, her Guild was forcing an edict against the alchemically-dyed material, and Domizio had offered her a huge relief.

"Very well. Thank you."

They stood ever so slightly apart and continued walking to Greta's home. To her relief, when Greta entered her house alone, she found all four of her charges fast asleep. Teodoro had not conspired to ruin her Guild tonight.

# Chapter 8 – Orodi 27 Alchimisti 230 Years After Implosion

When Marta came down to breakfast, Greta inspected her hands again and was relieved to see that they were almost completely healed. There was barely a trace of the sores that had covered them.

"Can I work today?" she asked hopefully.

"I have a special task for you," Greta told her. "Domizio Sarto will be coming over after trading to help with Ranieri's orders. If you could sort through the orders and see what still needs to be done, that would be very helpful indeed."

"Why can't *I* work on them?" Teodoro complained. "He was *my* Maestro!"

Greta glared at the insolent boy. "You're not an apprentice anymore, Teodoro. I'm only allowing you to do the mending out of charity. I could just as easily give it to my girls and turn you out on the street. Would you rather I do that?"

Teodoro visibly bit back a retort and stormed out of the kitchen.

"You wouldn't really, would you Maestra?" Marta asked worriedly. "It isn't his fault that Maestro Ranieri died after all."

Greta took a sharp breath. Marta was correct, but that didn't change the situation.

"If Teodoro showed any affection for the Sarti Guild or any respect for myself and Ranieri, I wouldn't consider it. But as things stand, he hasn't given me a reason to keep him any longer than strictly necessary."

Marta looked aghast. "Just imagine if you were struck down. If even *you* are struggling to take on another's apprentice, what hope would the three of us have?"

Annika and Sofia paused what they were doing and listened in on their conversation. Neither of them was very subtle about it.

"The difference would be in your attitude. You wouldn't give a potential saviour good reason to want to dismiss you out of hand. Teodoro seems to be going out of his way to irritate me."

Sofia glanced sideways at Annika. The look wasn't missed by the older girl, nor by Greta. Annika blushed brightly.

"I'm not as bad as *him*," she said firmly. "And at least I love the Sarti Guild. I wouldn't want to choose another Guild or dismiss the Sarti entirely. *He* doesn't seem to care one way or the other."

Greta stood and placed a hand on Annika's shoulder. "I'm proud of you, Annika. I truly am. You've grown a lot these past few days. Marta will help you with the cooking and the mending today after she's gone through Ranieri's orders for Domizio."

Marta nodded eagerly. Greta was thankful her girls were finally starting to get along as fellow apprentices should. It had taken a while and she'd been to blame for most of the problems herself. She should have tried harder to be a good Maestra. Domizio might be surprised when he arrived that evening. She wasn't struggling nearly so much as he assumed she would be.

She felt an unaccountable glow of pride. It shouldn't matter to her what he thought, but she was surprised to realise it did.

"What Guild Mark does Domizio have?" Marta asked. "Just so I know what he should be capable of doing for you."

"Copper," Greta replied.

Marta stared at her. So did Annika and Sofia.

"Copper is ... erm ... not what I was expecting," Marta stumbled over her words.

Greta grimaced. "It was help readily offered by a friend. He knows his limitations and is happy to draw up patterns or cut material to the pattern if that's all I can trust him on to start with. He may be better than we imagine, after all he's been a Sarto for years."

The girls nodded encouragingly, but Greta could see her doubts mirrored in their eyes.

***

Greta spent the day holed up in her workshop with only Sofia for company. The girl worked fastidiously and quietly. It was quite a change from Annika who chattered away about everything and anything as she worked. In fact, the workshop was so quiet that by mid-afternoon, Greta was starving for conversation.

"How are you going with your bodice, Sofia?"

Sofia stopped sewing and looked up, her golden-brown hair shone in the sunlight. "It's tricky working with so many pieces. I'm used to single items because of all the repairs."

"Ah, yes. The trick to it is just to work on it a little piece at a time," Greta told her. She demonstrated with the section of the bodice she was up to. "Try that and let me know if it's any better."

Sofia nodded and bent her head back down to work. And the silence continued. Greta could not stand it any longer.

"Tell me about yourself, Sofia."

Sofia paused again and looked up. Greta watched her out of the corner of her eye as she herself continued to sew.

"I already told you, Maestra. I lived somewhere far away when I was little – I don't know where. Then I came to an orphanage here. There isn't much else to tell you. I lived in the orphanage until you took me on as your apprentice."

Greta cursed herself for her foolishness. Sofia had had a difficult childhood. She shouldn't have brought it up again.

"Tell me something else, then. Like your favourite colour. Do you have one?"

Sofia smiled that infectious smile of her. "I love the colour of the sea during a storm."

Greta frowned. "You mean that slate-grey sort of colour?"

Sofia nodded. "It's so deliciously tragic a colour. It gives me a terrible sense of foreboding, like in an old folk tale. Don't you feel that way too?"

Greta paused and thought about it. "You're right, you know. But it's not something I've ever *wanted* to feel. Life has too many tragedies in it as it is. I don't need an extra sense of foreboding to tide me over."

"It makes me feel ... I don't know, comforted."

"Comforted?" Greta asked, her confusing growing.

Sofia shrugged. "Don't know how else to explain it. Makes me feel like I want someone to hold me, and then I imagine that. Can't really remember what it feels like, but I get all warm and happy inside. That's how the colour makes me feel. Am I making any sense?"

Greta watched Sofia's expression as she attempted to explain herself. The longing in her eyes for a simple embrace was devastating. Would it be overstepping her boundary as Maestra to give the girl a hug? Especially now, when she had no excuse? It couldn't hurt to be more affectionate with the girls, could it? There was always the chance one would feel more or less favoured than the others, which in itself could cause issues.

She caught Sofia's eye as the girl glanced at her. Greta just wanted to embrace the girl, to comfort her just like her favourite colour. Instead, she gave a small smile and picked up the bodice again. She was up to the back panels where the zipper and ribbon would eventually go.

"Come and watch while I do this section, Sofia. It's one of the most difficult parts of the bodice."

She waited until Sofia had finished her last stitch and dragged over a chair to sit beside her. The afternoon light from the skylight was strong enough that she should be able to see every detail.

Greta filled the silence of the workshop with detailed explanations of what she was doing and testing Sofia on her knowledge. It brought back memories of similar days she'd spent with Ranieri. Though it was nice to know she was now doing things exactly the way he had done them, the memory brought the pain of his death into sharp relief. She found herself talking ever more to try to push the feelings away, but it didn't work. By the end of trading, she was feeling utterly wretched.

"Maestra, you look like..." She paused. Greta looked up at her sideways, trying to disguise her grief. Sofia took a deep breath. "Like a turbulent sea."

Greta huffed. "I think I'm starting to understand why you like that colour."

Sofia frowned and placed her hand over Greta's. Greta looked down at their hands covering each other's. Without saying a word, Sofia put her other arm around Greta, in an awkward semblance of an embrace. Greta threw caution to the wind and enveloped Sofia with both arms, pulling her close. She'd expected tears from Sofia but found that *she* was the one crying instead.

The tears fell fast and hard. She couldn't stop them. She heaved in deep shattering sobs. Ranieri was gone and she was all alone. She closed her eyes and saw his bloated green body, covered in sores. The only truly recognisable part of him was his Sarti Guild Tattoo. With a strangled cry, she opened her eyes and wept uncontrollably, sucking in breaths where she could.

She could only see shapes through her tears, but felt Sofia let go of her and another set of arms take her place. These arms were longer, stronger. They held her tightly against a flat chest, one arm cradling her head and stroking her hair.

Greta didn't know how long she cried. She must've fallen asleep at one point because when she finally opened her eyes again, it was dark. She was lying curled up on the floor of her workshop. Her head rested in someone's lap. One of their arms was draped over her waist, the other was still gently stroking her hair all the way down her back. It was such a soothing feeling that she couldn't help but relax despite every fibre of her being rebelling against being allowed to feel pleasure.

"There you are, Greta," a familiar voice said softly. "We lost you for a while."

Greta looked up into the brown eyes of Domizio. She tried not to tense her body. They were in a very compromising position. Should any clients come into the workshop, they wouldn't be impressed with her lack of decorum. She closed her eyes with a sigh. It was dark and Domizio was here – trading was over, and she was safe.

"Where are the others?" she asked hoarsely.

All that crying had made her throat raw. It had also made her nose run, she realised as mucus dribbled into her mouth. She grimaced in disgust. Domizio pulled out a kerchief and wiped her face. Greta let him. Her limbs felt leaden. She didn't want to move, ever again.

"They went to bed a while ago. Annika came to say she'd left us a bowl of soup each in the kitchen, though it'll be cold by now."

Greta tried to sit up. It took more energy than she'd anticipated. Domizio took the liberty of looping his arm under her shoulders and around her back. He gently propped her up to lean back against her workbench.

"I'm sorry," she said. It was unfair to have allowed him to come to work for her when she couldn't keep herself together.

"You've nothing to apologise for," he told her firmly as he pushed stray hair out of her face.

The strands tugged against her cheeks where they'd dried to her skin with her tears. Greta couldn't help but feel embarrassed by Domizio seeing her like this. She tried to turn her face away, but he wouldn't let her.

"Greta, I'm being honest with you. You've *nothing* to apologise for," he repeated himself. "I don't know how you've been coping these past few days with the extra stress of everything else brought on after Ranieri's death. Anyone else would've fallen apart, let our Guild fall into ruin and let their own business flounder."

Greta frowned. It was always the same. In times of crisis, people thought she was handling everything well when she thought she was making a mess of things.

"Now, let me help you so things don't get out of hand. I've more than enough time to spare and you have too much on your plate."

Greta looked around her workshop, her heart beating faster. He was right. There was too much for her to do. So many orders to fulfil, so many apprentices to teach, so many problems facing the Sarti Guild.

Her vision started to close in around her. Her breath came in short gasps. Domizio's face appeared in front of her.

"Breathe, Greta. Slow breaths. In ... and out. In ... and out."

Greta followed his breaths. It was a simple thing to focus on and it forced her forget about everything else.

"And up we get."

Domizio pulled Greta to her feet and guided her into the kitchen. He sat her down at the table, then opened cupboards and drawers looking for the things he wanted, placing bowls of soup, cutlery, and cups of water for the two of them. Finally, he sat down across from her and picked up his spoon. Greta watched his every move.

He paused. Greta wondered why until he leaned across the table and put a spoon in her hand.

"Eat."

It was a simple request, just like breathing. Greta looked at the food and wondered how Annika had felt adventurous enough to cook something other than pasta. The chunky soup smelled delicious. It would've tasted delicious too, had it been warmer. As it was, Greta was grateful simply to have food in front of her. She ate small mouthfuls, not quite trusting herself to keep it all down.

Bite by bite, her bowl emptied. It felt good to have something inside her. Domizio was already washing his bowl when Greta finished hers. She took her dirty dishes to the sink and waited her turn. Domizio took them from her.

"You don't have to do that, you know," she said quietly.

It felt wrong for a guest to be doing the dishes.

"Payment for my meal."

He winked at her, and Greta smiled half-heartedly. Domizio frowned and quickly finished the dishes. Greta passed him a cloth to dry his hands, her fingers accidentally brushing his. There was the same tingling sensation from the night before. She drew her fingers back instinctively. Domizio was younger than her. This wasn't something he would want. And not something she should ask for in her current state of mind.

She walked to the other side of the kitchen and busied herself by lighting the stove to warm the kettle. It was as good an excuse as any not to stand next to him. Unfortunately, it didn't work. As she was sorting through her stores of teas, Domizio found the teacups and brought two over to her. She turned and found herself face to face with him.

Was he breathing faster than before or was that just her? Greta couldn't tell. She could feel her pulse racing again, but it wasn't panic this time. She swallowed and took a small step back.

"Which tea?" she asked, holding up two brown boxes.

Without taking his eyes off her, Domizio took one out of her hand and opened it. Greta put the other one away. She tried not to look at him, but it was impossible. If she didn't know better, she'd have thought he was trying to seduce her.

Domizio poured a measure of tea into the teapot. He stood where he was, so very close to her, ostensibly waiting for the kettle to whistle. Greta smoothed her skirt and Domizio took her hand. Greta looked up into his soft brown eyes. There was no laughter there now. He was all seriousness.

"You don't have to do this," she told him, gently wriggling her hand out of his. "I realise it's too late to work on anything now, but I can at least offer you a cup of tea before you leave."

"Greta, this isn't something I *have* to do. This is something I *want*." He hesitated. "I thought it was something you wanted too. I apologise if I was mistaken."

The kettle whistled. He leaned in past her and turned off the stove. Greta could smell the lavender oil he'd rubbed through his hair. She felt a moment of hesitation. Had he come here with the express intention of seducing her? Really?

Greta didn't move away as Domizio poured the boiling water into the teapot. He turned to face her. She didn't have time to think, time to step back.

He kissed her.

It was a soft kiss, full on her lips. Not an accident. Greta opened her mouth, just a little. Domizio took his cue and kissed her more deeply.

Greta's stomach lurched as she leaned in. It always did – every time she kissed someone she really wanted to. It was almost a painful lurch, but immediately gave way to a glorious sensation all over her body.

Domizio took his time with her. She sighed heavily as he kissed every part of her face then moved down the curve of her neck to her bodice. His broad hands held her up against his strong and taut body. She drew his face up, her lips scratching across the stubble of his cheeks until they found his mouth. She gently bit his lower lip and pulled softly. He groaned in pleasure and pushed his groin against hers, his arousal now obvious.

Greta allowed herself to enjoy the sensation of their bodies pressed against each other for long moments but a rustle above them made her pause.

"I can't," she mumbled. "They'll hear us."

"We'll be quiet," Domizio whispered. "Kissing doesn't make a sound."

Greta so very much wanted to give in to temptation. It'd been such a long time since she'd bedded someone she truly cared for. But since taking on apprentices, she'd never brought a man home. She'd always gone to his house. This was uncharted territory for her.

Domizio continued kissing her, running his fingers through her hair and gently pulling her head back to kiss her neck. But he didn't try to undo her bodice. Greta wished he would and remove the decision from her. Smoking Caldera, how she wished he would!

Throwing caution to the wind, Greta took Domizio by the hand and led him up the dark and narrow stairs to her room, locking the door behind them.

# Chapter 9 – Mercatodi 28 Alchimisti 230 Years After Implosion

The clattering of dishes woke Greta. She sat up quickly, realised she was naked and pulled the sheet up to cover herself. Domizio was lying on his stomach beside her. The sight of his bare form stirred re-awoken urges in her.

There would be time for that later. She smiled to herself at the thought. She got out of bed carefully so as not to wake him. By the colour of the sunlight, she could tell it was still early morning.

After last night's amorous activities, she needed a shower. She fished around in her wardrobe for a dressing gown, tied it closely and stepped lightly down the hall to close herself in the water closet.

Domizio woke once she'd returned and begun dressing for the day. She saw his unchaste smile, and let the robe slide teasingly slowly from her shoulders. He rolled over and stretched out an arm to her.

"Tonight," she promised him. "You can see me again tonight."

There was a hungry anticipation in his eyes that drew her towards him. Greta stopped herself just out of his reach and stepped back towards the garderobe. Her looking glass had shown the love marks along her shoulder and the curve of her neck. Freely loving anyone she chose was all well and good but parading it to potential clients and visitors was an entirely different thing altogether.

She selected her most conservative blouse with a high neckline, the well-worn leather work underbust corset and her most voluminous skirts. The skirts would restrict her movement in her small workshop so much that she would likely change into a narrower fit when Domizio was gone.

Domizio was dressed and ready to go before Greta had finished. Men's clothes were so much simpler to put on. As a Sarta, she'd managed to simplify women's clothing to a certain extent, but clothes as chaste as this would always have ridiculous amounts of buttons.

She'd considered putting zippers on her most chaste dress designs, but felt that would be counterintuitive. Those dresses, with their complicated rows of buttons and laces, were more common for young women who were technically of age and available, but either not ready or not willing to experience that side of life – sometimes it was their parents' decision rather than theirs.

Those dresses discouraged amorous young men. The skirts were too heavy to be easily pushed aside by eager young hands for their ultimate prize. The only way to bed the wearer was to undo every single button.

Most young men had neither the patience, nor the time to undo all those buttons before being caught by the young signora's parents or siblings, and they were forced to leave in frustration.

Greta's father had employed the same technique himself with her older sister, Nelia. He'd had little time to supervise Nelia and had often sent Greta herself in to disturb any young man who'd accompanied her sister home after an evening out.

Without fail, Greta would find her sister half undressed from the neck down. Sometimes, the young men would be caught fondling her breasts rather than continuing with the buttons, other times they'd be kissing her distractedly as they fumbled with the buttons. But never had they got enough buttons undone to rip the dress off Nelia before Greta was sent in.

Greta often wondered if her father had timed how long it would take to undo all those buttons. He never sent her in too early. He wasn't foolish enough to deny his daughter *every* pleasure. If he'd done that, she would've resorted to more drastic measures outside their home, and he knew it. This way, she felt some pleasure of being loved, without the danger of pregnancy.

Nelia had refused to join a Guild, preferring to work whatever shop job she could find instead. Had she fallen pregnant too young, it would've fallen to Greta's father to help look after the child and he barely had time to look after the two he had. Nor did he have any delusions about the young men Nelia brought home.

Greta had known that the real problem was that Nelia was reckless, too caught up in the feelings of the moment to be careful, and she was not discerning in her selection of young men. Her sister would open her legs for almost anyone at any time. An unwanted pregnancy wouldn't have made her think twice the next time.

None of them had been Guild men. They weren't responsible or stable and wouldn't have the money to support her or a baby, especially if they weren't committed – in Tor'Esint, commitment ceremonies were not seen as a necessity. It made for a freer life, but it meant teenage pregnancies were more difficult to deal with.

Since Greta's early years, the Alchimisti Guild had come forward leaps and bounds in their alchemical solutions making unwanted pregnancies a thing of the past. All one had to do was drink one of their contraceptive solutions within two days of bedding someone to ensure a pregnancy did not occur.

Greta always had a few of those solutions in her garderobe. She preferred to buy a decent supply at a time, that way she could maintain some semblance of privacy in her love life. She discreetly took the second last one out of her drawer and drank it. She wasn't certain if Domizio knew what it was, but he didn't ask questions. From his attentions last night, she assumed he was an experienced enough lover to have seen women drinking such solutions before, but one never knew how other women dealt with their romantic engagements.

"You're going to test my patience with this outfit tonight," Domizio said as he sidled up behind her and slipped his arms around her waist.

The girth of the skirts ensured that he could not move close enough to press his body against hers. Greta grinned. It was already working.

"I can offer you breakfast before you go," she told him. "Unless you've people waiting for you at your workshop."

Domizio turned her round to face him. He had a quizzical look on his face.

"You *do* know that I live alone, don't you?" he asked. "My workshop is tiny and there's only a single bedroom upstairs, but it's just me."

Greta thought how much more fun they could have had with each other had they spent the night at Domizio's house instead. The thought instantly made her blush. There was no hiding it from Domizio. His face was right in front of hers.

"You could come over to my house this evening."

He waggled his eyebrows at her in a very unsubtle way. Greta laughed.

"And stay the entire night? Leaving three young ladies alone with one disturbingly cavalier young man? I think not!" she scoffed. Then she added in a whisper. "You'll have to make do with being quiet for another night."

Domizio smiled mischievously and whispered back to her. "If I recall correctly, it was *you* who had to bite the pillow to stay quiet."

Greta blushed hotly and batted him away from her. "Begone then, or we'll never start our day."

"No." He shook his head. "I was promised breakfast, and breakfast I shall have. Then I will return just after trading to do a few hours of work for you before your children go off to bed. Then, my lovely signora, I'll do things that will make you wish you'd agreed to come to my place so you could make as much noise as you want."

Greta threw her head back and sighed loudly. "Enough! Enough. Go downstairs now. I'll be there momentarily."

She waited impatiently for Domizio to leave the room then hurriedly fetched the chamber pot from under her bed. She'd been in such a hurry to get dressed that she'd forgotten to relieve herself and was now bursting. Unfortunately, the dress she'd chosen to wear precluded her from using the water closet. There was no way she would even be able to close the door with such wide skirts.

When Greta descended into the kitchen, she found her apprentices silently eating their breakfast and staring at Domizio as he helped himself to a slice of toasted bread. Only Teodoro didn't seem to notice or care that there was an extra person in their household today.

"Good morning," Greta greeted them happily.

Sofia stared at her, then over at Domizio and back to Greta again uncomprehendingly. Marta and Annika didn't even meet her eyes. Greta wondered at their reactions. She'd never made it a secret before if she were going to a man's house and she knew she'd been quiet enough not to wake them last night.

It suddenly occurred to her that perhaps the girls weren't schooled in such matters. The thought shocked her. Surely, they knew the facts of life and love? Tor'Esint was a very liberal town. Was it possible they'd grown up without anyone telling them ... *anything*?

Greta bit her lip. If they didn't know, it was something she was going to have to tell them. Certainly, she wasn't their mother, but if no one else had bothered teaching them, then it was up to her. They'd be in her care for the better part of their teenage years, and she couldn't in good conscience allow them to become women without understanding the first thing about bedding.

"Did you make tea last night?" Annika asked as Greta bit into an apple.

Greta looked over to the benchtop where their forgotten tea still sat in its pot. She repressed the urge to shrug and say at least they hadn't knocked it over in their amorous attention to one another. She doubted that would go down well.

"Yes," Greta replied smoothly. "But something more important drew my attention away."

"Something more important than *tea*?" Sofia asked in surprise. "But you always say there's no bad time for tea."

Domizio laughed. "That's true, Signorina, but distractions are called that for a reason. It's not that it was a bad time for tea, more that Greta was distracted from the tea."

Greta smiled at him from behind her apple though that earned her disapproving glares from two of her girls. She rolled her eyes and bit savagely into her apple. She couldn't have the talk with Domizio here and it probably wouldn't help to have Teodoro in the room. Imagine if she had to explain the specifics to them! The girls would die from embarrassment.

As soon as Domizio was finished with his toasted bread, Greta beckoned him into the shop. It was still well before trading hours, so there was little chance anyone would pass by and see him.

"I think your girls may be lacking some education, my dear," he told her.

"And you thought it was up to you to educate them, did you Mizi?" she asked teasingly.

He huffed out a laugh then turned a serious face on her. "All jokes aside, Greta. I think your youngest really has no idea what happened last night. Your other two, well, I think they may've realised and simply not approved."

Greta bit her lip. "Yes, I'll talk to them. Just not with you still here."

Domizio nodded. He tried to lean in to kiss her lips but between her full skirts and her playful leaning away, he settled for kissing her fingertips.

Greta tried not to grin at the fact that her dress had already saved her more than once from his very welcome advances.

He let himself out and Greta locked the door after him, ensuring that the *Closed* sign remained that way. She smoothed down her skirts and re-entered the kitchen. The girls were whispering together in the corner farthest from Teodoro. She could just imagine where this was heading.

"Teodoro, clean the dishes before getting back to your repairs." She didn't give him a chance to reply before speaking again. "Ladies, if I could have a word with you upstairs before we begin our work for the day."

She'd debated talking to them in the workshop instead, but there was too great a chance that Teodoro would overhear, and it was not a conversation she thought the girls would appreciate an audience for. Better still, upstairs she could show them the alchemical solution that was required if they ever found themselves in need of it.

Instead of taking them into their room, she took them into hers. Greta only considered it might've been a mistake when Marta gasped. She turned to see a scowl darkening Annika's face. The only one who seemed genuinely confused about the state of her bedroom was Sofia. At least their reactions gave Greta some indication of the level of their education on such matters.

"Marta, help me change into a more practical skirt, then we can all sit down together" she told them, selecting a skirt that still worked well with the high neckline and leather underbust corset. "I think it's time we had a chat."

Marta walked over to help her, and Sofia sat hesitantly at the foot of the bed, but Annika stayed resolutely where she was, arms firmly crossed.

"I know what this *chat* is about, and I don't need it."

Greta nodded, as Marta unbuttoned the skirt. "Nevertheless, I want you to stay. You may know part of it, but I'd hazard a guess you don't quite know *everything*."

She could see the hesitation in Annika's face. Eventually, Annika sat where she was, on the floor. Greta knew that was the most she could expect from the girl and accepted that. She stepped out of the voluminous skirt and into the narrower one, then sat on her bed, leaving space for Marta.

"Now, I'm not certain how much each of you knows, so I'm just going to start at the beginning."

Annika rolled her eyes and made a loud attempt at an inconvenienced sigh. Marta and Sofia glanced at her, but Greta purposely paid her no heed.

"Does everyone know how babies are made?"

Marta and Annika nodded. Sofia started to shake her head, saw the others nodding and then awkwardly changed her mind. Greta saw right through it but did not wish to embarrass the girl. She would explain *that* part of it to her later.

"Right, then let's move straight on. I'm not sure what you've understood, but people in Tor'Esint are quite liberal in their views. Women and men can bed whomsoever they wish, as long as the other person is willing and uncommitted. I've heard of other places where they ridiculously expect everyone to remain pure until they are committed and then never bed anyone else in their life. Tor'Esint is not like that.

"You can bed who you want, when you want and not have any regrets about it. The general rule is that anything goes behind closed doors, just don't parade it on the street. In other words, if I wish to bed Domizio, or anyone else, I have the right to do so without being judged. We were discreet about it. Even the three of you wouldn't have known anything had taken place if he'd left when we were done.

"But bedding someone is nothing to be ashamed of. I was happy to bed him and will likely do so again. There used to be the danger of unwanted pregnancies, but with the Alchimisti's solution, one need never worry about that again if one acts in a timely manner."

Here, she went to her garderobe and pulled out the last vial of precious liquid.

"It's a contraceptive solution. Every Alchimista worth their Guild Mark will have a ready stock of these. So, when your time comes and you feel you are ready to take a lover, you can purchase yourself a small store of them to guard against amorous encounters."

She put the vial back in her drawer and turned back to the girls.

"Like last night," Marta asked hesitantly.

Greta nodded. "Exactly. Like last night. I like Domizio, probably more than I should. But I didn't expect to bed him. I honestly thought we'd work together for a few hours, and then he would go home. But then I..."

"Fell apart?" Annika said, not unkindly.

Greta nodded again. She didn't want to think of how she'd fallen apart. It made her worry that she'd do so again.

"That's all I'm going to say about it. You're all young ladies now and can do as you please. The only warning I'll give is that you'll remember all experiences – the good and the bad. Try not to open your legs to just anyone.

"My sister was that way and it got her into a world of trouble. Some men thought that because she was so free with her body, it gave them the right to do as they pleased with her. It was a hard lesson for her to learn and our father made sure every one of those men was punished and not always by the Amministratori."

Annika's harsh expression had softened, just a little. "What happened to her?"

"She moved to Tor'Selit," Greta replied ruefully. "It's a stricter society there but she didn't have a reputation, good or bad, for them to judge her with. I think she's happy enough, but we miss each other terribly."

"Did your papà send her away?" Sofia asked.

"No, dear," Greta said gently. She didn't want to make Sofia feel any worse about her own parents. "Nelia said she wanted to move. Papà helped her decide on a town and he moved there with her. He bought himself a small Gioielliere workshop and she is his shopkeeper."

Sofia frowned angrily. "So ... they deserted you then?"

Greta shook her head. "Of course not. I'd already started my apprenticeship with Ranieri by that time. Papà gave me the option of joining them, but I didn't want to." She clapped her hands together. "That's enough of this. Annika, I need you to go to Signora Loyola's house and tell her we're ready for a second fitting. I know it's Mercatodi, but she can come today if she likes, otherwise first thing Gildadi morning.

"Marta, help Annika get through that pile of repairs today. We've so much work now that I may need you to start working on Ranieri's orders while I continue with Signora Loyola's dress."

The girls made to leave the room, but Greta held Sofia behind. She couldn't in good conscience leave the girl so uneducated.

\*\*\*

As the Guild Hall clocks tolled eleven o'clock, Annika announced Signora Loyola's arrival. Usually, Greta wouldn't have invited a client to the shop on Mercatodi, but she was already running further behind on this dress than she'd like.

"Thank you, Annika. Show her to the dressing corner. Sofia and I will be with her shortly."

Annika nodded and withdrew from the workshop. Greta carefully took the satin and organza bodice from the mannequin and motioned for Sofia to bring the cotton skirt. Together they made their way to the dressing corner and waited for the impatient huff that signified the client's readiness.

"Good morning, Signora, and thank you for coming at such short notice for this fitting," Greta said as she helped the lady into the bodice.

"I'm as eager for you to finish this dress as I'm certain you are," Signora Loyola told her truthfully. "And don't you dare think I'll be leaving before seeing the progress in a mirror."

Greta did her best to hide her smile as Sofia held the skirt open for Signora Loyola to step into it, then pulled it up with some difficulty over the snug corset. Greta tugged the skirt to line it up with the bodice. It was a tighter fit than it should've been.

"I'll need to cut it here and pin it together. Sofia, fetch the pincushion for me and ask Annika to bring in the mirror."

While they waited, Greta took the scissors from her work corset and cut a slit in the skirt to find the right width. By the time the girls had set everything up, she was ready to pin the cotton skirt to the satin and organza bodice. There wasn't enough room for the four of them inside the dressing corner, so Annika graciously stepped out and gave Sofia a smile in passing.

Signora Loyola stood still as the cotton skirt was pinned around her. When Greta was done, she stood back to admire her handiwork.

"There now. We've purchased a selection of beads for the organza sections of the bodice and neckline. The neck will fasten with a loop over two or three beads. Then the skirt will have a zipper just here. I'll put a ribboned belt here, but it will be purely decorative. What do you think?"

Greta stood further back, giving her client a clearer view in the mirror. Signora Loyola delicately touched the bodice, her fingers dragging gently over the soft organza.

"It's beautiful," she whispered. "More beautiful than I'd dared to hope. I can only imagine how stunning it will be with the beading. I've never seen anything like this."

Greta let out a long breath. "It's a new design specifically created for you, Signora."

A light flush rose to Signora Loyola's cheeks. "When shall I come for the final fitting?"

Greta chewed her lip, making the mental calculations. It would still take at least four full, uninterrupted days to complete the dress and if the past week were anything to go by, she would not have that luxury.

"I'll send word when we're close to that point. There's still much work to be done."

For a moment, it looked like there'd be an argument, but Signora Loyola simply nodded. "I'll await your word then. As long as it's ready before my dinner party."

"Of course, Signora," Greta agreed.

She and Sofia helped Signora Loyola out of the bodice and skirt and took everything to the workshop. Greta returned to see Signora Loyola out of the shop and locked the door behind her. She couldn't afford any more distractions today.

"Sofia dear, I'm going to cut the skirt and loops and make the belt and laces today. You can watch me, or you can begin on the beading. Which do you prefer?"

Sofia's eyes went wide. "The beading?" she asked softly.

"If I draw a design on the linen sections of the bodice, do you think you can copy that onto the organza?"

"Of course, Maestra, but do you really think I'm good enough to work on an actual order?"

Greta smiled broadly. "I would never have given you the opportunity if I didn't think your stitch work was good enough. Now, fetch me one of each of those beads so I can sketch the dimensions closely enough."

\*\*\*

When Domizio returned after trading, Greta saw Sofia glance between the two of them and blush brightly. To save her apprentice any further embarrassment, she sent Sofia in to help Annika with dinner preparations.

"Good evening, Mizi." Greta nodded her head but didn't make a move to take his hand. Last night, that had led all too quickly to other activities and they couldn't afford to get distracted so early tonight.

"Good evening, Reta," he returned with a short bow, eyeing the change in her skirt from that morning. His chestnut hair flopped into his eyes. He deftly swept it out of his face as he walked over to her. "Did you receive your edict today?"

Greta nodded. "Ludovico sent one of his lackeys to my workshop this afternoon to search top to bottom for any sign of alchemically-dyed material. Apparently, he didn't believe me when I told him Lucrezia confiscated Ranieri's orders. He even had the hide to tell his lackey to search my warehouse. I told him if he insisted on doing that, he'd need to find a blazermobile to take us both there outside of trading hours."

"They didn't search my house. I gave them the one packet I had and that was it." Domizio frowned. "Are you certain you don't want to tell me what happened between the two of you the other night?

Greta shook her head. "It was nothing, really. A difference of opinions on how the situation should've been handled. That's all. Now, let me show you the orders and you tell me what you're confident to do."

Domizio raised an eyebrow at her. Greta blushed.

"I didn't mean it like that. It's just, I've never worked with you before. I don't know how you work, that's all."

She was surprised when he laughed.

"I'm a Copper Sarto, Greta, with little time and no money to create another Great Work. I'm competent enough, only not as skilled as you. Show me the orders then."

Greta led him to the other workbench where Marta had sorted through the orders yesterday.

"This is the most urgent one. Ranieri sketched the pattern on brown paper but hadn't cut it yet. This is the material that goes with it."

Domizio nodded to himself. "If I couldn't do that, I wouldn't be worth a Copper Guild Mark. You go back to your dress and leave me with this suit."

Greta tried not to heave a sigh of relief. It had been such a long time since she'd earned her Copper Guild Mark that she honestly couldn't remember what her skill level had been at that point. She doubted it would've mattered if she did – it all came down to Maestri.

She'd been fortunate enough to be training under one of the best Sarti Tor'Esint had ever seen. Domizio hadn't been quite so fortunate himself, but Flavia was a respectable Sarta and on her Electrum Guild Mark. She would've been a good Maestra.

They worked in silence for an hour or so before Marta popped her head in to call them in for dinner. Greta attempted to finish her current section before raised voices drew her to the kitchen. Sofia was backed up in a corner behind Annika who was glaring at Teodoro. Marta was standing between them with her hands outstretched to either side of her as though she could hold them the pair back from each other.

"What's going on?" Greta asked.

No one answered.

"Marta, explain," she ordered.

"I don't know. Annika was yelling at Teodoro by the time I came back," Marta replied looking from one to the other.

"Annika?" Greta asked with increasing frustration.

The older girl stood firmly, her hands on her hips, shielding Sofia.

"Ask *him*!" Annika growled.

"Oh, for Caldera's sake! Teodoro, what did you do?" Greta practically shouted.

"What?" he asked with mock innocence. "All I did was to ask your blonde girl there if she wanted to bed me tonight seeing as you'd be busy doing the same with this one again."

Greta couldn't believe her ears! Sofia was just barely fifteen and clearly had *no* desire whatsoever to bed this ash-sucker. Before she could stop herself, Greta stormed over to Teodoro and slapped him across the face. He glared at her angrily, hands balled up into fists.

"She's old enough," he said crudely. "I can bed her if I want to, and you can't say anything about it."

Greta pointed to the door. "Get out of my house now. You're no longer welcome. Take your things and go."

Teodoro stood firm. "You can't kick me out for that. I ain't done nothin' wrong."

"You don't belong to me," Greta replied coldly. "You don't even belong to my Guild anymore. And you've made it perfectly clear you have no love for it. Marta, get his things from your bedroom. Teodoro will be leaving us now."

Marta walked quickly from the room. Within a moment, she was back in the kitchen, holding out a small bundle. When Teodoro didn't take it, she placed it on the table and stepped back from him.

"I ain't going," Teodoro said resolutely. "You can't make me."

Greta didn't know what to do. Teodoro was at least seventeen and muscular. If she tried to physically push him out, he could probably overpower her, or at the very least make it an undignified display.

Domizio walked around her. Without a word, he picked up Teodoro's bundle of belongings and gripped the boy's arm tightly, pushing him towards the door. Teodoro looked like he would protest, but instead snatched his bundle from Domizio and stormed out of the kitchen. Domizio followed him into the shopfront.

Greta didn't let out her breath until she heard the door close and lock behind the errant boy. It was only then that she went to Sofia. The poor girl was trembling.

"Annika, make her a chamomile tea. Sofia, dear, come and sit with me."

She had just managed to coax Sofia onto the bench when Domizio came back into the room.

"I gave him an earful outside. He won't be back to bother you. And he generously gave up his claim to any money from Ranieri's repairs."

Greta nodded her thanks to him. She would have to tell Ludovico about this, but that could wait until tomorrow – and she could send him a note.

"Now then, Sofia, he won't bother you anymore," Greta said soothingly, rubbing the girl's back. "And like I told you this morning, it's *your* decision if and when you ever want to bed someone. You don't ever have to if you don't want to."

"It's not that I never want to bed someone," Sofia said quietly. "But the *way* he asked me – it was so crude. Like it was a sport to him. Something we could do to spite you. He made me feel *dirty*." She shuddered and looked up at Greta. "Does it always make you feel that way?"

"No!" Greta shook her head emphatically. "No. Not when you like the person. Not when they care for you. It's ... blissful."

She could have done with some privacy from Domizio right about now, but he didn't leave. Instead, he sat at the table across from Sofia, passing her the tea that Annika had just finished making.

"Listen to me, Sofia" he said gently. "Not all men are like that ash-sucker. Unfortunately, there are a lot of younger ones who will flatter you with words and gifts to persuade you and then leave you straight after. But you're a clever girl. You'll be able to tell which ones care for you by the way they treat you. *Those* are the ones who may deserve you but it's always your choice and none of them have the right to treat you the way he did."

Greta couldn't have put it better herself. She was thankful she hadn't told him to leave. She stretched her hand out across the table towards him. He took her hand in his and squeezed it gently. Greta could feel Sofia's eyes on them.

"You care for Maestra Greta, don't you?" Sofia asked.

He smiled his lopsided smile. "Very much so. I don't know if you've noticed, but she's a very special signora."

He winked at Sofia conspiratorially. Greta withdrew her fingers from his. She hadn't realised quite how deeply Domizio felt for her. She didn't want to have the talk with him – not yet. She didn't want to have to worry about any potential plans he had for their future.

"Doesn't it bother you that you're not the only person she's bedded?"

The unexpected question came from Annika. Greta purposely averted her eyes from Domizio. She didn't want to see the hurt in his eyes. It was one thing saying that Tor'Esint was liberal, it was quite another to have your own secrets spilled out to a current lover.

Domizio drew a deep breath. "I don't presume to be the only person Greta has ever bedded, nor do I expect she'll be content with me forever. I will cherish whatever amount of time we spend together and that is all."

Greta tried not to sigh in relief.

"How about some dinner?" Greta said before any other awkward conversations could crop up. Annika grinned at her.

Later that night, after she'd sent the girls up to bed, Greta bid Domizio farewell. Though she had been looking forward to his company all day, the unexpected turn of events with Teodoro had cooled her passion. Domizio didn't complain at being turned out. He simply bowed, kissed her fingertips, and departed with a promise to return tomorrow to continue his work.

# Chapter 10 – Riposidi 1 Inventrici 230 Years After Implosion

A pounding on the door woke Greta unreasonably early. It was Riposidi for Caldera's sake! She hurriedly covered her nightgown with a heavy woollen dressing gown, rushed down the stairs and opened the door.

"I believe *this* belongs to you," Ludovico said in a loud voice for so early in the morning.

He was holding Teodoro by the arm and shaking him none too gently. Greta straightened her spine and stood tall.

"Teodoro is no longer welcome in my household. He's neither my apprentice nor my ward."

Ludovico glowered at her. "You said you'd take him in until other arrangements could be made."

Greta lifted her chin even higher. "I signed no agreement to that effect. The boy overstepped his boundaries and, as he doesn't currently belong to our Guild, I have no obligation to him. Did he come crawling back to beg you for another apprenticeship?"

Ludovico curled his hand into a fist. Greta saw the motion but did not retreat. She would not be cowed on her own doorstep.

"He was found making a nuisance of himself," Ludovico retorted sharply. "Which he wouldn't have been at liberty to do had you not thrown him out last night."

"If he hadn't been so crude with my girls and so disrespectful of our Guild, perhaps I wouldn't have turned him out," Greta replied evenly. "Even if you had an apprentice spot ready for him, I wouldn't encourage you to give it to this ungrateful boy."

"Wouldn't want one anyway," Teodoro spat at her.

Greta rolled her eyes. "You make my point perfectly. Now, if you don't mind, Ludovico, I have other matters to attend to."

Without waiting for a reply, she shut the door and locked it on them. For a moment, she leaned back against the wooden door, trying to collect her thoughts. When she opened her eyes, Annika was there.

"I ... never realised how much you cared about us," she said quietly. "I'm sorry if I ever doubted you."

Greta stepped forward and patted Annika on the shoulder.

"I always did, Annika. Now it's your turn to show how much you care. You've come a long way in a few short days. I have faith in you."

"I think I made a mistake," Annika said softly.

The girl gave her such a pained look. Ice gripped Greta's stomach as she tried not to panic.

"What kind of mistake?"

"Yesterday, when the man from the Guild was here. He asked me for the key to your warehouse. He said it was Guild Business and I was to hand it over immediately."

"And did you give it to him?" Greta asked, nauseous with worry.

"Well, no."

Greta let out a long breath. "Then you haven't made a mistake."

Annika looked uncomfortable. "The thing is, I told him you wouldn't like anyone snooping around there without you. He gave me this funny sort of look, like I'd just given him a present."

"Caldera's smoke!" Greta swore.

She raced upstairs and got dressed as quickly as she could in a plain work dress. She took the keys for her warehouse and looped them onto her necklace. Annika was dressed and waiting for her when she got downstairs. The others were still in their nightgowns, looking sleepy and confused.

"I've got to go."

"I'm coming with you," Annika insisted. "It's Riposidi. The shop will be closed anyway, and Marta and Sofia are more than capable of managing until we return."

Greta didn't have time to argue. She hurried out of the shop, Annika at her heels. To the girl's credit, she didn't bother asking stupid questions. Greta practically ran to Aveline's workshop just a few doors down the street. It had never felt so far before.

She knocked loudly on the door until Nevio opened it.

"Signora Sarta, it's not even seven o'clock. What are you doing here?"

Greta brushed him aside and walked into the Inventrice's workshop. "I need to borrow Aveline's blazermobile as a matter of some urgency." The boy didn't move. "*Now*, Nevio."

Nevio hesitated only a moment longer, then raced up the stairs to where Aveline was presumably still in bed. Any sane person would be. Greta paced up and down, trying to formulate a plan. If the Sarti Guild, Ludovico in particular, wanted to harm her, all they'd need to do was show the Amministratori her warehouse and the Mercantili Guild would be able to prove she'd been trading around them.

Not *all* of her stock was illegally obtained, but enough of it to get her in trouble. What was she going to do? How was she going to hide it?

Long minutes later, Aveline came down the stairs looking the worse for wear.

"What's happened, Greta?"

Greta wondered just how close a friend Aveline was and wished she didn't have to guess.

"I need your blazermobile and ... no questions."

Aveline eyed her for a moment then turned to her apprentice. "Nevio, I'll be back ... later."

Greta put out her hand to stop Aveline. "You don't have to come."

"If you're doing what I think you are, you'll need my help," Aveline told her plainly. "Let's go."

Relief flooded Greta. "Thank you, Veli."

Aveline shook her head. "Don't thank me until you're safe. I'll drive."

The three of them hopped into Aveline's blazermobile. Greta clasped her hands together nervously as Aveline poured the blazer solution into the fuel cell.

"On second thoughts, *you* drive. I don't know where your warehouse is."

They switched seats awkwardly. Greta sped off as soon as she was settled.

"How did you know where we're going?" Annika asked Aveline.

"Just a hunch," Aveline replied grimly. "Another hunch tells me you're going to need somewhere to store certain goods you don't want the Amministratori to find, yes?"

Greta grunted.

"Good thing for you I've got a workshop in the warehouse district now."

That was a surprise. Greta didn't take her eyes off the road as she interrogated Aveline. "What does an Inventrice need another workshop for?"

"It's a … side project," Aveline answered evasively. "It's difficult to explain. I'll show you when we get there. I can't promise your wares will be completely safe, but I'll do my best not to burn them."

"Burn them?!" Greta cried out. "Veli, what in Caldera's smoke is going on?"

"Greta, if you're afraid the Amministratori are going to raid your warehouse, you'd lose more than just your illicit wares in the process. Surely you'd rather keep yourself and your Guild Status safe?"

There was no question about it. Aveline was right, but Greta wished she had another option to consider.

It had never seemed to take so long to drive to her warehouse before. Greta imagined they were being followed ten times over, but every other blazermobile turned off a few streets after joining them. Her paranoia was giving her butterflies.

Finally, they reached her warehouse. It was still early enough in the day that no one else was on the street. They tumbled out of the blazermobile and onto the quiet street.

"Annika, stay with the blazermobile. Make room for us. Veli, come with me."

Greta took the keys from around her neck and opened the warehouse. She closed the door quickly behind them. Even if the streets appeared empty, she didn't trust them. These days, anyone could be spying for the Mercantili Guild. They'd soon have reason to want to spy on her if they weren't already.

She went to open the roller roof to let in light but thought better about the noise at this time of day. Instead, she lit the glass lantern at the door and took stock.

"We'll need to move all my stores of silk and organza. The satin, I can probably pass off as having bought here in Tor'Esint without needing the Mercantili Guild. You'll find the organza in that box there. If the box is too cumbersome, we'll just take the material itself."

She left Aveline to deal with the organza and walked around her legal stores to the back wall where all her special items were. She'd managed to accumulate an entire wall of wares. How could she possibly move them all?

The door opened and closed as Aveline took the box of organza out to Annika. Greta was still staring at the wall when she returned.

"Veli, how am I going to move all of this? It won't fit in your blazermobile."

Aveline shrugged. "Not in one trip, no. But we'll do as many trips as it takes. Let's start with the smaller bundles so we can get rid of more of it."

Greta took a deep breath and nodded. Many of the bolts were in manageable sizes. Only a very few were rolled around long strips of wood. They each carried out four smaller bolts at a time, leaving Annika to arrange them in the back of the blazermobile.

It took them five trips to fill up the blazermobile. When they were done, Aveline took control.

"Annika, you come with me. My warehouse isn't far. You can help me unload the blazermobile while Greta arranges things here for the next trip."

Annika looked at Greta for permission. Greta nodded and disappeared back inside the warehouse, locking the door behind her. She walked around the warehouse. What could she possibly explain away? What could she afford to leave here?

It was difficult to choose. Most silks and even some satins were difficult to come by in the haberdasheries. Would the Amministratori believe she'd found them there without proof of purchase?

Greta tried not to let it all overwhelm her. There was nothing for it but to get rid of as much as possible before the Amministratori arrived. It might all depended on how angry Ludovico was with her. This morning's outburst would've only made things worse. She doubted it'd take more than a few hours for him to figure out the best way to harm her. She could only hope that he didn't try to have her stripped of her Gold Guild Mark or thrown in prison.

She shook her head. These thoughts would not help her. She collected the rest of the bolts and took them to the workbench at the front of the warehouse. There were still twelve of them to transport. That would take up at least half the room in the blazermobile.

Then there was the problem of the long rolls. The only way to fit them in the blazermobile was to shove them in from the back and have them poking into the front seats. It would make it difficult to drive the blazermobile, but there was no choice. It would take too long to take them off the rolls, though it would certainly make it easier to transport them.

Greta tapped her foot impatiently. They were taking a long time to return. Perhaps she'd have time to unroll at least some of the longer bolts. She looked at the remaining stores. If she had to choose one colour to save, it'd be the dark blue she was using for Signora Loyola's dress. It was by far the most expensive. In fact, all the blues were expensive. Her thoughts were not helping!

With a mammoth effort, Greta took down the long bolt and placed it on her turn table. The contraption helped her easily unroll as much of a particular fabric that she needed. This was the first time she was truly glad she had given in to the expense of it.

She tugged at the edge of the material. It came away easily – all she had to do was keep pulling. To keep the material in some kind of order, she held both arms out as far as she could and folded the material in long swathes as she pulled it off the roll. There was more on the roll than she had anticipated.

Cursing to herself, Greta placed the material on the floor. At least it was only dusty and not actually dirty. But it would still likely ruin that section of the material. She continued pulling the material and folding it atop itself.

When she was finally done, she folded the massive bundle over in half, to shorten the roll length, then attempted to wrap it in brown paper. There was a battering at the door. Greta froze.

"Who's there?" she asked from where she was.

"It's Veli and Annika. Open the door. Quickly!"

Greta breathed a sigh of relief and opened the door, letting them both in.

"We saw the Amministratori two streets away, checking Sarti Guild warehouses. We won't have much more time."

"Smoking Caldera!" Greta swore loudly. "Right, let's get these smaller bolts in first. Then we're going to have to slide the longer rolls in. I was trying to take them off the rolls, but we won't have time now."

Annika held the warehouse door open as Greta and Aveline ran back and forth to put in the twelve smaller bolts. By the time they were done, Aveline was looking quite pale.

"Veli, what's wrong?"

Aveline placed her hand across her stomach, visibly pale. "I don't think I can do this."

"Why?" Annika asked in surprise.

Greta had no time to explain. "Fine, you take Annika's place and keep the door open. This next bit will be more difficult anyway and I don't want you dropping the material. Annika, come with me."

Together, they picked up the swathe of material Greta had taken off the roll. There was no way she was leaving this one behind. They carried it awkwardly, the brown paper only helping so much to keep it from falling everywhere.

Back in the warehouse again, Greta didn't have time to prioritise one colour over another. They went from one side of the wall to the other, taking the heavy rolls and sliding them into the blazermobile from the back. They were just getting the last roll when Aveline yelled out at them.

"Hurry! I can see them on the street. I don't think they've noticed us yet, but it won't take long."

Greta walked as quickly as she could with the cumbersome load. She placed it none too gently on top of the other bolts and pushed. It was too heavy. She needed help.

"For Caldera's sake, Annika *hurry*! Help me shove it in there." Greta practically yelled at her apprentice.

Annika didn't reply. She just pushed harder.

"They've seen us!" Aveline said frantically. "Greta, lock your warehouse. Annika, help me close the door. Get in the blazermobile. Quick!"

Greta dashed to the warehouse door and fumbled with her keys to lock it. They'd managed to get most of the contraband items out, but that didn't mean she wanted the Amministratori snooping around inside unencumbered.

The blazermobile door slammed closed behind her. Greta finished locking the door and practically jumped in the vehicle.

"Stop! By order of the Tor'Esint Amministratori. Stop!"

She could hear their distant footsteps pounding down the street.

"Go, Veli, go!" Greta screamed.

"I'm trying!" Aveline replied angrily, fumbling with the blazer solution.

In seconds, the blazermobile roared to life. Aveline didn't bother putting the lid back on the solution before grasping it between her knees and hurtling down the street, away from their pursuers.

Greta tried to keep steady, but as Aveline careened around corners, she was pushed up against the side of the blazermobile, blazer solution sloshing over both herself and Annika. Annika grabbed the solution from between Aveline's knees and screwed the lid on. Greta was too terrified to thank her. She was covered in blazer solution, transporting illicit material, while being chased by the Amministratori. How had this happened?

True to her word, Aveline's warehouse was not far away by blazermobile. With any luck, it would take the Amministratori at least ten minutes of running hard to reach them – and that was presuming they knew where they'd gone.

Greta and Annika were forced to be more careful in moving the load of material from the blazermobile to Aveline's warehouse because of their blazer solution-soaked clothing. She didn't want to ruin her expensive fabric.

Aveline let them inside her warehouse. Greta looked around in surprise. It was practically empty except for a small wooden table at one end with a wooden box sitting atop it. All the bolts from the previous load had been unceremoniously dumped on the floor next to the door. Greta tried not to be angry about that. Aveline was right – better for it to get ruined than for her to get caught and face the consequences.

With Annika's help, Greta managed to unload the entire contents from Aveline's blazermobile much more quickly than they had loaded it.

When they were finished, Greta leaned up against the wall and breathed heavily. They were safe now.

"Let me just check this box," Aveline said walking to the workbench, "and then we'll go."

Greta started to follow her, but Aveline held out a warning hand.

"Stay back. I don't want you to get hurt."

"How would I get hurt?" she asked hesitantly.

"Just get behind the rubber wall there for a moment. I'll explain once I know it's safe."

Greta looked to the other side of the warehouse. She'd thought it was an actual wall painted black. It hadn't occurred to her to that it was made from an entirely different material. Without questioning the logic of it, Greta grabbed Annika by the hand and dragged her behind the rubber wall. Annika looked at her with a grimace.

"I'm sorry," Annika said quietly.

"Whatever for?" asked Greta, trying to get her breath back from all the running around.

"Well, they wouldn't even have known to look in your warehouse if I hadn't said something. Would they?"

Greta patted Annika's hand. "They would've come sooner or later," she told her. "Granted, it may only have been the Sarti Guild if you hadn't said anything and if Ludovico wasn't so furious with me. But it would've happened eventually. At least you had the good sense to tell me in time."

Annika nodded silently. Greta pitied the poor girl. She'd only recently begun to turn herself around.

"Why was Ludovico so angry?" she asked, chewing on her lip. "It doesn't sound like him."

Greta grunted. "I'd say there's a few reasons, but it mostly comes down to him feeling threatened. He thinks I'm the cause of all his current discomfort and would like very much to pass that discomfort to me."

"Does this have to do with Ranieri? Or the material?"

"Both," Greta sighed. "There are things about the Guilds that only Guild members know. Certain things that they want to keep secret from non-Guild members. Ranieri ... well, he left me something in his Final Testament that may not actually have been his to leave me. It could cause a huge problem depending on how it's handled."

Aveline came around the corner and looked down at them sitting on the floor.

"You make it sound so terrible, Greta. It was a wonderful gift."

Greta shrugged. "He left me everything else. He didn't need to complicate things by leaving me *that* too."

Annika looked at her in confusion.

"Leave you what?" she asked.

Greta exchanged glances with Aveline who shook her head imperceptibly. "Sorry, Annika. I can't tell you – at least not until you have your Copper Guild Mark."

Annika raised her eyebrow but did not argue. Greta turned her attention back to Aveline.

"Now, Inventrice, will you tell me what you've got in that box that's so dangerous?"

Aveline bit her lip and looked back at the box. "It's ... a bit of a secret, actually. Chide might not want me saying anything."

"Then by all means, don't tell me," said Greta drily. "Since when has he commanded your actions?"

"Reta, don't be like that," Aveline said, resting her hand on her belly. "It's a Guild thing. We may have found a new power source if we can only figure out how to safely harness and regenerate it."

Greta was interested despite herself. "A new power source that still uses fire or friction?"

"No," Aveline shook her head. "It's ... another source. It has shocking power but if we can't find a way to control it, we won't be able to sell it."

"But you mean it would be a safer option for me than using fire lanterns in my workshop? It's too dangerous with the material and a wooden workshop. Would it fix that problem?"

"Well, yes," admitted Aveline. "That's what we're hoping. It would revolutionise power. It would be a huge boon to the Inventrici Guild."

"And not bad for your pocket either," laughed Greta. Aveline laughed with her. "But would it generate enough wealth to start counteracting the Mercantili Guild?"

The Inventrice stopped laughing abruptly. "That's a dangerous thing to say. The Mercantili Guild is still too powerful. They have their hands in too many pockets. I wouldn't even know where to begin."

"But you've thought about it," Greta said. "I'm sure you have. I'm sure all of us have. We need to find a way. Even if it's finding which Amministratori they lined the pockets of. I don't know how they managed to get their Edicts in place, but we need to stop them. Soon."

Aveline shook her head. "We can't do it alone, Reta. They're too powerful. So many Alchimisti in my acquaintance have already disappeared or been thrown in prison. Some have even had their Guild Marks stripped. They can't earn enough to feed themselves, let alone their families if they don't have one."

"I know," sighed Greta. "But someone needs to do something about it. We can't just let them run every other Guild into the ground while they build themselves up. If we do, then we'll never get out from under their thumbs. It'll get to a point where we can't ever rebuild our Guilds. I don't want to be the one to bring down the Sarti Guild."

Aveline looked at her curiously. "Is that what's happened here? Why they're searching the Sarti warehouses?"

Greta shrugged. "Not entirely. Let's get out of here. I don't want them to find us together and accuse us of inter-Guild relations. Not when they already know we created the zipper together."

Aveline nodded and drove them home in her blazermobile.

***

The afternoon dragged by as Greta sat in her workshop, trying to concentrate on Signora Loyola's dress and failing miserably. If the Amministratori decided to search *all* warehouses, they'd still find her store of illicit materials in Aveline's warehouse. That could potentially be even more disastrous. Not only would they be able to prove Greta had been trading without the Mercantili Guild, but they'd accuse her and Aveline of inter-Guild relations. They wouldn't be able to explain away the evidence in a suitable fashion.

Sofia tried to talk to her a handful of times, but Greta couldn't focus. She was forced to unpick and re-hem the zipper section of the skirt time and time again. Finally, she put the skirt down and walked over to her youngest apprentice.

"How's the beading going?" she asked.

Sofia shrugged. "It's not really that much more difficult than doing repairs but for the intricacy of the pattern."

The conversation continued, but Greta was detached from it. She was saying all the right things, in all the right places, but she really couldn't focus properly.

"I'm going to make some tea," she announced finally.

Sofia looked at her oddly. "There's a pot right there."

She pointed to the far end of the workbench. Greta's shoulders slumped.

"I'm sorry, Sofia. I'm a bit distracted today. I'm going out for a walk to clear my head."

Time had slipped away from Greta. She didn't realise how late it already was until she met Domizio coming down the street as she exited her workshop and adjusted her coat. He smiled lopsidedly at her. She tried to return his smile but failed.

"Greta, what's happened?"

He maintained a decorous distance from her, even though today she was wearing a lower neckline with her work underbust corset and a simple but elegant skirt. She and Annika had had to shower and change when they returned home. The faint odour of blazer solution still surrounded them, but at least they were clean.

"It's been a long day," she told him. "I just need to get out."

Domizio hesitated. "Do you still want me to do some work?"

"Yes, if you don't mind," Greta nodded. "I've been practically useless today. At least you can help me from falling behind even further. I'll be back soon. I promise."

Domizio looked at her in concern. Greta could feel it, but she didn't have the energy to explain. Not right now. She kept walking past him, not turning to see if he was watching her. Her feet took her to Aveline's workshop. *This* was where she wanted to be. *This* was who she wanted to talk to. But could she? With Nevio around, did Aveline feel safe to talk in her own home? Greta had thought her own house was safe, but even a loyal apprentice could make a blunder without meaning to.

Greta swallowed her doubts and walked up the steps and into the workshop. Nevio looked up at her entrance. Aveline was not there.

"Signora Sarta, Aveline is not here. She left a message for you though, in case you came to call on her. I have it here somewhere."

Nevio passed her a slip of paper.

*Meet me at Chide's house.*

She turned it over in her hand. There was nothing on the other side. Well, that was it then. Off to Telchide's house. She'd never been there before, though she knew it wasn't far off Via dell'Oro. All she'd have to do was look for the Inventrici Guild symbol and hope there weren't too many on that street. What level was he now? Silver? Gold? Nevio might know. But she couldn't ask him outright. That would give her movements away and she didn't want anyone following her without her knowledge.

"Nevio, tell me, what Guild Mark does Aveline have?"

He frowned at her – he probably knew that she knew.

"Electrum."

Greta nodded thoughtfully. "And she's just come back from travelling with Telchide, correct? What level is he?"

Nevio stiffened at the mention of Telchide's name. "Signore Telchide is also now an Electrum Inventore. The new Guild Mark went up on his door just two weeks ago."

Greta raised an eyebrow. Now that was a surprise. "Well, that's ... good news."

Nevio gripped his tools a little tighter. "It doesn't make him better than Maestra Aveline."

"Well, of course it doesn't," Greta replied easily. "It only puts him at the same Guild level, that's all."

"Exactly," replied the apprentice, slightly mollified. "And his *two* apprentices won't be able to learn as quickly as me because there's still only one of *him*."

Greta frowned. "Certainly. You've got Maestra Aveline all to yourself and they'll need to share Maestro Telchide. I'll be off then. Thank you for the note."

Nevio huffed in a mollified way. Greta could tell he was angry, though just exactly what about she couldn't quite tell. Was he angry that Telchide had gone up to an Electrum Guild Mark? It wasn't a surprising elevation – Telchide's work was well-renowned. If only his manner wasn't so infamous, he'd have so many more clients.

Greta walked back onto Piazza Mercantile and headed down Via dell'Oro. Two blocks down, then a turn to the right. Another block or so along and there was Telchide's workshop, with a shiny new Electrum Inventrici Guild Mark screwed into the door. It looked no different from Aveline's, except hers showed slight signs of tarnish from years of weather exposure.

She hesitantly knocked on the door. Telchide had not invited her – Aveline had. She'd never walked into Telchide's workshop herself. It felt a little like spying. A young man with brown eyes opened the door for her.

"Good evening, Signora ... Sarta." He'd looked down her coat to find the Sarti Guild Mark brooch. "How may I help you today? Would you like to order a fine pocket watch? Perhaps a lovely music box? Or are you in need of a mechanical aide?"

Greta internally applauded his manner. It was smooth and efficient – more so than Telchide himself had ever been. If this was one of his apprentices, Telchide had done quite well for himself.

Another young man was working on a set of shelves in front of the street window. Telchide was leaning on a set of crutches next to him.

"Put that nail there, right there, no to the left a little."

The young man stopped and looked at Telchide. "Inventore, don't waste your working time with this. I am perfectly capable of hammering in some nails."

The first young man laughed at the spectacle, making Greta herself grin.

"I was looking for Aveline Inventrice," Greta told the brown-eyed boy. "She left a message for me to meet her here."

"Ah, you must be Greta Sarta." The boy held out his hand. Greta shook it warily. "I'm Florio. That's my brother, Gaspare. We're Telchide Inventore's new apprentices. Aveline is upstairs. She'll be down soon. Please, allow me to take your coat."

Florio waited patiently for Greta to take off her coat. She was thankful that there weren't so many buttons on this one. Telchide looked up as she walked over.

"Greta, welcome. Aveline will be down shortly."

She nodded and looked at his plastered leg.

"What happened?"

Telchide looked at her in confusion. She motioned to his leg.

"Ah, yes, an accident ... on the Caldera. Nothing to worry about. It will heal in time."

He proceeded to ignore her and hobbled his way to the workbench, leaning heavily on his crutches.

"Is that for Signora Loyola?" Greta asked.

Telchide's eyes widened in surprise. "Well, yes. But how did you know?"

"Veli is one of my closest friends, Telchide. She speaks of you often." She smiled at the sudden flush of colour on his cheeks. "In fact, it was fortuitous she did this time. It ensured that Signora Loyola could not demand a shorter timeframe from me than was necessary for her new dress."

"It was, erm, rather *difficult* to make her understand how long these things take," Telchide admitted.

"But if she insists on the best, she can't expect ridiculously short timeframes," Greta said. Telchide nodded. "I'm glad you stood your ground with her. This dress wouldn't have been possible in a shorter timeframe."

Telchide nodded and continued working on the music box. Florio joined her in watching the Inventore at work. It was an interesting process. He was hammering out little bumps in a metal disc – it looked like copper.

"What's that for?" she asked curiously.

Aveline didn't make music boxes. Greta had never seen such an elaborate creation before. The music box Telchide had traded her for Teresina's sleeves was much simpler than this one.

"Florio, can you answer?" Telchide asked, not taking his eyes off his work.

Greta bristled at his rudeness in not to answering himself, but as Florio explained the basic mechanics of the music disc, she realised it was a teaching strategy. Telchide corrected him only when he had made an actual error of fact.

"I'm done, Inventore!" Gaspare called out behind her. "But it rocks. How can I make it more stable?"

Greta turned to see Gaspare rocking the shelf back and forth. Telchide did not immediately respond. Florio walked over and watched his brother rock it back and forth.

"Spare, where are those metal strips I showed you yesterday? We'll need two of them."

Gaspare went to a set of drawers on Telchide's workbench. The Inventore himself didn't stop working but pointed to the next set of drawers across from that one. Greta thought he should pay a little more attention to his apprentices than he was, but it was not for her to say.

After a minute of searching, Gaspare returned with two metal strips that had holes punched through them. Greta wondered what in Caldera's smoke the boys were thinking of doing, and without their Maestro providing any guidance whatsoever! It was *not* how she thought they should be working. But she held her tongue.

Curious, despite herself, Greta paid close attention to the boys. Florio was holding one metal strip on the workbench with half hanging over.

"You hold that there, I'm going to hammer this side down."

"Stop!" Telchide shouted. The effect was instant. Both boys froze in position. "Two things. First. I'm working here on a very delicate process. If you start hammering away, my project will be ruined. Go and use the other workbench.

"Second, use the clamp. It will save your fingers should your brother's aim be off, and the clamp will hold it steadier than you possibly could."

"Yes, Inventore," they mumbled in unison. "Thank you, Inventore."

Greta reassessed her previous assumption. Telchide was taking in everything but by letting the boys make their own mistakes, he was allowing them to learn so much more.

A tumble of footsteps raced down the stairs, distracting Greta from what the boys were doing. Teresina, in a mock work dress with pockets all over it ran headlong towards Telchide. She stopped short when she saw Greta, her eyes growing larger as she looked her up and down.

"Oh Papá, look at her *dress*! And that corset – it's exquisite! Can nonna make me one like that?"

Greta smiled at the child's adoring praise. Telchide stopped what he was doing and looked over at Greta's attire. He shook his head.

"Teresina, your nonna isn't a Sarta. She can't do things like *that*." He waved his hand up and down, gesturing to Greta's outfit. "And besides, you're too young for a corset. Will Aveline be much longer?"

Teresina raised her eyebrows at her father but turned to Greta and smiled politely.

"Greta Sarta, Aveline is upstairs making tea. She's asked me to escort you to the kitchen if you've time to spare for a cup." Greta smiled at Teresina as the girl whispered out of the corner of her mouth, "Did I do that right, Papá?"

He smiled and held an arm out to her. Teresina ran into him and hugged him tightly. Telchide winced but didn't make a sound.

"Telchide, do you mind?" Greta asked him.

After all, it wasn't Aveline's house, but his. The Inventore waved her up the stairs. Teresina took Greta by the hand and led her upstairs. It felt more than a little odd to be walking into the living quarters of a mere acquaintance.

Greta looked around with envy. The entire property was larger than hers, but Piazza Mercantile was known for its smaller properties. It was a popular area and more people wanted to live there. But this property was almost twice the size of hers! Even if Telchide had sectioned off his ground floor the way she had, with a shopfront, a workshop and a kitchen, he would still have a larger working area than she did.

Teresina insisted on giving her a quick tour, pointing out the room the twins were sharing, her nonna's room, Telchide's room and finally her own.

"Can I show you my favourite thing?" she asked conspiratorially. "It's one of papá's inventions, but he wasn't allowed to submit it as a Great Work."

Greta found herself quite curious as so why this invention was disallowed.

"I'd love to see it."

Teresina bloomed into a smile, and she led Greta into her bedroom. She closed the door and drew the blind, making the room as dark as possible. Greta could barely see the girl's silhouette. And then she was glowing yellow as was everything else in the room. Greta walked over to the box that had illuminated the entire room with enough light to see by.

"This is marvellous! What is it?" she asked.

"It's a lightbox!" Teresina told her excitedly. "Papá made it to help keep my nightmares away – they're always worse in the dark. Each of the colours lasts a different amount of time. This is the shortest one. But there's one that lasts four hours!"

"What colour's that one?" Greta asked as the yellow light dimmed.

Teresina drew back the blind and opened the door. "Blue."

"And is it as bright as this yellow one?"

An idea was forming in her mind, but Greta didn't want to play her hand too soon – not even to a child.

"Of course," Teresina shrugged. "They're all as bright as each other. Sometimes, if I wake up and can't get back to bed again, I read by the lightbox. It's magnificent and it's all mine."

Teresina smiled like she had just shown Greta the greatest treasure in the world. And perhaps, without knowing it, she had. If Greta had a lightbox like this, she could work late into the night without fear of burning down her workshop. She'd need to talk to Telchide about it. Even if it hadn't been accepted as a Great Work, perhaps she could still commission one.

"Resi, did you get lost?" Aveline's voice called down the hallway.

Teresina grabbed Greta by the hand and dragged her down the far end of the hallway to the kitchen. Even with four bedrooms and a water closet upstairs, there was still enough room for a large kitchen. Greta's envy was growing by the second. It had been a wise move at the time to purchase a workshop in Piazza Mercantile, to gain a large customer base. But now that she had that customer base, and a Gold Guild Mark, she could potentially move to Ranieri's workshop, which was closer to this size. It certainly would be more comfortable a place to live than her own cluttered home.

"Reta, I'm sorry to give you the slip earlier," Aveline apologised, placing a tea tray on the kitchen table. "There are things we need to discuss, and it might be better here than at my workshop."

Greta raised an eyebrow. Nevio was an older apprentice than Florio and Gaspare. Was Aveline suggesting he wasn't as trustworthy?

Aveline sat across from Greta. "Serenita's out for a few hours, so we won't be disturbed."

Ah. Sebetine's mother, Greta thought to herself. The reason Aveline refused to contemplate a relationship with Telchide. Greta could understand – she barely coped allowing Domizio to stay the night.

In fact, she hadn't even managed that. It had led to Teodoro annoying Ludovico, which had only served to infuriate the Amministratore to the point of speeding up the searches of warehouses. Why he'd seen fit to include the Tor'Esint Amministratori in the process was beyond her. *He* was the one accusing her of damaging their Guild – well, now he was going to do more damage by getting the Tor'Esint Amministratori involved.

"Drink, Greta. You'll feel better."

Aveline poured her a cup of green tea and passed it over to her. Greta took it in both hands and breathed in the bitter aroma. Telchide had good taste in tea, which was odd considering Teresina had mentioned he preferred coffee.

She sipped at the tea and tried to relax. It didn't work. She was far too wound up by the events of the day.

"Can we continue our conversation now?" Greta asked, perhaps a little too recklessly. "How are we going to bring down the Mercantili Guild?"

Teresina drew in a sharp breath. Aveline shot Greta an exasperated look.

"Resi, why don't you go to you room and write a list of options for Gaspare to buy dinner for tonight?"

"Can I ask Eduardo if he has more of the solution for my lightbox?"

"I'm not sure that's a good idea," she replied.

Greta saw the look pass between Aveline and Teresina. The little girl jumped up and nodded.

"You're right. Gaspare helps me get back to sleep now. I'll be fine without it. Besides, it will be fun to think of something nice for dinner."

There was definitely something here that Greta was missing. She waited until Teresina had left the kitchen before making any comment.

"You certainly seem to have a good rapport with Teresina," she noted wryly. "Who'd have thought another woman's daughter would fall for you so easily."

Aveline put down her teacup. "Don't be cruel, Greta. Teresina is a sweet child who barely remembers her mother. And I'm not replacing her mother. She knows nothing."

"But you've become so close that a single look makes her know what you're thinking," Greta pointed out.

Aveline shrugged. "There are things going on that you don't know about. Things I can't tell you."

"Like what?" Greta asked. "You've already told me about the secret project. And the baby. What else could you have to hide from me? I thought we were friends."

Aveline did not respond immediately. She sipped her tea and refilled it, taking the time to refill Greta's cup as well.

"As your friend, I helped you hide things from the Amministratori and evade them this morning. I didn't ask questions, because you told me not to. I believe that works both ways. I told you about the project because you were in the same room as it and it might damage your goods. But you don't need to know everything else that's happening in my life."

Greta held her tongue. Aveline was right. She hadn't asked questions, though she must've been curious about the warehouse raid. Whatever had passed between Aveline and Teresina was nothing for Greta to stick her nose into.

"Back to planning then," Greta said, taking another sip of her tea. "What are we going to do about the Mercantili Guild?"

"There isn't anything we *can* do right now," Aveline told her. "The only way to bring down the Mercantili Guild is to beggar them, and I can't see a way to do that. Can you?"

Greta shook her head. "We could convince people not to trade outside of Tor'Esint. Then they wouldn't have to go through the Mercantili Guild. That would certainly hurt them."

"It may hurt them in the long term, but the Mercantili Guild makes a point of flaunting their wealth. I don't think we can't bring them down like that. It'll take too long."

"The Guild Ball."

Telchide was standing in the doorway. Greta had been so focused on the conversation, she hadn't heard the sound of his crutches. She looked behind him, but his apprentices weren't there.

"They're not hosting the Guild Ball this year, Chide," Aveline reminded him.

Telchide fiddled with his pocket watch. "I know. The Gioielliere Guild is. But the Mercantili Guild is bidding to host it next year."

"How does that help us *this* year?" Greta asked.

Truly, the man might be an inventing genius, but he didn't appear to have much common sense. What could Aveline possibly see in him? She saw him frown and look over at Aveline. The Inventrice smiled encouragingly at him.

"It takes a great deal of preparation to host a Guild Ball and the Mercantili Guild never spares any expense. What would happen if they won the bid for next year and we waited until all their plans were in place, novelties and foods paid for – then we force them to cancel the ball?

"In the meantime, what if we convinced the other Guilds to stop trading outside the city, just for a year, to decrease the Mercantili Guild's resources? They wouldn't have any way to recoup their losses. I don't think anyone would buy tickets for the Guild Ball with the Mercantili hosting it. Having us all in the one place makes it too easy for their Guild to have us all arrested."

Greta listened to him in disbelief. That would definitely hurt the Mercantili Guild. The plan probably wouldn't be enough to bring the Mercantili down on its own, but it would certainly go a long way to helping every other Guild while giving the Mercantili a slap in the face.

"That would take a lot of organising," Greta pointed out. "Where do you suggest we start?"

Telchide shrugged. "I'm ... not good at that side of things."

"But you just came up with a brilliant plan." Greta frowned. "How are you not good at that?"

Aveline lay a hand on Greta's arm. "Reta, Chide's mind works differently from ours. He can come up with the best plans, but it'll be better if someone else organises them. He gets distracted too easily. But if we need him to do anything for it, he'll be able to help."

Greta bit her lip. It would be dangerous. They'd need to involve every other major Guild and have as many people on board with the plan as possible – it wouldn't work otherwise.

"This year's Guild Ball will need to be magnificent," Greta mused, "to give the Mercantili Guild something to live up to. We'll have to help the Gioielliere Guild to make it spectacular and convince every Guild Member to purchase a ticket, then let enough of them know the plan that so the Mercantili bid for next year's ball is successful. Who do we know in the Gioielliere Guild? It's been such a long time since Papà left, I can't remember anyone from his Guild."

Aveline looked at Telchide. He shook his head.

"I only know Ciro Corallino, and he works more with corallo than jewellery itself."

Greta paused. "That could work. The Mercantili Guild don't control the bay. If the Gioielliere Guild focus on works of corallo for the Guild Ball so they don't need to import metals from outside Tor'Esint, they'll begin the crippling effect on the Mercantili Guild."

Telchide shook his head. "Not every Gioielliere is adept at working with corallo. It's a very specialised art. Ciro often complains of the argument to make the Corallini switch to the Artiste Guild, but he insists they create jewellery as much as art and if they are forced to switch, they'd be tried for inter-Guild relations for creating any jewellery items."

"Do you think you could talk to Ciro, set up a meeting for us?" Greta asked tentatively.

"I ... have no reason to see him," Telchide said softly. "I have no companion to lavish with gifts and Teresina is too young for such precious items as Ciro creates."

Aveline's expression fell. Greta suddenly felt she was intruding in a private household matter. She coughed uncomfortably and stood up.

"I'll ask around and see if anyone else has contacts within the Gioielliere Guild," she said. "Perhaps the Guild Amministratori all know each other. You could ask yours?"

"Certainly. Kesida would probably be glad to help," Aveline agreed. "And you can ask yours."

Greta's smile froze on her face. "I ... don't think that will be possible. I might see if I can get someone else to ask him. Ludovico and I aren't quite seeing eye to eye at the moment."

She avoided Aveline's concerned look and turned to Telchide instead. "You have two lovely apprentices, Telchide. May they bring you good fortune and increased business."

It was the customary congratulations to give someone training their first apprentice. She didn't understand why he'd waited so long to get one and then gotten two suddenly – perhaps the twins had refused to be separated. She wished she could warn him against her mistake but, she had to admit, he seemed to be doing a fine job from what she'd seen downstairs.

Telchide bowed his head politely and moved aside for her. Greta went to give Aveline a quick hug before departing but Aveline forestalled her.

"I'll walk back with you. Telchide and I are done for the day."

Greta glanced at Telchide and saw his forlorn expression. Clearly things had not been resolved between them.

Downstairs, they were greeted by the twin apprentices, Florio and Gaspare. They looked so similar, Greta could not tell them apart aside from the colour of their eyes.

"Did you enjoy your tea, Signora?" the hazel-eyed boy asked.

Greta nodded. "Yes, thank you. It was most enjoyable."

"It worked!" the other twin exclaimed excitedly. "Spare, look!"

He stood next to the shelf he'd created and tried rocking it back and forth. It didn't budge. His brother clapped him on the back.

Greta and Aveline went to put their coats on as the two boys began putting all of Telchide's creations on the shelf. It was beginning to look like a jumbled mess of junk.

Greta coughed politely. "Boys, may I suggest less is better than more? One of each item should do the trick. Or two if you insist – a simple one and an intricate one."

They looked at each other, then at the shelf and began taking off all the unnecessary items. By the time Greta was finished getting ready for the chill evening air, the shelf was looking much better.

She left the shop with Aveline but once on the street, turned back to look at the window display. Truly, Telchide really was an amazing Inventore. If Greta had to tell the truth, she wouldn't have been able to say who was better between Telchide and Aveline. Certainly, they both had their Electrum Guild Marks, but they specialised in such different items it was difficult to compare them.

Greta took Aveline's arm in hers and walked towards Via dell'Oro.

"Have you been to see Lucrezia?"

Aveline nodded. "It's as I feared. I'm definitely pregnant."

"Have you told Telchide?"

Aveline shook her head quickly. "I still haven't decided if I'm keeping it."

Greta nudged her shoulder. "He loves you, Veli. Anyone can see that. You should tell him. He might be able to help you decide."

Aveline refrained from answering. They walked in silence back to Piazza Mercantile. Greta left Aveline at her workshop and returned home alone. Domizio was hard at work, a lantern blazing brightly beside him. How she hated those lanterns in her workshop.

Sofia sat near him, working on her beading. Greta walked over to inspect her work. Knowing her routine quite well by now, Sofia held it up for her to inspect. It was coming along quite nicely. She was following the pattern Greta had drawn on the linen sections of the test bodice.

"Lovely, Sofia," she complimented her youngest apprentice. "You have a very steady hand there. Careful or I might get you to do the beading on every order from now onwards."

Sofia grinned widely and raised her eyebrows at Domizio as though there had been some question about her skill.

Greta didn't want Domizio to feel like one of her apprentices, but she couldn't, in good conscience, leave him to work completely unsupervised for an entire project without ever having seen his work before. Trying to appear inconspicuous about it, Greta peeked over Sofia's shoulder at the Copper Sarta.

In mock imitation of Sofia, he raised up his current work for Greta's inspection. She couldn't help but laugh, which caused Sofia to laugh, which only served to make Domizio himself laugh. Soon, Annika and Marta were in the workshop.

"What's so funny?" Annika asked, arms crossed. Greta couldn't help but feel that Annika thought they were laughing at her though she hadn't even been in the room a few seconds ago.

"Oh, nothing," Sofia answered between giggles. "Maestra Greta is only treating a Copper Sarto as an apprentice. Nothing else."

Annika's eyes bulged at the statement and then she too joined in the laughter. Marta didn't. In fact, she looked more sombre than the situation called for.

"Whatever's the matter, Marta?" Greta asked.

Marta forced a smile. "I have something for you, Maestra. It came not too long after you left."

She handed Greta a folded piece of parchment, sealed with the Tor'Esint seal. The smile fell from her face. This couldn't be good news.

Greta excused herself and went straight up to her bedroom. Once there, she lit the glass lantern and sat at her small desk. With trembling hands, she broke the seal and opened the letter.

*Greta Sarta, you are hereby summoned to bear testimony at the trial of the Alchimisti Guild in the matter of alchemically-dyed material. You will present yourself to the Tor'Esint Town Hall at nine o'clock in the morning on Gildadi 2 Inventrici. Bring with you any evidence you feel may be necessary for the trial.*

Greta read the letter over and over again.

This wasn't possible! Only the Sarti Guild and Lucrezia knew about the link between the deaths. Lucrezia said she'd deal with her Guild, but there'd been no mention of the Amministratori.

Her mind raced in circles, trying to understand what was going on. Someone must be attacking the Alchimisti Guild. That was the only explanation. But who? Greta drew in a sharp breath. Ludovico.

He was desperate to save his Guild, certainly, but was he desperate enough to shift the blame to another Guild and bring the Amministratori into it? Is *that* why they had been searching the warehouses? How could he have been so reckless?

Greta folded the letter and slipped it into her sash belt. She raced down the stairs and into the workshop.

"Domizio, I know I'm paying you to work, but I need you to come with me. Girls, stay inside and lock the door behind me. Don't open it to anyone. I'll take the spare key with me."

Their frightened faces stared back at her, but there was nothing she could think to say to allay their fears. She was too scared herself. Domizio didn't ask questions, but immediately put his work down and followed her into the shop.

"We're going to Lucrezia's house," she told him in a quiet voice as they put on their coats. "I've got to warn her if she doesn't already know."

"Know what?" Domizio asked just as quietly.

Greta checked to see none of the girls were listening through the open doorway. "The Amministratori are after the Alchimisti Guild. I've been called to a trial for them tomorrow morning – about the alchemically-dyed materials."

Domizio stared at her incredulously. "How do the Amministratori know about that?"

Greta shook her head. "If they didn't figure it out by themselves, I can only think of one person who might do this. But I won't speak ill against him without proof. Let's go."

Greta wanted to run to Lucrezia's shop, but she knew it would only attract unwanted attention. Instead, she took Domizio's arm and walked as quickly as she thought seemly towards the Alchimista's house.

When they finally arrived, all the windows were dark, the door was hanging off its hinges as though someone had broken in. Ice gripped Greta's stomach, but she forced herself to walk into the shop.

Bottles lay broken over the floor, their liquid contents creating a sickly odour. Greta tried not to step in the puddles as she walked further in.

"Lucrezia?" she called out, without much hope of response. "Anyone?"

Her voice sounded too loud in the abandoned shop. Greta followed Domizio into the workshop behind the shopfront. There were similar signs of struggle here too. Lucrezia's chair was lying on the floor far from her workbench. All the concoctions Greta had seen in progress a few days ago lay in a shattered mess.

"Let's try upstairs," Greta said softly. "She had five Alchimisti working for her plus her apprentices. They might all live here."

Greta walked hesitantly up the stairs, Domizio close behind her. Everything was dark. She called out again.

"Is anyone here?"

Even to her own ears she sounded afraid. A hand squeezed her shoulder. It was all Greta could do not to scream. She spun around and lashed out at the arm.

"Sorry, sorry," Domizio said quietly, retreating. "I didn't mean to scare you. I don't think anyone's here. The place is deserted."

Greta had to agree with him. There was no point searching all the rooms. What would she do if she found someone anyway? Her goal had been to warn Lucrezia – but she was too late.

They stumbled down the dark stairs and stepped awkwardly around shiny puddles on the shop floor. There was nothing else they could do here. By unspoken agreement they left the Alchimista's shop and walked back towards Greta's shop.

"This is all wrong," Greta said quietly, pulling back on Domizio's arm. "Lucrezia wasn't even involved until I brought her Ranieri's material to test. Why would they have gone straight to her house?"

Domizio shrugged. "She's the only Alchimista you mentioned at our meeting. Maybe one of the Sarti sent the Amministratori there in retribution?"

"No." Greta shook her head. "That doesn't make sense. They would've gone to their own Alchimisti if they wanted repayment for dangerous goods. Lucrezia was only the one who proved the material *is* dangerous."

"Ludovico then?" Domizio asked. "He wouldn't know any other Alchimisti who dealt with it."

Greta bit her lip. If Domizio had come up with the same culprit she had, perhaps the idea had merit.

"Let's go ask him," Domizio suggested, "so you know what's happening when you go to the trial tomorrow."

"I can't," Greta replied. "We aren't exactly on friendly terms right now." Domizio studied her by the light of street gas lanterns.

"Is this because of the Guild meeting or because you refuse to bed him anymore?"

Greta refused to feel ashamed of either action. "The Guild meeting, but I doubt he'd be happy about me bedding you now if he knew about it."

"Of course he knows," Domizio replied easily. "That little ash-sucker, Teodoro, would have told Ludovico when you threw him out."

Greta felt sick. She didn't know what to do – not now, not tomorrow. Should she try to warn any other Alchimisti? Should she try to defend their Guild tomorrow? Would it put her in the same position they were in? The last thing she wanted to do was harm the Sarti Guild, but she didn't want to ruin the Alchimisti Guild by protecting her own either.

"There's nothing more you can do tonight," Domizio told her. "Let's go back to your place and see what tomorrow brings."

Greta bit at a fingernail, then immediately stopped. It'd been a nervous habit of hers in childhood that had ended in painful sores more often than not. Instead, she took Domizio's arm with both her hands and walked with him back to her home. Where she no longer felt safe. Where she could not promise to keep her apprentices safe.

# Chapter 11 – Gildadi 2 Inventrici 230 Years After Implosion

Greta woke with Domizio curled up beside her. This time, they were both fully clothed. The stress of the night had prevented anything from happening.

She dressed herself in a respectable, if not entirely conservative dress, with her favourite work corset. Downstairs, she found the girls whispering in the kitchen. The whispering stopped as she entered. They looked at her, one and all, with wide-eyed fear.

Ice ripped through her stomach. She excused herself and ran up to the water closet. She reached it just as her bowels loosened uncontrollably. Greta squatted uncomfortably as she drew off her soiled undergarments. This had never happened to her before. She knew it was from worry but there was nothing she could do about it. Long, uncomfortable, and painful minutes later, she emerged from the water closet feeling sick and empty.

Sofia was waiting for her with a fresh change of clothes, undergarments and all. The girl was an absolute blessing. Greta took them with a word of thanks and disappeared back into the water closet to shower and change. This wasn't the first time she'd thanked herself for the extraordinary expense of installing a bath only just large enough to sit in with a movable shower head to wash herself.

When she returned to the kitchen, Marta placed a cup of chamomile tea in front of her and Annika poured her a bowl of honeyed porridge. Greta's eyes filled with unwanted tears.

"Thank you, girls." The words came out choked and soft. She coughed and beckoned them closer. "I don't know what's going to happen today, but I don't want you to worry. I'm not the one on trial. If they somehow see fit to strip me of my Guild Status or throw me in prison, I have more than enough money to see you all comfortably well off until a new Maestra can be found."

Sofia shook her head. "Don't worry for us, Maestra. If anything happens to you, we'll do everything we can to help, won't we?"

To Greta's surprise, even Annika nodded vigorously. Tears sprung into her eyes again. Greta wiped them away before they could do any lasting damage to her visage.

"If anything happens to Greta, you'll all come to live with me until the mess is sorted."

Greta turned to see Domizio standing behind her. She bit her lip and nodded gratefully at him. It was a generous offer. He knew as well as she did that anything could happen at this trial, even if it was aimed at the Alchimisti Guild.

He ladled himself a bowl of porridge and sat by her side. Greta sipped at her tea, not certain she could stomach any food.

"Even just a few bites, Greta," he said quietly at her side. "You'll need your strength."

Gritting her teeth, Greta forced herself to eat three mouthfuls of the sweet porridge. Annika had flavoured it with cinnamon – had she purposely done that because she knew Greta like it? To be honest, Greta wouldn't have been surprised anymore to know that Annika had done something nice for someone else.

The clock on the wall chimed eight times. Greta stared at it, unreasonably scared of the time.

"I want to go past Aveline's house first," Greta said suddenly. "She's my best friend. I ... just need to see her. Just for a moment."

Domizio nodded easily. "Let's go then. We don't want to have to rush at the end."

Greta rose and walked towards the shopfront, but before she got there, the girls ambushed her with an embrace so tight she could barely breathe. Greta returned the embrace with as much strength as she had to spare.

"Keep safe, Maestra," Marta sniffed.

"Don't let them badger you," Annika advised gruffly.

Greta waited for Sofia to say something before realising the girl was crying. She tried so hard not to succumb to her own tears.

"Look after each other today, girls. I'm counting on you to keep my shop running smoothly. Sofia, please continue with the beading. Annika and Marta, I need you to edge the skirt. Do it behind the counter, so you aren't in full view of any customers."

She disentangled herself from the girls and put her coat on without looking back. She was too afraid of never seeing them again.

It didn't take long to walk to Aveline's house. It was just two hundred piedi along Piazza Mercantile. Domizio supported her the entire way. Greta hadn't realised quite how much energy her violent bowel evacuation had cost her until she started walking.

"Perhaps we can borrow Aveline's blazermobile?" Domizio suggested. "You said she has one, didn't you?"

Greta nodded. The thought had crossed her mind as well. Aveline probably wouldn't mind in the slightest.

Domizio helped her up the stairs to Aveline's house and knocked firmly on the door. Trading hours had just begun but the door was still locked.

The door was opened by Nevio. Aveline never seemed to open her own door anymore. Although, to be fair, Greta rarely did either unless it was an unreasonable hour, like Ludovico's visit the morning before.

"Signora Sarta, what an unexpected pleasure." His tone hinted at something quite the opposite of pleasure. Perhaps he was unimpressed to be disturbed so early in the day.

"Is Aveline in?" she asked without her usual pleasantries.

"I'll get her for you," Nevio said. Greta went to walk into the workshop, but Nevio closed the door before she could enter.

"What's gotten into him?" Greta asked no one in particular.

Domizio only shrugged. He didn't know Aveline at all.

They weren't left waiting too long. Aveline opened the door, peered both ways down the street and bustled Greta and Domizio inside.

"Veli, what in Caldera's smoke is going on?" Greta asked as Aveline locked the door behind her. "Anyone would think *you* were the one appearing in a trial today."

Aveline froze. "What trial? What's happened?"

Greta tried to appear unconcerned, but Aveline knew her too well to fall for it. She smoothed her skirt and took a deep breath.

"The raid yesterday? The thing I wouldn't tell you? I think you need to know now."

Aveline forestalled her with a hand in front of her face.

"Nevio, would you go down to the market for me? I've a craving for an olive roll. You know, the one from Caffè Pasquale? Here's the money for it." She pulled a few coins out of her pocket and handed them to her apprentice. "Why don't you get yourself something nice to eat while you're there?"

Nevio looked suspiciously at them "I'd rather not," he said slowly. "Something's going on and you keep leaving me in the dark. I'm your loyal apprentice, Maestra and have been for *two years*. Please trust me."

Greta remained silent. This decision was Aveline's alone. If she didn't trust her apprentice, that was her own business. Until recently, Greta herself wouldn't have trusted Annika and she was her oldest apprentice.

"You realise any betrayal of me, whether I'm in the wrong or not, will result in you losing your home and your apprenticeship."

Nevio gave her an injured look. "I understand, Maestra."

Aveline bit her lip and nodded. "Alright, Greta. What's happened?"

Greta glanced at Domizio before replying. He nodded encouragingly. "It's been discovered that the new bright green material on the market has been alchemically-dyed with arsenic. At the best, it gives people sores, at the worst, it kills them. I only found out recently and told my Guild to stop using the material."

Greta related recent events to Aveline. The set of her face changed considerably at the state of Lucrezia's workhouse.

"After we left yesterday evening, Telchide heard noises at Eduardo's house too," Aveline informed her. "He went through the back fence when the noise stopped but no one was there. Not even his apprentices. Florio and Gaspare came to tell us as soon as they realised what had happened. We don't know who took them or where they took them. Even Chide is worried for him."

Greta frowned. "I thought he should be the first person worried for Eduardo. Aren't they quite good friends?"

Aveline shook her head. "They were. But if the Alchimisti Guild is on trial today, I doubt it's only because of the alchemically-dyed material. I'm coming with you. We'll pick up Chide on the way. Our apprentices will have to keep the shops for us today."

Nevio drew himself up to his full height. "I won't let you down, Maestra. I might even manage to finish that pocket watch without you hovering over my shoulder."

Greta thought it an odd comment to make at such a serious time, but it made Aveline smile.

The Guild Hall clocks chimed a quarter past eight. Greta grimaced. They'd already been here too long.

"Let's go," she said nervously. "I'd rather be early than late."

Aveline took her simplest coat off the coat stand and bustled them out onto the street. Greta could still smell the stench of blazer solution as she hopped into the blazermobile, Domizio close behind her. The smell only increased when Aveline opened the container to pour more solution into the fuel cell.

The blazermobile was such an incredible contraption, Greta wondered if she should purchase one now that she had a small fortune at her fingertips.

Aveline drove quickly to Telchide's house.

"Probably best you wait here. I won't be long," she said as she hopped out of the vehicle.

In truth, Greta was grateful to just sit down for a while longer. She was so tired. She lay her head on Domizio's shoulder and closed her eyes.

\*\*\*

Domizio gently shook her awake. "We're here," he said softly.

Greta struggled to open her eyes. She was so very tired. Aveline passed her a green capsule. She stared at it not understanding.

"It's a restorative. I take one every day after..." Aveline glanced at Telchide and hesitated. "It helps. Try it."

Greta needed no further prodding. She popped the capsule into her mouth and swallowed it without chewing. Domizio helped her out of the car and held out his arm for her to take. Greta noticed Telchide was not doing the same for Aveline. He was vomiting in the gutter, crutches held out to balance him.

"Did we have to take the blazermobile?" he groaned. "You knew I didn't have any ginger tablets left."

"Sorry, Chide, but we didn't want to be late," Aveline said in a very unapologetic tone. "Would you like a restorative too?"

Telchide shook his head firmly. "I don't like those things. You know that."

Greta drew closer to them. "Why don't you like them?" she asked, concerned that she had just taken something she shouldn't have.

Telchide looked at her as though he hadn't realised she was there. "Personal preference. That's all. Nothing more."

Greta frowned. She was missing something but doubted he was going to tell her what it was. If it had anything to do with the Alchimisti Guild, she'd probably find out today anyway.

The Guild Hall clocks chimed quarter to nine. There were fifteen minutes until she needed to be inside. Greta looked up at the Tor'Esint Town Hall. It stood on Corso delle Gilde, next to the Mercantili Guild. She tried not to think how convenient that must be for the Mercantili – all they had to do was walk next door to make any complaint or request any change in policy.

The four of them were not the only ones entering the Town Hall. Greta noticed a number of other Guild members, Sarti included. They nodded politely to each other and only a few whispered greetings were exchanged. There was a disquieting hush over the main foyer.

"Something's wrong," Greta whispered to her own small party. "There wouldn't be so many of us here if it was just about the alchemically-dyed material."

"Perhaps the Mercantili Guild is striking out over the Alchimisti's recent financial gain with their blazermobile," Telchide whispered back. "I hear they're quite expensive if you don't have friends among the Alchimisti."

Aveline looked at him in surprise.

"Come now, Veli, I'm not accusing *you* of anything."

Perhaps Telchide was correct.

"Do you know if Eduardo dealt with the alchemically-dyed material?" Greta asked.

Telchide shook his head. "He wanted nothing to do with that. He was very meticulous in his workshop, kept all his apprentices safe."

"For Caldera's sake, Chide, be quiet!" Aveline reprimanded him. He gave her an injured look. "If they call you, for any reason, *think* about your words."

"What did I say?" Telchide asked in surprise.

"You implied that the material was dangerous, and that Eduardo knew about it."

"But," Telchide hesitated, "he *did* know. That's why he refused to deal with it."

Aveline glanced at Greta. "What are we going to do?"

"I don't know," Greta said truthfully. "We need to help the Alchimisti Guild if we can. It could be any of our Guilds on trial next time. Whatever happens here will set an important example."

As the Town Hall clock stuck nine o'clock, the noise inside the foyer became almost deafening. If Greta hadn't been watching the hall doors, she wouldn't have heard them opening. As soon as the ninth chime rang through the air, the Ministro of Tor'Esint called them in.

"Those with letters, over on this side. Spectators, over here."

Domizio squeezed Greta's hand and left her to find himself a seat with Aveline. Telchide stayed next to Greta. She frowned at him curiously. He patted his pocket.

"I have a letter as well."

Greta longed to see what his letter said – if it mentioned alchemically-dyed materials or some other contraband item. But that would have to wait. For now, she wanted to get the best seat possible and that meant politely elbowing past people to reach the front. She hoped Telchide was following her. Greta claimed their seats only two rows from the front. She turned to see Telchide still fighting his way through the crowd with his ungainly cast and crutches. She waved to get his attention and he nodded apology after apology until he reached her.

"May I see your letter?" she asked, handing him her own.

He started at the request but obliged her. Greta read his letter thrice over, making sure she hadn't missed any details.

*Telchide Inventore, you are hereby summoned to bear testimony at the trial of the Alchimisti Guild in the matter of dispensing dangerous substances. You will present yourself to the Tor'Esint Town Hall at nine o'clock in the morning on Gildadi 2 Inventrici. Bring with you any evidence you feel may be necessary for the trial.*

"Dispensing dangerous substances – what's that mean?" Greta asked.

"It's a long story," Telchide replied curtly.

"Telchide, this is important. What's your letter about? What can they do with it?"

The Inventore sighed. "Eduardo gave my companion, and then my daughter, tablets to help them sleep and stop their bad dreams. They ... weren't meant to use them as much as they did. It caused them both memory issues and, in the case of my companion, it ultimately led to her death."

Greta stared at him in horror. "But he's your best friend," she whispered urgently. "You can't tell them that! You can't tell them he caused your companion's death. They'll strip him of his Guild Marks! They'll throw him in prison!"

Telchide looked at her with sad eyes and wrung his hands together. "I know. But what can I do? They'll ask me questions and I'll have to answer. I know he didn't mean for any of it to happen. But it did."

"So ... what will you tell them?" Greta whispered.

Telchide held up his hands in a useless gesture. It was exactly the way Greta felt. How could they save their Alchimisti friends and colleagues if the Mercantili Guild had their mind set on destroying the entire Guild?

She asked no further questions as the seats around them began to fill. In fact, the entire gallery was filling up. Word must have spread about the attack on the Alchimisti Guild. She wondered how many of these people were here to testify, or try to help, and how many were here out of some morbid curiosity to see how the Alchimisti Guild fared and how they could play it to their best advantage.

It was a cruel thought, but she knew people too well. When the Inter-Guild Edict was first issued, she'd seen too many people draw away from Guild members they knew were in the line of fire, refusing to come to their aid, and yet insisting that they got to watch their downfall. It was sickening behaviour.

A loud noise drew her attention to the front of the auditorium. Ministro Ercolano sat with a large wooden gavel, banging it on his bench. He waited until the talking had abated before speaking.

"I hereby declare the Alchimista Trials open. We have Severino Mercante for the prosecutor and Valeria Alchimista for the defence. Would the prosecution stand and state the case."

Greta strained to see the prosecutor from where she was sitting as he rose to his feet. His back was towards her, but she recognised that balding round head. It was *that* Severino – the Mercantili Amministratore who, by all accounts, was the right-hand man of Carlotta Mercantessa, a Maestra of the Mercantili Guild.

"It has come to our attention that the Alchimisti Guild is dealing with dangerous materials," he began in his nasal voice. "We won't stand for it any longer. Everyone knows about the Exploding Beakers tavern. We suspect the explosions are to keep out the Amministratori while secret meetings take place between various Guilds in direct contradiction to the Inter-Guild Edict.

"We now know that the Alchimisti Guild has been alchemically-dying material without proper safety testing. This has resulted in harm to many people and the death of at least five that we know of.

"It has also been noted that they've neglected to test various other concoctions, which they claim are medicines. This has resulted in dangerous side effects, occasionally ending in death.

"We move to disband the Alchimisti Guild, have all Alchimisti stripped of their Guild Marks and to imprison the main offenders."

The man promptly sat. Greta stared in disbelief. Disband the Alchimisti Guild? Was such a thing even possible? Surely not! She clenched her fists so tightly her nails bit into her palms. All around her, people were calling out disparaging remarks about the Mercantili Guild and the Amministratori. She was too stunned to join in.

Ministro Ercolano banged his gavel down over and over, trying to regain some semblance of order. Greta looked at him closely. He seemed somewhat surprised by the facts of the case.

"These are very serious accusations and quite extreme punishments you are requesting. I'm not blind to the fact that this would set a dangerous precedent for every other Guild, including the Mercantili Guild itself. Are you certain you wish to proceed with the trial?"

Severino Mercante rose to his feet once more.

"We are, Ministro Ercolano," he said firmly. "We won't stand idly by while the people of Tor'Esint remain in danger from this Guild."

Ministro Ercolano shook his head and blew out his cheeks. Greta wondered just how much control he really had of the city or if he was in the Mercantili Guild's pocket too. At least he seemed willing enough to stand up to them, even if in a small way.

"Very well," the Ministro said, turning his attention to the blonde woman seated at the other table in front of him. "Will the accused please state their defence?"

The defender stood and faced the Ministro. Greta had never heard her name before, and she could only assume Valeria was the Alchimisti Amministratrice.

"It's with a heavy heart we hear these accusations and proposed punishment. The Mercantili Guild has crippled every Guild in Tor'Esint other than their own with their ridiculous Trading and Inter-Guild Edicts and forced an exorbitant increase in the price for goods that should be more freely available.

"What they propose with these allegations is absurd. By stripping all Alchimisti of their Guild Marks and disbanding the Guild, they will deprive Tor'Esint of their healers, among other things. The Mercantili Guild is not immune to disease or accidents. Who do they think will come to their aid if the Alchimisti Guild no longer exists?"

The bald man stood and interrupted. "Signora Valeria is not stating a defence. She's merely stating the consequences of her Guild's guilt."

Signora Valeria looked at him sharply.

"Our defence is that we deal with each case of misconduct as it arises. When we discovered that some alchemically-dyed materials were dangerous, we withdrew them from circulation and ordered the testing of every other alchemically-dyed material.

"For every accusation about unknown side-effects or plainly dangerous concoctions, we investigate thoroughly. In fact, there are several investigations currently under way. When we have our results, we'll deal with the offenders as we see fit.

"This has *always* been the Guild way. If any of our members are found to be dealing with dangerous materials without proper testing, we propose that they are closely monitored in their workshops until such time as we feel they can be trusted to work unsupervised."

"That's not good enough!" shouted Severino Mercante. "They should be stripped of their Guild Marks!"

This outburst caused a riot in the gallery. People yelled and threw things at the Mercantili Amministratore, no matter how much the Ministro banged his gavel. Greta found herself swept up in the fervour and threw a thimble at the balding man. She was close enough that it pinged him on the head.

"This is outrageous!" he shouted hysterically. "Ministro Ercolano, we need *order!*"

The Ministro took a large conical shaped contraption from the side of his desk and put the narrow end over his mouth.

"Order in the auditorium! ORDER!" His words boomed out unnaturally loudly. The hubbub of insults and threats lessened but did not cease altogether. "If you do not desist, I'll be forced to call in the Amministratori to take you away. Now all of you *sit down and be quiet* so we can get on with this trial."

This had the desired effect. People all around Greta began to take their seats once more. Greta realised that Telchide had never risen out of his. His face was pale. When people beside and behind jostled his seat, he took no notice. Greta placed a hand on his shoulder.

"Telchide, are you quite alright?" she asked quietly.

He looked at her blankly, as though he hadn't heard her at all. She repeated herself hesitantly.

"Yes, yes. Quite fine. Thank you."

His reply was automatic, like it had been rehearsed. Greta removed her hand from his shoulder. He didn't look fine. But she had no time to worry about him. The first accused Alchimista was being brought in. Greta had only ever seen him once before.

Aveline had taken her to the Exploding Beakers to celebrate their success with the zipper. It had been an *interesting* experience. Every time an explosion went off, it was accompanied by a scented cloud which suffused the room. They'd met other friends there for a meal, which was pleasant enough, and drinks, which were of a kind Greta had only ever experienced when the Alchimisti hosted the annual Guild Ball.

"Nestore Alchimista, you are accused of intentionally exploding concoctions to cover the illegal inter-Guild meetings taking place in your establishment. How do you plead?" Severino Mercante said, loudly enough for all to hear.

Nestore narrowed his eyes at the Mercantili Amministratore. "I plead not guilty. My tavern is called *Exploding Beakers*. My patrons expect a certain number of explosions per day, or they'd stop coming. It's not now, nor has it ever been, a strictly Alchimista tavern. I've always entertained all manner of patrons and what they discuss is their own business.

"None of them have ever asked me to set off extra explosions to cover 'illegal inter-Guild meetings' as you call them. You can't stop people from various Guilds striking up friendships with one another. Many of these friendships were around long before your idiotic Edict came into place. If they want to share a drink or a meal together, I'll not stop them."

Severino Mercante rose, clasped his hands behind his back and walked over to where Nestore was sitting, in a booth next to the Ministro's desk.

"You freely admit to having people of various Guilds meeting in your establishment?"

Nestore's face flushed dark red. "That's the whole point of a tavern – to meet people for a meal or a drink. Do you expect me to turn paying customers away and ruin my business?"

Severino Mercante shrugged.

"Your witness," he said to the Alchimista Amministratrice as he walked back to his own seat.

Valeria Alchimista rose and walked determinedly to Nestore.

"Do you cook the meals yourself?" she asked him.

Nestore shook his head. "I ain't no good with that. I make the drinks."

Valeria Alchimista nodded. "Would you say you spend more time behind the bar or on the tavern floor?"

"Behind the bar," Nestore replied easily. "It takes time and patience to create my delicacies. A few have been known to explode right in front of me."

He winked at the gathered people, which earned him a small round of laughter. Greta didn't join in. She was too worried about her role in the trial, and Telchide's.

"And how close are the tables to the bar?" Valeria Alchimista asked.

"Er, not very close," Nestore admitted. "I wouldn't want any of my patrons being covered in broken glass now, would I?"

"As you say." Valeria nodded. "Now, this would lead me to understand that you couldn't readily eavesdrop on conversations to ascertain whether or not inter-Guild meetings were taking place, rather than a friendly dinner?"

Nestore clearly tried not to smile. "Of course not. I wouldn't have time even if I could – the drinks take up too much of my concentration to get *just* right."

"Thank you, Nestore."

She walked back to her desk and sat down.

Nestore was excused. Greta couldn't tell if he'd pleaded his innocence well or not. She thought he was being truthful, but without watching him for nights on end, how would one ever know?

"Your next witness," Ministro Ercolano said, waving at Severino.

He already looked tired. This didn't bode well for the rest of the day.

"We call Greta Sarta to the stand."

Greta clutched at her skirt in fear. Telchide covered her hand and squeezed gently. She looked up at him with a grateful sigh. That small action of solidarity gave her strength.

Greta rose and walked down resolutely to the stand before turning her attention to the Alchimisti and Mercantili representatives – the Guild Amministratori. It made her wonder if Ludovico was here somewhere too. She scanned the crowd and was unsurprised to see Carlotta Mercantessa, a Maestra of the Mercantili Guild, sitting behind Severino.

"Your witness, Severino." Ministro Ercolano waved dismissively.

Greta had never really thought much about the Ministro. She'd assumed he was in charge of the city until a few years ago. When the Inter-Guild Edict was brought in, she'd thought he was a Mercantili puppet. Now, she didn't know what to think.

Severino Mercante stood up and walked over to her. Greta found herself grinding her teeth without meaning to.

"Greta Sarta, is it true that Ranieri Sarto died from arsenic poisoning from alchemically-dyed material?"

Greta raised an eyebrow. This wasn't what she'd expected them to ask her.

"I don't know," she replied truthfully.

He stopped and stared at her, eyebrows raised high.

"Did you not tell your entire Guild that he was killed from arsenic poisoning from alchemically-dyed material?" Severino changed his line of questioning.

Greta shook her head. "I said it was *probable*. Not definite. I'm not one of the Amministratori investigating his death."

Severino's face went dark. "So, you withheld this information from the Amministratori then?"

"The Amministratori are the ones responsible for investigating Ranieri Sarto's death, not me. I may be entirely wrong about this."

Greta fought not to bite her lip. That was technically true, but she didn't believe it herself. She doubted Severino did either.

"Very well," he continued, his nasal tone grating on her nerves. "Is it true you asked Lucrezia Alchimista to test a swatch of fabric for toxins and then had your own Guild ban the use of this type of fabric because it was deemed poisonous?"

Only a Sarti Guild member or Lucrezia herself could know that. She knew Lucrezia wouldn't have been stupid enough to embroil herself with the Mercantili Guild, so that left the Sarti Guild. There was a spy in her Guild. There was no way around answering that. She couldn't lie and she couldn't dissemble.

"Yes."

"Thank you, Greta Sarta," Severino said in his arrogant voice. "You've just proved the Alchimisti Guild was selling poisonous material without proper testing. No further questions."

He walked back to his desk and sat down. Greta saw the thin smile Carlotta gave Severino and wanted to protest. She hadn't said that at all! Severino was twisting her words.

Valeria stood and walked over to her.

"Greta Sarta, have you ever purchased alchemically-dyed material?"

"No."

"Before you inherited everything from Ranieri Sarto, had you ever seen alchemically-dyed material?"

"No."

"Do you know where Ranieri Sarto purchased his alchemically-dyed material?"

"No."

"Do you know if any Sarti Guild member has purchased alchemically-dyed material from an Alchimista in Tor'Esint?"

Greta shook her head. "I don't know where the material came from. It could have been imported into Tor'Esint by the Mercantili Guild for all I know."

"Hearsay!" shouted Severino as the crowd erupted into angry cries.

Greta saw the small smile on Valeria's face and couldn't help but smile herself. They'd managed to turn one of the Mercantili Guild's strongest points against them. Greta couldn't understand why Severino hadn't called another Sarta – one who'd actually purchased the alchemically-dyed material themselves. Perhaps the spy wasn't at the Guild Meeting? Perhaps they hadn't seen who else had some of this highly contentious material. But who else could have known what was going on?

Ministro Ercolano banged his gavel until the room descended into quiet once more.

"Greta Sarta, you are excused from the stand."

Greta looked at Ministro Ercolano in surprise. Not that she wanted them to ask her more questions. If they did, they might find out about her illegal store of materials in Aveline's workshop. That wasn't something she wanted to reveal.

She stood up and walked past Valeria Alchimista and Severino Mercante on her way back to her chair. The tension between them was palpable.

"We call Lucrezia Alchimista to the stand," Severino said, getting to his feet.

Ministro Ercolano raised an eyebrow. "I don't believe I said you could call your next witness yet and this is *my* trial room. I wish to call *you* to the stand, Severino Mercante."

There was a murmur of surprise around the auditorium.

"This is highly irregular, Ministro Ercolano," the Mercantili Amministratore said, not moving from behind his desk.

"Nevertheless, I'm calling you. Come to the stand. *Now*."

Severino stood slowly and walked stiffly to the stand. He paused a moment before walking around to a position Greta doubted he had ever been in before.

"Severino Mercante," began the Ministro, "you've accused the Alchimisti Guild of knowingly dealing with toxic alchemically-dyed material. Greta Sarta makes a good point – it may have been imported by the Mercantili Guild rather than created by any Tor'Esint Alchimisti. Do you have any proof that it wasn't?"

Greta clutched tightly at her skirts as Severino found her among the crowd and glared at her. Telchide patted her arm awkwardly. It didn't help.

"The Mercantili Guild keeps meticulous notes of all imports and exports, Ministro Ercolano," Severino replied, nose in the air. "I can assure you that should you wish to peruse these notes, you won't find a single mention of alchemically-dyed material."

Ministro Ercolano rapped his fingers on his desk while absently nodding his head. "Are you telling me that you personally oversee every one of your Guild member's account books every week?"

"Well, of course not," Severino huffed out. "I don't have time for that."

"Then how can you be so certain that none of your Guild members have imported this material to Tor'Esint?"

Severino tilted his chin up. "No one in the Mercantili Guild has been afflicted with sores or died under strange circumstances."

Valeria raised her hand. Ministro Ercolano nodded at her.

"Ministro, no one in the Alchimisti Guild has been afflicted with sores or died under strange circumstances either," she pointed out. "By his own reasoning, that means the Alchimisti Guild is innocent of dealing with alchemically-dyed materials as well."

Greta laughed. She couldn't help it. So did half the auditorium. Severino's bald head turned as dark as a beetroot. It was an impressive sight.

"Your point is well taken, Signora Valeria," Ministro Ercolano said with a badly hidden smile. "Severino, you may resume your seat and call in your next witness."

Severino stood, fists clenched at his side, and stormed back to his desk.

"I call Lucrezia Alchimista."

Lucrezia was brought in by an Amministratore. She walked with her head held high, fire in her eyes. The Amministratore tried to help her into the stand but was glared into inaction. Lucrezia stepped up to the stand and faced the auditorium, her eyes scanning the crowd. She paused when she met Greta's eyes. Greta wished she could tell her what had transpired. She doubted Lucrezia had been allowed to listen to the trial as it progressed.

Severino stood, hands held behind his back, and strolled lazily over to Lucrezia.

"Did Greta Sarta bring you some material to be tested for poison?"

Lucrezia nodded.

"Was it poisoned?"

"It was," Lucrezia answered without providing any more information than was strictly necessary.

"Did you sell her this material?"

"Of course not, you lavalump!" Lucrezia spat.

Severino immediately protested with an annoyed gesture. Ministro Ercolano raised an eyebrow but said nothing. The Mercantili Amministratore puffed up his chest and renewed his attempts at questioning.

"Have you or anyone you know sold unsafe alchemically-dyed material?"

Lucrezia rolled her eyes at him. "Severino, how stupid do you think I am? *I* haven't sold anything unsafe or untested. I can't speak for the rest of my Guild, but I can only assume we all take the same precautions with our solutions."

"Then how do you explain the alchemically-dyed material we found in your shop?"

Severino practically danced on the spot in his excitement at having caught her out. Lucrezia watched him impassively until he stood still. The entire gallery held their breath.

"You explained it yourself – Greta Sarta brought me some material to be tested. That was the first I'd seen of it. I was trying to find a suitable method of disposal for the contaminated material, which is the only reason it was still in my shop when you raided it, disrupted all my works in progress and unlawfully detained myself, and all my apprentices and hired Alchimisti."

Greta clutched at her skirts again. What was Lucrezia thinking?

"There was *nothing* unlawful about it," snarled Severino. "You were presumed to be guilty of inter-Guild relations and endangering the people of Tor'Esint."

Lucrezia raised her eyebrows at his outburst.

"As you can see there were no inter-Guild relations, and I was not endangering the people of Tor'Esint. I demand that you release me, my apprentices and my workers, and pay me for the damages to my workshop."

Severino clenched his fists tightly at his side. "You have *not* been proven innocent and your arrest was perfectly legal. Should you wish to claim any damages, you'll need to pursue that in a separate proceeding."

"Severino Mercante, have you any actual proof against this Alchimista?" Ministro Ercolano asked, elbow on his desk, chin in his hand.

"She had toxic alchemically-dyed material in her workshop," Severino pointed out.

Ministro Ercolano sighed. "Other than the material she was testing for Greta Sarta, at both their admission, did you find any *other* toxic alchemically-dyed material in Lucrezia's workshop?"

"Well, no," admitted Severino sourly.

"Very well then. Lucrezia Alchimista, you are excused from the stand unless your own Guild has questions for you."

"We do," Valeria said, putting up her hand. "It won't take long."

Ministro Ercolano nodded for her to stand. Greta questioned the move – surely it would be better to let Lucrezia off the hook as it seemed she had exonerated herself.

Severino sat heavily in his chair and crossed his arms petulantly across his rotund belly. Greta felt angrier than ever that such a querulous Guild could have garnered so much power in their town.

"Lucrezia, can you please explain the actions you took once you realised you might be in possession of a toxic material."

"I cleared my workshop of all my workers and tested the material thoroughly. Once the results were confirmed, I placed the contaminated material in a box with strict instructions that no one was to touch it.

"I went directly to Greta Sarta to give her the results of the tests, knowing she would alert her Guild. I then alerted the Alchimisti Guild of the potential danger so they could issue an edict forbidding all Alchimisti from producing or trading in arsenic-dyed material.

"I took the precaution of stating that we should test *all* alchemically-dyed material to ensure its safety before allowing any Alchimista to continue producing or trading in it."

As she spoke, Valeria slowly paced the floor back and forth, nodding occasionally.

"In short, you forced the Alchimisti Guild to put the safety of all Tor'Esint residents at a higher priority than their own financial gain."

Lucrezia nodded.

"That will be all, thank you."

"Lucrezia Alchimista, you are excused," said Ministro Ercolano.

Greta breathed a sigh of relief. Although excusing her didn't amount to an exoneration, at least Lucrezia appeared to have dodged flowing lava.

Ministro Ercolano sat straighter in his seat.

"Severino, I sincerely hope the rest of your accusations are not as baseless as they have been so far. The Mercantili Guild may wield a great deal of power in Tor'Esint, but if I find you've been wasting *my* time, it will come at a heavy cost to you."

Greta couldn't believe her ears.

"Telchide Inventore, take the stand," Severino demanded angrily.

Greta wished she were more familiar with Telchide. At least then she'd have felt comfortable giving his hand a squeeze or patting his arm or back for encouragement. Instead, she offered him a weak smile. She would have traded places with Aveline now if she could. The two of them clearly had an understanding that was beyond what Greta thought she could ever have with the Inventore.

Telchide laboured down the stairs, nearly toppling a few times as his crutches threatened to trip him up. Up on the stand, he immediately began fiddling with his pocket watch. Greta was starting to understand that the poor man simply couldn't stand – or sit – still. He naturally gravitated towards doing something with his hands, whether fiddling with his pocket watch or twisting his coppola until she was certain there was no shape left in it from the hatter.

"Telchide Inventore, is it true that Eduardo Alchimista gave your daughter untested medicine to make her sleep?"

Greta held her breath. Eduardo's career, and possibly freedom, were in Telchide's hands.

"Erm, no, not exactly," Telchide replied awkwardly.

"Do you dispute the fact that is was untested?" Severino demanded.

Telchide clutched and unclutched the pocket watch almost spasmodically. "Well, now, it wasn't untested, and it wasn't really to make her sleep."

Severino sighed heavily. "What was it for if not to make her sleep?"

"It was meant to calm her dreams. She has terrible nightmares," Telchide attempted to explain. "And the medicine was tested. Eduardo himself told us it wasn't meant for frequent use."

Severino stopped pacing and stared at Telchide. "He *knowingly* gave your daughter something that he knew wasn't safe?"

"No! Not at all," spluttered Telchide. "That's *not* what I said. It was perfectly safe in the amounts he instructed us to give her."

Severino held his hands together behind his back and walked over to the stand.

"If that's the case, then why did you go to the Amministratori to have your companion declared dead, citing the fact that new circumstances had come to light about a certain medicine she had been taking? Wasn't this the very same medicine Eduardo prescribed to your daughter? Isn't it safe to assume that if it killed your companion, it could easily kill your daughter?"

Telchide's face went a sickly shade of green. "Eduardo didn't know how often my companion was taking those tablets. And he took away my daughter's store of tablets when he realised that she was taking too many. He was diligent. He was careful. He never meant to hurt either of them."

"Hmm. But you *do* admit that his tablets killed your companion."

"No," Telchide replied firmly, standing just that little bit straighter. "The tablets themselves didn't kill her. They ... had an unintended side effect that caused her to lose her way on a long journey. That's all. We must presume she is dead. But it wasn't entirely Eduardo's fault."

"Do you admit she wouldn't be dead if she hadn't taken the tablets?"

Telchide's shoulders slumped. This wasn't looking good.

"I'm sorry, but you'll need to answer the question, Inventore," Ministro Ercolano said gently.

Telchide looked up at him with such a piteous look Greta wished the entire trial were over.

"Probably not."

Severino tossed his balding head up triumphantly. "No further questions." He resumed his seat once more. Valeria put up her hand.

"*I* have some questions."

Ministro Ercolano nodded for her to proceed. Greta couldn't see how the Alchimista Amministratrice could possibly get Eduardo out of this mess. Valeria picked up a piece of paper and walked over to Telchide.

"What did Eduardo tell you when he gave you the tablets for your daughter?"

Telchide paused, lost in thought. "He told me to give her one before bed. That it would calm her dreams."

"Did it, in fact, calm her dreams?"

"Yes."

Greta waited for him to elaborate, but he didn't.

"Did he tell you to use them every night?"

Telchide shook his head. "No. He said to use them sparingly. They weren't for regular use."

Valeria nodded and gave Severino a pointed look.

"So, in fact, he gave you specific directions, which your family disregarded. Ministro Ercolano, how can Alchimisti be held responsible if their instructions are not adhered to?"

Ministro Ercolano said nothing. He didn't look entirely convinced.

"Inventore, when Eduardo Alchimista realised his instructions were not being adhered to, isn't it true that he confiscated the rest of the tablets? That your family searched the house for more tablets and continued a prohibited treatment for your daughter?"

Telchide fiddled so much with his pocket watch that it sprang open, all over the floor. He reached out after the flying pieces in horror. Had it not been such an important moment in the trial, Greta would've laughed at the absurdity of it. But she didn't. Neither did anyone else. The gallery was so silent, every fall of a cog or screw could be heard until they all settled.

"Well?" demanded Valeria.

"I ... was away at the time."

"Weren't you told what had happened in your absence?"

"Erm, yes, well, that's what I was told happened."

"Isn't it also true that Eduardo tried to visit your daughter on a number of occasions after he confiscated the medicine, only to be turned away for fear he'd discover what was happening?"

Telchide's hands fell still. "So I've been told."

"No further questions from the Alchimisti Guild, Ministro Ercolano."

Valeria didn't smile on her way back to her desk. Even if Telchide's testimony was true, it didn't completely absolve Eduardo from wrongdoing. His tablets were still unsafe in certain circumstances, and he hadn't told Telchide's family of the possible side-effects, whatever they were. Greta was still unclear on that point.

"Telchide Inventore, you're excused," Ministro Ercolano told him.

Telchide rose inexorably slowly and tried to kneel to pick up the remains of his pocket watch. With a flick of his wrist, Ministro Ercolano motioned for two Amministratori to help him. Telchide was bundled off to the side as the Amministratori picked up every loose spring and cog.

Once they'd handed the pieces to Telchide and he'd pocketed them, he limped back to his chair, head hung low. Telchide and Eduardo had been friends for years – even Greta knew how close the two of them were. Whatever the argument had been between them, Greta knew Telchide couldn't help but feel worried about his erstwhile friend.

"Call out Eduardo Alchimista and let's get this over with," Ministro Ercolano said in a sour voice.

Telchide took his seat beside Greta. He didn't meet her eye. She tried to think of something comforting to say, but there was nothing. A door opening at the front of the hall caught her attention.

Eduardo walked in, escorted by an Amministratore, and searched the crowd. His eyes fell on Telchide, but when the Inventore didn't look up at him, he looked to another part of the hall. Greta followed his line of sight and saw Aveline. Her friend shook her head almost imperceptibly. Eduardo's shoulders slumped and he walked slowly to the stand.

Greta thought his stance did not bode well for him. He was practically shouting out to all of them that he thought himself guilty, that he should be punished. That was no way to take the stand.

Severino stood and began to walk towards the old Alchimista, but Ministro Ercolano held up a hand.

"I'm tired of these games. We're talking about people's lives here – their livelihoods. *I'll* be asking the questions."

Valeria nodded easily, Severino, not so easily. His head had turned a deep shade of red once more.

"Eduardo Alchimista, do you test your potions and tablets before dispensing them?"

"Yes."

"Do you ever sell or dispense any knowing they have faults or side-effects?"

Eduardo looked up hopelessly. "Ministro, *every* tonic or tablet has a fault or side-effect. Most rarely occur, but that doesn't mean they don't exist."

Ministro Ercolano raised an eyebrow. It was news to Greta too. She wondered how many people were aware of this.

"Do you tell your customers and patients about these faults or side-effects?"

Eduardo shrugged. "Some are not worth mentioning. Others, well I tend to tell them how to take the tablets or tonics to minimise any unwanted outcomes."

"Let's narrow it down to these two cases then," Ministro Ercolano said with a heavy sigh. "How did you come to prescribe Telchide's companion with the tablets that ultimately led to her death?"

Eduardo sighed heavily. "She was having trouble sleeping because of her bad dreams. She was overtired because of their new child. The tablets I gave her were meant to calm her dreams. I told her not to use them for more than a few days at a time. I gave her enough to last a few months' worth of that type of use.

"It was only recently that I realised she must've been taking one tablet a day since the very first tablet. And she didn't tell me the tablets had stopped her dreams altogether."

Murmurs ran around the auditorium. Greta looked at Telchide, but he was only looking at his hands and playing with the gears he'd gathered from the floor.

"How did you recently come to realise that effect?" Ministro Ercolano asked. "Did the same thing happen to the daughter?"

Eduardo nodded.

"Did anything else happen to the daughter?"

Eduardo nodded again but didn't elaborate until Ministro Ercolano prompted him.

"Her memory has a few holes in it," Eduardo said carefully. "She remembers things, just not everything. It seems the continual lack of dreams has an effect on memory. I didn't know about that, because I've always prescribed them for only a few days at a time. And everyone else *listens* to me."

Telchide clenched his fists. Greta laid a hand on his arm. No matter what had happened, being told your family was at fault for their own misfortune was never easy to hear. Whether true or not.

"Have any of your other products had such adverse effects on your customers?" Ministro Ercolano asked.

Eduardo shook his head. "No. And I've retired that product for modification. I won't sell it again until I'm certain it only calms dreams, not stops them altogether."

"Very well. Eduardo Alchimista, you're excused." Ministro Ercolano rose from his chair. "We'll take a break there. This is a difficult case. I need time to deliberate. I'll pass judgement this afternoon at four o'clock. The rest of you, get back to work. Tor'Esint will grind to a halt if every Guild member stops working for every case."

Greta stared at the Ministro. *Tor'Esint will grind to a halt if every Guild member stops working.* There was something important in that thought. Could that somehow be the key to harming the Mercantili Guild? If the other Guilds stopped working, there wouldn't be any work for the Mercantili Guild.

The auditorium began to empty but Telchide didn't move. Greta stayed seated next to him until Aveline and Domizio joined them. With a small start she realised Filippo Falegname, a maestro of the Falegnami Guild and companion of Carlotta Mercantessa, had walked over with them. Aveline sat by Telchide's side, completely unperturbed to be accompanied by Filippo, and lay a hand over his fretting ones.

"Chide, let's go," she said gently. "Teresina will be missing you, even with Florio and Gaspare to keep her company."

At the mention of his daughter, Telchide raised his head. He seemed surprised to see everyone looking at him.

"It's all my fault," he said softly. "If I hadn't told the Amministratori about Sebetine, they wouldn't be investigating Eduardo."

Greta huffed. "By your logic, it's *my* fault Lucrezia and the entire Alchimisti Guild was under fire because of the alchemically-dyed materials. All I wanted was to keep myself, my apprentices, and my Guild safe.

"We weren't the ones who created these alchemical things, Telchide. And we weren't the ones calling for a trial. That's all down to the Mercantili Guild."

She stole a glance at Filippo only to notice him nodding.

"Honestly, I'm surprised it took Lotta and her ash-sucking Guild this long to pounce on the Alchimisti considering what she already suspected with Eduardo," Filippo said bitterly. "Come Chide, Aveline, let me treat you to a bite before returning you home. It's the least I can do for the trouble my companion has caused you. Signora Sarta, you're more than welcome to join us."

Greta shook her head before she could stop herself.

"I think I'd best be leaving before they decide to charge us with inter-Guild relations for simply talking to one another. I'll see you here this evening."

She took Domizio's arm and walked out of the auditorium.

Ludovico was waiting for Greta outside the auditorium. His eyes narrowed on her hand resting on Domizio's arm.

Greta didn't miss a step as she walked towards him. "What do you want, Ludovico? I've got a busy day."

"Your warehouse needs to be searched for alchemically-dyed material," he told her snidely. "It appears you added an extra lock, and we can't get in without you, unless you're happy for us to break down the door."

Greta took a deep breath. She refused to let him anger her. Or frighten her. Everything illegal had been moved to Aveline's workshop. She was surprised he hadn't mentioned her flight from the Amministratori. Was he saving that as blackmail for another time or did he not know?

"Very well, your Amministratori can come and collect me at my workshop at their leisure today, with a blazermobile. I don't have time to waste tramping around town when I should be working on orders."

Ludovico glared at her but had no authority to do anything else and they both knew it.

"Come, Domizio, let's get back to work."

Domizio obliged her by shouldering his way past Ludovico and not looking back. Out on the street, they walked in silence until they'd turned off Corso delle Gilde.

"Sorry about that," Greta said in a huff of annoyance. "Seems his nose is quite bent out of shape because of me lately. You don't have to work on my orders during the day – that was just my way of telling him how busy I am."

"I can though," Domizio told her. "I don't think you've quite understood my position. My workshop isn't really that at all. It's just my home. I don't have many clients of my own. Most of the time, I hire out my services to Sarti who need extra hands. Most Copper and Silver do the same. Not every Sarta is as ... fortunate as you."

"Oh." Greta didn't know what else to say. She knew she and the other Gold Sarti were well set up, but she'd owned and run her own workshop successfully from her Silver Guild Mark onwards. It came as a shock to realise not every Sarta was like that.

"In that case, may I hire your services until further notice?"

Domizio tipped his hat to her. "It would be my honour, Signora Sarta."

Greta laughed at his formality but could not dislodge the chord of discomfort he'd struck by explaining how fortunate she was. If the matter of Ranieri's testament was sorted in a way that allowed her to receive his patent fees, her fortunes would grow significantly. It would certainly make her the richest, if not the most sought after, Sarta in town. She would need extra hands.

It finally dawned on her why Lucrezia had not only apprentices but fully fledged Alchimisti working with her. She was one of the few and popular Gold Alchimisti in Tor'Esint. Without the extra hands, she'd never be able to keep up with her workload, just like Greta was already starting to find. If things went well with Signora Loyola's dress, she'd be inundated with orders from recommendations.

"Until further notice could be quite some time," Greta warned him belatedly.

"I don't mind," Domizio assured her. "It'll be nice to have some level of stability in my hired work."

Greta smoothed her skirt. She'd never been in such an unstable position as it appeared Domizio was in. And to know that was common with Sarti was unnerving.

"Tell me, would you happen to know any other decent Sarti who might be willing to join us for a time?"

Domizio grinned. "Indeed, I do. But we can talk about that after the trial."

Greta readily agreed. She'd hoped to be much further along in Signora Loyola's dress by now. It was a good thing she'd insisted on four weeks instead of three – it gave her an extra week up her sleeve for delays such as this. Signora Loyola appeared to be sympathetic to the current troubles of Guilds, but if Telchide's music box was ready for her on time, Greta wouldn't be able to delay the dress any further.

\*\*\*

By the time they returned to her workshop, there was already an Amministratore blazermobile waiting outside. Greta acknowledged them with a wave and quickly disappeared inside her shop with Domizio. The girls ambushed her with questions and hugs. Greta had a difficult time extricating herself from them.

"There's an Amministratore blazermobile waiting for me outside to search my warehouse. I'll be back soon. Hopefully. Domizio will be working with us until further notice and can answer all your questions. I must go."

Before they had a chance to bombard her with even more questions about the Amministratore blazermobile, Greta found the keys to her warehouse and left Domizio to deal with the aftermath.

The Tor'Esint Amministratori introduced themselves as Ubaldo and Arlo but offered no further information. The ride to her warehouse was silent and bumpy. The blazermobile had two rows of seats, which was rather unusual as far as blazermobiles went. Greta sat in the back seat, the two Amministratori taking the front. She didn't mind so much. It meant she didn't have to worry about accidentally leaning up against a stranger when they rounded a corner. The cobblestone roads had not been designed with blazermobiles in mind. They were durable enough for the horses and carriages that plodded along at slower speeds, but they didn't handle the fast-moving blazermobiles well, especially around corners.

They stopped in front of her warehouse. Arlo remained in the blazermobile as Ubaldo quickly stepped out and opened the door for her. Greta took the offered hand to step down to the street.

"Is this your warehouse?" he asked pointing to Greta's door.

She nodded and walked towards it, with the Amministratore a step behind her. Greta couldn't help the nervous flutter in her stomach. These were not Sarti Amministratori, but Tor'Esint Amministratori. They wouldn't turn a blind eye for any reason.

Greta unlocked the door and opened it wide, trying to intimate that she had nothing to hide. Ubaldo brushed past her into the warehouse. It was dark inside. He looked around for a moment before turning to Greta.

"Do you have a light?"

"Wait a moment," she told him.

Beside the door, there was a pulley system linked to a separate covering on the roof. She pulled the chains down, hand over hand, allowing the covering to move aside. As it pulled back, light flooded the warehouse, leaving nothing in shadows.

Ubaldo thanked her and walked around, meticulously noting each and every item in a notebook. Greta wondered if every other Sarta had been so thoroughly investigated but decided it wouldn't be prudent to ask. She knew there was no contraband left here. Every item currently in the warehouse had a receipt from a local haberdashery. Greta had refused to go through the Mercantili Guild since their idiotic edicts and exorbitant fees were set in place.

"Is this your only warehouse?" Ubaldo asked once he was finished the laborious task of listing all the items.

"Yes," Greta replied easily. "How many warehouses do you think I need?"
The Tor'Esint Authority raised an eyebrow at her.

"You were seen yesterday placing items from your warehouse into
a blazermobile. You were then hailed down but refused to stop for
the Amministratori. Why did you flee and where did you take those
items?"

Greta paused. How was she going to get herself out of this one?

"I apologise, but I didn't hear anyone hailing me down. You know how
noisy Tor'Esint can be in the warehouse district."

Ubaldo glared at her. "Do you intend to tell me you weren't fleeing the
Amministratori with contraband items?"

"Of course, I wasn't," Greta gasped and put a hand to her exaggeratedly
heaving chest. "How dare you accuse me of such a thing?"

"I see," he replied wryly. "Then you won't mind if we search Ranieri's
properties in your presence? I understand he passed everything to you,
which includes his warehouse and workshop."

Greta's breath caught in her throat. She had no idea what materials might
be there.

"You may, of course, search those properties, but I cannot and will not
be held accountable for anything you find within. Ranieri passed away less
than a week ago. I've not set foot in his properties since then. Anything he
may or may not have purchased cannot be faulted against me."

The Amministratore gave her a tight smile. "You don't make demands.
*We* are the Amministratori and we'll do as we see fit."

"Of course, Signore." Greta swallowed hard and gave a brittle smile. "Shall
we go there now?"

There was no point delaying. If they were going to search his properties, it
wouldn't matter if they did it now or later and Greta preferred to get it over
with. After all, how much worse could the day possibly get?

Greta closed the ceiling vents of her warehouse and locked the door
behind herself. Ranieri's warehouse was conveniently located next door to
Greta's. He'd organised it for her himself when she'd gained her Copper
Guild Mark. His forward thinking had helped them both in busy times.
They'd often shared materials and worked on projects with each other
using a hidden adjoining door. Greta hadn't bothered to point it out to the
Amministratore. He didn't need to know.

Signore Ubaldo asked her for the key to Ranieri's warehouse when she'd
locked her own door. Greta frowned at him.

"I don't have the key," she told him. "As I've already explained, I haven't
been to either property yet. The only one who's been inside is Ludovico.
I wouldn't even know where to look for the warehouse key if the Sarto
Amministratore doesn't have a spare one himself."

That, at least, made Ubaldo pause. He turned to Arlo in the blazermobile and had a quiet word with him. Greta couldn't hear what they were saying. Ubaldo finally turned his attention back to her.

"Do you have the key to the workshop?"

She shook her head. "Ludovico found Ranieri's apprentice and brought him, along with Ranieri's outstanding orders, to my workshop.

"If you don't mind, I have work to do. So, unless you plan on going all the way back to the Sarti Guild Hall, to Ranieri's workshop and then back to the warehouse, I suggest you take me home. I'm certain we all want to see how the trial is resolved, and we all have work to do."

Ubaldo narrowed his eyes at her. "*This* is our work. We *will* go to the Sarti Guild Hall to fetch Ranieri's keys. We can't help it if that means you'll miss out an entire day of work. That's not our problem."

Greta smoothed down her dress. Ludovico must have paid them to search her properties so thoroughly. She was certain there were other people more deserving than herself to be so closely scrutinised.

Nevertheless, she got into the blazermobile without another word and held on tightly as the Amministratori drove her all the way back to the Sarti Guild Hall. Greta watched the houses go by in a blur. She wasn't paying attention, so their arrival took her quite by surprise.

"Come with me," Ubaldo said brusquely.

Greta didn't bother objecting. It seemed it was going to be an entire waste of a working day. There was no point making things more difficult than necessary. Together, they walked into the Sarti Guild Hall.

The foyer was a bustle of activity. Greta tried to understand what was happening, but there were too many people running around for her to comprehend anything. She walked with Ubaldo to the front desk.

Agata Sarta was standing there, hands on hips, yelling at Ludovico.

"If you don't get these ridiculous searches over with quickly, you're going to grind the entire Sarti Guild to a halt. Is that what you want, you officious little oaf?"

Greta couldn't help but smile. This was probably the first time she and Agata had ever seen eye to eye.

"Good morning, Agata," Greta greeted her from behind. "Tell me, did your Amministratori go through every single item in your warehouse noting them all down in a book? Or did they just look for alchemically-dyed materials as was the original plan?"

Agata turned to glare at the Amministratore next to Greta. It was an odd experience having Agata's sharp stare directed at someone other than herself. She found she rather enjoyed it.

Greta turned to the Amministratore. "Ludovico, this Amministratore would like to search Ranieri's warehouse and workshop, but I don't have the keys for them. Apparently, even though I've yet to take ownership of the properties, I'm to be held responsible for anything he finds within them. How *I* would have been the one purchasing any of the goods is a mystery to me!"

Agata turned and slapped Ludovico across the face. The action stunned everyone, most of all Greta.

"Signora Sarta, acts of aggression are not tolerated in Tor'Esint," Ubaldo told her firmly. "You will kindly refrain from assaulting Ludovico Sarto."

Agata eyed Ubaldo narrowly. "I'll refrain from slapping him again if you refrain from charging Greta with anything found in Ranieri's properties. She doesn't even have a key to the properties so how could she *possibly* be held responsible for what's inside?"

Greta felt a strange sense of gratitude, but it was quickly quashed by suspicion. If Agata was being so vocal in her support of Greta it could only mean one thing – Agata knew that Ranieri had more alchemically-dyed material in his private stores. It wasn't a great leap of reasoning, considering it was one of Ranieri's current orders that had prompted this entire situation. Had they been working together?

Greta fought the urge to shake her head. Ranieri *knew* how much she and Agata disliked each other. Why would he work with her on anything?

Ludovico disappeared while Agata and Ubaldo had words. He returned soon after with two keys and handed them both over to Greta.

"The large one's for the warehouse, the smaller one for the workshop. I'm done with the entire affair now. His money has been transferred to your vault and you now have possession of both his properties. I wash my hands of this affair."

Greta gave him a hard stare. She knew he wasn't only talking about Ranieri's testament, but it grated on her that he thought to presume *he* was the one ending their own affair. *She'd* ended it months ago, in a much friendlier way, or so she'd thought.

"This *affair* isn't over. There are still certain items in Ranieri's testament that I wish to discuss with the Sarti Guild Maestri. I believe it will be of interest to most Gold Sarti."

Ludovico turned white with fury. Greta marvelled at how just a few days ago, *he'd* been the one championing her case. Now, everything she said seemed to infuriate him, not that she cared at all.

"Indeed?" asked Agata curiously.

Greta nodded. "Indeed. Ludovico, make me an appointment to see the Maestri tomorrow morning. Agata, you're welcome to join us. In fact, I would welcome *all* Gold Sarti members at that meeting."

"The Maestri are not free tomorrow morning," Ludovico said immediately, without consulting his appointment book.

Greta leaned over the desk and pulled up the appointment book. She flipped over to the next page, it was empty. Without hesitation, she took the pen out of Ludovico's shaking fingers and wrote her name at half-past seven.

"We can discuss it before the day's trading. I know I'm not the only one who is losing an entire day because of the Alchimisti trial and these ridiculous searches."

Up until that point, Ubaldo had remained silent – their discussion hadn't involved him – but now Greta had offended him directly.

"Signora Sarta, it's time to search your properties. If anything is found in these *ridiculous* searches, you *will* be held responsible."

Greta felt her anger rising. There were almost certainly contraband items in Ranieri's properties and she had no way to get rid of them before the search. It wasn't fair!

"I'd like to propose an agreement with you," Greta said suddenly. "I think it a certainty that there will be alchemically-dyed materials in Ranieri's workshop. After all, that's why the searches are being carried out in the first place. I'm willing to give all these materials over to the Amministratori with no request for reimbursement in exchange for a promise of fair treatment.

"Nothing in Ranieri's properties was purchased by me. I shouldn't be held responsible for anything within them."

Ubaldo smiled snidely. "You're in no position to make demands or agreements. We'll search the properties and you'll be held accountable for everything found within. Are we clear on that matter?"

Greta felt a wave of dizziness wash over her. She put out a hand to steady herself on the front desk.

She found she couldn't answer him or even nod. Ubaldo didn't seem to care. He grabbed her roughly by the arm and escorted her out of the Sarti Guild Hall. In a way, she was glad because her legs felt so weak she doubted she could've walked out by herself. The mounting fear made her feel ever fainter.

By the time they reached the blazermobile and she was bundled inside, Greta doubted her legs were working at all now. Her vision swam and she slumped against the window of the carriage.

There was a muffled argument outside the blazermobile, then someone joined Greta in the back seat. Her vision was so blurred that she couldn't tell who.

"I'm coming too."

That was Agata's voice. Greta was certain of it. What was her fiercest competitor doing helping her? The blazermobile roared to a start.

"Breathe slowly, Greta. Your vision will soon clear."

Greta struggled to take long, slow breaths. It took a minute or two for her vision to clear sufficiently. She looked around to confirm that it really was

Agata sitting beside her. The world had gone up in smoke and ash if Agata was currently her ally.

There wasn't time to ask why the change of heart nor if Agata had a plan. Ranieri's workshop was only a few blocks away on the opposite end of Piazza Mercantile from Greta, down past Aveline's workshop, nearer to the west side of Via Mercato.

When they pulled up outside, Arlo stayed in the blazermobile, as he'd done at Greta's warehouse. Ubaldo opened the door for Agata and Greta to get out. It wasn't so much a social nicety as a demand for them to comply with.

Agata got out first and held a hand out to Greta. She took it gratefully. If Agata was her ally now, she wasn't going to do anything so stupid as dismiss her kindness and risk alienating her.

Greta took the smaller key from her pocket and opened Ranieri's workshop. The last time she'd been here, Ranieri had been alive and she'd come to share a cup of tea. This time, she was too frozen to think.

She pushed the door open and walked in, keeping the door open for both Agata and Ubaldo. They joined her in the workshop. Greta didn't open the shuttered windows. If the Amministratore was going to hold everything against her he could open the smoking windows himself.

And he did. Without any difficulty. Sunlight streamed in through the dusty windows, shedding light on every surface. Greta's eyes fell on the seat where she'd spent so much time mending clothes for customers who didn't take enough care with delicate materials.

Though she'd been the sole apprentice most of her time with Ranieri, it wasn't a boring apprenticeship. They'd spent hours talking with one another with relative ease, right from the beginning. Perhaps it was because Greta had already seen the harsher side of life and was prepared to work herself to the bone to ensure she was never in that position.

Without any family in Tor'Esint, Ranieri became her pseudo-father and Greta had always gotten on well with her father. Her relationship with Ranieri had been no different, except there wasn't the constant expectation that she'd look in on her sister to ensure she wasn't getting herself impregnated by her current favourite dandy.

Greta shook her head, trying to distract herself from her memories. There were more important things to focus on right now. Ubaldo walked around the shop, methodically writing down every material he found, followed assiduously by Agata.

Greta walked apart from them, wondering just where Ranieri kept his contraband items. There'd been no such thing as contraband Sarti items when she was an apprentice. Since the ban, everyone she knew had a secret compartment somewhere in their house to conceal things. She only hoped Ranieri's secret compartment was well hidden.

Trying not to appear as flustered as she felt, Greta sat on one of the waiting chairs and watched as Ubaldo and Agata walked around the shop area. Their initial search came up with no contraband, but Ubaldo didn't let that stop him from writing everything down.

Greta followed them into the back section of the shop when they were done with their initial search. Almost every available wall was covered with Ranieri's own Silver Great Work – adjustable fabric wall mounts. There was nowhere for her to sit out of the way, so she walked to the back wall and leaned against a wall mount with a foot against the wall.

She heard a soft click and slowly, unobtrusively, looked down. A small wooden panel had popped out from the wall. Her skirts were hiding it from Ubaldo's eyes, but Greta didn't want to take any chances. She immediately released pressure and then pushed the panel back in. There was another soft click, but Ubaldo didn't notice.

Not trusting her luck to hold any further, Greta moved away from the wall and followed Agata's example in shadowing Ubaldo's movements.

"I don't see any alchemically-dyed material. Have you found any?" Greta asked more confidently than she'd felt all day.

Ubaldo growled at her. "It'd be a lot easier for me to search this place if the two of you weren't standing so close to me."

"Oh, I do apologise," Greta said, pulling Agata back with her. "We'll just go and fetch a glass of water."

Agata frowned at her but followed, nonetheless. In the kitchen, Greta whispered as softly as she could.

"I found his secret compartment. Ubaldo won't find anything here."

Agata's shoulders sagged in relief. "But what about his warehouse?"

"I don't know," Greta replied nervously. "I can't think of a way to stall him until I've had a chance to look there myself. And I'm certain Ranieri has things there he shouldn't have. *All* of us do."

Agata gave her an odd look. "You do, do you?"

"Well, not anymore," Greta replied evenly. "But I did."

Agata thought for a moment. "Have they already searched your warehouse?"

Greta nodded.

"And they have no reason to go back there?"

"He took as detailed notes there as he's taking here. I don't think there'll be *any* reason for him to go back."

Agata bit her lip. "How much do you trust me?"

Greta tried not to laugh. Until today, she'd have answered "not at all". But everything was different now.

"What are you thinking?" Greta asked.

"Your warehouse is next door to Ranieri's isn't it?"

"Oh." Greta tried not to make any loud sounds. "Did you already know about the adjoining door?"

Agata grinned. "No, but we're talking about Ranieri here. I assumed he had backup plans all over the place. He didn't trust these ash-suckers one bit. Do you have the key to that door?"

"Yes." Greta heaved a sigh of relief. "Do you think you'll have time to get there and move everything incriminating before we arrive?"

"Not without a blazermobile."

Greta tore a scrap of paper from her pattern book and scribbled a quick note on it. She wrapped two keys within it.

"Go to Aveline Inventrice's workshop, on the north side of Piazza Mercantile across from Via dell'Oro. She can take you to my warehouse and you can get into Ranieri's warehouse from there. You might need her apprentice to help move things. She's in a ... delicate situation."

Agata frowned. "She's *pregnant*?"

Greta didn't answer. She wasn't certain if Aveline wanted people to know, though if she did not end the pregnancy, it would be a matter of months before everyone knew anyway.

"Just give her this note. She'll know what to do." She handed the small parcel to Agata. "I'll stall him as long as I can. And Agata?"

The other Sarta looked at her expectantly. Greta pursed her lips.

"Thank you."

"Don't thank me just yet," she replied, taking the parcel and putting it in her pocket. "I'll do what I can."

Greta filled two glasses with water and led Agata out into the shopfront again. The older Sarta huffed noisily.

"How much longer is this going to take? I haven't got all day to stand around watching you make lists."

She roughly took the glass from Greta's hand and sloshed water all over the floor before taking a long sip. Ubaldo looked at her in disgust.

"It'll take as long as it takes," he replied testily. "I must be thorough, or I may need to come back again. No one invited you to come and no one cares if you leave, Signora Sarta. This isn't *your* workshop."

Agata glared at him. She really was quite a good actress.

"Greta, you're on your own. I've got orders to fulfil."

Greta took the glass that was thrust at her, spilling more water on the floor. She pretended to be flabbergasted, opening and closing her mouth without saying anything. From the corner of her eye, she saw Ubaldo rolling his eyes.

"So dramatic," he mumbled as Agata slammed the door closed behind herself. "Signora, you'd best clean up that mess before I search that side of the shop."

Greta bobbed her head in mock acquiescence. "Of course, Signore Ubaldo."

It was difficult not to narrow her eyes in annoyance, but she took herself off to the kitchen to relieve herself of the glasses before she gave in to such a childish impulse.

As she cleaned the glasses, she wondered what the most obtrusive way to clean the spill in the workshop would be. A thick cloth would be the fastest and easiest, so she dismissed that idea immediately.

Greta stepped into the workroom and started opening cupboards and searching through them as noisily as she could, muttering to herself the entire time. "Where does he keep his mop? He moved it since I was an apprentice here."

She took her time, after opening six incorrect cupboards she finally opened the one she knew contained the mop and bucket. She pretended to struggle, pulling them out of the cluttered cupboard. Eventually, she hauled them out and swung them around in an exaggerated circle to the middle of the room, narrowly missing Ubaldo who watched her in horrified fascination. Doubtless he'd never seen anyone struggle so ridiculously with a simple mop and bucket.

Greta swiped a stray curl out of her face and dropped the heavy wooden bucket onto Ubaldo's foot. She tried to hide the smile behind her false attempts to help him as he yelped and hopped around on one foot, holding the injured foot with both hands.

"Oh, I'm sorry, Signore," Greta gushed uselessly. "Can I help you? A glass of water?"

The entire time, Greta walked slowly towards him, herding him towards the puddle on the floor. He stepped back from her and into the puddle, lost his footing and fell flat on his back, knocking his head on the stone floor.

He screeched in pain and shouted at her as she knelt by his side. "Don't touch me! Get away from me!"

Greta held her hands up innocently and moved away from him. She righted a chair that had fallen in the kerfuffle and sat down, trying to look contrite. It felt ridiculous to act so helpless and sorry, but it appeared to be doing the trick. Ubaldo couldn't possibly think that she was purposely trying to stall him from searching the warehouse now. She only hoped it bought Agata and Aveline enough time to clear Ranieri's workshop of everything incriminating.

A minute or two later, Ubaldo sat up and inspected his injuries. Blood came away on his hand when he probed his head injury.

"I'm sure Ranieri had some bandages or blood staunchers if you'll allow me to look for them," she offered. "He used a pepper cream on me any time I pricked my fingers on unforgiving needles. There's bound to be a jar around here somewhere."

166

Ubaldo tried to stand but swayed on his feet. Greta immediately went to his aid and helped him to a chair.

"You stay here. I'll fetch you a glass of water and see if I can't find that pepper cream. Just wait."

She gave him no chance to object before she disappeared into the kitchen once more. The pepper cream would be upstairs if he really had any. Greta returned with a glass of water, which she carried with exaggerated care to him.

He accepted it warily, but Greta was done being purposely clumsy. She hadn't really meant for him to get so badly hurt. It wouldn't do to have the Amministratori accuse her of anything else.

"I'll go find the cream now. I shan't be long."

Ubaldo sipped slowly at the water as she disappeared once more into the kitchen. From there, she climbed the stairs. It took more emotional strength than she'd anticipated. She hadn't been up these stairs in years – not since she'd reached her Silver Guild Mark. She'd stayed on with Ranieri after her apprenticeship to save money for her own workshop.

As a Copper Sarta, she'd earned a small wage and diligently saved as much of it as possible so that when she earned her Silver Guild Mark, she was almost ready to purchase her very own workshop. She'd had no idea that Ranieri intended to help her in that venture.

The memory of that day still brought tears to her eyes. He'd found the small workshop in Piazza Mercantili where she still lived, not far from his own workshop, as well as a warehouse next to his own.

Without giving her the option, he'd negotiated with the Sarti Guild to help her purchase both but have only *her* name on the properties.

"It's my parting gift to you," he'd told her affectionately. "You're the best apprentice I ever had – the closest to a daughter I'll ever have. I want to give you every chance to be successful that I can. Please, let me do this for you."

Greta had wanted to argue that she wasn't his daughter, that he owed her nothing, that his gift was the years he'd spent teaching her to hone her skills. Instead, she'd hugged him as tightly as she could and cried into his shoulder. The reaction had surprised both of them and they'd laughed about it many times over the years.

"No more laughter," she whispered to herself as she climbed the stairs.

It felt wrong to be in this house without him. The workshop was one thing, but the living quarters was quite another. Greta hadn't set foot in here since she'd moved out. Even when she came back to visit, they'd remained downstairs, enjoying a cup of tea in the kitchen or the more comfortable armchairs in the shop.

She walked straight to the cupboard next to the water closet. That was where he kept all his medicines and oddities. She opened it up and was not at all surprised to see a jar of pepper cream right in front. It was almost empty but would have enough for Ubaldo's head. Greta wondered if every other apprentice of his had pricked their fingers quite as much as she had. Honestly, if Ranieri hadn't been so certain of her, Greta herself would've given up on being a Sarta.

She tried not to think so much about Ranieri as she descended back into the workshop with a cloth to administer the cream. Ubaldo stopped her as she tried to put the cream on his head.

"*I'll* do it," he said firmly. "I don't need any more of your help. Thank you."

He took the cream-smeared cloth and wiped it on the back of his head. He gasped at the pain, but continued until there was no more blood. The Alchimisti deserved a great deal of credit for their work. Their creams, solutions and tablets worked wonders. Sometimes different wonders than expected, but wonders nonetheless.

As Ubaldo was seeing to his wounds, Greta picked up the mop and bucket and soaked up the spilt water with as much efficiency as she dared, to keep up the illusion of her incompetence with those instruments. She noticed that Ubaldo didn't move from his seat until she'd packed everything away in the cupboard once more. It was a clever, if paranoid, reaction.

Greta decided she'd forcibly stalled him enough and went to make herself a cup of tea – Ranieri always kept some of her favourite. By the time she returned, Ubaldo had resumed his work, much slower than before. She was glad of the delay but did regret how much pain she had caused him. It really hadn't been intentional.

After a good hour, Ubaldo did a sweep of the workshop and finally put away his notebook and pencil. Greta looked up at him expectantly.

"Did you find anything?"

He glared at her suspiciously. "There are certainly things here I wouldn't expect to find in a Sarto's workshop, but no alchemically-dyed material. As for the warehouse, it's time to see about that."

Greta nodded apprehensively. Ludovico and the Amministratori seemed out to get her, and she wasn't certain if it was just because of the alchemically-dyed material or not. This was starting to feel much more like a personal attack.

She could almost understand, though not condone, Ludovico's sudden turn against her, but she hadn't done anything to irk the Amministratori.

"Letizia di Bibiana is certain we will find something in Ranieri's workshop or warehouse to explain his sudden and violent death. She's linked the other similar deaths to Ranieri. It turns out they'd all ordered clothing from him in the past. Each had an article of clothing that had been arsenic-dyed. If we can find his orders proving he created those particular items for them, then..."

He smiled cruelly. Greta stared at him incredulously.

"Then what? You charge him with their murder? There's no point if he's already dead. And how could it possibly be murder if he then died from it himself?"

Ubaldo shrugged. "Presumably, the Ministro will repossess his property and goods, and use them to reimburse the dead people's families for their loss."

"His property and fortune have already been passed to me, as you've so kindly pointed out to me numerous times today," Greta said firmly. "As *I* have done nothing to these people, I doubt there's any way you can legally take all of my money and property to give to these other families."

"That's not for me to decide," Ubaldo told her, clearly showing what his preference would be. "I'm certain the Ministro will decide the right thing to do."

Greta smoothed down her skirt. "That's *if* you find anything linking them in the first place. You can't be so certain to do so."

Her heart was thumping loudly in her ears. She knew exactly where Ranieri kept his paperwork. It wasn't in the secret panel, but surely she could move it there before they found it. He didn't even keep it in his workshop – it was in a chest, under his bed, hidden by false planks. If she could prevent the Amministratori from looking upstairs, she could search them later and destroy the evidence.

"Shall we be off then?" she asked, trying not to sound too eager.

Ubaldo grunted his assent and preceded her out of the workshop. Greta locked the premises behind herself and tucked the key in her pocket alongside its larger warehouse counterpart.

Social niceties had obviously completely been dispensed with for when Greta turned to the street, Ubaldo was already in his seat beside Arlo without even bothering to open the back door for her. She made an excessive fuss about opening the door herself and gathering her skirts to step up into the blazermobile without any assistance whatsoever. Ubaldo and Arlo appeared not to notice or care.

Greta tried to keep her breathing steady the entire way to the warehouse district. She was reasonably concerned about the contraband they might find. However, she was more concerned that Agata and Aveline would be discovered moving goods from Ranieri's warehouse to her own. Both were taking an enormous risk for her. Who knew what trouble they'd get into if they were found?

When the blazermobile pulled up in front of her warehouses, Greta looked for any sign of them. Aveline's blazermobile was nowhere to be seen and she could see that the ceiling partitions of the warehouses hadn't been pulled open. It was almost too much to hope that they'd moved everything already.

Greta's own workshop had needed more time than this to move and she'd known where everything was. Unless Agata was intimately familiar with Ranieri's warehouse, it would've taken time for her to find the items that needed removal and transport them through to Greta's warehouse.

Out on the street, Greta took as much time as she dared finding the warehouse key and unlocking the door. Ubaldo shoved her none too gently out of the way.

"Find some lighting. It's too dark in here."

Greta shrugged helplessly. "Signore Ubaldo, really, how many times must I say it? I haven't been here in years, and I can't remember what sort of lighting system Ranieri had, if any. You're just going to have to make do with what you have."

Ubaldo growled at her, his temper growing darker by the minute. "Fetch the lantern in the blazermobile."

"I'll do no such thing," Greta insisted. "What in Caldera's smoke are you thinking of, bringing flames into the warehouse district? You'll start a fire that will ravage the whole of Tor'Esint!"

"What do you propose then, *Signora Sarta?*" His snide voice was almost too much to bear.

Greta smoothed her skirt. "Surely you have a friction light handy. I understand all Tor'Esint Amministratori were given them when they were invented by Ugo Inventore."

Ubaldo growled and searched his pockets for his friction light. Greta was thankful she knew about the mandate because of her friendship with Aveline. If Ubaldo had started a fire in Ranieri's warehouse, accidental or not, it would have been devastating for more than just herself.

The Guild Halls struck two o'clock. Ubaldo didn't seem to notice.

"I need to be back at the Town Hall before four o'clock," Greta told him.

"That's not my problem," he replied callously.

Greta gritted her teeth. "It *will* in fact be your problem if I'm not there. I was called as a witness to the Alchimisti trial. If I'm not there at four o'clock and they need to call on me again, Ministro Ercolano will want to know who prevented me from being there."

"Oh." Ubaldo paused. "Well, if you help me, I'll have you back in time."

Greta raised an eyebrow at him.

"Just keep the friction light going while I take notes."

"Oh, very well," Greta relented. There was no point in being obstinate about it. If Agata and Aveline had gotten rid of everything, good. If not, well, there was nothing more she could do to protect herself now. Purposely making the search process go slower would be a pointless exercise and cost her the chance to see how the Alchimisti trial unfolded.

Greta led Ubaldo down the many rows of material. He was still making notes, but to Greta's eye, they were becoming less and less detailed. Instead of listing every colour of every material, certain materials were being grouped together. *Cotton, various colours. Wool, fine, various whites. Wool, coarse, dark colours.*

Well, that was one thing in her favour. If he were keeping less meticulous notes, she wouldn't have to find receipts for everything. How could she when there was no positive description of each item?

"Is this satin or silk?" he asked her, pointing to a shimmering material.

"That's satin," she replied quickly.

"Local or other?" he enquired hopefully.

Greta sighed in frustration. "Signore Ubaldo, I really *don't* know how to tell you any other way. This is only my warehouse by default. I haven't worked with Ranieri since I gained my Silver Guild Mark. That was simply *years* ago. I haven't set foot in this warehouse since that time. I honestly don't know where he sourced his material from and would have a hard time finding any receipts if he even bothered keeping them."

He stopped and looked at her closely. "You really don't know, do you?"

She shook her head emphatically.

"Fine then. It's getting late. Let's just see if there's any alchemically-dyed material and be done with it. I don't want to spend any longer on this than necessary."

Greta took a deep breath. She led the way up and down the rows of material. Ubaldo opened any boxes they came across. Some had fine materials such as organza inside, but he paid them no more notice than the more common cotton and wools. Either he didn't know that these materials were from other islands, or he was past the point of caring. Either way, she wasn't going to point the rarity out to him.

In the distance, the Guild Halls struck a clamouring of chimes for three o'clock. One hour until the verdict.

"What's this?" Ubaldo asked, looking inside a small box.

Greta wound the friction light up again and brought it closer to the box. As she did, the inside of the box glittered silver. It was an effect she hadn't seen before on anything other than crystal beads. But these weren't beads. They were small shiny discs.

"Is it from an alchemically-dyed material?"

Greta shook her head. "Those leave behind a power residue. This isn't powder, it's metal."

"Then I don't care about it," he proclaimed. "Let's keep looking. We haven't much time left."

Eventually, they came upon an empty box with green power on the inside. Greta was careful not to touch it but saw Ubaldo reach out towards it.

"Don't!"

She pulled his hand back, but it was already covered in green power.
"Wash it off, now."

"With what?" he asked her, panicked eyes darting back and forth.

Greta shook her head. There weren't any taps in the Sarta warehouses.
Nothing that could wash up such a disaster. She ran to the cheap cottons
and tore off a strip for him.

"Use this to wipe it off. Then take me back to my workshop. I've got
something there that can help you."

She turned to leave.

"What about the box?" he called out behind her. "It's the only evidence I
have. I can't leave it behind."

Greta didn't want to help him in his Guild hunt, but she didn't want him
to return at another time to retrieve it either.

"If I help you now, you promise *in writing* not to charge me with anything
you've found here or in Ranieri's workshop."

Ubaldo blanched at her suggestion. Did he have specific instructions to
the contrary?

She smoothed her dress down with care. They weren't *her* hands being
damaged by the second. "Who knows how deadly that arsenic is? It could
be enough to kill you."

Ubaldo quickly wiped the arsenic powder off his hands and dropped the
cotton cloth on the floor. Greta raised her eyebrow at that. She'd have to
deal with it later. How did one even deal with arsenic? Could you burn it?
Or would that only help it enter your body as you breathed in the fumes?

"Well?" she asked casually. "What's it to be?"

Ubaldo pursed his lips. "Fine. I promise, and I'll sign a document to
that effect, that you will not be charged for anything found in Ranieri's
warehouse..."

"Or workshop," Greta added meticulously.

"...or workshop," Ubaldo added through gritted teeth. "Now pick up that
box and let's go."

Greta looked carefully around the warehouse. Whatever she used would be
ruined. Eventually, she decided on a coarse woollen cloth and wrapped the
wooden box within it, careful not to touch the wood with her bare hands.

***

The Guild Halls were striking half past the hour by the time the
Amministratori blazermobile pulled up outside Greta's workshop once
more. She had half an hour to sort out Ubaldo and get to the Town hall.

Greta entered her workshop and was confronted with a hive of activity.
Annika and Marta were talking with relatively subdued customers while

Domizio stood behind the front counter, trying to deal with an explosive personality.

"Ah, Signora Loyola, how lovely to see you again," Greta called out to her.

The loud woman turned to face Greta with a red face. "Are you using alchemically-dyed material for my new dress?" she demanded loudly. "I won't have it, do you hear me?!"

Greta straightened her back at the assumed insult and turned to Marta.

"Marta dear, take this man and give him some of that cream you used on your hands the other day. There's a good girl."

Marta, thankfully without question, took Ubaldo through to the kitchen while Greta stayed behind to deal with Signora Loyola.

"Signora Loyola, I *never* use alchemically-dyed material. Your gown, along with every other order, including all of Ranieri Sarto's incomplete ones, will be made using naturally dyed material.

"However, as you must know there have been numerous disruptions to the Guilds this week, your second fitting will be delayed. It will still, however, be finished within the agreed timeframe."

Signora Loyola harrumphed at that but said nothing further. She swept out of the shop like a tidal wave, dragging the other customers along with her. They must have been friends or lackeys. Either way, Greta wanted nothing more to do with any of them today.

She had very little time to draft an agreement between herself and Ubaldo and get down to the Town Hall before the verdict was given over the Alchimisti trial.

"Mizi, can you handle things until I return? I'm sorry I took so long. I'll explain it all later."

Domizio nodded easily. Greta thanked him, went through to the kitchen and placed the cloth-wrapped box on the table. Marta had given Ubaldo the cream and was instructing him as he proceeded to slather it over his hands.

Greta tore a page out of her pattern book and wrote their agreement on it.

*I, Ubaldo of the Tor'Esint Amministratori, do hereby declare that Greta Sarta will not be held responsible for any items found in Ranieri Sarto's warehouse or workshop. She is not to be punished for the actions of her former Maestro. I give my word on pain of imprisonment myself.*

"That should do it," she said, reading over the agreement.

She handed it to Ubaldo to read. Again, he blanched, but held out his quickly healing hand for her pencil. Greta could see Marta trying to catch her eye. She looked up at the girl and shook her head. There was no time for an explanation now.

Once the agreement was signed, Greta escorted Marta and the Amministratore back out to the shopfront, Ubaldo clutching the cloth-wrapped box.

"Ubaldo will take me to the Town Hall for the verdict of the Alchimisti trial. I don't know when I'll be back. Domizio's in charge until I return."

Domizio took her aside before she could leave.

"Greta, are you certain the streets will be safe for you by the time the trial finishes?" he asked in undisguised concern.

Greta knew it was a well-founded fear, but she didn't want to leave her girls alone when it appeared she had enemies out to get her.

"I'm certain Aveline will be there. I'll ask her to walk home with me. She's just a few doors away after all." She glanced meaningfully at Ubaldo. "I'm certain the Amministratori will have no problems allowing two old friends to walk home together."

Ubaldo shook his head. "I think they've more important things to worry about at the moment than two friends walking home together."

Greta was impressed by how much his manner had changed since she'd helped him, and they'd made their deal. Would she be able to rely on him for help if or when she needed it? She stopped the thought there. It would be nice to think she had his friendship, but what she really had was a binding agreement that could send him to prison.

"Let's go," she said before anything else could delay her further. There was too much on the line for her to miss this verdict.

\*\*\*

Greta arrived at the Town Hall a few minutes to the hour. The front steps were already packed with people wanting to hear the verdict. Ubaldo left her at the entrance, and she pushed her way through to the auditorium. This time, she had to make do with a seat towards the back of the gallery. There was no separation for those who were to stand witness and everyone who was here to gawk.

The Guild Hall clocks struck four o'clock. Ministro Ercolano walked into the auditorium along with Severino Mercante and Valeria Alchimista. The three of them took their seats as everyone else settled down.

Once the gallery was quiet, Ministro Ercolano rose in his chair.

"Bring out Lucrezia Alchimista and Eduardo Alchimista."

The doors leading out to the detainment area opened. Lucrezia walked in, head held high, staring defiantly at Severino Mercante. Eduardo walked in as though all his years had been heaped on him in one day. He didn't look up at anyone. It was a depressing sight.

"The Alchimisti Guild has been accused of negligence and reckless behaviour. Behaviours that could be potentially dangerous and have already cost some people their lives. I find it difficult to condemn an entire Guild for the actions of a few. Therefore, the Alchimisti Guild in and of itself will not face any penalties."

A murmur of relief went through the crowd. Greta herself sighed heavily. It seemed the Mercantili Guild didn't have *everyone* in its pockets. That, at least, was something. Ministro Ercolano banged his gavel for silence.

"Lucrezia Alchimista, step forward." She did. "You were accused of using and trading in alchemically-dyed material. I find you innocent of these charges as you were the one who tested the toxic material to reveal the extent of the danger. You wouldn't have done so had you already been dealing with it yourself."

"Nice of you to notice," Lucrezia said drily. Ministro Ercolano shot her a warning glance.

"I command the Alchimisti Guild to withdraw all alchemically-dyed materials from the market. In addition, I think it necessary to impose strict testing for all future alchemically-dyed material. I decree that Lucrezia Alchimista will carry these tests out and deem them toxic or safe. Her reputation, her Guild Status, and potentially her freedom, will rely on her honesty and integrity in this matter."

Greta let out a breath she didn't realise she'd been holding. It wasn't the best outcome, but it was the best they could've hoped for. And it would keep the people of Tor'Esint safe.

"Eduardo Alchimista step forward."

Lucrezia stepped back as Eduardo shuffled forward. He kept his eyes on his feet.

"Eduardo Alchimista, you've been charged with knowingly dispensing dangerous medicines. I find this a difficult case. On the one hand, I understand that all medicines have some unintended effects and not all are necessarily known about until after widespread or frequent use. On the other hand, if there was even the shadow of a doubt after Sebetine di Serenita had taken the same medicine and disappeared, it was irresponsible of you not to come forward yourself to mention your fears that she might be dead. Not only that, but you dispensed the very same medicine to Teresina di Sebetine, causing grave damage to her memory.

"If it weren't for the fact that you tried to stop the child taking those tablets once you realised something was amiss, I would have you stripped of your Guild Status and imprisoned. That one act was your saving grace.

"In this matter, I'll hand you over to your Guild for observation. You'll have a Guild Amministratrice or a Gold Alchimista shadowing you in your workshop. Every item you manufacture yourself will be thoroughly tested for safety. Every dispensation will be checked before it is received by customers.

"This will continue for one year. If we are satisfied that you're competent after that time, you'll be allowed to resume work as normal. If not, you'll be stripped of your Guild Status."

There was silence in the hall. Eduardo was a well-respected Alchimista. He was more well-liked than Lucrezia as well, which likely gave him more customers. When word of this got out, how many of those customers would stay with him? And who was to pay for the Guild Amministratrice or Gold Alchimista to shadow him? It would cripple his business, even without stripping his Guild Marks.

Severino stood up and bowed his head towards the Ministro. "Thank you, Ministro Ercolano."

Ministro Ercolano stared at him until he sat once more.

"As for *you*, Severino Mercante, I'll be sending my own personal accountants to the Mercantili Guild. You'll show them every record of every ship, funicolare and blazermobile that has entered Tor'Esint in the past three years. If I find *any* hint that the Mercantili Guild was guilty of importing alchemically-dyed material, an imploding volcano won't save you from my wrath."

"Yes, Ministro," Severino replied smoothly. "I'll await your accountants there."

"No, you'll escort the accountants there yourself, now," Ministro Ercolano countered. "Forgive me if I don't trust you not to destroy those records before they get there."

Even from the back of the hall, Greta could see Severino's bald, shiny head once again turn a dark shade of red.

"The rest of you, clear off. Any more days like this and Tor'Esint really will grind to a halt. Go home and rest. I want every workshop open for business tomorrow. No exceptions!"

He banged the gavel and left the room. Greta tried to find Aveline, but the crush of people forced her out into the bursting foyer before she had a chance. There, she fought her way through to the street. She'd be safe waiting here. It was still relatively early, and the streets were flooded with people exiting the Town Hall.

"Greta!"

She looked around as someone called her name. Across the road from her, Agata was waving wildly. Greta gently pushed and prodded her way through the crowd to her fellow Gold Sarta.

"How did it go?" Agata asked in as quiet a voice as she could.

Greta grinned. "I don't know how you did it, but all we found was one box with powered arsenic inside."

Agata's face fell at the mention of it. "Smoking Caldera! I thought we got rid of it all."

"No, it's fine," Greta assured her. "Ubaldo got the powder all over his hands and I exaggerated how dangerous it could be. We came to quite a beneficial agreement that I'd give him the cure if he'd protect me against anything found in Ranieri's properties."

Agata's mouth gaped open. "You did *what*?"

"Very little persuasion is needed when one thinks one will die without appropriate alchemical attention." Greta shrugged. "However, this entire situation has put me quite a bit more in your debt than I'd ever thought to be."

Agata patted her arm. "You don't know the half of it. Come with me. Aveline's waiting for us back at Telchide's house with her blazermobile."

"Telchide's house?" Greta asked in confusion. For Aveline not wanting to commit to the man, she was spending an awful lot of time with him.

Agata shrugged. "It's closer to the Town Hall than her house and she needed to speak with him about something important."

Greta smoothed her skirt. This day was turning into a smoking mess.

She linked arms with her fiercest competitor and walked the few short blocks to Telchide Inventore's home. It was the second time in days that she'd had cause to visit the workshop, though she'd never previously set foot inside it.

When they got there, Greta saw Aveline looking up and down the street through the shuttered windows. She was clearly worried.

Agata bundled Greta up the stairs where Aveline opened the door and dragged them both into the empty room. Greta didn't even have a chance to unbutton her coat before Aveline launched into a tirade.

"What's wrong with all of you? Forcing the Amministratori to perform searches of your warehouses when you have such ridiculously contraband items in your possession!"

Greta held out her hands in a placating manner. "Aveline, it wasn't my warehouse."

Aveline shot daggers with her eyes.

"It *is* your warehouse now!" she yelled and then lowered her voice. "And this is *twice* in two days that I've been forced to help you move contraband items."

Greta stared in shock at her best friend. Aveline was absolutely livid.

"Honestly, Veli, I didn't mean for the Tor'Esint Amministratori to do the search. It should've been the Sarti Amministratori. They were to collect alchemically-dyed materials and confiscate them. I don't know why Ludovico changed the plan."

Agata rolled her eyes. "Would it have anything at all to do with your current bedmate?"

Greta felt the blush rising all the way from her toes to the tip of her head. "Who I decide to bed is of no concern to you."

"It is when it causes a spate of jealousy so severe that our entire Guild is being forced to pay the price."

Greta had no retort. It was true. But Ludovico's jealousy was not her fault. She'd stopped bedding him months ago. Surely, he'd understood she wouldn't return to his bed again. Surely.

"Whatever the reason, I still don't understand why you're both in such a state over some contraband material."

There was silence in the workshop. Greta stared from one to another.

"This ... isn't about contraband material, is it?" she asked slowly.

Aveline shook her head and looked to Agata to explain.

"Ranieri was more of a rebel than either of us thought. I knew about the alchemically-dyed material and some of the illegally imported material because we went in on some of them together – he knew you wouldn't want to. But I didn't know he had a project on the side."

Greta felt the blood drain from her face and looked around for a chair. She dropped down onto it before her vision gave out. The blood rushed noisily through her ears, making it difficult for her to hear anything else.

A glass was shoved into her hand and guided to her mouth. She drank tiny sips until her vision returned and the sound of rushing blood abated.

"What project?" she asked hoarsely.

"It looks like a machine to sew automatically," Agata told her. "He must've been working on it for months, maybe even years."

"Sew automatically?" ask Greta, confused and *angry*. Why hadn't Ranieri told her about this?

Agata nodded eagerly. "From the looks of it, yes. And it belongs to you now. We moved it into your warehouse to be safe. If the Tor'Esint Amministratori find out about it, they'll know he was collaborating with Inventrici."

"Which Inventrici?" Greta asked, looking at Agata and Aveline in turn. They both shrugged.

"I can assure you it isn't anyone I know," Aveline told her. "I have regular meetings with some Inventrici – no one's mentioned this."

Greta shook her head, trying to clear it, but it didn't work.

"Can you take me there to see it?" she asked Aveline hopefully.

Aveline shook her head. "It's late, Greta. We've all had a busy day and this baby is only making me more tired." Greta startled at the blatant mention of it, but Aveline continued without pausing. "Tomorrow. And then you need to see about getting a blazermobile for yourself. I'm certain Lucrezia will be only too happy to help you after the trial today."

"I doubt it," Greta replied. "If I hadn't sent Marta to her in the first place to get the cream for her hand, she never would've been dragged into this mess. And what about Eduardo?"

There were heavy steps on the stairs as Filippo descended, with Telchide close behind him on some sort of chair contraption attached to the stairs.

"Eduardo will never forgive me," Telchide said sombrely. "I should never have cast suspicion on him the way I did. It was unfair."

"No," Aveline said firmly, walking over to him. "What was unfair was the Amministratori taking such extreme measures. You did what you had to do for your family. For *Teresina*. Eduardo will forgive you ... eventually."

Telchide looked at her sadly. "Eventually could be an awfully long time away. Who knows if he'll still be an Alchimista by the time Resi chooses her trade? Will she even have him as a choice if she wants him?"

"You know Resi would have to add her name to the list of hopeful apprentices like everyone else, Chide," Filippo told him. "And by that point, perhaps the damage Carlotta is causing will be a distant memory."

Greta glanced uncomfortably at Agata. It was clear this was a personal conversation. She didn't need nor want to be part of it.

"I'm going home," Greta said a little louder than she intended. "As you said, it's been a long day. My poor girls must be beside themselves by now. I'll come past your workshop tomorrow and we can go to my warehouse from there."

Aveline looked over and nodded. "Will you walk together with Agata? Chide and I have things to discuss."

Greta looked at Agata in as much alarm as she looked at Greta. "I think we've trespassed on each other's good graces enough for one day. It's only a few blocks away on well-lit streets. We'll be fine."

Aveline took a pair of knuckle-dusters from her coat pocket and handed them to Greta. "Take these, just in case. You can give them back to me tomorrow."

Greta looked down at the heavy items and backed away from them. "I'll be fine, Veli. It's still early."

Aveline's over-precautions always worried Greta. She'd never been attacked herself but knew Aveline had. Unfortunately, those few wretched incidents had been with someone she knew or had met that night who assumed he had a right to her body because they'd shared a drink or two. It was unfair that women should not feel safe out at night.

"I'll see you tomorrow," she said before Aveline could force the issue. "Good evening, Agata. And ... thank you for your help today. I'll see you tomorrow morning at the Sarti Guild for my meeting."

There was nothing else to say. They both knew Greta was in their debt, but there wasn't anything that could be done about that now. Tomorrow would shed some light on what kind of favours Greta could afford to bestow on either of them.

Greta stepped out of the house and walked quickly to Via dell'Oro. It was only two short blocks to Piazza Mercantile. And it was still quite light out. If she kept to Via dell'Oro, she'd be fine.

There were a lot of people out on the streets for a weekday evening. Greta made way for couples and small parties that took up the entire walkway. She frowned at the ever-present fashion of such wide skirts that impaired a woman's ability to walk. She only rarely used them herself but knew many adopted this fashion to keep unwanted suitors at arm's length or further. They were extremely cumbersome to make and required such large hoops that Greta barely had room to make them in her small workshop. She'd thought to create a quick release mechanism for these skirts for a Great Work, but then reasoned if every Sarto knew about it, the secret would soon be out, and then the voluminous skirts would be pointless.

She arrived back at her house without incident. From Aveline's caution, Greta had almost expected something to happen and was surprised, and relieved, when nothing did. Domizio and Annika were still in the kitchen when she arrived. Greta found them talking quietly over a cup of hot cocoa. It was an odd sight. Annika was usually so uptight and rude to *everyone* that Greta had never seen her have a companionable cup of anything with anyone.

Annika looked up at her entrance. "I boiled the kettle for you, in case you wanted tea. It should still be warm. And dinner is keeping warm in the oven."

"Thank you, Annika," Greta said, divesting herself of her coat. "Are the others in bed already?"

Domizio nodded. "It was a long day for everyone. With the trial going on, Signora Loyola wasn't the only one asking whether you use alchemically-dyed material."

Greta sighed. Such a lot of trouble over something she'd never meddled in herself.

She felt the teapot – it was still warm enough. Going through her usual motions, Greta made herself a pot of tea and brought both pot and a cup to the table before fetching her dinner out of the oven.

She sat down to eat the roast vegetables and sea bream.

"Who made this?" she asked. "It's delicious."

Annika grinned. "I made it, but Domizio helped me. Who knew he was skilled with more than just a needle?"

Greta smiled and looked fondly at Domizio. He was skilled at more than Annika would ever know. Annika, more perceptive than Greta gave her credit for, looked between her and Domizio and stood up from the table. She quickly washed her cup and bid them both goodnight. Greta waved at her as Domizio nodded in her direction. They waited for her footsteps to recede up the stairs before discussing anything further.

"So, tell me, how did you really get on without me?" Greta asked, not certain she'd been told the whole truth.

Domizio slid closer to her. "You've got a good lot of apprentices, Greta. They would've been fine, even without me here today. They're loyal to you, to a fault. You must know that."

Greta shrugged demurely. She knew her girls looked up to her, even Annika now, but that was normal for maestri and apprentices. After all, that's how it had been with her and Ranieri.

"No, Greta, you don't understand." Domizio shook his head. "I've been in a lot of workshops, hiring out my services to any Sarti who need help. Most have a decent working relationship with their apprentices, even sometimes a modicum of respect, but what your girls give you – what they get from you – it's rare. Don't take it for granted."

Greta frowned. "I don't take them for granted anymore. Nor you. I don't take *you* for granted."

That earned her a glowing lopsided smile and Domizio slid even closer to her. Greta bit her lip in anticipation of their evening recreation. But first, there was food and tea. She wasn't going to allow every evening pot of tea to go cold to satisfy another hunger. With precision and care, she poured herself a cup of tea and sipped at it as Domizio ran his hand up her back. Even through the material, she could still feel the heat of his touch. It sent pleasant shivers down her spine.

"Mizi," she murmured as he kissed the side of her neck, "do you know the *special circumstances* around Great Works?"

Not every Guild Member found out about the patent fees until their Silver, or even Electrum Guild Mark if their Great Works weren't popular enough to be used by others.

"Just that they earn you Guild Marks. What else is there to know about them?" he answered, planting small kisses down her neck and along her shoulder.

Greta ate her dinner and took another sip of her tea, not certain whether she should tell him. Perhaps it was best to wait until things were resolved one way or the other tomorrow morning. It seemed the patent fee was more secret than she'd realised. Perhaps it shouldn't be. It would make Sarti, and other Guild members for that matter, work harder for their first Guild Mark, so they could earn enough off it to purchase their own workshop sooner.

Once his lips were inhibited by the neckline of her dress, Domizio pulled gently at the material. It only gave way so much. Gently, but deliberately, he took the cup from Greta's hands and drew her to her feet.

"Let's go upstairs," he suggested in a low voice. "I've had you on my mind for days now. I don't think I can take this much longer."

Greta bit her lip and pushed herself up against him. "But I want my tea."

"And I want *you*," he growled softly, kissing her firmly on the lips. Greta tasted the cocoa on his tongue that he'd just finished drinking. It didn't go well with her tea. There was no point drinking any more of it now that she had a sweeter taste in her mouth.

"Take me then," she told him. "But don't you dare ruin my dress!"

Domizio grinned at her with lustful eyes. He took her by the hand, led her up the stairs and into her room. There, he lit a glass lantern and turned around to kiss her again. Greta almost regretted the fact that she'd chosen a less cumbersome outfit today than she'd worn a few days ago. Almost. Domizio was still taking his time, a kiss for every button, each slightly lower than the last. The suspense of it almost drove Greta to distraction.

By the time he reached her corset Greta was helping him along by pulling loose the laces as he continued with the buttons.

At some point she realised Domizio would be fully clothed by the time she was naked and decided to rectify that. He didn't object, nor did he help her. He continued his mission to de-robe her as slowly and with as many kisses as he could. Greta sighed in delight. This was definitely worth waiting for.

# Chapter 12 – Ramedi 3 Inventrici 230 Years After Implosion

The next morning, Greta woke early. Domizio lay tangled in her sheets. It was quite the sight. She was glad of her initial decision to bed him, but it was looking increasingly likely that it would lead to unwanted attachments later.

It happened, though most men took it better than Ludovico. With Domizio, it could be worse – there appeared to be a genuine sense of attachment from him. She couldn't deny that she was also growing attached to him. Well, it would be fine while they were working together. Perhaps she could end it after that.

It was a sobering thought. Was she any better than her sister, really, if that's how she viewed him? The main difference between them was that her sister's lovers lasted two nights at the most and were not few and far between. Greta's tended to last at least a few weeks or months, but she would not then fall into another man's arms for months or even a year afterwards. Did that make so much of a difference?

Domizio opened his eyes and saw her staring at him.

"That's a very pensive frown for so early in the morning," he teased her.

She smiled to distract him and leaned down for a kiss. He pulled her down on top of him, trying to untangle himself from the sheets at the same time. Greta let him kiss her for longer than she should have. It had been such a long time since she'd found so dedicated a lover. He did everything he could to please her, and she showed her gratitude as well as she could. But she didn't have time this morning. It seemed she didn't have time *any* morning these days.

"I've got an early meeting," she told him, coming up for air from a lengthy and knee-quivering kiss.

He rolled her off him and lay atop her, trying to kiss every inch of her. Greta closed her eyes and let him. The meeting was at half past seven. It couldn't be later than half past six now. What harm would there be in enjoying another few minutes with him?

A few minutes turned into much longer. Greta heard the Guild Hall clocks strike seven o'clock and realised she really was going to run late if she didn't hurry. With a last kiss, she tore herself away from him, dressed herself in the simplest dress she owned, fastened on her leather work corset, and combed through the tangles in her curly hair. Her nightly activities were making her morning routine more cumbersome than usual – not that she was complaining.

Thankfully, Domizio stayed out of her way as she made herself presentable for the day. He pulled on his own clothes and shoes, ran a comb through his annoyingly tangle-free hair and was ready – in a fraction of the time it took Greta! She knew she had only herself to blame for her tardiness and difficulty in getting ready. After all, she was a talented Sarta. If she wanted simpler clothing, she had but to make it for herself.

Her kitchen clock showed ten past seven. Greta grimaced. Aveline was right – she should really get her own blazermobile. It would make it so much quicker for her to get around Tor'Esint.

She took the piece of buttered toast Sofia handed to her, and a quick sip of the tea Annika had prepared.

"I've got a meeting this morning at half past seven with the Sarti Maestri. With any luck, I'll be in the workshop most of today. I'll have to visit the warehouse district again, but I might leave that until later tonight. Otherwise, I don't know when in Caldera's smoke I'm going to ever get around to working on Signora Loyola's gown. Annika, you're in charge until I return. Sofia is to continue the beading. I need you and Marta to finish edging that skirt for me this morning otherwise I really will start to run late. If you've time after that, back to mending."

She took a long sip of her tea and started on her toasted bread as she walked out into the shopfront to get her coat. The clock struck a quarter past seven. She would have to hurry now.

Greta walked as quickly as her tired legs could take her towards the Sarti Guild Hall. At a leisurely pace, it usually took fifteen minutes. As she didn't wish to arrive just on time, she walked faster, until she feared people would think she was actually running on the streets.

On Corso delle Gilde she met Agata.

"Cutting it a bit fine, aren't you?" Agata asked with a smirk. "Did Domizio keep you up too late last night?"

"No." Greta blushed despite herself.

"Oh, then he occupied you for too long this morning, did he?"

Greta gritted her teeth but did not break her stride. "Do you think Ludovico invited the other Gold Sarti as I requested?"

Agata shrugged. Her stride was longer than Greta's – she didn't struggle to keep pace with her.

"With Ranieri dead, there's only four of us. If Erico and Amelia aren't here this morning, we can easily tell them ourselves what the issue at hand is. Which reminds me, what exactly *is* the issue?"

Greta shook her head. They were only a few piedi away from their Guild Hall now. She didn't dare to speak of it out on the street. Few people knew about patent fees in the first place. It was the best kept Guild secret in Tor'Esint.

They quickly ascended the steps and banged on the large wooden door until Ludovico opened it. He scowled at the sight of Greta but stood aside to let both her and Agata in.

"Are Enrico and Amelia joining us?" Greta asked once they door had closed behind them.

"Not everyone is as free with their time as you are," Ludovico sneered. "Some are busy fulfilling orders. Perhaps your workshops don't have any."

Greta didn't rise to the bait, neither did Agata. It was such a ridiculous comment. He knew they were two of the busiest and skilled Sarti in Tor'Esint. And there were only four Gold Sarti after all.

"Fine then, take us to see the Maestri," Greta ordered him.

Technically, Ludovico was beneath her in Guild rank and he was forced to obey her. By the look on his face, he knew it too. Without a word, he spun on his heel and walked down the Hall of Great Works, clearly expecting them to follow.

The Maestri kept council on the second level of the Guild Hall. They all lived here. They must have workshops somewhere, Greta reasoned, or they wouldn't be able to maintain a comfortable lifestyle.

She amended that thought. Perhaps their patent fees paid enough for them not to work anymore. Perhaps Maestri had to give up being working Sarti. It suddenly made sense to her why Ranieri had never became a Guild Maestro. He loved his trade too much, as was evidenced by his latest creation. He would never have given it up.

Halfway down a long hallway, Ludovico paused and knocked at a wooden door.

"Enter," said a voice.

Ludovico opened the door and escorted Greta and Agata inside. The three Sarti Guild Maestri, Carlo, Michele, and Rosa, were seated and waiting. Ranieri's testament was open on the table in front of them.

"Leave us, Ludovico," Carlo said.

Ludovico shot Greta a murderous look as he turned to leave the room. Greta tried not to roll her eyes at how childishly he was behaving. Honestly, she wouldn't care one bit if he were to bed another woman. She'd be surprised if he hadn't by now. He was a needy lover – she doubted he would last long without finding someone to warm his bed at least a few times a week.

It was one of the reasons she'd stopped bedding him herself. She didn't like the assumption that because they had bedded twice, it was his right to request access to her any time he liked. His hand on the small of her back in public, the way he stood too close to her, all of it felt suffocating and possessive. She was not *his* nor would she ever be.

She belatedly realised that the Maestri had asked her and Agata to sit. The chair closest Michele was still free, so Greta sat there.

"We've read Ranieri Sarto's Final Testament in minute detail," Carlo told her. "We understand that Ludovico has already given you the keys to the properties and transferred Ranieri's funds into your Guild account."

Greta nodded.

"Very well. We'll need you to sign a transfer deed to complete the transaction. We understand you now own two warehouses and two workshops – the warehouses, we will let be as they are adjacent to one another and we've no doubt Ranieri managed to link them somehow.

"As to the matter of the workshops – you don't need two. No Sarta does. Ranieri's workshop is bigger than yours by far. If you'd prefer to relocate yourself there, we take no issue with that. As specified in the testament, however, we will repossess the unwanted workshop and allow another Sarta to purchase or rent it. They're both in good locations in Piazza Mercantile and any Sarta would be lucky to have either."

Greta sat still, taking in everything. She hadn't really expected to be granted the choice of one workshop or the other. Ranieri's will stated that the Sarti Guild could sell or rent one whichever she didn't want, but she'd assumed the Maestri would pick one for her.

"May I," she coughed. "May I have a moment to think about that?"

Carlo smiled kindly. "You may have two days. It's a big decision and if you move, it will be cumbersome. We don't want to force your decision one way or the other, but specialised Sarta workshops are rare, and we'd like to free one up for purchase."

Greta smiled gratefully. She hadn't been in many meetings with the Maestri and was surprised by their kindness.

"What's the other issue?" Agata asked gruffly. "I'm sure Greta didn't ask me here to help her with the decision of which workshop to keep. We should all be so lucky!"

The Maestri exchanged glances with one another then all eyes turned on Greta.

"I thought it important that the Gold Sarti were present for this discussion, though it seems Ludovico didn't agree with me on that matter."

Rosa raised her eyebrows. "That would've made things easier, I must say. We'll just have to inform them of our decision posthaste."

"Have you made a decision then?" asked Greta, hating the fact that her voice was trembling.

It was so important. Whatever decision the Maestri made here could potentially be enacted in every other Guild or kept a Sarti secret to make their members richer or poorer.

"We're in disagreement over the matter," Michele stated. "I'm against it, Carlo is for it and Rosa insists on abstaining."

Greta looked from one to the other of them. "Well, where does that leave us?"

"At an impasse," Michele replied sourly.

Agata stomped her foot on the carpeted floor. "Would someone *please* tell me what this is all about?"

"Ranieri left everything to Greta," Michele began.

"That's no surprise to anyone," Agata interrupted, throwing her hands in the air. Michele stared her into silence.

"*Everything* including his ongoing patent fees," Michele explained. "His patent fees were quite substantial, as I'm sure you would've surmised had you ever bothered to look at his submissions in the Hall of Great Works. The question at hand is whether he had the right to give his ongoing patent fees to anyone or whether they should discontinue on his death as everyone's always has."

Greta looked over to Agata. She'd gone very still.

"Is there a law against it?" she asked in an oddly neutral voice.

"No," replied Carlo, "which is why I'm in favour of it."

"It's unfair to everyone else whose Maestro has died," Michele interjected. "Any one of them could have been singled out for the honour Ranieri bestowed upon Greta."

It was a fair point. Agata was at least ten years Greta's senior. Her Maestro must be dead by now too. Would he have left Agata his patent fees if he'd thought about it?

"Maestra Rosa, why do you abstain?" Agata asked.

Greta was glad for her fellow Sarta's confidence – she'd never have asked the question herself.

"I think it too complicated a matter," Rosa replied carefully. "If we agree to this, we set a precedent and all Sarti will choose their favourite apprentice to bestow this honour on. That's all well and good, and may even encourage apprentices to be more respectful, but what happens when *they* die? Can they pass on their own patent fees as well as the patent fees they inherited? It could go on forever, creating a massive divide between the wealthy and poor Sarti.

"Not only that, but if the other Guilds get wind of what we've allowed, would they then allow the same thing, thereby creating such a divide in their own Guilds? The rift in Tor'Esint could become even worse than that which the Mercantili Guild have created."

The other Maestri scoffed at her last comment. It was unimaginable that anything could cause a greater rift the Mercantili Guild's Trading and Inter-Guild Edicts.

"May I ask a question?" Greta said timidly. Carlo gestured for her to go ahead. Greta smoothed her skirt over her knees. "Imagine an apprentice puts forward a Copper Great Work that is so fantastic that it earns ongoing patent fees. Is there a time limit for how long they would receive those patent fees, or do they go on until that person dies?"

The Maestri looked at one another, a shrug here, a cocked eyebrow there.

"I'll presume every Sarta earns their own patent fees until their death. If we assume a death age of perhaps eighty, with a minimum age of twenty to submit a Great Work, that could potentially be sixty years of patent fees. So, why not put a year limit on it, no matter whether the patent fee is passed on or not?"

Silence greeted her suggestion. Greta couldn't tell if that was good or bad. She'd obviously suggested something they hadn't thought of themselves.

Agata shook her head. "No, sixty years is ridiculous. What if Ranieri had died when he was ninety instead of sixty-one? Then even if he passed his patent fees on to you, you'd never receive a single coin. Or what if he died when he was fifty instead? Then you'd get his patent fees for another thirty years.

"No. The only way to make it fair is to allow the patent fees to be passed on to someone, but with a defined timespan after the original patent-holder's death, say twenty years. Then you'd get Ranieri's patent fees for twenty years after his death. Only if you die in those twenty years could you pass on the patent fees to someone else, but then they'd only get the remainder of those twenty years."

Greta stared at Agata in awe. It wasn't just a clever idea – it was a *brilliant* idea. There was just one flaw.

"What about the Maestri who died before now and never got a chance to pass on their patent fees to anyone?" Greta asked.

Rosa tapped her fingernails on the arm of her chair. "We do a secret ballot. Everyone whose Maestro has died in the past ten years can come together to vote on who they think would have received the patent fees if there'd been the option in a Final Testament. The only rule would be that they cannot vote for themselves, or we'll never get anywhere with this. I think the only exception to this would be if there was a family left behind – then the family would be part of the secret ballot. After all, one would assume they also know about the patent fees."

Greta frowned. "Does that mean you've changed your vote?"

Rosa smiled. "Indeed. I vote *for* the passing on of patent fees. We shall discuss the timespan today and come to a conclusion by the time we're ready for the secret ballots. I'd ask both of you not to mention this to anyone. We wouldn't want any bribery around the secret ballots to ensure one winner over another."

Greta sat back in her chair, in a daze. She was already wealthy beyond her imagining. This would tip her over the edge of reason. She could afford to purchase a blazermobile and hire as many Copper or even Silver Sarti as she required for her workshop.

"May I ask one more question," she said in a voice barely above a whisper. "Theoretically, can a Gold Sarta submit a Great Work?"

"Why?" asked Michele sharply.

Greta risked a glance at Agata. She only shrugged at her.

"What if you have something truly amazing that would bring in even more patent fees, but you've already obtained your Gold Guild Mark? Can you submit another Great Work or are you limited to four?"

"Do you have such a thing?" Carlo asked curiously.

"Not at this moment," Greta replied uneasily. "But I'm still young. It's possible that I could create any number of Great Works in my trade life. Am I limited to four Great Works, or can I submit more?"

The Maestri looked at each other uncertainly.

"Why don't you leave that matter with us? We'll discuss that while we figure out the legalities of the patent fee issue. We'll have everything ready by Legaramedi which, don't forget, is how long you have to decide which workshop you want to keep."

Greta nodded uncomfortably. It wasn't something she wanted to think about. Not now. Not with everything going on. Not with all the work she had to complete. But now she had no other option. Perhaps the girls could help her with the decision.

Greta rose, along with Agata and the Maestri. Their meeting was at an end. With any luck, she and Agata would get a decent amount of work done today. She wasn't certain about her fellow Sarta, but Greta knew she needed a quiet working day.

\*\*\*

Before the day's trading began, Greta was back in her workshop. With barely a greeting to her household, she went straight to Signora Loyola's dress. The skirt was on her workbench, edged and ready for her to work on. Sofia was still beading the bodice. It would take her at least another day or two to complete.

Greta began on hemming the side of the skirt for the zipper and focused on her work all day, only stopping for food and tea when Sofia coaxed her out of the workshop.

It was just after trading when she finished work for the day. Much as she would've loved to continue with the dress, there were more pressing matters at hand. She called the girls and Domizio into the kitchen for a discussion.

"I know it's been a difficult week for all of us. Ranieri's death, the Alchimisti trial – everything has been thrown into chaos. With any luck, it will eventually slow down again and become somewhat normal. We just have *one* more decision to make this week."

"We?" asked Sofia. "How can we help?"

Greta smiled. Yes, Sofia was almost certainly the one she would leave everything to in her testament.

"I'm glad you asked." Greta smoothed her skirt. "I don't know what I've told you and what I haven't, so let me tell you everything."

She explained in as much detail as she dared about Ranieri's testament, only leaving out the issue of his patent fees. Her apprentices would learn about that in good time and Domizio ... well, it wasn't her place to tell him. Most Sarti found out by their Silver Guild Mark. There was an unwritten rule that the issue of patent fees was not to be discussed with those who didn't already know about them.

"All that remains is for me to decide which workshop I prefer. And for that, I'd like your help. I ... am very familiar with Ranieri's workshop, but it isn't my home anymore and it's never been *your* home. I don't want the hassle of switching workshops if no one thinks it's a good idea."

Domizio coughed. "Do *you* think it's a good idea?"

Greta paused. She'd barely allowed herself think about it.

"It's a larger workshop with larger living quarters above it. It's set up in a different way, one which is very efficient but could never work in this smaller space. Both workshops are in Piazza Mercantile – Ranieri's is on the opposite side, closer to the north end of Via Mercante.

"Can we see it?" Annika asked.

"Ooh yes! Can we?" Marta asked excitedly. "We could go there now, couldn't we?"

Greta bit her lip then nodded. "Get your coats then. I'll take you to the workshop and then we can all go out for dinner. My treat."

Domizio bowed his head and retreated a little.

"You too, Mizi," she told him. "You'll be working with us for as long as we need you, so don't you think you're getting out of this."

He grinned at her and joined the girls in getting a coat. With another qualified Sarto in her household, Greta was starting to feel like she didn't have too many apprentices anymore. It was an unexpected advantage.

Greta donned her own coat and met her household on the street. Domizio offered her his arm and she took it gratefully. The girls linked arms with each other and followed behind them. Greta walked along the shopfronts and paused at Aveline's workshop.

The blazermobile wasn't parked at the front. Greta resolved to pass by on her way home and beg a delay of borrowing the blazermobile until tomorrow.

She led her companions through Piazza Mercantile, past Via dell'Oro all the way to Via Corallo. Corner shops were quite sought after, especially those in the Piazza. Aside from the discomfort of being in her dead Maestro's house, she was finding fewer and fewer reasons not to take it. Her last obstacle was if any of her apprentices strongly objected to the move.

Greta stopped outside the door. Unlike most shops, the door was not in the middle of a wall, but on the corner of the house with large windows on each streetfront. She unlocked the door and pushed it open. She didn't have a chance to hesitate. The girls swept in from behind her and opened all the blinds to let in as much evening light as they could.

They gushed over the size of the shop and called each other over to look at every interesting item they found. Greta couldn't help but smile. Their enthusiasm and noise muffled the memories trying to engulf her.

"Shall we?" Domizio asked, gently pulling her arm forward as he stepped towards the threshold.

Greta took a deep breath and stepped over the threshold. It almost felt like home again with her own household inside.

"There are friction lights in that drawer if you want to look around a bit more. The bedrooms, water closet and kitchen are all upstairs."

"But there's a kitchen here," Marta pointed out. "Look, behind this door, there's a sink, a bench and stove, and a small table."

Greta almost laughed at her simple expectations. "That was just because of Ranieri's fondness for tea. The *proper* kitchen is upstairs."

The girls squealed in delight and took a friction light each, leaving just one for Greta and Domizio to share. Greta wound it up and set it on the table, knowing it would provide light for about five minutes before she had to wind it up again.

"What do you think?" she asked, gesturing around the room.

Domizio shrugged. "There's no question it's a better workshop, and a larger house. It's even in a slightly better location. But we knew all of that before you brought us here. The question is will *you* feel comfortable here?"

Greta bit her lip. "I don't know. It feels strange, but better with the girls."

"Let me phrase it another way then. Weeks or years down the track, would you regret it if you let someone else have this workshop? If it was one of Agata's old apprentices perhaps."

Greta instantly shook her head. "I don't want any of them to have this workshop."

"Then I think you have your answer," Domizio pointed out. "You've made your own workshop function admirably for its size, but this will be so much better for you, for the increased business of a Gold Sarta with Signora Loyola's recommendation and Ranieri Sarto's clientele."

Greta huffed in embarrassment. "I don't have her recommendation yet."

"From what I've seen, it won't be long in coming."

Greta blushed, glad that Domizio couldn't see it in the darkness. He was right and she knew it. There was no false flattery there.

"This workshop is also better suited to having more qualified Sarti working for you. I drew up a list of names for you today." He passed her a small piece of paper. "These are the Copper and Silver Sarti I know who will work for a daily fee. I've made a mark next to those who I think will suit you best, but I'm not certain how many you want or can afford."

Greta tried not to laugh. She could now afford to hire every Copper Sarta in Tor'Esint if she chose, but she wasn't going to tell Domizio that. Some people had *interesting* opinions about money. She didn't want his opinion of her to change, nor his amorous feelings to become more ambitious than genuine. Greta took the slip of paper and tucked it in her pocket.

A few minutes later, the girls came thundering down the stairs and almost ran straight into Greta.

"Oh Maestra, it's wonderful!" Sofia exclaimed excitedly. "Could we really live here if you say so?"

Greta nodded. "I have until Legaramedi to make a decision. But if we decide to take it, the Guild will allow us more time for the move."

"I'd take it if I were you," said Annika in a matter-of-fact tone. "I won't feel like I'm constantly stepping on someone else's toes here."

"Yes, there's so much space! *Four* bedrooms! *Four*!" Marta squealed in delight.

Greta shook her head. "Don't get too excited, Marta. I haven't made a decision yet."

"Why not?" asked Annika, a little of her former insensitivity showing.

Sofia elbowed her. "Imagine going back to live in your family household but your parents aren't there anymore."

"This wasn't her family household," Annika replied in a quieter voice.

"You're right," Greta told her. "It *wasn't* my family household, but I lived here for almost as long as I lived at home. It's the same thing, really."

Annika's mouth formed an O of understanding. Marta raised her hand timidly.

"I know it might feel strange, but it really does seem the better place. What do *you* think, Maestra?"

Greta found herself nodding without meaning to. "It *is* the better place. And it doesn't feel quite so strange with the three of you here."

"So?" all three girls asked in pleading unison.

Domizio laughed and Greta joined in.

"I suppose that settles the matter. I'll take this workshop instead. Mind you, it won't happen overnight. There'll be things to sort out with the Guild and everything has to be packed to move. I don't even want to think about that tonight. Now, let's go to dinner before you collapse from hunger."

She shooed them out of the workshop and took a long look around the large room before closing and locking the door. It was absurdly strange to think that she would be living there again. Would she be a better Maestra in this workshop? Would her girls be happier in this house? Would *she* be happier in this house? She'd always felt confident here, but that was probably more because of Ranieri than anything else. She'd have to build her own confidence and keep it for herself.

Greta turned to see the girls eyeing the restaurants in Piazza Mercantile with their tables spilling out into the square. It wasn't often she took them out for dinner. It would be a treat for all of them.

The next afternoon, Greta set out for Aveline's house just after trading finished, determined to reach the Inventrice before she disappeared again. She stepped lightly into Aveline's workshop. Both Nevio and Aveline looked up at her entrance. Aveline looked more worn than the day of the Alchimisti trial.

"Veli, you look like you need more rest," Greta pointed out none too gently.

Aveline shook her head and looked back at her workbench covered in metal parts. "I'm still an Inventrice, Reta," she pointed out. "I still have orders to fulfil and new inventions to create. I wouldn't be worth my Electrum Guild Mark otherwise, would I?"

Greta shrugged in reply. One reason she didn't want an actual family herself was that she didn't want childbearing and rearing to interfere with her work. Even though she could probably afford never to work another day in her life, she couldn't imagine the thought of never creating another gown or suit again. It was unfathomable.

"Do you want to come for a ride to the warehouse district or are you happy for me to drive your blazermobile myself?"

It was a loaded question, and she knew it. Aveline was very possessive of her blazermobile and only let Greta drive it herself when she really was not at liberty to be a chauffeur.

"I'll drive under the condition that we pass by Lucrezia's on the way back to order one for yourself," Aveline said firmly.

"Fine," sighed Greta. She'd already resolved to order a blazermobile, but having Aveline along for that conversation would hopefully lower the price or speed the process. Greta was under no illusions about her own relationship with Lucrezia, especially after the alchemically-dyed material incident.

"Wait, is she back home again?"

"Yes. They let her go directly after the hearing. The Alchimisti Guild had nothing to hold against her. She's extremely careful with everything she does."

There was an edge to Aveline's voice that Greta couldn't quite place. She knew something that Greta didn't. Well, Greta knew better than to ask. Some secrets were better kept than told. Before they left for Lucrezia's workshop, Greta returned home quickly to retrieve her empty bottles of contraceptive solution. She'd need Lucrezia to fill them today if she planned to spend any more time with Domizio.

***

Out at her warehouse, Greta opened the ceiling panels to let in the afternoon light. Aveline pointed out all the boxes and bolts of material she and Agata had shifted from Ranieri's warehouse. There was surprisingly less contraband material than she'd thought there'd be. But none of that interested her right now. All she wanted to see was this new invention. If Agata had ascertained its use correctly, then Greta could be sitting on another goldmine.

"It's over here," said Aveline, pointing to a large device covered by a thick white cloth. Together, they unveiled the device. Greta gazed at it from every angle. It seemed like an ordinary table with a metal contraption on top, but at a closer examination, it was connected. The table was like a regular workbench with a metal ruler along one edge.

Part of the table edged out further than the legs and drawers beneath it. This section looked like it was collapsible for smaller projects. The drawers were small, but the perfect size for spools of thread, needles, buttons, and other little items needed for sewing.

The base of the table was all metal. It had a panel underneath that looked like it would move up and down with foot pressure. Greta pulled up a chair and sat at the table. She placed her foot on the panel and pushed. To her surprise, the needle on the top contraption went down as she pushed with her toe and went up when she pushed with her heel.

"This is extraordinary!" she cried. "Do you know how it works?"

Aveline was already studying it. She moved wheels and levers on the top contraption, testing out theories. Greta had never really watched Aveline at work. She knew her friend was more than competent, but she'd never seen her try to figure out someone else's invention.

"You can see the thread goes here," Aveline said, pointing to a wheel on the side of the sewing machine. "Then when you use the pedal there, it rolls the thread onto this tube. It looks like you put the tube here, where the needle is, and another here underneath this trapdoor. Then up here, you put a normal spool of thread and take the thread through all these loops and hooks down to the needle."

Greta listened as she explained it. "None of that makes sense. Why would I need *three* threads to sew something?"

Aveline shrugged. "You're the Sarta, not me. I didn't invent this. I'm just telling you what I can see. We won't really know how it works until you ask the Inventrice responsible."

"Who invented it?" she asked impatiently.

"I don't know, Reta!" Aveline threw her hands up in the air. "There's dozens of Inventrici in Tor'Esint, if he even used one here."

Greta bit her sharp retort. Perhaps inventing wasn't like sewing. Greta could tell who had made each dress by the style and how it was sewn. But then, there were only four Gold Sarti in Tor'Esint. She'd watched them carefully throughout their careers. She knew all their sewing traits as she was certain they knew hers.

"How many Inventrici are there in Tor'Esint, Gold and Electrum?"

Aveline counted them out on her fingers as she named them quietly to herself. "There's six Gold Inventrici and I think twelve Electrum Inventrici now, including me and Chide."

Greta nodded. Eighteen to sort through then. "Would any Silver Inventrici be capable of this?"

Aveline shook her head slowly. "If they could make something like this, they wouldn't still be on their Silver Guild Mark."

"Do you recognise anything at all about the workmanship?" Greta asked. "Eighteen Inventrici is a lot to get through to find the right one.

Aveline looked at the machine carefully again and bit her lip in frustration.

"Reta, I only just became an Electrum Inventrice a few months ago. The Gold Inventrici barely deigned to speak to me when I was still on my Silver Guild Mark. I'm good friends with some of the other Electrum Inventrici, but I only really know one Gold Inventore – my old Maestro, Giacomo. And there's Telchide's Maestro, Ugo, but I don't know if they're still in contact."

Greta stood up and paced back and forth. This sewing machine could be quite a windfall if she could figure out how to use it properly. But how could she ask any of the Inventrici about it without being accused of inter-Guild relations?

She stopped pacing and looked at Aveline speculatively. Aveline's eyes grew wide. "No. Not now, Greta."

"But you're in a *much* better position than I am to be asking these questions," she reasoned. "If I go asking around and the Mercantili Guild finds out, they'll lock me up for inter-Guild relations. After all that's happened this week, I'm sure they're itching for a reason to incarcerate me."

"And if *I* go asking around about it, I'll give every Inventrice in the city the idea of creating a machine that sews automatically," Aveline retorted. "Then when I finally get to the Inventrice of *this* machine, they'll want to strangle me for giving their idea out to all the Inventrici in Tor'Esint."

Greta paused. She had a point there.

"Can you at least ask if any of them had anything to do with Ranieri? If there were any secret projects going on? You don't need to mention what it was."

Aveline sighed. "I'll see what I can do. In the meantime, I suggest you try to figure it out on your own. Now, let's get you to Lucrezia's and order you a blazermobile so I don't need to escort you around Tor'Esint every other day."

\*\*\*

They arrived at Lucrezia's shop at sunset. A sign on the door indicated it was still open for trading, though only emergencies would bother her at this time of the evening. Greta reflected that put her and Aveline squarely out of their minds.

Aveline didn't even bother knocking on the door before pushing it open and walking in. Greta followed in her wake. She was getting more than just an inkling that Lucrezia and Aveline were something other than mere professional acquaintances.

"Agnese, be a dear and find Lucrezia for me. My friend here needs to order a blazermobile."

The apprentice's eyes lit up at the mention of a blazermobile. She bobbed her head and quickly fled the room only to return moments later with Lucrezia herself. Greta nodded awkwardly as Lucrezia's eyes bore into her.

"Right, Agnese, tell the others you can all have the night off. You deserve it after the week we've had. Take three coppers each from the till."

"Yes, Maestra!" Agnese said happily and went to find the other apprentices.

Lucrezia motioned for Aveline and Greta to sit in the waiting chairs until the workshop was empty. It took all of five minutes. The apprentices insisted on getting dressed up for the occasion, while the hired Copper Alchimisti hurried them on. They exited in a flurry of excitement, leaving the room in complete silence.

Greta smoothed down her dress to fill the moments. Lucrezia continued to stare at her.

"For Caldera's sake, Lucrezia, it's not as if I told the Amministratori anything about your involvement. I told my Guild that you'd tested the material – that's all."

"Then you have a snitch in your Guild," Lucrezia surmised. "I'd get it seen to sooner rather than later."

Greta rolled her eyes. There wasn't really anything she could do about it right now.

"Crez, be kind. At least you didn't end up like Ardo," Aveline pointed out.

Lucrezia scoffed. "It's his own fault. He went in looking guilty. How could they ever have found him innocent?"

"Crez, be *kind!*" Aveline scolded her. "The same thing could've happened to you."

Lucrezia shook her head. "No, it couldn't. I'm more careful than Ardo, in *every* way."

There was a stormy silence between them. Greta did not try to understand what it was about. They both clearly knew something she didn't and if they weren't going to tell her, she wasn't courageous enough to ask. Instead, she cleared her throat.

"I'd like to order a blazermobile," Greta said, drawing the attention back to herself. "Aveline swears by your work, so I was hoping you can help me."

Lucrezia raised an eyebrow. "They're expensive, you know."

Greta narrowed her eyes. "If you hadn't heard, I've recently come into an inheritance, and I now have two properties in the warehouse district. I can't keep borrowing Aveline's blazermobile every time I need to tramp across town."

Lucrezia eyed her carefully. "Do you already have a carriage?"

Greta shook her head. So did Lucrezia.

"A brand new blazermobile will cost you one thousand gold pieces."

Greta choked on the spittle in her mouth and coughed loudly. She knew blazermobiles were expensive, but she hadn't been expecting quite so much.

"Too expensive for your taste?" Lucrezia asked jeeringly.

"Of course not," Greta replied angrily. "One thousand gold pieces, on delivery."

Aveline placed a hand on her arm, but Greta shook it off in annoyance. Why hadn't she bothered to ask how much it would cost in the first place? She could afford it, but that was a fifth of her inheritance from Ranieri. Was it really the best use of her money? Ranieri himself hadn't thought it worthwhile enough to purchase one.

"Crez, why do you always have to be like this?" Aveline said angrily. "Reta, it isn't a thousand gold pieces, it's only five hundred. Lucrezia is just being difficult."

Greta looked sideways at Aveline, then across as Lucrezia who stood, hands on hips with her head held high. The Alchimista sniffed and smiled cruelly.

"You put me through a lot of trouble. I *should* be charging you a thousand gold pieces."

"But ... you *won't*?" Greta asked, her voice oddly high pitched. She hated how desperate she sounded.

"No, I won't," she replied, rolling her eyes. "Five hundred will do."

Aveline rolled her eyes. "Lucrezia Alchimista, it's amazing you have any customers at all given your manner with them! I only hope your apprentices don't learn your arrogance alongside your skills."

"I should say the same for Chide's new apprentices," Lucrezia jibed. "Though they seem more affable than he is, so perhaps they'll teach him a thing or two."

Aveline bit her lip. Greta wondered if it was to stop herself insulting Lucrezia or because she knew what the Alchimista said about her lover was true.

"Have you told him about the baby yet?" Lucrezia asked.

"You're keeping it?" Greta asked in surprise.

Aveline nodded. "I told him last night."

"Did he renew his offer?" Greta asked before she could stop herself.

"Yes," Aveline said softly.

"And?" Lucrezia asked.

"Our problems haven't disappeared, Crez," Aveline replied sourly. "His dead companion's mother lives with him and that isn't going to change anytime soon."

"Foolish girl!" Lucrezia threw her hands up in the air. "He loves you, Veli. He had his companion declared dead and practically ruined Ardo's career all for *you*. He's willing to turn his entire life upside down to accommodate you. Why can't you see that?"

Aveline's eyes narrowed. "Why can't *you* see that I don't want to live with Serenita? You know what she did. You know it was *her* fault. I don't know how anyone could forgive her. It's difficult enough the times I'm forced to go there for work or other reasons. Can you imagine if I *lived* there?"

Greta followed the argument back and forth, trying to keep up.

"So, who will look after the child while you're working?" she asked. "You can't very well ask Nevio to do it."

Aveline shrugged. "I'll figure it out. But I *am* keeping it. Just because I can't figure out how to make things work with Serenita in the picture, doesn't mean I shouldn't have some modicum of happiness. And Teresina will be a wonderful big sister."

There was a long pause. It seemed even Lucrezia could think of nothing to say about Aveline's situation.

"Now, Greta, I think it's time we head back home. Lucrezia will doubtless inform you when your blazermobile is ready. She may be arrogant, and rude, but she makes the best blazer solution. Don't go to anyone else for it. Those liquids are highly unstable. It's not safe to trust just anyone with them."

Greta now had a sinking feeling about this entire endeavour. She hadn't known quite how dangerous blazer solution could be. She hoped she wasn't making a mistake, but blazermobiles were better than carriages and she needed *something*.

Before they left, Greta had Lucrezia restock her supply of contraceptive solution. She was certain to need it in coming days.

\*\*\*

Aveline drove Greta back to her workshop and promised to discretely ask around which Inventrice might have been working with Ranieri. Greta was going to bring the metal spool to a few of the Gold and Electrum Inventrici to see if any had seen it before. That could lead them to the creator of the sewing machine just as easily as Aveline's line of investigation.

They agreed to have tea on Mercatodi to discuss their findings. But for now, Greta was exhausted. All she wanted was to go inside, have a nice warm meal and fall asleep with Domizio's arms around her. She didn't care if that meant she was becoming too comfortable with him. It had been a trying week – she deserved all the comfort she could get. It would be foolish to push him away right now.

If she were truthful with herself, *that's* what she missed the most about Ranieri – the fact that he'd always been there for her, no matter what the problem was. And now ... well, now he wasn't. And he never would be again. True, Greta had her father and her sister, but they weren't even in the same town. She had friends, she had apprentices, but she'd lost the one person she felt she could always rely on.

She was no fool. Domizio would gladly be that person for her, but she didn't want him to be. She didn't like the idea of being tied down in such a way. She didn't want anyone expecting things of her. She didn't want to be anyone's companion – ever.

Domizio was waiting for her when she arrived. The girls, once again, had long since gone to sleep. It was just the two of them now. He sat her down at the kitchen table and warmed the leftovers of Sofia's soup on the stove. Sofia was a far better cook than Annika, but she would never point that out to the girls.

Greta sat quietly, watching Domizio's confident movements around the kitchen. He'd so quickly become accustomed to life in their little household. And he fit in so well. Without her requesting it, Domizio even made a pot of Greta's favourite tea – chamomile. He brought both the soup and the tea to the table and poured a cup of tea for himself as well.

He sat across from her with purpose. Greta knew there would be a *conversation* now. She didn't feel equal to the task, but Domizio had done so much for her lately that she felt she couldn't refuse this now.

"Have you had a chance to look at those names I gave you?" Domizio asked.

Greta had to stop and think what he was talking about. She stalled by taking a spoonful of the soup. He smiled at her deflection.

"The names of the Copper and Silver Sarti I think would work well with you."

"Oh, *those* names," Greta said slowly. "Erm no. I haven't. Sorry."

Domizio sighed. "Greta, I know you've been busy, and worried, but you need more help. Sofia's working steadily on your big order, but that will still take the better part of a week to finish properly.

"Annika and Marta are doing their best to get through all the repairs, but there's a lot of them. Especially with the extras from Ranieri's workshop. And then there's Ranieri's proper orders – I can't work on all of them alone. I need help. *We* need help."

Greta ate her soup as she listened to him. He was right but she simply hadn't had time to organise everything. And then there was the move to her new workshop to consider.

"Do you think they'd be willing to help me move everything from this workshop to Ranieri's?"

Domizio considered this for a moment. "As long as you pay them and promise to employ them as Sarti for a minimum of one or two weeks afterwards, I don't see why not."

Greta continued to eat her soup until the bowl was practically empty. She used a chunk of bread to mop up the remainder.

"I'll look over them tonight," Greta promised. "Tomorrow, I'll need to let the Maestri know I've chosen Ranieri's workshop over mine."

She frowned slightly at the idea.

"It's the right decision, Greta." Domizio covered her hand with his and squeezed it gently. "And I'll be here for you, whenever you need me. This isn't something you need to do alone. We're *all* here for you."

Greta's eyes prickled with the pressure of unshed tears. She retrieved her hand and sipped her tea slowly, hoping the steam would hide any trace of emotion on her face.

For the first time in days, Greta felt rested. She wasn't worried about the Alchimisti trial, or her own illicit goods being discovered. She wasn't concerned about Ranieri's apprentice abusing her girls or being a bad influence on them.

No. All she had to do today was tell the Sarti Guild Maestri of her decision to move to Ranieri's workshop, hire some new Sarti to help her, and work on finishing Signora Loyola's dress in time for her dinner party in two weeks.

Greta laughed at the thought. When Signora Loyola had come to order the dress and Greta had decided upon such an intricate design, that alone had made her fret. But the last few days had made her re-assess her life. Making a complicated dress was nothing in comparison with warehouse raids and bearing witness at a trial – and none of it compared to losing a most beloved friend and Maestro.

Before going downstairs, Greta sat at the small desk in her room and wrote a note to the Sarti Maestri. She didn't want to waste her time trying to get an appointment with them through Ludovico. That would be a needless worry. She sealed it with her own personal seal – the Sarti Guild Mark with a G for her name – with gold wax. Only four Sarti in Tor'Esint were allowed to seal their letters with gold wax. Ludovico wouldn't dare open it.

Domizio and her girls were already seated at the kitchen table, chatting easily with one another. Marta placed a bowl of cinnamon porridge at an empty seat for her. Greta placed the letter in the centre of the table and sat down to eat. Everyone stared at the letter.

"Is that what I think it is?" Sofia asked, not taking her eyes off the letter.

"If you think it's a letter to the Sarti Guild Maestri alerting them to my decision to take Ranieri's workshop and give them mine, then yes, it is."

The girls squealed in delighted, Sofia and Marta bouncing in their seats.

"Are you taking it to the Sarti Guild yourself, Maestra?" Annika asked.

"Actually, I'd really like to spend the entire day working on Signora Loyola's dress. Would one of you mind taking it for me?"

"I will!" Annika and Marta answered at the same time.

Greta laughed. At least Sofia hadn't also volunteered.

"Very well, you can both take the letter," she told them. "However, I want you to insist that you're not allow to place it in anyone else's hand but one of the Maestri themselves. Understand? Ludovico will try to take it from you and tell you they're too busy.

"Don't take no for an answer. You tell him you're willing to wait until they're not busy. If he really does make you wait, I want you to walk up and down the Hall of Great Works and look at all the submissions.

"When you return, I want you to tell me which you think is the most important Great Work and why. Don't forget, one day you'll need to submit a Great Work of your own to earn your Copper Guild Mark, and every Guild Mark after that."

She watched their reactions carefully. Both nodded, Marta more eagerly, but Annika's reaction was the more impressive. A few weeks ago, she'd have sneered at the idea of doing any sort of work while out of the workshop. Now, she seemed more than a little interested in the task.

With the promised excitement of going to the Sarti Guild Hall, Marta and Annika finished eating quickly, washed their bowls and took everyone else's bowls almost before they were finished.

Greta sent Sofia ahead into the workshop to continue her cotton dress. She wanted to discuss the list of Copper and Silver Sarti with Domizio. Before going to bed last night, she'd rummaged around in her pockets to find the list he'd given her. She didn't recognise any of the names on it. She should have taken more of an interest in the younger Sarti, but there were simply too many of them.

"I don't know anyone on your list," she said, pulling the paper out of her pocket and placing it on the table. "Who would you recommend? I think we could do with another three Sarti to start with. If we need more, we can always hire more. And I don't think it's fair to only employ them for a week. If they work well with us, I'd want them to stay for at least a month."

Domizio twisted his lips sideways. "If you plan on keeping them that long, perhaps a trial day would be in order. Ask them to come for a day, when you'll pay them for their time, give them a few different tasks so you can assess their skills and see how they'll fit in with the girls. If you like them, you can extend the contract for a month. If not, you can pay them for the day and thank them for their time and be done with it."

Greta stared at Domizio with newfound respect. She wouldn't have thought of that herself, at least not until she had tried and failed in hiring a few Sarti who didn't work out. He laughed at her expression.

"I told you, Greta, I've hired out my services many times before. The more successful Sarti always give me three tasks before I start working for them. Different tasks, depending on what they think they'll need me for, but three tasks nonetheless."

She kissed him lightly on the cheek. "Thank you, Mizi. In that case, choose the three you think will work the best and invite them one day after the other, starting tomorrow if possible."

"You have *no* preferences?" he asked in surprise.

Greta shook her head, then stopped. "Actually, yes. I don't want all of them to be male or all of them to be female. I want my girls and my customers to know that anyone can be a Sarta, no matter what their gender."

"And *that's* why you only have female apprentices." Domizio nodded knowingly.

Greta elbowed him gently. "I only have female apprentices because Annika was at the top of the list to start with, and I didn't want any teenage dalliances to worry about under my own roof. I had enough trouble..."

She broke off and went silent. Domizio didn't need to know about her sister. Her sister had moved away and built herself a new reputation in Tor'Selit. Thankfully, Domizio didn't press her on the matter.

"I'll ask Nicolina first," he said easily. "I've worked with her before. She's very capable and I think you'll like her. She's a Copper Sarta but has a lot of experience."

"Then why is she still a Copper Sarta?" Greta asked warily.

Domizio laughed at her naivety. "Greta, really, I've tried to explain – not all Copper Sarti have the time and resources to create another Great Work while they struggle to make ends meet. We weren't all so lucky to have Ranieri as our Maestro. Some of us were kicked out of the workshop as soon as we gained our Copper Guild Mark. Our Maestri would rather take in a new apprentice for the free labour rather than keep a moderately skilled one and start paying them."

"Oh." Greta didn't know what to say. It hadn't occurred to her that other Sarti didn't work the same way as Ranieri. Teodoro would've worked better with one of those Sarti than Ranieri. He didn't deserve her old mentor for his own.

Greta couldn't believe how much it stung her to know that Ranieri had taken in such an ungrateful lump of a boy. True, she had Annika, but they'd turned that situation around. Annika was a golden child compared to Teodoro.

She smoothed down her skirt. There was no point getting angry over that boy. He wasn't worth her time or energy.

"Right then, Nicolina. I'll write a letter to her now. Could you please deliver it to her before you start work for the day?"

Domizio nodded. It looked like he wanted to say something else, to placate her feelings, but Greta didn't give him the chance. She went straight back up to her writing desk and began to compose a letter for Nicolina.

*** 

Later that morning, Domizio returned with a reply from Nicolina.

*Dear Greta Sarta,*
*I would be pleased to come for a testing day tomorrow.*
*My testing rate is five coppers. If the contract is extended, I will accept nothing less than three coppers a day. If that is acceptable to you, I would be glad to join your workshop.*
*Nicolina Sarta*

Greta's eyebrows rose steadily as she read the letter. She hadn't discussed wages in her letter to Nicolina – perhaps she should have. Thankfully, these wages were reasonable, but she'd need to make sure that none of her hired Sarti earned more than any others or it could cause trouble between them.

She placed the letter in a drawer of her workstation and got on with her work. She was close to finishing the dress now and would need one final fitting with Signora Loyola to measure the correct length before she hemmed the skirt.

Most of the time, the skirt was the easiest part of a dress, but in this instance the entire dress was difficult. From a good hand's length below the waist, there was a pseudo-corset lace at the back, going up to a hand's width above the waist, widening as it went up. It was a clever, if difficult, idea for the dress. It meant that if Signora Loyola changed weight between now and the next time she wore the dress, it would still fit her.

Greta admired the bodice before she took it off the mannequin to attach the skirt to it. The back was mostly open, panels rising from the corset waist to meet in a graceful curve where the neckline was clasped together at the back with the same ornate beading that traced around the neck and then down the centre of the delicate organza bodice insert. The navy satin flowed over the shoulders, demurely covering the breasts and leaving only a finger's breadth of bare organza on either side of the beading before meeting the decorative belt.

It really was a very intricate and gorgeous dress. She hoped Signora Loyola realised that when it was presented to her as complete. It wouldn't do to have everyone else expecting such elaborate evening gowns in short timeframes.

"I'm done with the bodice, Maestra," Sofia informed her. "What would you like me to do next?"

"Be a dear and go around to Signora Loyola's house. Inform her maid, or whoever she has working there, that she needs to come in early next week for a final fitting. Tell her if she doesn't come, her dress won't be completed in time for her precious dinner party."

Sofia's eyes bulged at that. Greta smirked.

"You can omit the word 'precious' if you see fit."

Sofia broke out into a grin. "She might take it from you, but I doubt she'd take it from me. But why next week? It looks like you're almost done."

"I am," Greta agreed, "but we agreed on four weeks. If I ask her to come in for a fitting now, she'll expect it next week and demand a shorter timeframe next time. Besides, we have a lot of other orders to work on and I need to help you with your dress."

"Thank you, Maestra. I can't wait to finish my first dress!" Sofia dimpled. "I'll go now and be back before trading ends."

Greta nodded. "Send Annika and Marta in on your way out."

Sofia nodded and carefully tidied her workstation before walking out to the shopfront. Greta's two other apprentices soon appeared.

"Did you deliver my letter?" Greta asked.

Annika smiled mischievously and handed her a sealed envelope. "I gave Ludovico an earful before he finally got one of the Maestri down for us. She read the letter right in front of us."

"Yes, she thinks you made a wise decision and will give you two weeks to move everything across before you hand back your key," Marta added quickly. "They'll draw up the paperwork for you so all you'll need to do is sign once you've moved everything over."

Two weeks. It was a generous offer and would hopefully be plenty of time to move – especially if she had help from Domizio and another three Sarti. She'd need a full day in Ranieri's workshop to make space for everything from her own. Greta closed her eyes and breathed slowly. Two weeks would be plenty of time. She didn't need to do it all in a day.

"Now tell me, Annika, what do you think was the most important Great Work in the foyer?"

"The needles," she answered easily. "If it weren't for the needles, we wouldn't be able to sew anything."

Greta nodded. It was an obvious answer though. She'd hoped Annika would choose for something more intricate.

"What about you, Marta?"

Marta thought about it for a while. "The needles and pins *were* very important, but I think some of the more important ones are to do with the patterns. How someone came up with things like circle skirts, or petticoat rings, I'll never understand. And the corset!"

"Marta!" Annika cried out. "Just pick *one*!"

Marta blushed brightly. "Fine, the petticoat rings. Without them, you wouldn't be able to have a nice full skirt that didn't weigh you down so much that you couldn't walk."

Greta was surprised by her answer. It most certainly didn't make the top ten on her list of important inventions, but she couldn't deny that she found them useful when making ballgowns.

"Interesting," Greta said aloud. "Both good options and, yes, both important inventions."

"What would you have said?" Annika asked her curiously. Marta's eyes opened wide in expectation.

"The mannequin," Greta answered easily. "I find the expandable mannequin particularly invaluable when working on a new design. See here."

She pointed to the dress now hanging on the mannequin.

"Even without an expandable one, you'd still be able to see how the bodice will fall over a bust and I can adjust the height to get the correct length for the skirt. Without the mannequin, I'd need my customers to come in for more fittings and risk irritating them.

"I'll be able to finish the entire dress other than the hem before Signora Loyola comes in for another fitting. All because of the mannequin."

She stood back again and admired the ensemble. She'd have to make herself something spectacular for the Gioiellieri Guild Ball – it wouldn't do to be envious of all her clients.

"Now, who wants to take a break from mending to cook dinner?"

There was a groan from both girls. Greta laughed.

"Right, you can both take a break to cook dinner. Ask Domizio if he'll be eating before he goes home."

Annika startled at that remark.

"Won't he be staying here again?"

Greta raised an eyebrow. "He doesn't live here, Annika. And he'll need to go home eventually at the very least to change his clothes."

The girls left the workshop in the awkward silence that followed. A few minutes later, she heard the racket of pots in the kitchen. If Annika had reacted like that to her question, she wondered how Domizio had reacted and was suddenly glad she hadn't been the one asking.

She enjoyed their amorous evening activities as much as she was sure he did, but she really didn't want him to get too comfortable here. He wasn't her companion – he was her current bedmate and that was all. She sincerely hoped this wouldn't put a damper in their relationship, such as it was.

Finally alone with no chance of being interrupted, Greta unsealed the envelope from the Sarti Guild Maestri.

*Legaramedi, Fifth day of Inventrici*
*Two hundred and thirtieth year After Implosion*

*Dear Greta Sarta,*
*Thank you for alerting us of your decision to relinquish your workshop and takeover Ranieri Sarto's workshop. You have two weeks to complete the transition.*
*With regards to the matter of your inheritance, we have agreed that Ranieri's patent fees will be passed on to you for twenty years and have instructed our*

*Amministratori in the matter. We ask you to keep this as secret as you keep your own patent fees.*

*In the coming weeks, we will be organising secret ballots to allow other Sarti similar opportunities and alerting all Sarti currently earning patent fees of the new arrangement, should they wish to amend their Final Testament.*

*As to the matter of earning further patent fees after earning your Gold Guild Mark, we feel it will tilt the balance unevenly in favour of those who already have more wealth than others. We do not wish to create such a rift within our own Guild. However, you will always be free to enter a submission for the Guild Awards.*

*Kindest regards,*

*Carlo, Rosa and Michele*

*Sarti Maestri*

Greta read the letter over and over again, her fingers trembling. Ranieri had managed to change the way the entire Sarti Guild worked with this Final Testament. With his patent fees, in addition to her own patent fees and his vast fortune which had already been transferred to her, Greta was, without a doubt, the richest Sarta in Tor'Esint. She could have anything, *do* anything, and would never want for anything.

She folded the letter carefully, walked up to her room and placed it in her cabinet of secret treasures. She locked the cabinet securely and placed the key back in a hidden drawer. It would not do for anyone to find that letter.

***

The Guild Halls clocks clanged four chimes to signal the end of the trading day. Greta looked up from her work in surprise. She hadn't heard the smaller tinkle of the doorbell to signal Sofia's return. With a growing sense of dread, she ran to the kitchen and saw only Annika, Marta and Domizio there.

"Has Sofia returned?" she asked quickly.

They exchanged worried glances, which only made Greta more concerned.

"Annika, Marta, stay here. I'm going to look for her."

Domizio rose. "Not by yourself you're not. If something's happened to her, you'll need help."

Greta wanted to argue, but it was pointless. If something really had happened to Sofia, she mightn't be able to help the girl by herself.

"Let's go then. Girls, lock the door behind us and don't let anyone but me, Domizio or Sofia back in, do you hear me?"

They nodded, faces pale as smoke. Greta ached at the sight. She'd really thought she was done with drama.

She took her lightest coat and ran down the front steps, Domizio only a few steps behind her. Signora Loyola's house was in the wealthier section of Tor'Esint where the land sloped upwards from the bay towards the peak that ran along the spine of Beltigura. Many of the prosperous townspeople lived up there. It gave them an uninhibited view of both the sea and the town below them.

Greta wished she already had her blazermobile. Instead, she gritted her teeth and walked as quickly as she could up Viale Despina towards the peak. Domizio tried to offer her his arm, but she was too much in a hurry to take it – it would only slow her down.

They looked down every side street on the way to Signora Loyola's house, but Sofia was nowhere to be seen. Greta refused to give in to the dread trying to suffocate her. When they reached the expansive villa, Greta paused a moment to catch her breath. She wouldn't be able to speak if she were spent. When she'd composed herself, she knocked heavily on the door. Again, and again. The door opened to reveal a red-faced girl staring angrily at them.

"I'm not a doorman, you know. This is a big house. It takes *time* to reach the door."

Greta winced at her words. "My apologies, Signorina. I'm looking for my apprentice, Sofia. She was meant to come here to ask Signora Loyola to come for a fitting next week and I haven't seen her since."

"Well, she ain't here," replied the girl sullenly.

Greta smoothed her dress frantically. "Yes, but has she been here? I simply want to know if she arrived safely or if she never made it here in the first place."

The girl's face softened a little. "She came, but she left mebbe an hour ago."

Greta bit her lip to stop it from trembling. At a brisk walk down the hill, it should have only taken Sofia fifteen minutes to return to the workshop, twenty if she was dawdling.

"Do you know which direction she took when she left?" Domizio asked when it was apparent that Greta could say no more.

The girl pointed back down the street they had come up. "Down that way. I told 'er the apple scrolls are nice today from Giovanni's Pasticceria. Mebbe, she went past to get one or two?"

"Thank you," Greta said hoarsely.

She immediately headed towards Giovanni's Pasticceria. It was just on Viale del Maestro, off Via Mercato. It had a good enough reputation that it didn't need to be on the main street. Domizio kept pace beside her. It was easier walking downhill and they made much better time. In just under five minutes, they were standing outside Giovanni's Pasticceria, banging on the door. It was well after trading now, so he had no obligation to be open.

"Giovanni!" Greta shouted. "Giovanni, *please*, I need to talk to you."

"Just a minute, just a minute," a voice said patiently.

Greta stood back and listened as the locks behind the door were unlatched. It opened inward to reveal a stout, middle-aged man with short, brown, receding hair circling a round face.

"Greta Sarta," he said in some surprise. "What can I do for you?"

"Giovanni, have you seen Sofia, my youngest apprentice? Did she come here?" Greta asked, the words falling out of her mouth so quickly she didn't know how to stop.

Giovanni nodded. "I saw your apprentice a few minutes before trading ended. She was quite keen to get her hands on some of my apple scrolls. But I told her I was all out and asked if she would settle for an orange one instead."

The continued conversation baffled Greta. She listened along and understood that Sofia had indeed been there but was no longer present.

"Do you know where she went when she left?" Greta asked desperately, hope slipping away.

Giovanni looked at her closely with kind eyes. "Sorry, Signora. I thought she was going straight back to you."

Greta stared at him silently, her thoughts straying away in a dizzying whirl.

"She didn't go straight back," a voice called out from within the bakery. "I saw her arguing with her brother."

"Her ... *brother*?" Greta asked, baffled. "She doesn't have a brother."

"I dunno." A scruffy-haired boy shrugged his shoulders as he joined Giovanni. "She was arguing with him like he was her brother. He led her away by the elbow, so I thought mebbe she was in trouble."

Greta closed her eyes. Sofia *was* in trouble, just not the sort this dim-witted boy assumed.

"Did you see which way he took her?" Greta asked as patiently as she could.

"Nah, just away."

Greta's shoulders slumped. Now she had no leads.

"Thanks for your trouble," Greta said quickly before half dragging Domizio out the door. "Mizi, it must've been Teodoro. If we find him, we'll find Sofia."

"Do you know where he lives?" Domizio asked.

Greta shook her head. "But Ludovico might. Teodoro went there after I threw him out. That's really what started this whole thing with Ludovico, though, so I'm not sure he'll help me."

"It's a start," replied Domizio half-heartedly. "It'll be getting dark soon, so we'll have to hurry. I don't want Sofia out on the streets at this time of night, especially not with someone like *him*."

Greta swallowed the bile in her mouth. Teodoro was far more worldly than Sofia. Just his leering at her had made the poor girl tremble. With a deep breath, she walked swiftly towards the Sarti Guild Hall.

Instead of heading straight down to Corso Delle Gilde, they walked back across Via dell'Oro closer to the warehouse district before cutting down towards Via Mercato. The streets were still busy enough at this time of day, but already there were no women walking alone.

Almost.

Greta saw a bundled heap of clothing shivering in a doorway along Viale Ignazio. She stopped and looked back. The colours of the cloth were familiar. And those bright blonde streaks in chestnut hair were unmistakable. It was Sofia. Greta knelt beside her.

"Fia?" she called out softly.

The shivering stopped, but she didn't look up. Greta tried again.

"Sofia, you're safe now. Look at me, dear."

Sofia still did not lift her head. Greta sat beside her on the sunbaked cobble street and stroked her hair until Sofia's tension began to melt away, but the girl still did not look up.

"Mizi, do you think you can carry her?" she asked.

He'd been standing silently, watching over the two of them but as soon as he was needed, he sprang into action.

"If she'll let me, of course," he answered valiantly. He really was a treasure.

Greta tried to convince Sofia to raise her head, but she wouldn't.

"Sofia, Domizio's going to carry you back home. Is that fine by you?"

There was a sniffle and a small nod. So small, Greta almost missed it. But it was all she needed. She placed a hand under Sofia's arms to lift her up so that Domizio could lift her properly.

He managed to get one arm under her shoulders, the other under her knees. Greta's heart wrenched in her chest as Sofia clung to him tightly – it was the same way Nelia had clung to their father. For all her recklessness, Nelia had never deserved *that*, but at least she'd experienced the pleasure of bedding before it happened. Sofia was a complete innocent. It was so unfair. How could Teodoro do this to her?

When they reached her workshop, Greta knocked loudly. She saw Marta peeking out from the window to see who it was before opening the door. Good girl. When Marta saw Domizio holding Sofia, her face went pale. Greta could hear her struggling with the latches behind the door.

"Annika!" Marta screamed out hysterically. "Boil the water."

Finally, she managed to unlatch the final lock and opened the door. Domizio walked in and turned to face Greta.

"Upstairs, if you can manage it," she told him. "She'll be more comfortable in her bed than anywhere else." She followed Domizio into the kitchen as Marta latched the door behind them. Annika turned and froze at the sight of them. "Annika, bring that water upstairs when it's boiled."

Greta took the friction light off the wall and lit it to get up the dark, narrow stairs. In the girls' room, she lit their glass lantern and helped Domizio put Sofia down on her bed.

"Thank you, Mizi. I thank you more than you can understand. But I need you to leave this room now and not return to it."

He kissed her gently on the forehead. "I know, Greta. She's lucky to have someone like you looking out for her."

Greta waited until he left before whispering, mostly to herself, "I should never have let her go out by herself. This is *my* fault."

She turned to Sofia and sat by the girl's side. Sofia didn't move. But she cried. Then the soft sounds turned into sobbing. Marta came up the stairs, but she stopped at the doorway when she heard Sofia's pain. Annika had to nudge past her with the boiling water.

"Marta, go and find a towel, something soft," Greta told her.

Marta didn't move. Greta's anger rose, but she swallowed it down. Marta had never experienced this before. She didn't know what to do or how to deal with it.

"Marta, go downstairs. Annika, find something soft to wipe Sofia down."

The girls nodded and left the room. Annika came back shortly after with some towels and facecloths. Greta was thankful for the help. She didn't want to have to do this by herself.

At first, she drew back the tangled mass of hair from Sofia's face. It was matted and stuck to her face with dried tears. She used the warm water to clean the tear and dirt-streaked skin. It had been one thing doing this for her sister, but another matter entirely to do this for her apprentice – a girl *she* was responsible for.

Sofia started to unclench her fists and relax her shoulders under the gentle ministrations. Greta took the opportunity to survey her further. Her clothes were not ripped – not anywhere – and there were no traces of blood or other fluids on her dress or skin. It might not have been what Greta had feared. Sofia might have escaped the worst.

"Fia, was it Teodoro?" she asked.

Annika looked up sharply at the name, but Greta shook her head to dissuade any questions for now. Sofia nodded.

Greta hesitated. She wasn't quite certain how to phrase the next question.

"Did he ... well, did he hurt you? Or, erm, did he try to force himself on you?"

Sofia didn't answer but clenched her fists again. Greta looked at her hands closely. Her nails weren't torn or bloody.

"He dragged me into a small alley and..." She swallowed hard, "He pushed me against the wall so hard I hit my head. I couldn't think or see for a bit, but when I came to, he … had one hand under my skirt. He was trying to undo the buttons with his other hand, but he couldn't. Especially when I started pulling his arms away. They were sewn on well – they didn't break when he tried to just rip them off."

She paused and took a deep breath. Greta thought she was preparing herself to say the worst, but she didn't say anything else.

"Did he rape you?" Annika asked, unable to contain herself.

Sofia shook her head vigorously. "An older man came up and pushed him out of the way, like he was competition and pushed himself against me, lifting my skirts. Teodoro punched him and they started fighting, so I ran. I didn't know where I was running, but when I got to a busier street, I couldn't go any further. My legs gave out. I was just too scared to do anything. I'm sorry."

Greta frowned and hugged the girl tightly. "You've nothing to be sorry for. You didn't do anything wrong. This was Teodoro's fault, not *yours*. When we find him, we'll have him charged with, with … something."

Sofia sniffled and hugged Greta fiercely, trembling all over. "I'm sorry I made such a big fuss when I wasn't raped."

Annika looked at her aghast. "Just because he was interrupted by someone else who wanted to rape you too, doesn't mean he wouldn't have done so himself if given the chance. He was halfway there with everything else he did."

Sofia nodded miserably. The warm water sat mostly unused by her bed. It hadn't been needed for more intimate ministrations. Greta was thankful for that. But she wished Sofia hadn't been such an easy target. So early in the evening, she shouldn't have been, but Teodoro must have been watching out for any opportunity to hurt Greta. The boy had already shown his disrespect and disregard for both her as a maestra, and for her Guild. He had tried to take advantage of her youngest apprentice under her own roof. And now this. This was a dangerous escalation. His attempt to rape Sofia had almost led to an even more brutal one at the hands of a grown man.

Greta breathed shakily at the thought of it. At least Sofia had had the presence of mind to run when they'd started fighting over her. It had saved her.

She left Sofia talking softly with Annika about the experience and went down to the kitchen. Marta was finishing the dinner preparations. Domizio was helping her. It was very sweet of him. She was thankful that not every man was like Teodoro.

He looked up at her entrance with questioning eyes. She shook her head.

"You don't have to stay, you know," she told him.

She'd meant he shouldn't feel obliged to stay. It was clear he thought she didn't want him to stay.

"I was helping Marta, and I wanted to know how Sofia is," he replied in a hurt tone.

"It wasn't as bad as we feared, but it wasn't good."

She knew he'd understand what she was saying. She didn't want to be explicit in front of Marta – it wouldn't help any of them.

"Do you ... will you be making a complaint against him?" he ventured.

Greta shrugged. "It'll depend on Sofia, but I think so."

"Is she hurt?" Marta asked in an oddly hushed voice.

Greta tilted her head. "She has few bruises and a lump on her head. You can go and talk to her if you like. Annika's keeping her company. Why don't you bring up some food for the three of you on a tray? As a special treat. You can even get some of the special biscuits out of that secret tin I know isn't so secret anymore."

Marta gave her a small smile and immediately went to fetch the biscuit tin. Greta ladled out a bowl of pasta with oil, garlic and herbs for herself and Domizio. It was simple, but delicious. She set the plates across from the table from each other and moved around Marta to make tea and fetch the cutlery.

Before the kettle had boiled, Marta was out of the way with her tray of food. Domizio looked at the bowls set at the table and walked over to Greta.

"I thought you didn't want me to stay," he said softly into her ear.

Greta sighed. "I don't want you to stay the night, but the least I can do is offer you a meal. Especially after all you've done."

Domizio took a step back out of her space.

"Mizi, you know me. What we're doing, this isn't a courtship. I enjoy your company, but I'm not going to want it every evening. You do understand, don't you?"

He smiled with a twinge of sadness. "I know, Greta. I'm happy for any time you're willing to spend with me, in the workshop or the bedroom. That doesn't mean it won't hurt when you so very clearly don't want me."

"I'm..." Greta paused. She was going to apologise before she thought better of it. She had no reason to apologise for her actions. He knew what he was getting into before he bedded her that first time. She refused to feel guilty over his hurt feelings.

"I understand," she said carefully. "But I think we'll need to be more discreet with more Sarti starting work here from tomorrow. I don't want them to get any ideas that they have rights to my body because they see you with me. It might sound silly, but that's the way I feel about it."

Domizio took another step away and sat down at his bowl.

"It's not silly," he conceded. "Now you're making me wish I hadn't suggested hiring other Sarti."

Greta laughed at him as she sat across the table. They both started eating in an effort to dispel the awkward moment.

"Have you thought about the three tests you'll give Nicolina tomorrow?" he asked between mouthfuls.

"Blind hemming," Greta replied after some careful thought. "It's a difficult task and will show her skills or lack thereof."

Domizio nodded approvingly. "It's not a common one, but it's certainly not unheard of. What else?"

"Drawing and cutting a pattern from a picture or description," she said eventually. "If I'm to get more orders after this dress for Signora Loyola, I don't want to worry about my hired hands messing them up."

"That's a good one." Domizio gestured approvingly with his spoon. "And last one?"

Greta shrugged. "What do you suggest?"

"Something to do with dresses," he replied. "You make a lot more of those than other Sarti. More elaborate too."

Greta thought of all the things she was having to do with Signora Loyola's dress and made up her mind.

"Beading. Thankfully, Sofia has a deft hand with beading but if I get as many orders as I hope to from Signora Loyola's dress, then there might be a lot more beading to come."

Domizio raised his eyebrows. "Your third-year apprentice? You're letting her do the beading on an *actual* dress?"

"Well, of course." Greta frowned. "What's the point of having apprentices if they don't work on actual orders? They'll never get any proper experience otherwise."

He looked at her appreciatively. "You're a good Maestra, Greta."

She tried to huff and wave his compliment away. She was far from the Maestro that Ranieri had been.

"Give yourself some credit, Greta. I know you think you took on too many apprentices too quickly, but you're still a better Maestra than a lot of others out there. You're skilled and thoughtful. You don't only think of yourself, but of your apprentices as well. I don't know any other Sarti who would've trawled the streets looking for their missing apprentice unless they were still missing the next morning."

Greta smiled. She was loath to admit it, but his words made her feel so much better. Greta got up to wash the dishes. She appreciated it when Domizio rose to help her, especially when there was no chance he'd be invited to stay the night.

When they were done, he kissed her cheek fondly and bid her farewell with little ado. Greta locked the door behind him and double checked every latch.

On the way to her bedroom, she checked in on the girls. They were talking softly amongst themselves. Marta had pushed her bed right next to Sofia's so they could be near each other. It broke her heart – this was exactly the way she and Nelia had coped after her sister had been attacked. Greta had hoped never to have to deal with the aftermath of an assault ever again.

# Chapter 15 – Orodi 6 Inventrici 230 Years After Implosion

The next morning, Greta got the girls ready for what to expect that day. Sofia was, thankfully, composed enough to work with Greta, though she didn't want to stay in view of everyone. Greta was happy to keep her in the workshop where she could help the girl with her cotton version of Signora Loyola's dress.

Nicolina arrived at the start of trading, only a few minutes after Domizio. He quickly busied himself with one of Ranieri's orders in the kitchen, drawing and cutting out the pattern for Greta to direct him on later.

Greta heard the bell tinkle with her arrival. Marta came in to announce her with an eager smile. She seemed unaccountably pleased that there'd be more Sarti in their workshop and that they'd need a trial. When she thought about it, Greta realised that Marta would've been offended had the Sarti not been tested. Greta tried to assess her apprentices on a regular basis – the latest was when she asked them to darn stockings and Annika had proven that her stitching could do with some practice.

"Nicolina is here for her testing day, Maestra," she said loudly enough for Nicolina to hear it too.

"Thank you, Marta," Greta replied in a quieter voice. "Please show her in."

Marta grinned and retreated into the shopfront. Nicolina entered the workshop and looked around appraisingly. Greta didn't mind. She'd have done the same thing herself if she'd hired out her services to another Sarta.

"Good morning, Nicolina," Greta greeted her warmly. "I'm so pleased you could come at such short notice. You've met my apprentices, Marta and Annika, in the shop, and Sofia is making a dress in the workshop today."

Nicolina nodded at Sofia, who only glanced up at her. Greta was glad Nicolina was female – she wasn't sure what Sofia's reaction would be to a Sarto. She might need to rethink her strategy on that.

"Your workshop comes highly recommended by Domizio Sarto," Nicolina told her. "If I'm up to your standards, it will be a pleasure to work with you. What tests will you have me perform today?"

"A blind hem to begin with," Greta replied decisively.

Nicolina's eyes bulged. "Of ... of course."

"Then you can draw and cut a pattern from an order. Lastly, you can do a bit of beading. Sofia, be a dear and show Nicolina the beading you've been working on."

"Yes, Maestra," Sofia replied quietly.

She walked over to the mannequin and pulled aside the covering cloth to point out the organza she'd been working on for the past few days. Nicolina walked over and felt the cloth delicately in her hand, seeming afraid to break it. Greta wondered if she'd ever seen organza before – it wasn't a common material in Tor'Esint.

"You did this?" Nicolina asked Sofia incredulously, turning the neck over to see the stitching on the back.

Greta knew it was just as neat on the underside as on the front. Sofia was extraordinarily meticulous in her stitching.

"Sofia has a very steady hand," Greta explained. "She's my youngest apprentice, but I think she may have more talent than my other two combined."

Sofia blushed at the compliment. Greta was happy she could show Sofia how good a Sarta she was becoming. It wouldn't surprise her if Sofia gained her Silver Guild Mark before Annika and Marta. Of course, she wouldn't be able to apply for her Copper until she'd finished her five years of apprenticeship, but that would be the only thing stopping her.

"Shall we begin?" Greta asked brightly. Nicolina nodded apprehensively. "Good then. Blind hemming. You'll find different coloured threads in this drawer, scissors are here, and you can use any scraps of coloured cotton from over there. Let me know when you're finished, and I'll give you an order to work from. Please excuse me now. I need to help Sofia with her dress today."

She motioned for Sofia to continue her work. She'd already tacked together the bodice of the cotton dress. Greta helped her dress the mannequin and watched as Sofia tried to figure out how to fit it properly, only offering suggestions when necessary.

The shop bell tinkled, and Greta heard Signora Loyola's voice.

Greta didn't bother waiting for her to be announced. She left Sofia and Nicolina in the workshop and walked past the curtain into the shopfront. Nicolina would be more nervous with her there and be more likely to make mistakes. She wasn't testing her on skills under pressure – she only needed to know what she was capable of in the first place.

"Signora Sarta," Signora Loyola said in a delicate voice as Greta stepped into the shop. "I heard your apprentice went missing yesterday. Is she…"

"She's had better days, Signora, but it could have been worse." Greta didn't have to elaborate. She was certain her client knew exactly what she meant.

"I should have sent my page to escort her home. I'm truly sorry." She wrung her hands together despairingly.

Greta was touched by her care. It appeared Signora Loyola had a heart after all.

"I know you said to come next week for a fitting, but could I possibly see the dress now? My curiosity is hot as lava."

Greta hesitated. "I suppose it can't hurt to have a quick fitting now before I make the final adjustments to it. I'll still need you to come back next week for a final fitting."

Greta ushered her behind the curtain and went to find Sofia. When Signora Loyola was ready, they entered the curtained area to help her with the unfinished dress. Greta breathed a silent sigh of relief when she saw how well it sat on her. With Sofia's help, she pinned up the neckpiece and checked the fitting of the zipper and lace between the skirt and bodice.

When she was done, she stood back and surveyed her work. It really was a magnificent dress – or it would be when it was finished. But even now, it was still beautiful.

Signora Loyola turned to look at herself in the mirror. Her eyes went wide, and she froze. With gentle fingers, she felt at the beaded organza and traced the smooth satin down the bodice and skirt. She turned to look at her back, but couldn't quite manage it.

"Sofia, ask Annika to help you bring in another looking glass so Signora Loyola can view the back."

Her apprentice left the curtained area and Greta took the opportunity to admire her handiwork.

"Greta, Signora Sarta, it's..." she floundered, lost for words. "It's *spectacular*. It really is. I can't begin to tell you what this means to me."

Greta smiled. She loved working on new dress designs, but she couldn't deny that the incentive of extra business was nice too.

Sofia returned with Annika and a long mirror. They set it up across from the other mirror so that Signora Loyola could see herself reflected in both. She turned this way and that, admiring every inch of the dress.

"You can't tell in these tight quarters, but it's a full circle skirt, that way it swirls around your ankles, but will fan out magnificently when you turn."

Signora Loyola smiled more broadly than Greta had ever seen.

"When will it be ready?" she asked in excitement.

"We still have two weeks until the promised time, signora, and I have neglected many other orders to work on this dress. I'll send a note early next week to call you for a final fitting before we complete the dress. By that point, I should only need to hem it."

Signora Loyola sighed reluctantly. "I suppose I won't be able to wear it before my dinner party anyway – it will ruin the surprise for everyone else. Mind you don't show this design to any other customers."

Greta promised easily. It was a standard request from her clients. Every dress she made with a new design was kept secret from society until they'd had a chance to reveal it in their own time.

Only after that was Greta allowed to create more dresses from the same pattern, albeit with minor alterations to ensure none of them would feel awkward by wearing the exact same outfit as their friends or rivals.

"Sofia, Annika, take the mirror away while I help Signora Loyola to disrobe."

The girls immediately obeyed her and closed the curtain behind themselves. Greta remained behind and carefully helped Signora Loyola out of the dress. The zipper made things so much easier. It meant Greta really only needed to be careful with the pins at the neckline so that she could put the beads and loop in the right place.

She sighed in satisfaction – she had outdone herself this time. Ranieri would have been so proud of her for this dress. Now, she'd have to be proud of herself and be happy with that.

The rest of Tor'Esint would soon be clamouring at her door for new dresses for the Guild Ball. It was only three months away now. How many dresses could she possibly make in that time, even with the help of hired Sarti?

She took the pinned dress back into the workshop while Signora Loyola re-dressed herself. Nicolina looked up at her entrance, but Greta paid her no mind. She knew the poor girl would be nervous with her going in and out, but there was nothing she could do about it. If she was nervous now, it wasn't going to get any better when they were busy and Greta was working in amongst everyone else.

"I'm almost done with this customer," she told Nicolina, barely glancing her way. "I'm not expecting many other customers today who need my attention, so there shouldn't be too many disruptions."

Nicolina nodded and bent back down to her work. Greta wanted to peek but restrained herself. There would be time enough for that. For now, she returned to the shopfront and awaited Signora Loyola.

The influential signora walked to the front counter where Greta was waiting.

"When you're ready for the final fitting, send *two* of your apprentices to tell me. I don't want to feel responsible for anything that happens to them on their way to or from my house."

Greta thanked her for her concern. It was unexpected and kind, in a selfish sort of way, but it was still kind. Signora Loyola left the shop with little pomp and ceremony. She knew Greta had seen through her highbrow manners – they were past false pretences now.

When the door closed behind her, Greta heaved a large sigh of relief and smoothed down her dress. It was always a relief when customers left her in peace to get on with her work.

"Sofia, we've got work to do," she called out to her.

"No, Maestra." Sofia shook her head and walked into the shopfront. "You've got tea to drink and a Sarta to see to. Marta was doing a blind hem out here the same time as Nicolina and she's finished. Your Copper Sarta should be too."

Greta looked at her middle apprentices in surprise. "Marta, why were you doing a blind hem?"

Marta shrugged. "We wanted to see how good we were compared to a Copper Sarta. Sofia's already shown you her beading. I did the blind hem and Annika was going to draw and cut a design today. Then we thought we could switch tasks for any other Copper Sarti you trial."

"I see," Greta replied slowly. It was a wonderful idea. She couldn't decide if she was more impressed with the girls for coming up with it or annoyed that she herself hadn't suggested it to them. Either way, it meant that she had a good way to test her apprentices at the same time as the Copper Sarti Domizio had found for her.

"Well then, Sofia, bring in a tray of tea and ask Domizio to mind the shop. Marta, Annika, come into the workshop when Domizio relieves you."

Greta entered the workshop and sat down at her own workbench and picked up a mundane, but tricky repair. She noticed that Nicolina was still working on her blind hem. She should have specified how long or how wide to make the hem. Then again, Marta hadn't needed the instruction, so Nicolina shouldn't have either.

Marta and Annika entered the room, the former with a small bundle of material. Greta immediately noticed she'd taken a swathe of spare cotton, the same quality as Nicolina was working with. How had the girls come up with their plan so quickly? Or had Sofia given her the same material to be fair? Either way, it made it easier to judge how they had fared against each other.

"Here's my blind hem, Maestra." Marta held out her bundle of material. "I couldn't get the hang of it until about halfway through, but I think the last half is my best effort yet."

Greta took the proffered material and examined the work closely. Marta's self-assessment was accurate. The first half of the hem was anything but blind. Greta could see where she'd started to understand how to do it and by the final few stitches, it looked flawless. Of course, it wouldn't be good enough for actual customers until every stitch was flawless, but this was admirable work.

"You're definitely getting better at it, Marta," she acknowledged. "When you can do it like this the whole way, I'll let you start working on customer hems. Keep practising and you'll be there soon."

Marta beamed proudly. "Thank you, Maestra. I'll work on it between my repair jobs."

Greta nodded her agreement to the plan. She was pleased with how much initiative her apprentices were taking lately. It was certainly making her job a lot easier. Perhaps having three apprentices wasn't such a bad idea, as long as some of them already knew what they were doing.

Sofia came in with a tray of tea for everyone and passed the cups around, forcing Nicolina to put down her cloth. Sofia took the opportunity to bring the unfinished blind hem to Greta. Nicolina tried to protest but couldn't with a cup of tea in her hands.

"Let's see what you've done so far," Greta said, taking the cotton from Sofia.

"I haven't finished it yet." Nicolina held out a hand in protest. "I haven't had to do a blind hem in months."

Greta tried not to react to that nugget of information. It signified that Nicolina hadn't been working with Gold Sarti, possibly not even Electrum Sarti, and she hadn't bothered to hone her own skills in the meantime. She tried not to think badly of Nicolina, but she couldn't help it. What kind of self-respecting Sarta wouldn't practise these skills on a regular basis, even if they didn't have need for it in their current employment.

"Domizio hasn't done one in months either," Nicolina added pointedly.

Greta looked up sharply, eyebrows raised. She didn't approve of finger pointing, no matter who it was at.

"Domizio has already proven his worth to me," Greta replied calmly. "Don't be so quick to undermine yourself. I've not yet had the chance to review your work."

Nicolina bit her lip, then blew on her tea, her eyes not leaving Greta. Greta reminded herself that she was a Gold Sarta – one of only *four* in all of Tor'Esint. Every other Sarta was beneath her and she had every right to assess them as she saw fit to determine whether could work for her.

She was not obliged to respond to Nicolina's claim that Domizio hadn't done a blind hem in months. She wasn't asking *him* to do one. She'd watched him like a hawk when he'd cut his first pattern for her. He was capable at that, so she'd leave him with that for now. If she wanted him to do anything else, she'd test him on those things beforehand.

If she was honest with herself, she knew she should test him on blind hems and beading before the next potential Copper Sarta came in. It would only be fair. But not now. Not while Nicolina was here. This Copper Sarta would not be given the satisfaction of knowing how her comment had made a Gold Sarta think twice about her methods.

Finally, she turned her attention to the blind hem. It started better than Marta's and got better a lot faster. More than half of it was truly blind. For her claim of not having done it for months, it really wasn't a bad effort. It would need work before she could be trusted on actual orders, but Greta would check all the orders before they went out anyway. If she had time, she would check them at each stage.

"This is a decent effort," she conceded aloud. "Another hour or so of practice, and you'll be ready to work on the blind hems for orders. Now, drink your tea and, Sofia, dear, bring out some biscuits before we perish."

Sofia grinned and returned quickly with a tray of biscuits she must have already prepared in the kitchen.

Nicolina looked confused. "So, you're not ending my trial?"

"Of course not," Greta replied, equally confused. "You still have the pattern and beading to do."

"But ... my blind hem wasn't perfect."

"Neither was mine when I was a Copper Sarta," Greta told her plainly. "But you have great potential. With practice, your blind hem will come along quickly. Here, look at Marta's and tell me the difference."

She handed both cloths to Nicolina. The Copper Sarta put down her teacup and took both pieces to study them.

"Well, Marta's one takes longer to become blind than my one. In fact, it starts off a little worse than mine as well."

Greta nodded. "Marta is my fourth-year apprentice and you are a Copper Sarta. Those results are as they should be. Now, as I understand it, the girls have taken it upon themselves to complete the tasks alongside you. Your beading will be compared to Sofia's and Annika will join you now in drawing and cutting a pattern. To save time, as we're quite busy now, you can work off one of Ranieri's standing orders. Nicolina, you may have first pick of a shirt or trousers, Annika will take the other."

"Trousers," Nicolina decided immediately. "I've done a lot of trousers in the past few months."

Greta raised her eyebrows. "You give a lot of yourself away, Nicolina. How do you know I won't judge you more harshly now because I know you've had a lot of recent practice?"

Nicolina paused, her eyes widening. Greta shook her head in disappointment. Was she ever so naive as this young Sarta?

"Sofia, take the tea dishes back to the kitchen, Marta, relieve Domizio in the shop and Annika, ask him to show you which of Ranieri's orders need to be done next. You can use that for your test."

The girls scattered to do her bidding. Sofia returned before Annika, so Greta immediately set her to work on her cotton copy of Signora Loyola's dress.

"Now, Sofia, tell me what you think we might need to do next."

Sofia looked at the cotton bodice on her workbench, tilting her head in concentration.

"I think I'd like to try the neckline. Do you want me to bead the linen organza section?"

Greta patted her gently on the back. "No, Sofia, not unless you want to. You can use my pattern as a guide for the linen organza and then make your final measurements on me."

"Linen organza?" Nicolina asked from her corner of the room. "What's that?"

Greta looked over and saw she was still waiting for Annika to return with the order they were to work from.

"Sofia's creating a copy of my current order. She's using linen where I'm using organza, so the difference in materials is still noticeable."

"But what's organza?" Nicolina asked again. "Is it the softer fabric on the dress?"

Greta beckoned the Copper Sarta over and held out the remaining scraps of organza. Greta hadn't wanted to show how much she had stored in her warehouse. It wouldn't do for everyone to ask for such fine material. She'd soon find herself in trouble with the Mercantili Guild or disappointing customers, neither of which was a favourable option.

"It's so soft without the beading," Nicolina commented as she felt the material between her fingers. "Where did you get it?"

Greta debated telling her the truth but settled on a half-lie. "It's the last of my own personal stores from Isola Rustal. With the Trading Edict in place, it'd be too expensive to import anymore, unless my customers were desperate and willing to pay the cost and potentially wait weeks for its arrival."

Annika returned at that moment with the order. It wasn't very specific. There were the measurements for Signore Daniele di Gianni but little else other than "narrow fit" written in the margin of the order form.

"What style would you like me to make?" Nicolina asked.

Even Annika looked at her in surprise. Nicolina went red in the face.

"You choose, dear," Greta told her. "I'm not fussed about it as long as you do a decent job. That goes for you too, Annika."

"Yes, Maestra," Annika replied quickly. She showed Nicolina where the brown pattern paper was and got started on her own work. Greta turned her attention back to Sofia and the neckline.

"This is a tricky section, so try but don't be afraid to ask for advice. I'm almost done with this repair, then I'll start work on the dress again."

"Yes, Maestra," replied Sofia and brought over a chair to work beside her.

Working on the lengthening was easy for Greta. She found it relaxing to do such a simple task – it gave her time to think. She'd need to revise how she was paying Domizio. A percentage of the price for a commission might not be as much as Nicolina had requested.

Greta hadn't asked him to complete all these tests, but perhaps she really ought to. She'd initially thought to pay all her hired Sarti the same rate, but perhaps she ought to be paying them according to their skills. It felt strange to think that Sofia was certain to be better at beading than Nicolina but she wouldn't be paid for her work at all.

Of course, Sofia was given free food and lodging. That should count for something. But it didn't stop Greta feeling bad about the situation. Perhaps she'd buy Sofia a nice gift or make her a new dress when this order was finished. If Signora Loyola favoured her with anything extra, she could perhaps share it with Sofia. Surely she'd appreciate that.

Greta lost herself in her work and didn't resurface until the pants were lengthened. It must have been at least half an hour later. She stretched her arms up to the ceiling before turning to Sofia.

"How's the neckline going?"

"I'm done, but it's messy. I'm not very good at sewing along a circle."

Sofia handed it over for inspection. She was right – it was very messy.

"Don't be too hard on yourself, Fia. It's the very first dress you're working on. I'd be surprised if you didn't have some trouble with it. My first dress was so atrocious I thought Maestro Ranieri would terminate my apprenticeship. Necklines are tricky and take a lot of practice. Why don't you begin on the skirt now?"

"Yes, Maestra," Sofia replied with the hint of a smile.

Sofia took the bodice to her workstation. Greta took the opportunity to check how the pattern making was going. Annika had drawn a rough design for the shirt and was part way through drawing her pattern, checking it against the measurements on the order.

Nicolina was taking a different approach. She hadn't drawn out a design first but was drawing a pattern from her head. Greta watched from a distance, arms folded to stop herself fidgeting. It was clear that Nicolina was repeating a pattern she'd done countless times in the past few months. It was a safe option – one that Greta wished she hadn't taken. Any Copper Sarta would be able to do that. This test was meant to allow her to showcase her originality. Perhaps the pressure of a Gold Sarta looking over her shoulder was too great for Nicolina.

Reflecting that was probably the case, Greta took Signora Loyola's dress off the mannequin and brought it over to her workbench.

"Sofia, I'm just going to quickly finish the neckline. Could you bring me the beads you used for the bodice?"

Sofia immediately put down her work, went to the bead cabinet and pulled out the three drawers of beads they'd bought specifically for this dress.

Together, they selected which ones to use with the loop. Greta took three silver cut glass beads and showed Sofia how to sew them in a tight cluster to hold a small loop from the other side of the neckline. In less than half an hour, she was done.

All that was left now was the hem of the skirt and she wouldn't do that until after she called Signora Loyola in for her final fitting next week. It would afford her some much-needed time to work on Ranieri's orders and the more complicated repairs that her apprentices couldn't handle.

"I'm finished, Signora Sarta," Nicolina said from across the room. "One pattern for narrow fitting trousers."

Greta looked up from her work and joined Nicolina at her workbench. She studied the pattern, taking note of the measurements and mentally picturing how it would all fit together. It looked exceedingly familiar.

"Is this Giacomo Sarto's design?" she asked casually. "The one he brought out last year to gain his Electrum Guild Mark?"

Nicolina looked at her in surprise. "Well, yes. I worked with him two months ago and have been using his patterns since. Is that a problem?"

Greta shook her head. "Not for testing purposes. However, we won't be able to use this pattern for Ranieri's order."

"I'm sure Giacomo won't mind," Nicolina pointed out hopefully. "He said I could use it as often as I liked as long as I ... oh."

She hesitated and looked at Greta's apprentices then back at Greta herself. "I see how it might be inappropriate for a Gold Sarta to use an Electrum Sarto's pattern."

Greta nodded and smiled thinly. Nicolina had obviously found out about patent fees and had *eventually* realised that Greta wouldn't want to pay Giacomo anything when she didn't have to.

"As I said, for testing purposes, I can see you've done a fine job from memory. I'm impressed that you can do that, but if you're to work with me, you'll be expected to use your own original pattern or one of mine or Ranieri's. I don't want you using another Sarta's patterns in this workshop. Is that understood?"

"Yes, Signora Sarta," Nicolina replied meekly.

Greta eyed her for another moment before nodding. "Very well. We'll break for lunch and then you can begin your beading task. Annika, how are you getting on?"

Annika didn't lift her head. "Well enough, Maestra. I've done the front and back and the collar. The sleeves are giving me a bit of trouble. I was trying to give them a little flare around the cuffs and shoulders, but I can't manage it."

Greta walked over and drew a few lines lightly over Annika's pattern. "If you do this here, and move this line over ... here, you'll get the effect you're looking for. You'll need to put darts in to create the flares properly. I'll show you how to do that when you get up to it."

"When *I* get up to it?" Annika asked in a high-pitched squeal.

Greta smiled. "Make it out of the test material first, but if I'm happy with it, you can make it out of linen for the actual order. You're a fifth-year apprentice now – it's about time you start working on proper orders by yourself."

"Thank you, Maestra!"

Annika threw her arms around Greta, pinning her arms unexpectedly to her side. Greta was not used to such affection from the girl. It was a startling experience.

"Yes, well, let's go and eat some lunch before we all expire. Annika, ask Domizio to clear the kitchen table so we can eat."

Annika released her and disappeared into the kitchen. Greta turned to Sofia who was still busy with her cotton skirt.

"Fia, leave it until later. Your fingers will get too sore if you don't give them a break."

"Just a few stitches, Maestra, just a few more," Sofia pleaded.

"*One* more, then put it away."

Sofia nodded without looking up. Greta shook her head, knowing that Sofia would work all day long if she was left to her own devices. It reminded Greta of herself. Ranieri had often had to force her to stop working when she was his apprentice – more so when she'd earned her Copper Guild Mark. Little had changed now that she was a Gold Sarta, but today she had more to worry about than Signora Loyola's dress. If she didn't spend time with the Copper Sarta, it would be a waste of a day and she would never manage to hire any extra hands.

"Your apprentices take their work seriously," Nicolina observed from beside her. "And they respect you more than other apprentices I've seen in the workshops I've worked in these past few years. It's..."

"Nice?" Greta asked when Nicolina paused for so long.

"Unusual," Nicolina corrected her. "Most apprentices either fear or loathe their Maestri. Some have no feelings towards them whatsoever, but I haven't seen any with such respect for them."

Greta frowned. "Whose workshops have you worked in?"

"Mostly Electrum and Silver Sarti. The Gold Sarti don't usually take on more work than they can manage, and they have enough apprentices not to need hired hands. I'm guessing the only reason you need extra help is because you've got the workload of two Gold Sarti rather than one right now."

Greta didn't answer – Nicolina was correct. She'd never have hired anyone if it hadn't been for the sudden increase in orders. She wasn't even certain she'd require them after they'd moved workshops and Ranieri's orders were all completed.

It would depend on whether his regular clients moved to her without question or trial. She knew she'd get more orders based on Signora Loyola's recommendations alone, but that mightn't require extra hands.

Her apprentices were becoming quite skilled and if she made her clients wait the regular timeframe rather than rushing every order, she'd have time to teach them all the things she needed to – like the flared cuff and shoulder for Annika's shirt, and the blind hem for Marta, and everything she'd neglected to teach Sofia in the three years she'd been there.

"You're done, Sofia. Let's eat lunch."

Sofia reluctantly put down her work and followed Greta and Nicolina into the kitchen. Domizio had cleared away his pattern work and was helping Annika lay the table for a light lunch. Raw vegetables, cheese and bread, and an orange were set out for each person. It was reasonable fare for a working day.

"Marta, turn the sign and join us for lunch," Greta called out into the workshop.

The six of them sat elbow to elbow around the table.

"Good thing the kitchen table is bigger in Ranieri's house," Annika said tactlessly. "Especially if there'll be more of us soon."

"You can eat in shifts," Nicolina pointed out. "That's what they do in most of the workshops Mizi and I have worked in. It's the only way to ensure everyone gets fed and the shop remains open."

Mizi? Their familiarity with each other shouldn't have bothered Greta, but it did. She retreated into her thoughts and ate her food in silence, letting her apprentices take the lead with the conversation.

They asked a hundred questions about the different workshops Domizio and Nicolina had worked in together and how they differed to Greta's workshop. Greta listened on with interest – she would have asked the questions herself had she felt more comfortable in Nicolina's presence.

"I worked for Agata once, but it didn't last long," Nicolina admitted. "Even though I passed her tests, we didn't exactly see eye to eye, so I left after a week. I doubt she missed me at all. I know I didn't miss her."

Greta smiled to herself. Until recently, she'd never seen eye to eye with Agata either. Perhaps Domizio had been right that she and Nicolina would work well together. If they had one adversary in common, at least that was a start.

"Domizio, how are the patterns coming along?" Greta asked when there was a break in the conversation.

"I'm almost done with the fifth one now," he answered. "That leaves three to go. Do you want me to start cutting and edging the material so it doesn't fray?"

Greta nodded. "I think so. We'll soon have help with cutting the patterns if I manage to hire all the Sarti I need. Marta and Annika can help you with that this afternoon. I think we'll need all hands on deck with that before we can start working on the actual tacking."

"Would you like me to start on the tacking when each piece of material has been edged?" Sofia asked.

"No," Greta replied firmly. "You're not to do anything other than that dress until it's done. It's important you work on your dress from start to finish otherwise it'll never get done and we'll be back in the same situation we were in before where I didn't take enough time to teach you everything."

Sofia's cheeks dimpled as she nodded amiably. Greta remembered how excited she was to work on her first dress. But that was in her second year, not her *third*.

"If I may, Signora Sarta, if my testing goes well, would you like me to return tomorrow to begin work?" Nicolina asked.

It was a bold question, to assume she'd be returning, but it *had* gone well enough so far that Greta already thought she'd be hiring Nicolina.

"I thought to do all the days of testing this week without the other Sarti present. I haven't done this before and don't want to make anyone feel awkward."

Nicolina smiled kindly at her. "You're even nicer than your reputation suggests. I can assure you no testing Sarta will mind other hired Sarti being present at the same time."

Greta mulled the idea over but still didn't like it. There wasn't enough room in this workshop to have so many Sarti and apprentices. They'd be on each other's toes all day. But that could be avoided as soon as they moved to Ranieri's workshop.

"As you may have gathered, we're soon moving to Ranieri's workshop. I'm going to need as much help as possible for that. Would you be averse to helping with the move?"

Nicolina startled at the question. "It's ... not usual, but I'm certain I can help if you tell me what you need."

"Thank you. I'll sit down tonight to make plans. I'd like to minimise the disruptions to the workshop as much as possible."

"We can help, Maestra!" Marta exclaimed. "Even today! Annika and I can help Domizio move all Ranieri's cut patterns back to his workshop and start working on them there. In the *new* workshop!"

"Oh yes!" Annika agreed excitedly. "That will make room for all your testing Sarti and let us get used to the new workshop. *Please* Maestra!"

Greta laughed loudly at their enthusiasm. "Yes, fine. As long as you return at the end of trading *with* Domizio. I don't want either of you walking the streets alone right now."

"Yes Maestra!" they chorused in unison.

"What about me?" Sofia asked quietly.

Greta shook her head. "I'm sorry, Sofia. I don't want even a copy of that dress going out of this workshop until it's finished. I can't imagine what I'd tell the client if anyone saw it or if the surprise was ruined before she'd even had a chance to wear it.

"However, as soon as you finish your cotton dress, you may join the others in edging in Ranieri's workshop until we figure out how to move everything."

"Can you borrow Aveline Inventrice's blazermobile again?" Marta asked.

It wasn't a bad idea, but Greta had borrowed it so many times lately, she wasn't certain Aveline would agree to it.

"We have two weeks from yesterday to move," Greta replied. "I'm sure we can do without Aveline's blazermobile until my own arrives. Besides, the Maestri might give me more time to move if I need it."

There was silence in the room. Everyone stared at Greta. She sipped her tea, trying not to bring too much attention to herself.

"Aren't they very expensive?" asked Annika in a whisper.

"Indeed," Greta replied. "But I can't keep borrowing Aveline's blazermobile and I now have *two* warehouses. I thought it a prudent purchase. It likely won't be ready for at least a month."

Domizio exchanged glances with Nicolina. It looked like they were debating which of them was going to ask the question they wanted answered. Nicolina lost the debate.

"Signora, I don't mean to pry, but are you certain you'll be able to afford four hired Sarti after such a purchase?"

Greta stared at her in surprise. "Why would I hire you if I couldn't afford you?"

Nicolina shrugged. "We get hired by a lot of Sarti who don't realise exactly how much money they'll be spending to keep us. Then they let us go when they run out of money. Sometimes *after* they run out of money, even, and we don't get paid."

Greta put down her cup slowly and carefully. "I assure you, I'll have enough money to hire ten Sarti for an entire year without running out of money even if I don't get paid by a single client."

The room fell silent again. Greta cringed at how indiscreet she'd been and closed her mouth. She'd wanted to reassure Nicolina, not brag about her fortune.

Unfortunately, she'd done just that. Well, she supposed it wouldn't be a secret for long anyway. Once she moved into Ranieri's workshop, it would become obvious to everyone that she'd inherited everything from him, and everyone knew Ranieri was wealthy in the first place – though possibly not the full extent of his wealth. It would only stand to reason that they'd assume she now had that fortune.

"Well, are we all done? Yes? Good then, back to work everyone. Nicolina, I'll show you where all the beads are kept so you can begin your final test."

Nicolina followed her into the workshop and immediately sat down to her task. Sofia entered soon after and sat straight down to her cotton dress. Greta returned to the kitchen to find Marta and Annika clearing away the dishes while Domizio gathered all the cut material for Ranieri's orders.

"Will we need to bring anything from here?" he asked her.

Greta shook her head. "Other than food, Ranieri's workshop is completely stocked with everything you could possibly need. Here's the key. Look after my girls for me."

The last she added in a quiet voice. Domizio squeezed her hand gently as she handed him the key.

"I promise," he whispered back, then spoke to the girls in a louder voice. "I'm ready when you are."

"Ready!" they cried out.

They fought over the hand towel, eventually negotiating to use one side each. Greta left them to their devices and returned to the workshop. She heard the bell tinkle a little while later to signify their departure. It felt odd to have her shopfront empty of apprentices. She couldn't leave it empty but needed the extra space in the workshop to do her work.

"Nicolina, would you mind doing the beading out in the shopfront? I don't like to leave it empty," she said raising her head to look at the Copper Sarta.

"Of course, Signora," she replied easily. "I'll take these out and finish the task there."

Greta nodded her thanks. It was an improvement that Nicolina hadn't asked what design she should bead, or which beads she should use. It mattered little what she did – it wouldn't be sold to a customer in any case. In fact, she should have Nicolina unpick it once she was finished so they could use those beads again for the next testing day.

A few hours later, Nicolina popped her head into the workshop.

"I'm done, Signora. Would you like me to bring it to you or would you rather come into the shop?"

"I'll come there."

Greta got to her feet and took the beading from Nicolina as she entered the shopfront. She examined it closely. It was well done. The design was in the shape of a star with well-chosen beads for each shape needed. She turned it over to look at the back. She smiled in satisfaction – the stitching was neat and tidy. No unnecessary knots or overlapping where there shouldn't be.

Nicolina had clearly practiced her beading in the past. Greta was pleasantly surprised that it was better than Sofia's, but so it should be. Sofia was only a third-year apprentice. She shouldn't be working on actual customer's orders until at least her fourth year. Even Annika hadn't been allowed to work on them yet, though she was finally trying her hand at it now with the shirt. If she hadn't palmed off her work to Sofia so often, perhaps *she'd* be the one working on the beading right now instead of edging material with Marta and Domizio.

"Well, that's the end of your testing," Greta said. "I think we can safely say that you can join us. Come tomorrow morning and hopefully I'll have organised how to move workshops, otherwise I'll have you working on one of Ranieri's orders."

Nicolina frowned. "You don't want me to stay the rest of today? You're paying me for the entire day – you may as well make use of me."

Greta hesitated. She hadn't considered that Nicolina would want to stay after her tests.

"Well, you could work on some repairs for me here. I can't bring Sofia to the front room to work on the cotton version of her dress. My client will be furious with me if she finds anyone has seen her order before her dinner party."

"Of course," Nicolina agreed with a grin.

Greta showed her the pile of repairs and left them with her. She was clearly competent enough to work unsupervised.

The rest of the afternoon passed blissfully uneventfully. Greta worked with Sofia in the workshop while Nicolina continued the repairs. Soon after trading ended for the day, Domizio returned with Annika and Marta. The two girls were animatedly discussing Ranieri's workshop.

"We hope you don't mind, but we rearranged some things around the workshop so that we could work together. We pushed some of the tables together to make larger ones. It made it easier," Annika told her.

Greta tried not to care, but she did. That workshop held a lot of memories for her. She still wasn't certain she was doing the right thing even if that workshop *was* the better of the two.

"Of course, I don't mind," she lied. "I'm certain we'll have to make some changes when we move in. The least of which is deciding which bedroom belongs to who."

Her words caused all three girls to stare at her. She couldn't understand what she'd said wrong.

"Won't we be sharing anymore?" Annika asked hesitantly.

Sofia and Marta looked at her just as expectantly as Annika.

"Well, you can if you like, but I thought you'd want a room each. There are certainly enough of them."

"But you'll take the largest one, right?" Marta asked.

Greta immediately shook her head. "That's Ranieri's room."

"Girls, let's not bother Greta with all your questions," Domizio quickly interrupted. "Why don't the three of you make some dinner and Nicolina and I will help Greta finish up for the day."

He bustled the girls into the kitchen before anyone could object. Greta stared at him and the ease with which he'd read her. It hadn't gone unnoticed by Nicolina either, though there was no jealousy in her look, only understanding.

"You don't have to take Ranieri's room," Domizio said in a gentle voice when the kitchen door had closed behind the girls. "It would do just as well for you to take one of the smaller rooms for yourself and let your apprentices bunk together in Ranieri's room, as they do here. You could use the extra two rooms as board for your hired Sarti if they need it, or extra workrooms for all the extra work you're expecting."

His words soothed her. She didn't have to take Ranieri's old room. She could even take her own old room. Perhaps she'd feel more at home there.

"I suppose we have time to figure it all out," she answered hesitantly. "I still don't know how I'm going to move everything from this workshop to that one. How would I transport it all – even with a blazermobile?"

"Boxes, like hatters use," Nicolina answered easily. "Or woven baskets. I'm sure we can find some larger ones to transport all your bolts of material and kitchen things. You might even be able to borrow flat trolleys from the Falegnami. Surely they'll have something to transport all their wood."

Greta nodded slowly. It was a good idea, but she didn't know any Falegnami. But Telchide did. Aveline had spoken about his interesting relationship with them before.

"Could I ask one of you to stay with the girls while I quickly pop over to Aveline's shop?"

They both nodded and Greta hastily put on a coat before running down the street to Aveline's shop. The door was still open for business when Greta arrived. Aveline and Nevio looked up at her brusque arrival.

"Greta, is something wrong?" Aveline asked worriedly.

"No, I simply need your help," Greta replied.

"Again?"

"Again." Greta smiled. "But for a different reason. I've decided to take over Ranieri's workshop and I need help moving. My blazermobile won't be ready in time, so I can't rely on that.

"Nicolina, my new Copper Sarta, suggested asking a Falegname to borrow a trolley but I don't know any, and I noticed Telchide appears to be friends with one."

Aveline's eyed widened. "You're ... moving?"

Greta paused. "Well, yes. It's not far. Ranieri's workshop is still in Piazza Mercantile on the corner of Via Corallo. Depending how you walk, you could pass me on the way to Telchide's house whenever you work with him."

"Oh, yes, I suppose so," Aveline agreed quietly. "So, you want to borrow my blazermobile then?"

Greta shook her head. "No, not again. I've borrowed it enough lately. I was hoping Telchide could introduce me properly to Filippo Falegname so I could borrow a trolley or two."

Aveline frowned and put her tools down. "You're going to walk a trolley up and down Piazza Mercantile with all your possessions in the open for the world to see?"

Greta swallowed. When she put it that way, it didn't sound like such a good idea.

"Maybe I could put everything in boxes first. Nicolina suggested that too."

Aveline laughed. "And did Nicolina also tell you how expensive it'll be to purchase boxes? Or how long it will take for them to be made?"

"Erm ... no," Greta admitted.

Aveline walked over to Greta and took both her hands. "I'll help you. So will Chide and our apprentices. I'll wager even Teresina will be able to lend a hand."

"Really?" Greta asked incredulously. "Are you certain?"

"Absolutely!" cried out Nevio from his workbench. "I'll help Marta, and Florio and Gaspare can help Annika and Sofia. Many hands make light work, as they say."

Greta rolled her eyes. Nevio would do anything to spend time with Marta it seemed. But in this case, it might actually be more helpful than harmful.

"Very well then, I'll need a few days to start packing things and I won't want to start moving everything until I've hired all my new Sarti."

Aveline laughed. "Reta, I'm here to help. I'll come by on Riposidi to help you sort through things. And don't forget you wanted to see if you could find the owner of a peculiar bobbin."

Greta couldn't contain herself. She gathered Aveline into a quick embrace and whispered a word of thanks into her ear. Aveline returned the embrace easily.

When Greta returned to her house, she outlined the plan to her extended household. Nicolina and Domizio agreed to help with sorting and packing, even though it was not part of their regular tasks as hired Sarti. They were both just as keen as the girls to work in a larger workshop.

"I'll buy pizze for everyone that helps."

Domizio nodded eagerly. "I'm always happy to help out in exchange for a meal."

Nicolina hesitated at first, but when she saw how excited everyone was, she quickly agreed. "I'll come tomorrow for my first proper day of work and will help you with sorting on Gildadi."

Greta nodded her thanks to everyone. "Right, well, let's see what the girls have cooked for dinner."

# Chapter 16 – Mercatodi 7 Inventrici 230 Years After Implosion

Greta tapped her foot and looked out the window for the tenth time. The Mercatodi stalls were already popping up around the edges of Piazza Mercantile. Annika, Marta and Sofia were setting up hers. A few stalls down, Telchide's apprentices and daughter were setting up next to Aveline's stall but the Inventrici themselves were nowhere in sight.

Neither were her own hired Sarti. Greta stood back from the window, clenched her fists, and then double checked that the peculiar bobbin case was in a pocket of her work corset.

It wasn't often Greta allowed herself the opportunity to go shopping for pleasure, but today was different. She was determined to find the Inventrice responsible for the automatic sewing device in Ranieri's warehouse. If she made a few purchases along the way, then the Mercantili Guild could never accuse her of inter-Guild relations.

The door opened. Greta turned in time to see Domizio stop in his tracks at the sight of her, causing Nicolina to walk straight into him.

"Mizi! What are you doing?" She looked around him to Greta and broke into a smile. "Oh, Greta, you look divine. What's the occasion?"

Greta looked down at herself and shrugged. Today she'd chosen a forest green skirt and a cream blouse under her work corset with forest green slitted sleeves. Instead of her usual tight braid, her wavy hair was kept out of her eyes with a beaded trinzale and green brocade lenza.

"I'm taking advantage of the fact that my apprentices can tend the stall while my hired Sarti continue with our workload. I haven't been shopping on Mercatodi in such a very long time!"

"I'd be more than happy to accompany you," Domizio said a little too eagerly.

Greta rolled her eyes. "I don't think that will be necessary and besides, you'll get bored. I'm curious to see what new inventions are out there. If you need me, I'll be in Zona Inventrici."

Nicolina unbuttoned her coat and nodded. "Are you happy for us both to work here today? Or does Mizi need to work in Ranieri's workshop?"

"I don't mind," Greta replied easily. "If you could get on with some of Ranieri's standing orders, that would be most helpful. I'd like at least one of you to stay here with Sofia in case she has questions about her dress while I'm out."

Nicolina raised her eyebrows at Domizio.

"I'll go and fetch one of Ranieri's orders from his workshop and bring it back here. I think Sofia would appreciate more people around her at the moment."

His attention to the people near and dear to her touched Greta. She lay a soft hand on his arm.

"Thank you. I'm certain she'll appreciate that. Now, I'll be back by midday to check on everyone."

She fetched her cream parasol from the hat stand and walked out into the street. The final stragglers were hurrying to set up their stalls as the Guild Hall clocks struck a quarter past eight. Greta bid her girls farewell and walked along the footpath, behind the stalls towards Via dell'Oro.

It was only from this angle that she could see Telchide holding Aveline's hand between their stalls. She was glad that they'd come to some sort of agreement as to how to proceed with their unusual circumstances.

Aveline's eyes widened as she saw Greta coming and she shook her hand free from Telchide's. Telchide turned in alarm, but his shoulders only sagged when he saw her. So perhaps they weren't being quite so open about their relationship as Greta had assumed.

"Veli, I'm going shopping in Zona Inventrici this morning, but I was hoping you or Telchide might be able to assist me with something else. I'm determined to commission something pretty for myself. Would you happen to know where I might find that Gioielliere you mentioned who is skilled with corallo?"

Telchide scribbled down an address and handed it to her.

"Ciro Corallino. He's the best I know of in Tor'Esint."

Greta took the proffered scrap of paper and studied the address. It was on the boundary between Zone Gioiellieri and Artiste – a decidedly uncomfortable position for any corallino to be.

"Thank you, Telchide." Greta pocketed the address. "I don't suppose you'd like to join me when I pay Ciro a visit? I confess, I've never purchased anything made of corallo. I wouldn't know the first thing to look or ask for."

Telchide shook his head so violently, Greta thought he'd fall off his chair.

"No, thank you. My leg, you see, it's still broken, and I can't walk so far on crutches."

"Perhaps Veli can escort us in her blazermobile?" Greta suggested before remembering Telchide's aversion to the vehicle. He turned a sickly shade of green. Aveline patted his hand and shot Greta a sharp glare.

"If you're desperate for company, I'll join you this afternoon," Aveline told her.

"I am *not* desperate for company," Greta stated plainly. "I'll be seeing you tomorrow in any case to start packing and discuss our findings."

Greta didn't wait for a response but opened her parasol and walked casually past the stalls throughout Piazza Mercantile and began her journey down Via dell'Oro, towards the docks, and into Zona Inventrici.

Her search lasted hours and, in the end, she was none the wiser. Every Gold and Electrum Inventrice barely knew what a bobbin was and didn't recognise the odd bobbin case. They'd clearly never worked with a Sarta before.

All she had to show for her extensive excursion were three pattern books for her girls and a friction-powered heating rod that, when inserted into a yellow solution, lit up the liquid. It was a novel idea for lighting – Liquid Sunlight. Cornelio Inventore had promised the heating rod would retain its heat for at least half an hour at a time. Greta had only purchased the Liquid Sunlight after he'd demonstrated how bright the solution would become in a dark setting. It would allow her to work, or even dine, much later than usual without fear of burning down her workshop.

After a short and increasingly loud negotiation, it was agreed that Cornelio's apprentice would escort her back to her workshop with the Liquid Sunlight in a large wicker basket slung on his back. Greta outright refused to carry it all the way back herself.

On the way back, she insisted on stopping in at Delfina's Pasticceria to buy something nice for lunch. The apprentice had agreed to wait for her in exchange for a small olive loaf.

When they arrived at Greta's shop, the apprentice helped her set up the Liquid Sunlight in the workshop. He demonstrated to everyone how the heating rod worked.

"Oh, that's like the toasting rod!" Sofia exclaimed. "Are there more things that use this sort of friction rod?"

The apprentice rolled his eyes as though Sofia was simple. "Signorina, almost *every* heat or mechanical invention is friction powered. That or steam, but friction is safer in such a wooden town as this."

Greta stepped in before Sofia said something she might regret. "Yes, thank you. Here's your olive roll. Thank you and farewell."

The apprentice took his cue, and his olive roll, and left the premises.

"Maestra, this is wonderful," Sofia said, examining the Liquid Sunlight. "I wonder how far the light will spread in somewhere as large as Ranieri's workshop."

Greta hesitated. Perhaps she ought to have purchased two Liquid Sunlights. Domizio closed the ceiling shutters and drew closed the curtain between the workshop and the shopfront.

"I think one will do very well indeed," he stated confidently. "It's lighting up this entire room well enough for all of us to do our work."

Nicolina nodded her agreement but kept on with her work. Greta appreciated her dedication.

"I'll go and relieve Marta and Annika so they can have a bite to eat," Domizio offered. "I'm certain they won't be impressed if I eat everything from the Pasticceria and leave them nothing." He winked conspiratorially, reopened the shutters, and walked through to the shopfront, leaving Greta laughing in his wake.

***

Later that afternoon, on the border between Zone Gioiellieri and Artiste, Greta walked into the oddest workshop she'd ever seen. There was a bench along one wall with such interesting instruments, she couldn't help but stare. In one corner of the room, a massive wicker basket held a treasure trove of bright red and light pink corallo. Another, smaller basket held an assortment of conch shells in all shapes and sizes. Next to the door was a glass topped desk, but Greta was too far away to see what it contained.

Sitting on a stool in the brightest window seat was a vecchietto, holding a wooden pole against a notch in his cramped workbench, carving away at the tip of it as he whistled a tune. Coming out of a back doorway was another vecchietto, only slightly younger, carrying two coffee cups. He placed one on the workbench and kept the other for himself. Neither of them seemed to notice Greta standing in the doorway until she coughed politely.

"Ah, signora, please, come in. Come in."

The older man looked up from his work as the younger ushered her in and closed the door behind her.

"Please, come and watch Ciro at his work. He's so close to finishing this one!"

Ciro sipped his coffee with puckered lips as Greta was practically pushed towards him.

"Seppe, leave the poor signora alone. She made the decision to come in all by herself. If she wants to watch me, she'll watch me. Now, drink your coffee and leave me in peace and quiet for Caldera's sake!"

Seppe huffed loudly but sat at one of the longer workbenches and sipped his coffee. Much as she wanted to, Greta did not immediately walk up to watch Ciro working. She so hated it when anyone looked over her shoulder as she worked. Instead, she walked around the workshop, eyeing the different pieces on display.

On the long workbench was a strip of wood no more than a hand's width high. The same curved notches were cut out of it at regular intervals. Resting in some of these notches were the same devices Ciro was currently using – a short wooden pole with a bulge at the end. Greta leaned in and realised the carvings were not part of the wood, but only attached to it with a glob of wax. The carvings themselves looked to be out of exceedingly delicate stone. She looked closer and realised it wasn't stone at all, but the back of a shell.

She gasped involuntarily. "They're beautiful!" she exclaimed.

Ciro chuckled to himself as he continued working. "Well, I should hope so. They wouldn't sell half so well otherwise! And I'd have wasted all those hours carving them."

Greta felt her cheeks grow hot at her naivety. She squared her shoulders and walked calmly to Ciro's workbench.

"You were recommended to me by Telchide Inventore as the best Corallino in Tor'Esint. I've never purchased anything corallo for myself, but I'd like to do so now."

Ciro calmly finished the section he was carving, put his tools down and looked at her squarely in the eyes.

"Telchide Inventore, you say?"

Greta nodded. Ciro mimicked her nod.

"His father was one of my closest friends growing up. Telchide is a lot like him, you know. Such a shame what happened to his young companion." Ciro sighed. His eyes misted over with old memories. "Well, let's see if we can't help you find something you like, signora."

He slowly got to his feet and shuffled over to the wooden desk with a glass cover. He lifted the glass and propped it open with a wooden lever. Inside was a vast array of corallo jewellery and the cammei that were becoming increasingly popular in Tor'Esint. Greta tentatively reached out to touch one of them but stopped short.

"They're not so delicate that you can break them merely by touching them, signora. Please, go ahead."

Ciro picked up a piece of coral carved into a rose and placed it in her palm. Greta smiled at the beauty of it. The rose looked so simple but like any of her simple dresses, it still would have taken hours to create.

"A design like this can be set into a ring or hung as a pendant on a necklace," Ciro told her. "I'd hesitate to create a brooch with it. Too heavy, you see. It will only overbalance, and the beauty of the rose won't be seen."

Greta held it above her finger but scrunched her nose at the size of it. Something like this would only get in her way. She put the rose back in the desk and ran her fingers along a necklace made entirely of corallo balls.

"Perhaps signora has an apprentice she wishes to favour with something?"

"My girls *have* been working very hard lately. Especially Sofia." Greta picked up a coral choker. "How much are these necklaces?"

Ciro looked at her closely, his gaze lingering on her Gold Sarta pin before travelling back up to settle on her eyes.

"Signora, first, let me show you how these particular necklaces are made. Come with me."

Greta curiously followed as Ciro shuffled to the wicker basket full of corallo. He picked up a piece roughly the length of his finger and brought it over to one of the odd machines on the first workbench.

"Here, you see, we find the correct measurement for this piece of corallo, then we cut it evenly."

He sat down, worked the machine with a foot pedal until the saw was moving fast enough. With practised ease, he held the coral steady and cut it into smaller pieces. He picked up one of the small cuttings and moved across to a grinding wheel off the edge of the workbench.

Without being asked, Seppe immediately began to turn the handle, making the grindstone spin. Ciro held the small coral cutting in metal prongs and held it against the grindstone, pulling it back and rotating the coral every few seconds until he was satisfied with the shape.

Careful not to drop it, he carried the ball over to another machine on the long workbench and began working the foot pedal on it. This time, a sharp needle-like instrument whirled around quickly. Greta watched in fascination as Ciro placed the bead in a curved groove and brought the spinning needle down to puncture it perfectly. He held it up proudly for her to see.

"You see, each piece of corallo has to be cut, shaped and pierced perfectly. On those necklaces, there are a minimum of one hundred corallo beads. Now, perhaps you will understand the price of two gold coins."

Greta smiled faintly. Six gold coins was quite a bit more than she'd planned to spend on her apprentices.

Ciro tilted his head with a small smile and walked back to the glass-topped desk. "They are perhaps more than a mere trinket to favour an apprentice with. However, these corallo pendant necklaces, I can sell you these for ten silvers a piece with a silver chain or an electrum for a gold chain instead."

Greta looked at the selection. Some were raw branches, simply cut from a length of coral and polished, with a hole drilled through them for a chain. Others were larger pieces of corallo, shaped into various designs – some encased in silver or gold, some plain.

She took her time and picked out a large, polished heart; an extraordinarily detailed rose; and a silver dragonfly with detailed corallo wings.

"I think the girls will love these. On silver chains please."

Ciro took the pendants from her and selected three fine silver chains to match them. Seppe held open a small white box with a bed of cotton for Ciro to place the finished necklaces into. The box was placed on the workbench while Seppe found a roll of twine to tie it closed.

Greta pulled out two electrum coins and held them out to Ciro. He frowned at them.

"Signora, forgive me, but you said you wished to purchase something for yourself." He paused. "You're a very generous person, thinking first of your apprentices, but you must think of yourself once in a while. What can we do for *you*?"

Greta blinked and stared at the corallino. "I ... wouldn't know what to get for myself."

Ciro took the coins and patted her hand gently. "Perhaps we can trade? I'll make a cammeo brooch of your likeness, or the likeness of anyone you choose, if you make Giuseppe a new shirt. He doesn't like to complain, but any fool can see how threadbare it is."

Greta shook her head. "I cannot accept such a generous trade. Allow me to make a shirt for you as well and then we're in agreement."

Ciro looked down at his shirt in surprise. "My shirts are in good condition."

"But do you have one suitable for the Guild Ball, Signore Corallino? I'll make you one of such fine quality, you'll be the envy of every other Gioielliere."

Ciro's smile froze on his face. "A Corallino cannot afford to make enemies within his own Guild, Signora Sarta. Not when half the Guild already thinks we don't belong. If you insist, a simple shirt for everyday will do well for me."

"Agreed," Greta said instantly, inwardly cursing herself. "Forgive me, I was not aware how tense the situation is."

Ciro shrugged casually and walked over to a set of drawers, pulled out the third from the top and sorted through the contents until he found what he was looking for. He sat Greta by the window and took the pencil from behind his ear. With the ease of a true Artista, he sketched her likeness onto the white side of an oval shell piece and held it up for her approval. It was so detailed Greta couldn't imagine how he'd be able to do it justice.

"Your skills astound me, Signore Corallino. Now, allow me to begin my side of our trade and let me take measurements for you and Giuseppe."

The two men stood patiently and held out their arms when instructed. Greta took their measurements and wrote them down in her pattern book. She would transfer them to her order book when she returned to her workshop.

Seppe reverently held out the white box to her once she was done.

"When would you like the shirts?" she asked. "I could have them ready in a week. Will that suit you?"

"Signora, we're not in a rush. Our shirts won't wear through anytime soon. Take your time. Two or three weeks will be soon enough. I'll have your cammeo waiting upon your return."

Greta left the Corallino's workshop with a smile. She'd always admired cammei – now she'd have one over her very own!

*\*\**

She arrived home just in time to help the girls pack up the stall. They'd replaced thirteen buttons, accepted five repairs, and taken measurements for two young women who wanted matching sleeves.

"Annika, I asked you not to take any orders until things settle down." Greta sighed in frustration.

"Don't worry, Maestra, I told them we won't have them ready for three weeks unless they're happy to have apprentice-made sleeves."

"Oh. Well, what did they say?" Greta asked, a little surprised that Annika had come up with such a good solution.

Annika looked at Marta and they shared a smile. "They agreed to let Marta and I make them in two weeks in exchange for ten silvers apiece rather than an electrum apiece. After all, you won't let substandard sleeves out of your workshop, and they know that."

Greta nodded appreciatively. "That was a good idea, Annika. Better than good – it was clever and resourceful. Now come inside, I have something for the three of you."

The girls brought in the last items of the stall and hurriedly packed them away as Greta strolled through her shopfront and workshop to make sure all was in order. Domizio and Nicolina were packing their things away for the day and Sofia was hard at work on her skirt.

"Will you be joining us for dinner?" she asked them.

Nicolina shook her head. "Sorry, Greta, but my mother will be expecting me. Her eyes aren't what they used to be, and she relies on me heavily especially in the evenings."

"I'll stay," Domizio said. "Under the condition that we can start to organise things for the move while the girls cook."

Sofia turned at that statement. "Oh Maestra, please can I keep working on this dress? I'm almost finished this section of the skirt."

Greta walked over to inspect her work. The stitching really was excellent. All those years of Annika forcing Sofia to do her share of the repairs had worked in Sofia's favour.

"Very well, but first I have presents for the three of you."

Annika and Marta came through to the workshop at those words, eyes sparkling in anticipation. Greta placed the pattern books she'd purchased earlier that day on her workbench.

"You've all been working so hard lately, and I want to show you how much I appreciate it. I bought you a pattern book each, so you can draw in them whenever you like without asking for a page from mine."

The girls eagerly took a book each and flipped through the pages in delight.

"Thank you, Maestra." Annika glowed with happiness. "I can't wait to start working on ideas for my first Great Work."

Greta nodded and pulled out the little white box from her skirt pocket and held it close to her chest.

"Those pattern books are presents, but they're necessary for every Sarta. *These* are your real presents. They were made by Ciro Corallino, reputedly the best corallino in Tor'Esint."

Greta opened the box and laid out the three necklaces on a clear corner of her workbench. The girls came over to look, as did Domizio and Nicolina from a distance.

"Oh Maestra, they're gorgeous!" Marta exclaimed, gently touching them all. "Which one's for who?"

Greta raised her eyebrows at that. She hadn't considered that when she made her purchase.

"I don't mind," she told them. "You can each pick your favourite."

Annika shook her head. "No, Sofia should choose first. She's been working the hardest. Then Marta."

Marta eyed her suspiciously. "Why me next?"

Annika huffed and bit her lip. "It's my way of saying sorry. Just pick. They're all beautiful. I won't mind which is left."

"Go on then, Fia," Greta encouraged. "Which is your favourite?"

Sofia carefully picked up the silver dragonfly with detailed corallo wings.

"I like this one," she said softly. "But Maestra, they must've cost you a small fortune. Are you certain you want to give them to us and not keep them yourself?"

Greta shook her head, gently took the chain from Sofia, and fastened it around her neck so that the dragonfly sat just below her collarbones. The girls admired it appreciatively before Marta chose the polished heart.

"It's simple, but beautiful," she said, holding it out to Greta.

Greta obligingly fastened the silver chain around her neck and watched Annika out of the corner of her eye. Her oldest apprentice picked up the detailed rose and examined it closely.

"Do you like it?" Greta asked hesitantly.

Annika looked from the rose to Greta and took a deep breath. "It's exquisite – more than I deserve. *You* keep it."

Greta shook her head. "I ordered something for myself. This is for you."

Without giving Annika a chance to object, she took the chain and fastened it around her neck. The silver setting kept the rose in position, facing the world. It really was a lovely piece. Annika deserved it after the lack of attention Greta had paid her over the years and the problems that the neglect had, in itself, caused.

"Now, Sofia, if you insist, back to your dress. Annika, Marta..."

"Dinner!" the girls chorused together.

They gave Greta a brief embrace and headed off to the kitchen. Sofia gave her a much longer embrace.

"Thank you, Maestra," she whispered. "Thank you."

Greta patted her back and sent her back to work. She turned to find Domizio and Nicolina staring at her from the doorway to the shopfront. They moved into the shopfront as she approached them.

"What's the matter?" she asked them quietly. "Did something happen today I should know about?"

Nicolina shook her head. "I hope your apprentices realise how lucky they are to have a Maestra like you. I know a lot of Maestri, but none who would favour their apprentices with such gifts."

Greta frowned. "I'm sure you don't mean that. I remember Ranieri giving me a pattern book and little gifts when I'd done particularly well on a task."

Nicolina shook her head about to protest and Domizio lay a hand on the Copper Sarta's shoulder.

"What Nicolina means to say is that you have a big heart and we'll both treasure the time we spend in your workshop. Now, let's get to work organising or we'll never get anywhere tonight."

Nicolina raised an eyebrow at Domizio's statement but then shrugged and nodded.

"I'll be back first thing Gildadi."

Greta thanked her and placed eight copper coins in her hand as payment for her testing day and first day of actual work. She waited until Nicolina had left, then locked the door behind her and closed all the curtains.

Domizio walked up behind her, spun her around to face him and kissed her long and thoroughly. Greta's stomach flipped at the unexpectedness of it but leaned forward as he pulled away from her.

"Sorry, Greta, I couldn't help myself," he told her. "I just love how innocently you do such wonderful things and expect that everyone should be as generous and kind as you are. Now, we really should start organising that workshop of yours."

He walked into the workshop, leaving Greta alone with her confused thoughts and a sudden urgent longing to be kissed again.

# Chapter 17 – Riposidi 8 Inventrici 230 Years After Implosion

Greta gave her apprentices two copper coins each and told them to enjoy themselves after obtaining their promise that they'd keep together. She was pleased to see they were all still wearing the pendants she'd given them and not at all surprised they'd found clothes to appropriately show them off.

She closed the door behind them and thought back to the previous night. This was where Domizio had kissed her by surprise. She'd expected him to spend the night after such a show of affection, but after dinner, he'd excused himself with a promise to return on Gildadi. Greta had renegotiated his wages and paid him for his days of service and watched in confusion as he left her alone, unsatisfied.

It was an uncomfortable situation for her. She'd never been so fond of a lover before. And had certainly never had one leave her longing for his presence when he was gone.

A dull thud at the door disrupted her musing. She opened it to Aveline who bustled in past her, carrying an armful of wicker baskets, looking decidedly better today. The pills Lucrezia had given her must have been doing their job.

"I thought we could start packing your least used items so they can be carried over earlier and allow you to still work. Unless you'd prefer to do it another way?"

"No, that sounds the best way," Greta confirmed. "Mizi helped me organise things a little last night but there's still a lot to do."

Aveline raised an eyebrow. "Mizi, eh? Isn't he a little young for you?"

Greta blushed. "Considering he's the one who seduced me, I'm sure he'll be fine. Now, let's get to work."

She led Aveline through to the workshop where swathes of material had been sorted into some semblance of order. They worked together to pack the material into the baskets.

"The movable material racks in Ranieri's workshop will come in handy for all of these," Greta huffed. "If I'd had enough space in here, I'd have used that system myself."

Aveline paused in her work and cocked her head to the side.

"You keep calling it Ranieri's workshop. You know it's *your* workshop now."

"I think it's going to take a while before I think of it as mine." Greta shrugged and changed the subject. "Did you have any luck finding the Inventrice we were looking for? I visited so many Gold and Electrum Inventrici yesterday, but none of them even knew what a bobbin was, let alone the odd case holding it."

Aveline shook her head. "It's going to be more difficult than we thought to find the Inventrice. After all, we don't even know if Ranieri was working with someone in Tor'Esint to develop it or if he commissioned it from an Inventrice in another city."

"Wouldn't we have heard about it if it was already in production?" Greta asked.

"Not necessarily." Aveline shrugged. "The only time the Inventrici from other cities show us their new inventions is at the Inventrici Convention and I missed the last one because of my expedition. Perhaps Ranieri heard about it then and ordered one from there."

"I suppose that's possible," Greta admitted hesitantly. "But if I can't find the Inventrice responsible, I won't be able to get it working or know who to contact if it breaks."

"We'll figure it out, Greta. After the move, after things settle down. We'll have plenty of time to figure it out later."

"Speaking of figuring things out later, have you figured out anything else to do with the baby?"

Aveline repositioned herself on the floor and rested a hand over her stomach.

"I told Nevio, you know, just after I told Chide." She bit her lip. "He was very supportive but was clear about the fact that he doesn't know the first thing about children or babies. And, well, neither do I."

Greta placed the last swathe of material in an already overstuffed basket. She sat by Aveline's side and placed an arm around her shoulders.

"We'll all help, Veli. Telchide's household, my household and Nevio. I'm certain even Lucrezia could be persuaded to help in desperate times." She wiped a stray tear from Aveline's cheek. "Does the rest of Telchide's household know yet?"

Aveline nodded. "Teresina's so very excited to be a big sister," she said in a trembling voice. "She doesn't understand why I won't live with them but insists that she'll teach the child to read and will come over every day to visit. If she was old enough, we wouldn't need any other help, but it's unfair to burden her with such responsibilities."

An unbidden thought occurred to Greta. "Have you considered asking Serenita to help with the child during the workday? She could look after the baby at Telchide's house."

Aveline shook her head forcefully and Greta moved to sit across from her so she could see her face. "No, I refuse to do that. There are reasons ... I can't tell you. But I won't change my mind on this."

"Well then have you considered hiring a wet nurse? Or a nursemaid?" Greta asked, changing tack.

"Mamma hired a nursemaid for me," Aveline recalled bitterly. "I was largely ignored by her my entire childhood. I don't want to do that to my own child."

Greta faltered. She hadn't known. Her own motherless childhood seemed a joy in comparison. At least her father had been loving and thoughtful.

"It doesn't have to be like that, Veli. It's up to you how much time you spend with your child, even if you hire a nursemaid to help while you're meant to be working and training your apprentice.

"Besides, you have months to prepare. Now, let's have a nice cup of tea and see if we can't organise how to do this move without disrupting too many working days."

She drew Aveline to her feet and escorted her into the kitchen.

Not long after, the girls arrived home. Aveline excused herself, claiming she needed to rest. Greta farewelled her best friend and settled down for a quiet afternoon, sipping tea and hearing about the girls' day.

# Chapter 18 – Gildadi 9 Inventrici 230 Years After Implosion

Pietro arrived for testing at half past eight. Greta was unimpressed with his tardiness. She'd already sent Marta and Annika with Domizio to Ranieri's workshop. She didn't want a full house for her second day of testing.

Sofia was edging the material for her copy of Signora Loyola's skirt in the workshop and Nicolina was out the front working on one of Ranieri's standing orders. She popped her head into the workshop to announce Pietro's arrival when he finally appeared.

Greta smoothed down her skirt and walked out into the workshop ready to face the tardy Copper Sarto.

"Greta Sarta." He tipped the hat he should have taken off the moment he set foot inside. "I'm here for my testing day."

Greta raised an eyebrow. "You're late. I hope this isn't an indication of how you'd proceed if I hired you."

Pietro pulled back his lips into a small snarl which only turned Greta's feeling towards him from bad to worse. Well, she'd promised him a testing day, so she'd better get on with it.

"You can work out here today," she told him, not wanting to expose him to the still fragile Sofia. "I'll bring you what you need for your first task."

She disappeared into the workshop and reappeared a few minutes later with an unfinished sleeve, some thread, and needles. She placed them on the smallest workbench in the shopfront.

"I'd like you to sew a blind hem on this sleeve using whichever needle and thread you deem appropriate. You have half an hour."

As she turned to re-enter the workshop, she caught the twinkle in Nicolina's eye. She'd clearly noticed that Pietro had been given a time limit when she hadn't. Greta saw no need to pay favours to such an uncouth man – she wouldn't do him the courtesy of calling him a gentleman.

"What's he like?" Sofia whispered when Greta re-entered the workshop.

Greta frowned. "Late. We'll see if his skills improve his manner."

She doubted they would, but it was only fair to let him try. She was paying him after all. Half an hour later, Greta walked back into the shopfront and over to Pietro.

"Are you finished?" she asked not unkindly.

Pietro held up a sleeve that was almost entirely hemmed. Greta took it from him and studied the cuff. It was neat and even the whole way around. It wasn't blind – but it was close. Greta had to admit that she was impressed. She glanced quickly at the Sarto brooch on his collar and confirmed it was Copper. Technically, he should be at least as good as Nicolina. His skills might be, but his manner certainly wasn't.

"Is that up to your standards?" he asked snidely.

Greta drew in a sharp breath, momentarily angry that Domizio had recommended him. "Signore Pietro, your skills are not the only things being tested today. If your manner does not improve, I shan't hire you even if you surpass my other expectations. I am one of only *four* Gold Sarti in Tor'Esint and deserve to be treated accordingly.

"*You* are merely a Copper Sarto, so your skills are barely higher in my regard than my apprentices. Don't make the mistake of thinking I'll value you more than them, especially if you remain so ill-mannered. Am I understood?"

He stared at her, open-mouthed. Nicolina suppressed a laugh, badly. Greta almost wished she hadn't. Pietro needed to be taken down a peg or two.

"Yes, Signora Sarta," he replied in a restrained manner. "Please accept my apology. What would you like me to do next?"

Greta smoothed down her skirt. "Beading. We make a lot of dresses in this workshop and, leading up to the Guild Ball, we'll need as many hands as possible to do the beading on them. I'll bring out the chest of beads and a spare bit of cloth for you to display your skills. You can have until lunch for this task."

She took the sleeve with her into the workshop and found the small chest of beads. Sofia wouldn't be beading her cotton and linen bodice, so wouldn't miss the box. Greta found the same bit of cloth Nicolina had used on her testing day. She'd had the Copper Sarta unpick it before leaving so that she wouldn't need to waste another piece of material for today's testing. It had been well worth the effort.

Greta took them out into the workshop and placed them on Pietro's workbench.

"What pattern would you like me to bead?" he asked.

She glanced over to Nicolina and winked. "Your skills and your imagination will be tested here. My third-year apprentice has been working on the beading of a very important dress this past week. She helped design it herself after assisting me in choosing the beads. I don't have time to hold hands in my workshop.

"Perhaps after your test, I might allow you to view it as comparison. But I warn you, don't take the fact that she's a third-year apprentice as a sign that she's incompetent. I will be comparing your beading to hers."

Nicolina piped up at this point. "I'm not afraid to say that she's almost as good as I am at beading."

Pietro raised an eyebrow at her but said nothing. He simply opened the chest of beads to make his selection. Greta returned to the workshop and was surprised when he poked his head through the curtain.

"Signora Sarta, may I have a scrap of paper to draw my design? I don't want to make mistakes if I can help it."

She noticed Sofia stiffen at his appearance, but Pietro paid her no mind. Greta rose swiftly to find him some paper but purposely made her actions calm and measured so as to not alert him to Sofia's discomfort in him being there. The assault could be a bigger problem than Greta had anticipated. Domizio had been trusted even before the event and had helped bring her back home to safety. Pietro was an unknown entity, though at least his tone was more respectful now.

Greta handed him a pencil and a scrap of paper. Really, he ought to have both in a pocket or pouch, but she knew not all Sarti carried these tools around with them as she did. She even carried a needle, thread, scissors, and a measuring tape with her everywhere. She felt lost without them. It was a habit Ranieri had instilled in her. Greta hadn't realised it until recently, but her apprentices had taken to doing the same thing. If they didn't have pockets in their work dresses, they often wore a half apron with a pocket in front to carry everything.

Pietro thanked her for the tools and returned to the shopfront.

"Sofia, will you be happy for me to hire a Sarto?" she asked gently.

Sofia shrugged. "I wasn't expecting him to come back here. That's all."

"Yes, I understand. But I don't want to hire anyone who will make you uncomfortable."

"You can't make all your decisions based on what makes me uncomfortable," Sofia said quietly.

Greta didn't reply. At the end of the day, it wasn't Sofia's choice who she hired – that decision was all down to Greta. Pietro's manner was already a black mark against him. If his skills weren't better than Nicolina's, then she wouldn't hire him. If they were … well, she'd cross that bridge when she came to it.

"Now let me help you get your skirt ready. You need to line up the sides perfectly, and leave space for the zipper, otherwise it won't sit properly."

It took a few minutes for Sofia to line up the skirt to Greta's satisfaction. She was doing an admirable job considering it was her first dress.

"I'm going to start working on another order until you're done with that. We have some alterations that need my attention. Will you be alright in here by yourself for a few minutes?"

Sofia nodded without looking up. Greta walked out to the shopfront and over to Nicolina.

"Where's that alteration for Alberto di Gregorio? I understand Gregorio brought him in last Gildadi to have his trousers lengthened."

"Lengthened?" Nicolina asked in confusion. "How can you lengthen them?"

"He requested that I make them with a long hem so that they could be lengthened to keep pace with his son's amazingly fast growth spurts."

Greta smiled to herself. She'd encouraged the decision. It wasn't fair to have her loyal customers paying for new clothes every time their children grew a few inches. They'd probably have multiple visits to the Calzolai as well during those times.

"But ... aren't you cutting yourself out of a lot of business like that?"

"Only in the short term," Greta replied easily. "They'll be more loyal for the fact that I helped them during their children's time of rapid growth when other Sarti might not have."

Nicolina gave her a funny look. "You really do care for your clients, don't you?"

"Well, of course." Greta frowned. "Why shouldn't I?"

Nicolina shrugged but didn't answer. She handed Greta Signorino Alberto's trousers. They had been chalk-marked on the inside of the hem so Greta knew where to make the alteration. She took the trousers to the workshop and began work.

It was a soothing job. She found most alterations easy enough, especially when she'd made the clothes herself. It was more difficult when she had to alter someone else's handiwork. First, she had to figure out how they'd put the piece of clothing together before she could take it apart and fix it. But that wasn't the case here. She'd made Alberto's trousers herself and was the best person to alter them.

By the time she finished, she realised it was past lunch time and no one had bothered to tell her. She set down the trousers and watched Sofia at work for a moment. The girl was so intent on getting it right, she had the tip of her tongue poking out the side of her mouth.

"Sofia, put that down. We need to eat," she told her apprentice.

"Erm, you go ahead. I'm not hungry right now."

Greta walked over to Sofia and placed a hand on her shoulder. "This won't do, Fia. If you can't work side by side with him, I can't hire him."

Sofia pursed her lips and looked up at Greta just as Pietro walked into the workshop. He must have realised that he'd interrupted something because he backed out almost immediately, leaving his beading on the nearest workbench.

"I'll go and tell him," Greta said. "It isn't fair to continue the trial day if I've no intention of hiring him."

She walked out into the shopfront feeling miserable. She'd glanced at the beading on her way out and it really was very good. It was in the shape of a large wave with such colours that Greta could see the froth on top of the crest. Pietro would have been an asset to her workshop.

"Pietro, I..."

"Wait!" Sofia called.

Greta turned to find her standing next to Nicolina, as close to the curtain of the workshop as possible.

"Don't do it, Maestra. Look at his beading – it really is magnificent."

Nicolina took the beading from Sofia and raised her eyebrows appreciatively.

"I hate to admit it, but this is better than mine."

Greta looked from Nicolina to Sofia, torn with indecision. At least Sofia had braved coming into the shopfront to stop her making a mistake.

"Fine, let's have a quick bite to eat, then back to work. You too, Pietro. Turn the sign."

He did as he was told and didn't ask what had happened, though Greta could see the curiosity in his eyes. Lunch was a quiet affair. Sofia kept as far away from Pietro as possible trying not to make it obvious what she was doing. Greta doubted it fooled anyone in the room and the atmosphere was becoming increasingly awkward. Greta was relieved when Sofia finished her tiny meal and fled into the workshop. It didn't take long for the conversation to start once she had departed.

"Is she always like that?" Pietro asked, rather bluntly, though without his previous sneer.

Nicolina shook her head. "She wasn't last week."

They both turned to look at Greta. How could she explain this without violating Sofia's privacy?

"I don't know what to tell you," Greta replied truthfully. "Sofia ... had a difficult week and she doesn't know you."

Pietro chewed his bread thoughtfully for a few moments. "You were going to tell me not to bother with the rest of today, weren't you? Just before she stopped you."

Greta shrugged. There was no use in denying it.

"Was she ... attacked?" he lowered his voice.

Greta didn't want to answer. It hadn't happened to *her* – perhaps Sofia wouldn't want everyone knowing, especially strangers. It didn't matter. Her silence answered the question as well as words would have.

"I'll understand if you don't want to hire me," he said rather more kindly than Greta would have expected.

She met his steady gaze and bit her lip. It would be unfair of her to dismiss him when he hadn't done anything wrong.

"Let's just finish up the day and see what happens. Your stitch work really is quite good for a Copper Sarto. How long ago did you receive your Guild Mark?"

"Seven years ago." Pietro laughed. "I was a Copper Sarto for five years before I had the time to design another Great Work. I haven't enough time or money to make it though."

Greta frowned. "I simply don't understand. Why bother taking on apprentices at all if you don't plan to keep them until they can support themselves?"

Nicolina laughed loudly. "Oh Greta, you were so spoiled with Signore Ranieri. Very few Sarti keep on their apprentices once their apprenticeship is over. It isn't financially viable.

"Imagine you're a Silver Sarta and you get to have one apprentice. You've worked hard to get where you are and finally can afford to rent or buy a workshop of your own, but you can't take enough time to create another Great Work for your Electrum Guild Mark. If your apprentice does their five years with you, you won't suddenly be able to start paying them for doing what they were doing for free – even if you wanted to. You'd have to turn them out and get a new apprentice."

Greta frowned and shook her head. "No. You should at least still be able to keep your old apprentice until they can earn their Silver Guild Mark, even if you can't afford to employ them yourself."

"You wouldn't though," Pietro insisted. "If you only had enough money to rent or buy a small workshop, there wouldn't be enough room for yourself, an apprentice and a Copper Sarto to live. And you'd have to start charging them board to cover the cost of feeding them if you insisted on that courtesy. At that point, they may as well live somewhere else."

"I won't do that," Greta insisted. "When Annika earns her Copper Guild Mark, I'll employ her myself if she's willing to stay on."

"But Signora, you can afford to do that," Nicolina reminded her. "Not many Sarti are in your position. Most simply cannot afford to keep on their apprentices after they earn their Copper Guild Mark."

Greta crossed her arms angrily across her chest. It wasn't right. It wasn't *fair*. If it was such a problem in Tor'Esint, why did they allow so many people to train as Sarti? Or why didn't the Guild offer more shops for rent instead of forcing Sarti to purchase them outright when it was too expensive?

"Well, I won't do that with my girls," was all Greta said about it in the end. "Let's get back to work. Pietro, I've got an order for you to cut. It's your final test for today."

There was nothing else she could say. She knew she'd have to decide later, but she didn't want to think about it right now. It really did seem that Pietro was too great an asset to dismiss because he made Sofia feel uncomfortable. But Sofia's comfort was Greta's responsibility – she couldn't ignore it.

When she returned to her workbench, Greta checked on Sofia's progress. It was steady, but not fast. At this rate, the skirt wouldn't be ready until the next afternoon.

"Are you happy to keep working on that, or would you like some help?" Greta asked, leaning across Sofia's shoulder.

"No, I want to do it all myself," Sofia replied without looking up. "Besides, you have a lot of other orders to work on."

Greta knew she was right. She found another of Ranieri's orders and began working on it. They worked in silence but for the sound of fabrics brushing together. Eventually, Nicolina popped her head through the curtain.

"He's finished," she told Greta. "He doesn't want to come in to tell you himself."

Greta shook her head at Nicolina – she didn't want Sofia to feel more uncomfortable, but it was too late. Sofia looked up and grimaced. Greta gave her a short smile and went into the shopfront.

"Signora, I'm finished," Pietro said.

He stood behind the tiny workbench, hands behind his back, looking proudly down at his handiwork. Greta was pleased he took pride in his work. And his manner had certainly improved over the course of the day. He was much more respectful now – to all of them.

She picked up the order to see what he should have done. It was the trousers that Nicolina had tried the day before. The order hadn't been too specific other than it was to be a narrow fit. It looked vaguely familiar, but Greta didn't think it was a patent fee pattern, still she needed to check.

"Is this your own design?" she asked.

"Not entirely," he confessed. "But it's different enough not to have to pay patent fees, if that's what you're concerned about."

Greta shushed him. "My girls don't know about patent fees yet and you shouldn't talk about them so freely. What if someone had overheard?"

Pietro looked down, ashamed. "I'm sorry, Signora. All the workshops I've been in recently don't have apprentices. We all know not to use other Sarti's designs. I thought everyone knew. I haven't been an apprentice for so long I forgot."

Greta nodded. "Well, that's understandable. As long as you know how not to cost me money with your patterns, we'll leave it at that."

Greta inspected the workmanship. It really was quite good. She'd have been hard pressed to find anything wrong with it.

"It's very fine work," she told him. "I'm certain when you have time to complete it, your next Great Work will earn you your Silver Guild Mark with ease."

"So, does that mean you'll hire me?" he asked hopefully.

Greta glanced back at the workshop with indecision. The shop door opened, and Domizio walked in with Annika and Marta.

"We're starving!" he announced before he saw Pietro in the room. "Pietro! How's your testing going?"

Annika and Marta peered around Domizio's shoulders on either side, curious to see the next possible addition to their workshop.

Pietro shook Domizio's hand in greeting and looked sidelong at Greta. "We were just discussing that."

"Well, Greta, what do you think? Are you hiring him?" Domizio asked her tactlessly. He looked around the room and had a sudden thought. "Why were you working out here today? Surely there's more room in the back."

Nicolina coughed at the question. Domizio looked at her in confusion then seemed to finally notice the odd tension in the air.

"What's going on?" Domizio asked.

Annika elbowed him in the ribs. "Sofia," she whispered.

"Oh." Domizio went silent for a moment. "Is that going to be a problem, then?"

Sofia walked into the shopfront and stood behind Nicolina, again. All eyes turned on her.

"It won't be a problem," she said firmly, eyes just low enough she didn't need to meet their gaze. "Pietro didn't attack me and I doubt he'd think of it with all of you here to protect me anyway. Hire him, Maestra. You'd be a fool not to."

Pietro raised his eyebrows, paused a moment, and then walked over to Sofia. She visibly tensed at his approach, but Pietro stopped well away from her. He inclined his head towards her and spoke gently.

"Signorina Sofia, I promise never to lay a hand on you. If I can help find the scoundrel who hurt you, I'll make him wish he'd never touched you."

Ever so slowly, Sofia smiled. It wasn't so broad a smile that her dimples showed, but it was true enough that it reached her eyes. Greta took that as the best sign she was going to get.

"You're hired," she told Pietro. "You'll receive the same wages as Nicolina and Domizio. If any of you earn your Silver Guild Mark while you're working here, your wages will increase. Agreed?"

"Agreed," the three of them chorused enthusiastically.

\*\*\*

Later that afternoon, Greta continued arranging everything in her household to be moved. It wouldn't do to wait until the last moment to do it. The wicker baskets Aveline had sourced for her had been a good idea, but there weren't enough of them. Nicolina saw what she was doing and volunteered to go with her from house to house asking to borrow more baskets.

When Pietro and Domizio heard what they were doing, the two of them went as well. Between the four of them, they managed to take back twelve baskets of varying sizes. Greta hoped it would be enough. She hadn't moved homes since Ranieri had helped her find this very workshop. It had been easy to move then – all she'd had were her clothes and a very few Sarta tools. It had all fit neatly wrapped up in a swathe of cotton.

Cotton would do for many things, even with the baskets. She'd have to remember that when she began packing.

Back at home, the girls had made a large pot of pasta with legumes. It wasn't Greta's favourite dish, but it was filling. She invited the Sarti to stay for dinner, but they all declined.

"We'll be back tomorrow, Greta," Domizio told her patiently. "Remember, we aren't your apprentices – you've no obligation to feed us every night."

Greta made to protest, but he shook his head and motioned to Nicolina and Pietro. If she didn't want them knowing about the two of them, it would be best to keep their professional and personal business separate.

"Very well, then," she relented. "We'll see you tomorrow."

They left the house in a flurry of activity. Greta locked the door behind them and leaned back against it. Today had been exhausting. She didn't know how much more of this extra activity she could endure. All she wanted was one quiet day. But tomorrow was another day of testing.

"Who's coming tomorrow?" Marta asked, as they all sat down to dinner. "Is it another Copper Sarta?"

Greta nodded. "I had no idea so many qualified Sarti remain on their Copper Guild Mark for so many years. They're more skilled than I expected them to be. I think Nicolina and Pietro will be quite an asset to our workshop. The one coming tomorrow for testing is Elia."

"What do you know about her?" Annika asked.

"Not much, to be honest," Greta admitted. "Domizio has worked with all of them before. It's at his recommendation that I agreed to test these ones."

Annika frowned. "You put an awful lot of faith in him. Are you sure that's wise?"

Greta twisted her mouth to hide a grin. Annika never used to be so protective of her and their workshop. It was heartwarming to know how much she cared.

"I test them all with difficult skills, Annika. If they don't come up to my standards, I won't hire them. I almost didn't hire Pietro today, even though he's a better Sarto than Nicolina."

She bit her lip. She shouldn't have said that. It would only make Sofia feel uncomfortable.

"I'm glad you hired him," Sofia said firmly. "His beadwork was magnificent. It really was. He's so much faster than me as well. Imagine what an asset he'll be with all the ball gowns you're certain to have commissioned from you for the Guild Ball."

Marta threw an arm around Sofia's shoulder and hugged her tightly. The younger apprentice smiled shyly, her dimples popping adorably into her cheeks. Her character reaffirmed every day that Greta would leave a significant portion of her Final Testament to Sofia.

# Chapter 19 – Ramedi 10 Inventrici 230 Years After Implosion

The next morning brought a full workshop. Domizio, Nicolina and Pietro arrived one after the other a full quarter hour before trading started. Greta had to admit that she was surprised Pietro wasn't late again. Perhaps it was unfair of her to judge him so harshly, but his initial manner the day before had given her such a bad impression. He was clearly working hard to diminish that effect.

"Pietro, are you happy to go with Domizio, Annika and Marta to Ranieri's workshop to continue the pattern you cut yesterday? The girls will help you with the edging and tacking. Nicolina, if you don't mind remaining in the shopfront and continue on our repairs, that would be most helpful."

The bell tinkled as Elia opened the door. She poked her head in hesitantly, then smiled broadly when she saw the Copper Sarti. She took off her hat and nodded a greeting to them as she walked past to Greta.

"Good morning, Signora Sarta. My name is Elia. Thank you for offering a day of testing. I hope I'm up to your standards."

She said the words quickly, with little emotion, as though she had rehearsed them a hundred times. Her hat was held firmly in front of her. Greta nodded politely.

"You'll be given the same tests as Nicolina and Pietro – blind hemming, beading and pattern work."

Elia started at the list. "Really? That's..."

"A good list," Pietro interrupted her. "Greta Sarta has high standards – *Gold* standards, in fact – and expects all of us to do our best work for her."

Greta tried not to laugh at his defence of her. He'd argued against the list himself initially.

"Thank you, Pietro." Greta silenced him with a quick wave of her hand. "Domizio, please organise to take everything you'll need for today to Ranieri's workshop. And if you can see your way to taking some of the baskets Aveline and I packed on Riposidi, I'd be most grateful. We'll see you back here at closing. Don't forget to bring some food for lunch this time."

Annika and Marta laughed at that.

"*We'll* organise the food," Annika told him. "*You* organise the material for Pietro."

They bustled around the lower level of Greta's house so much that there was little point doing anything until they had left.

"Can I offer you a cup of tea, Elia?" Greta asked.

"Uh, yes, thank you, Signora," Elia stumbled over her words. "May I enquire as to why they're going to Ranieri's workshop?"

"There's more room there," Greta replied simply. Then realised Elia didn't understand the full situation. "Ranieri left me his workshop. It's much better suited for a Gold Sarta than this workshop. We've already started moving some things there. I have just over a week until this workshop is handed back to the Sarti Guild."

"I see," Elia said slowly, as apprentices and Sarti continued to bustle around her.

Greta took Elia gently by the elbow and showed her into the kitchen where she proceeded to boil a kettle of water. Taking no heed of the girls under her heels finding bits and pieces of food for their lunch, Greta set about selecting a tea to share with Elia, Sofia and Nicolina. By the time she'd prepared everything, including a tray with four teacups and saucers, the kettle finally boiled.

"Farewell, Maestra! We'll see you this evening!" Marta shouted out from the workshop.

Greta heard the bell tinkle furiously as the four of them exited the workshop. She didn't bother replying – they wouldn't have heard her anyway. She poured the water into the teapot and lifted the tray.

"Follow me," she told Elia.

She followed quickly on Greta's heels. Greta noticed her hat was still firmly held in her hands and her coat was still on. Instead of going straight through to the workshop, Greta detoured through the shopfront.

"The coatrack is there. Make yourself comfortable and then join me in the workshop."

She placed the tea tray on the shop counter and poured a cup for Nicolina. The Copper Sarta thanked her with a nod. Greta took the lighter tray into the workshop. As soon as she placed the tray down on her tea table, Sofia took over the tea duties, pouring the remaining three cups and taking the empty teapot into the kitchen.

When Sofia returned, she brought Elia with her. The young Sarta looked so nervous, Greta thought she'd faint on the spot.

"Sit here, Elia. Have some tea while you tell me about yourself."

Elia sat where she was directed and held the cup and saucer in both hands. She looked from Greta to Sofia and back again.

"I ... I'm a Copper Sarta," she said, hesitantly.

Greta waited for her to continue, but she didn't.

"Who was your Maestra?"

"Giovanna Sarta," Elia replied without extra details.

Greta smiled and sipped her tea, trying to hide her displeasure. Giovanna was still a Silver Sarta. If Elia had trained under her, that didn't bode well for her skills.

"And when did you earn your Copper Guild Mark."

"A little under two years ago, Signora."

Greta frowned. Why had Domizio suggested such an inexperienced Sarta to work with them?

"Have you worked with Domizio, Nicolina or Pietro before?"

Elia nodded, almost spilling her tea. "We all worked together for Signore Biagio last year.

"Biagio, really?" Greta mused aloud. He was a Silver Sarta with more money than sense. Greta disliked him intensely. It was rumoured he used his apprentices and hired hands poorly. "Did you like it there?"

Elia sipped her tea, avoiding the question with a shrug. She seemed quite a nervous character. Greta thought it would be cruel to press her any further. She finished off her own tea and went to find the sleeve she'd had Pietro work on the day before.

"You can blind hem the other side of this sleeve. You'll find everything you need in that cabinet there. You can work in here, or out in the shopfront with Nicolina."

She handed the sleeve to Elia and pointed out the cabinet with all their needles and thread. Leaving Elia to her own devices, Greta walked over to Sofia who was already hard at work on her copy of Signora Loyola's skirt.

"You're almost ready to attach the skirt to the bodice now," Greta told her approvingly. "Now, take the cover off that mannequin and look at how I did it. See if you can't figure out how to do your one from that."

Sofia eagerly put down her skirt and went to uncover the mannequin. She drew the cover off carefully and let out a content sigh at the near-completed dress. There was a gasp from behind them.

"That's exquisite!" Elia blurted out.

Greta nodded at her compliment, but Sofia positively glowed with pride. She'd never had so much to do with an order before. It was likely she wouldn't again until her fourth year. Especially now that Greta had hired Sarti working for her.

Sofia studied the join between the skirt and the bodice.

"Did you just sew this on the inside?"

Greta shook her head. "I first sewed the outside, then the inside to create a neater seam. That makes the stitching invisible from the outside. It's a technique Ranieri taught me in my fourth year, and I've been using it ever since. Now it's your turn to try it."

She watched and explained by turns then eventually left Sofia to her work and turned to Elia.

"Are you done with that hemming?" Greta asked the Copper Sarta.

The girl startled so badly she pricked herself with her needle. Greta stared at her. Could she really be so very nervous as that?

"I'm not happy with it," Elia mumbled, sucking on her bleeding finger.

"Well, you've been working on it for over half an hour. Let me see what you've done so far."

Elia held tightly to the sleeve. Greta disliked her attitude. She stalked over to Elia and forcibly took the sleeve from her. Elia was right to be nervous – it was not well done at all. She could see the stitching more clearly than even Marta's worst blind hemming.

Greta cleared her throat to cover her disappointment. "Blind hemming doesn't appear to be one of your strengths. Let's try the beading and see how you go with that."

She tried not to make up her mind about Elia straight away. She'd almost done it with Pietro and that would have been a mistake. Perhaps blind hemming was the only thing Elia was bad at. Greta knew she was putting off the inevitable. If Elia couldn't blind hem, she'd be almost useless with the more difficult orders.

"Sofia, show Elia the beading material while I double check everything on this dress."

Greta wasted no more time on the Copper Sarta. Instead, she concentrated on Signora Loyola's dress, checking every section to ensure it was perfect. She wasn't entirely convinced the loop was the right size for the beads they'd chosen to fasten the neck.

She carefully took the dress off the mannequin and unpicked that side of the neck to redo it. She noticed Sofia come over and watch her but didn't stop what she was doing. This was an important process for her apprentice to watch. Poor Sofia had been given too few opportunities like this before, but Greta placated herself that this dress alone was making up for so much that Sofia had missed out on in the past years.

"You really don't notice the time, do you?" Nicolina said, popping her head through the curtain. "My stomach's been rumbling since midday. We need to eat."

"You go ahead," Greta said without looking up. "Sofia, turn the sign and have lunch with Nicolina and Elia. I'm going to keep working on this. I'm almost done."

"No," Sofia said firmly. "I'm not leaving while you finish it. I want to see how you do it. Can't you stop just for a little bit?"

Greta shook her head. "I don't like stopping when I'm so close. I'll eat later."

"You go ahead, Nicolina," Sofia said authoritatively. "You and Elia can eat now, and we'll eat later. I hope."

Greta grunted at her comment. Sofia knew her too well. Apparently, Nicolina was coming to as well. When she and Elia had finished eating, she brought in a slice of buttered bread for Sofia and a cup of tea for Greta.

"At least drink something," Nicolina instructed her. "What would we do if you collapsed from exhaustion just as you were cutting the final thread off that dress? You'd ruin it without a hope of fixing it before it's due."

That got Greta's attention. She stopped what she was doing, gently placed the dress on her workbench and took the offered teacup. Nicolina grinned at her. Greta rolled her eyes and drank her tea, noticing that Nicolina had snuck a biscuit on the saucer to force her to eat just a little something. She grudgingly ate it and passed the cup and saucer back to Nicolina.

"Now, if you don't mind, I'll get back to work."

Greta continued working until the neck and loop were finished later that afternoon. She dressed the mannequin again and stood back to admire her handiwork. It really was a stunning dress. The full circle satin skirt with the satin and organza-beaded bodice was such a wonderful combination, it took her breath away.

"Maestra, it's amazing!" Sofia hugged her suddenly. "Thank you for letting me help. I'll remember this forever."

Greta patted Sofia on the back and waited patiently for her to let go. Neither Annika nor Marta had ever reacted like this to a dress.

"We need to get a message to Signora Loyola to come try on her dress tomorrow so I can make any minor adjustments before hemming the skirt."

Sofia stared at her with wide eyes. It only took Greta a moment to realise why.

"Take Nicolina with you. She's one of us now."

Sofia breathed a sigh of relief and smiled gratefully. "Yes, Maestra. We'll go now."

Greta waited for her to leave before covering up the dress and approaching Elia. The Copper Sarta tensed at her approach.

"May I see your beading?" she asked calmly.

Elia held it up to her, eyes downcast. Greta took it from her without much hope. The design was uninspired – concentric circles. She turned it over and bit her tongue to stop from gasping at the mess of threads on the back. It was the most atrocious piece of beading Greta had seen in a long time.

"Elia, I'm sorry. I don't think I can hire you."

"But I'm not finished testing yet. What about the pattern?" she asked in a trembling voice.

Greta shook her head. "As a Copper Sarta, I should be able to trust you with any task and I simply can't. Even if your blind hemming wasn't as bad as it was, your beading isn't even close to satisfactory. You saw the beading on our latest dress. My *third-year apprentice* did that. If she's more skilled than you, I ought to be paying her twice as much as you. I'm sorry, Elia. I'll have to ask you to go."

Greta handed her five coppers.

"This is for today."

Elia took the coppers with downcast eyes. It seemed like she really had her heart set on working here, but Greta couldn't allow it.

By the time Sofia and Nicolina returned, Elia was gone. Greta didn't mind. She already had three qualified Copper Sarti working for her. It would be much easier now to complete her orders in a timely fashion, even if they increased twofold because of Signora Loyola's dress.

"Where's Elia?" Nicolina asked, looking around the empty workshop.

Greta shook her head. "Her work was, quite frankly, atrocious. I sent her away."

Nicolina frowned. "But Elia's the best of all of us. We always get her to do her testing last if we have a choice, so they don't compare our work to hers."

Greta narrowed her eyes. "How long has she been a Copper Sarta?"

"Ten years."

Greta felt faint. Something was terribly wrong.

"She told me she'd only been a Copper Sarta for two years. Her work was terrible – worse than an apprentice's." Greta put aside the repair she was working on. "Who was the last Sarta who hired her? Was it the same as all of you?"

Nicolina shook her head. "Domizio was working elsewhere, but the rest of us were with Domenico."

Greta felt sick. "Did Domenico ask you to come and spy on me?"

"No!" Nicolina said forcefully. "I would *never* have done that!"

"But perhaps Elia would. And even Pietro may have," Greta said quietly. She sat down before her legs gave way under her. "You saw the way he treated me to start with. Is he always like that? Or was he purposely trying to get fired?"

Nicolina bit her lip. "He's not always like that. He can be a bit of a pain, but he's not normally *that* rude. He changed his mind quickly enough though."

The bell tinkled and the rest of Greta's household and staff entered. They stopped when they felt the tension in the room. Domizio was the one who approached her first. Greta hadn't even considered that *he* could be a spy, but Domizio was the one who'd recommended Elia.

"Domizio, have you ever worked for Domenico like the others?" she asked as he tried to take her hand.

"No, Greta. I wouldn't work for that ash-sucker even if he paid me double rates."

Greta breathed a sigh of relief until she noticed Pietro looking nervous.

"What about you, Pietro? Did he offer you something to spy on me?"

Pietro drew himself up to his full height. "He did. And I considered it. It was a hefty fee for telling him who your clients are and what you're making for them. It wouldn't have been too difficult. But I changed my mind after I saw the way you treat everyone here. It wouldn't have been fair to you."

Greta smiled mirthlessly. "Apparently, Elia didn't share your view."

Pietro turned on Nicolina. "Coli, why didn't you stop her?"

"Me?" Nicolina asked angrily. "I didn't know what she was doing! Domenico didn't ask *me* to spy. Why didn't *you* stop her?"

Pietro turned red. "I ... didn't know he'd asked her too. Besides, I wasn't here watching her make a mess of things."

"She was back there," Nicolina said, motioning to the workshop. "I couldn't see what she was doing either, or I would've called her out on it."

Greta's stomach clenched. Without a word, she fled to the water closet and locked herself in. She clutched at her stomach as her bowels emptied painfully. Minutes later, when she was certain nothing else could possibly come out, she left the water closet.

Sofia was waiting for her with a small metal hot water canister wrapped in thick wool. She took it gratefully and held it to her stomach. Warmth flooded through her, but she still felt sick. Sofia offered her an arm to help her back down the stairs. Everyone was waiting for them in the kitchen.

"Do you want us to find her?" Domizio asked as soon as she sat down. "She might not have spoken to Domenico yet."

Greta looked up at him desolately. "Find her if you can, but the damage may already be done. Signora Loyola didn't want anyone to know I was making a new dress for her, especially not in this style. I should never have let any of you into my workshop without making you promise not to speak a word of it."

"Even had you sworn us to silence, Elia mightn't have kept that promise if she'd already promised to spy on you," Nicolina reasoned. "I don't understand why she'd agree to it in the first place. Nor *you*." She glared at Pietro.

He shrugged. "For the money, obviously. He was offering ten electrums. It was a ridiculously good offer for such an easy task and would've given me the luxury to create my next Great Work."

Greta felt tears rolling down her cheeks. She buried her head in her arms and refused to look up at them – *any* of them. Her three apprentices and her three hired Sarti. This was meant to be the start of something wonderful – how wrong she had been!

She cried softly on the table, clutching the hot metal canister to her stomach with one hand. Sofia slung an arm over her shoulders and held her tight. Greta could tell it was her by the smell of lavender wafting over her. Sofia insisted on putting lavender flower sachets in her clothes drawer to keep them fresh.

A while later, a plate was placed noisily in front of her.

"Greta, you must eat something," Nicolina told her. "All you've had today was a biscuit and your breakfast. Someone please tell me she ate breakfast!"

No one answered. Nicolina pulled Greta up by the shoulder when she didn't move.

"Your girls warmed you a plate of pasta. Domizio and Pietro are out searching for Elia. Eat."

Greta looked at the legume pasta in front of her. It was the leftovers from yesterday. She hated leftover pasta. Even when the girls warmed it on the stove the next day, it never tasted as good. But her family had also been poor enough that she refused to waste food if she could help it.

She took the fork, speared a piece and brought it to her mouth. She chewed it slowly, trying not to feel sick again. Sofia took her fork away.

"I'll toast some bread for you. We'll eat the pasta instead, won't we girls?"

Annika and Marta barely hesitated before nodding. Greta tried not to cry at their kindness but couldn't stop herself. She regretted it as saltwater fell into her mouth and made the pasta taste even worse.

Sofia used the heating rod to toast some bread for Greta. She buttered it generously and served it up. At a nudge from Nicolina, Greta picked up the toast and nibbled away at it. She watched silently as Annika ladled out pasta for Marta and Sofia, taking Greta's discarded plate for herself. She offered some to Nicolina who declined, reminding them that she'd have dinner with her mother later.

The apprentices sat down with her to eat. Sofia brought over the tea she'd made and poured some out for everyone. They ate in silence. Greta tried not to think of how Elia could ruin her with a single day of watching her workshop. Aside from the tiny amount of organza in Signora Loyola's dress, she couldn't have seen anything suspicious. Besides Signora Loyola's name – had they mentioned it? – she couldn't have found out about any other customers. Perhaps it wasn't so bad. Perhaps Domenico would pay her and that would be the end of it. He might be able to use her pattern, but Elia had not been left in the workshop alone so Greta knew she couldn't have seen exactly how the dress was made.

She took a deep breath. Perhaps it really wouldn't be as bad as all that. She could warn Signora Loyola when she came in tomorrow for a fitting. Surely Greta couldn't be held accountable if Domenico stole her design. He couldn't possibly make the same dress before Signora Loyola's dinner party.

Greta would have to be more careful in the future. Ranieri's shop didn't have a hidden workroom. She might need to put in a folding screen to hide any orders she didn't want visitors to see. That should be easy enough.

By the time the men returned, dinner was finished, and all the dishes had been washed and cleared away. Greta had relocated herself to the workshop and sat curled up in her favourite armchair with her hot metal canister held close to her stomach and the new Liquid Sunlight glowing beside her. Sofia kept her company, but the others were in the kitchen playing a game of cards to pass the time.

Sofia turned at the sound of the bell over the door. Greta didn't move. Domizio and Pietro would come to her soon enough. And so they did, after a quick detour through the kitchen.

"We found her," Pietro told her. Greta didn't look at him. She kept her eyes firmly on Signora Loyola's covered dress. "She'd already been to Domenico and told him everything she could. He was an ash-sucker to her, paying only a tenth of his promised price."

At that, Greta turned a hard stare on him. "You think I care that an ash-sucker herself was used so badly?"

Pietro coughed uncomfortably. "No, of course not. I only meant to tell you that the information she passed him cannot have been so valuable as he was hoping for. She can't have ruined your business."

Greta paused. He was correct, of course. She should be thankful for that, but she was still afraid.

"And what of you?" she asked pointedly. "Do I have any reason to keep you on, knowing that you could turn spy at any time?"

"Greta, that's unfair," Domizio interjected. "He didn't have to tell you that Domenico tried to hire his services. You can trust him."

Pietro knelt in front of Greta and pricked his finger with a needle.

"I swear by my blood that I will do nothing to hurt you or your workshop. You've been kinder to me than you had any reason to be. I'm sorry I didn't tell you about Domenico's offer before. I would have if I'd thought he'd made the same offer to Elia."

Greta took a square of white cloth from a hidden pocket in her dress. It already had three drops of blood on it. Now, she added Pietro's to it.

"What's that?" Sofia asked looking curiously at the cloth.

"It's a promise cloth," Domizio answered. "A vow to always look out for the best interest of that person, never take advantage of or harm them in any way."

Sofia looked at the cloth as Greta laid it out to dry.

"Who else's blood is on there?" she asked.

"My father's, my sister's and Ranieri's," Greta replied quietly. "I gave them all a drop of my blood too."

"Does that mean you need to give Pietro a drop of *your* blood now?" Sofia asked, clearly confused by the ritual.

"No," Pietro replied firmly. "Never. She hasn't any reason to."

Sofia looked at him in confusion. "I don't understand."

"One day you will," Pietro told her. "It would be like me offering you a blood promise to keep you safe because of yesterday. You shouldn't give me a blood promise for anything because you never wronged me and have no great affection for me."

Sofia nodded slowly. Greta could see her doing the mental calculations. All three of Greta's previous blood promises had been out of affection, but Ranieri had exchanged blood promises with her just before she submitted her first Great Work. It had been just as much for his sake as hers. She was sworn never to go against him as he was sworn to help her as much as he could. They had both kept their word. They would have even without the blood promise.

There was a long moment of silence.

"What do we do now?" Sofia asked.

Greta finally stood up. "We go to bed. Tomorrow, we begin moving in earnest and we've barely begun to pack. We'll have to wake up early to get things ready. Good night."

She walked calmly to her room and locked herself in. Only then did she succumb to tears again.

# Chapter 20 – Argentodi 11 Inventrici 230 Years After Implosion

Greta woke to the sound of pots banging and muffled curses. She picked up her pocket watch and muttered her own curse. It was almost eight o'clock. So much for her waking up early to get things organised.

She dressed quickly, refreshed herself in the water closet and went downstairs. Her house was full of commotion. Aveline and Nevio were in the kitchen, taking cutlery and plates out of drawers and stacking them carefully into wicker baskets. Telchide's daughter and apprentices were clearing out the cupboards and packing things into wooden boxes.

"Good morning, Greta." Aveline paused what she was doing and got to her feet. "We're almost finished in here. Your girls were quite insistent that only *they* should be allowed in your workshop.

"They've stolen Chide and your new hired Sarti to help move things across the Piazza and are taking the precaution of covering everything with a large sheet of cotton. Though Chide is helping more to organise where things should go as they move them – he can't actually carry anything with his leg."

Greta took in the flood of information.

"I suppose I'll start upstairs then," she said.

Aveline shook her head. "I'm under strict instructions to ensure you eat something first. Your girl, Sofia, will have my head otherwise. Sit there, Florio will get you something."

Greta sat, with Aveline gently pushing her shoulders down. Aveline went back to work with Nevio, and Florio served Greta a bowl of hot porridge with honey and cinnamon.

"Sofia told me this is your favourite and you're going to need your strength for today, even with all of us helping, " Florio said jovially as he put the kettle on the stove and found the tea stores. "She's quite beautiful and has such a lovely smile. I never knew a girl with such wonderful dimples in *both* cheeks. And her hair!"

The other young man groaned. "What my brother is trying to tell you is that he's fallen in love with Sofia at first sight."

"Quiet, Gaspare," Florio waved a hand at him. "I haven't fallen. I'm still on my feet."

"Oh, *my apologies*." Gaspare bowed mockingly. "You're only smitten. The falling head over heels will come shortly."

At that moment, Sofia walked through the door. Florio gave her a dazzling smile, which made Sofia's cheeks turn a bright shade of red.

"Maestra, we're about to make the trip to the other workshop. Do you want us to put things in order, or just take everything over and sort it out later?"

Greta couldn't help noticing that Sofia kept glancing at Florio as she spoke, her smile growing larger by the second. It gave her hope that Sofia's wariness around men might be temporary.

"Just take everything over and we'll sort it out later. If you can keep like things together, that would help, but otherwise, I trust your judgement."

"As well you should, Signora," Florio expounded. "She's a very clever girl, your Sofia is."

"Florio, serve the tea and get back to work or I'll make you read aloud to all of us," Teresina ordered the boy.

Florio nodded and instantly closed his mouth. Greta wondered how the child had come up with such an odd threat and why in Caldera's smoke it had worked.

Sofia backed out of the room, favouring Florio with another smile. Greta wondered if the two of them might become fast friends. She found the idea pleasing. Telchide was teaching his apprentices well and they had a wonderfully amiable manner that made it difficult to dislike them.

Greta finished her breakfast and drank her tea. She tried to take her dishes to the sink, but Gaspare intercepted her, promising he'd take good care of them and she could take good care of things upstairs. Greta gave Aveline a bemused look, but the Inventrice only laughed.

"You get used to them after a while. There's no point arguing when they're in a helpful mood."

"Or a talkative one." Nevio heaved an exaggerated groan. "Do you have any idea how long it takes us to set up our stalls on Mercatodi these days with the two of them jabbering away with each other?"

Greta coughed to cover a laugh. It seemed that Aveline's new arrangements really might work out. She could tell from Nevio's tone that he actually quite enjoyed spending time with the twins, but the idea of living separately was probably the only reason things hadn't become strained between the apprentices. Seven of them under one roof would have been unimaginable!

To avoid further discussion, Greta returned upstairs with a stack of baskets to sort out the bedrooms. She began with her own. It was mostly clothes and a few personal belongings. They would work just as well if she left them in the cabinets and took them together, but there were cabinets enough at Ranieri's house. No, best to take everything out and put it in baskets. The cabinets could stay here.

It took her more time than she'd anticipated. There were more personal belongings in drawers and cabinets than she had thought. Many of them were keepsakes from when she was younger and living at home with her father and sister. Some were from her time in Ranieri's workshop. Others, she blushed at the memories, were from previous lovers who wished to favour her with trinkets.

Those, she wrapped carefully in one of her old skirts. They were not necessarily things she wanted everyone to see. Some of the trinkets were more expensive than they should have been and showed how deep a signore's regard for her had been.

She would've liked to have some items on display, but knew awkward questions could be posed about when she'd acquired them or from whom. And those were questions she didn't want to answer – not to her apprentices, not to whichever lover was in her favour. In her experience, it would only serve to make a lover insecure or angry, neither of which was conducive to a pleasant intimate experience.

Would Domizio care if she selected a few favourite items to display? Perhaps her new, larger bedroom would be the perfect excuse to display a few favourite items.

When she'd finished her room, she went to the girls' room. It was much easier to pack up their belongings. They only had five dresses each, a selection of sleeves to mix and match with them, a handful of stockings and undergarments, and very few personal belongings. Greta promised herself that she'd allow the girls to make their own clothes whenever they had spare time. After all, they couldn't edge material forever.

She brought the baskets downstairs, one at a time. Who knew clothes could be so heavy? The basket of bed linen was the lightest of them all! She took a smaller basket for the water closet. There wouldn't be much in there, but she'd need to pack it anyway.

By the time she'd finished, the kitchen was empty of people and baskets. Greta brought the last three baskets into the shopfront and deposited them with all the other baskets. It looked like most of her house had been packed away already.

Aveline had sent Nevio, Florio and Gaspare along with the others to bring things to Ranieri's workshop. Only Teresina and Aveline remained in the workshop. Teresina ran around wildly, looking at all things Sarta related.

Greta noticed with some amusement that she was wearing an identical dress to Aveline's, pockets and all.

"That's a lovely dress you have, Teresina," Greta told the young girl.

Teresina puffed out her chest and stood tall, grinning broadly.

"Nonna changed it when I asked her to. I told her I wanted one just like Aveline's with *lots* of pockets. One *must* have pockets on a work dress or it just isn't useful, don't you think?" Teresina barely paused for breath. "I wish I could have another dress, with a zipper this time, but Papá says I already have too many clothes. Four dresses are plenty for any young signora, and besides, I'm going to grow out of them so quickly he doesn't want Nonna making me too many. I suppose he's right, but that doesn't make me happy."

Aveline lay a hand on Teresina's shoulder. The girl reacted immediately. She clasped her hands in front of her and shut her mouth. Though Greta noticed there was no shame in the action. Aveline must have coached her quite well to not allow the girl to feel she shouldn't be talking so much.

"Perhaps I can do something about that," Greta told the girl conspiratorially. "As payment for helping me move, you understand. I can make you a dress with plenty of room to grow so you can use it for years and not feel like it was a waste to make it."

Teresina's mouth gaped into a large circle. Greta smiled and nodded. Aveline rolled her eyes at Greta.

"You don't need to, Greta," Aveline said softly. Teresina heard her and looked as though she was about to cry.

"It's not problem," Greta insisted. "It won't take me long. In fact, if Teresina agrees, I might even have my apprentices work on it for experience. What do you think, Teresina?"

Teresina's eyes went wide. "Oh yes, Signora Sarta. That would be wonderful! Perhaps I can become a Sarta one day and make my own dresses."

Aveline shook her head. "Resi, you're already torn between being an Inventrice and an Alchimista, let's not add Sarta to the mix or your poor papà will fall over himself to give you everything, which we both know is impossible."

Teresina deflated slightly. "You're right. I probably don't have the patience to be a Sarta anyway."

The door opened, but no bell tinkled. Greta looked up and realised the bell was gone. It made sense. There was no bell at Ranieri's workshop. There never had been. She hadn't missed it while she'd apprenticed there, but now that she was used to it, she realised she'd miss it if she didn't bring it along. One of the girls must have though the same thing and taken it with them.

Signora Loyola walked in and looked around in surprise. "Signora Sarta, I hope you didn't call me down here needlessly!"

Greta moved to welcome her in.

"Of course not, Signora Loyola. We're moving across the Piazza to Ranieri Sarto's old workshop. However, I made certain not to allow anyone to move your dress until after your final fitting."

That made the signora pause, mouth open. She closed her mouth and looked mollified.

"Very well, let me try it on then. Is it almost finished?"

Greta smiled. "Indeed. I only need to measure the perfect length to hem the skirt. Now, if you'll undress behind the curtain here, as usual, I'll bring you the dress."

Signora Loyola secluded herself behind the curtain and Greta quickly went into the back workshop. The dress was still covered on the mannequin. She breathed deeply and closed her eyes. She fervently hoped Signora Loyola would be pleased with the final product. Greta drew off the cover, undressed the mannequin and brought the dress to the curtain, ensuring it was hidden from street view the entire time.

She passed the dress through the curtain and waited for Signora Loyola to put it on. It was a long wait. Greta smoothed down her dress in anxious anticipation.

"Isn't that the signora who ordered that big music box from papà?" Teresina whispered to her. Greta nodded. "What kind of dress did you make for her?"

"An evening gown," Greta whispered back. "For her dinner party to show off the music box."

Teresina grinned. "The music box is ready too. Papà doesn't want her to know otherwise she'll keep trying to order things too quickly. He's so tired these days with the extra..." she broke off and bit her lip. "He's got a lot of work."

Greta looked at Teresina in surprise. She was being evasive the same way Aveline had been earlier.

"Veli, you and Chide had better finish your project soon," she said quietly. "You're all so bad at keeping secrets, it'll be out soon."

Aveline raised an eyebrow at Teresina who gave her an injured look of innocence.

"Signora Sarta, I'm ready for you."

Greta left the two of them to attend her client. She stepped through the curtain and marvelled at her work. It really was the most magnificent gown she'd ever made. She checked every seam, every measurement to ensure everything was perfect, pinning the hem at the end.

"How's the length? Will you be wearing heeled shoes or flat shoes?"

Signora Loyola grasped her hand. "The length is perfect. The dress is perfect. How can I ever repay you?"

Greta squeezed her hand gently. "Your happiness and continued custom are all I wish for."

"May we see the dress?" Teresina shouted from behind the curtain.

Greta's eyes widened in horror.

"Teresina, quiet!"

She heard Aveline's reprimand, but it was too late. Signora Loyola had clearly heard them. Her face was an impassive mask.

"Tell me, is that the Inventore's daughter out there?"

Greta nodded. "And my best friend."

"Is she a Sarta?"

"She's an Inventrice," Greta replied with a shake of her head, then remembered with a sickening lurch to her stomach that she needed to tell Signora Loyola about Elia.

"Very well then. If they come back here, there can marvel at your work without anyone else seeing."

Greta couldn't believe her ears. Signora Loyola's manner had completely changed since the first time she'd come in to order this gown. Before she could change her mind, Greta opened the curtain and beckoned Aveline and Teresina back to them.

Teresina raced over and stopped dead in her tracks when she saw the dress, her mouth gaping open.

"Oh Signora Sarta, it's the most amazing gown I've ever seen!"

Aveline joined them at a more reserved pace. But even she gasped.

"Signora, I don't know what your guests will marvel at more – your dress or your music box," Aveline stated.

Signora Loyola smiled in a very pleased manner. "They're both magnificent. I don't understand how Telchide Inventore hasn't got his Gold Guild Mark yet."

Aveline choked and began coughing. Greta patted her gently on the back. Teresina looked at them all confused.

"Papà can't lodge so many of his Great Works because of the silly edict."

"Teresina!" Greta shouted at the same time as Aveline. The girl realised her error and clasped both hands over her mouth.

"Don't tell papà I said that!" Teresina whispered, horrified.

"You should be thankful Signora Loyola is sympathetic to our plight and no one else was around to hear you," Aveline scolded her. "Go and stand back out in the shopfront and keep your thoughts to yourself."

Teresina turned her back to them, eyes full of tears. Greta almost felt sorry for the girl, but she really did need to learn to watch what she said.

"Don't be too hard on her, Signora Inventrice," Signora Loyola told her. "She's only a child."

Aveline shook her head. "Even a child can ruin a career with a misspoken word these days. What would she do if her words landed her papà in prison?"

There was a tense moment of silence as they all contemplated that scenario. It was not a pleasant one. Greta thought it might be the best opportunity she had to raise the issue of Elia.

"Signora Loyola, there's something I must tell you," she confessed. "I've been testing Sarti this week before hiring them to help me with my increased workload. Unfortunately, several of them were asked to spy on me by a fellow Sarto. One of them accepted the offer and reported back last night.

"She wasn't alone with your dress at any point in time, but she did see it for a few minutes and would still have been able to describe at least the front to the Sarto. I cannot recall if she knew it was for you, and in any case, she cannot have known it was for your dinner party. I'm sorry, Signora. I didn't know until she had already left."

Aveline made the smart move to remove herself from their discussion. Greta couldn't blame her – she didn't want to be there herself.

"I'll understand if you want to pay a reduced price for the dress," Greta offered. "After all, one of the conditions was that no one know the details of this dress until you wore it at the dinner party."

"Signora Inventrice, a moment please."

Aveline reappeared at the request of Signora Loyola.

"Do you know how close Telchide is to finishing my music box?"

Aveline glanced at Greta dubiously. Greta only shrugged.

"Will you promise not to insist on the same timeframe for any other orders?"

Signora Loyola nodded. Aveline bit her lip.

"It's done. He'll want another day to finish the paintwork on the wood, but that's all."

"And how long will it take you to finish the dress?"

Greta quickly did the mental calculations. "I think I could finish it by tomorrow evening."

"And there's no chance your ash-sucking Sarto will be able to create a dress like this in that time?"

Greta almost laughed. "Of course not. Even if he already had the material at his fingertips."

"Very well then. I shall move my dinner party to the night after tomorrow night, Orodi. That should give everyone enough time and still not spoil the effect on my friends."

Greta nodded. "I'll bring the dress to your house myself that morning and make any final alterations there."

"Very good. Bring that young apprentice of yours as well. I have a little something for her."

Greta quickly agreed. She didn't mention anything about the cost again. Whatever Signora Loyola agreed to would be all she could expect at this point. She should have been more careful with who she invited into her back workshop.

She closed the curtain for Signora Loyola and led Aveline back into the shopfront.

"Is he really ready?" she whispered as quietly as she could.

Aveline nodded and whispered back just as quietly. "It's been ready for days. He just hasn't told her that. Even the paintwork is done. I only said it wasn't to give you more time."

Greta couldn't contain herself. She hugged Aveline fiercely. She was still hugging her when Telchide walked in with Domizio and Nicolina. He looked at them suspiciously.

"Telchide, you'll need to finish that music box for Signora Loyola tomorrow," Aveline said loudly, pointing to the curtained off area behind her.

Telchide looked at her in confusion and was just about to speak when Signora Loyola herself emerged in her day clothes. His eyes grew so large, Greta thought they would pop from his head.

"Signora Loyola, what a pleasure to see you here," he said quickly, taking his cap off only to lose his balance as his crutch fell to the floor. Aveline was instantly there to prop him up and retrieve it.

Greta smiled at their mutual insecurity and was thankful she wasn't quite as bad or as obvious about hers.

"We've had a little hitch in our plans and Signora Loyola needs to bring forward her dinner party," Greta explained. "I'm sorry for the inconvenience Telchide. I hope I can make it up to you by allowing my apprentices to make another work dress for your daughter."

Teresina couldn't help herself – she ran at Greta and hugged her legs so tightly they both almost fell over.

"Erm, yes, of course, that's too kind," Telchide replied, confused by the turn of events. "She has so many dresses already."

Teresina glowered at him. "*Four*, papà. I have only *four* dresses."

"Yes, well."

Telchide twisted his cap even further. Signora Loyola took this opportunity to exit.

"I shall see you in two days, Signora Sarta," she said as she passed her. "Signore Inventore, I shall come past to pick up the music box myself as soon as you tell me it's ready. Thank you both for your discretion in this matter, even though it must have caused you both such grief."

Greta nodded silently and noticed that Aveline had taken Telchide's arm to prevent him saying anything he shouldn't. Once Signora Loyola had left, everyone let out a collective breath. Greta started laughing, so did Aveline. The others stared at them incredulously.

"That was fortunate," Greta said, wiping a stray tear from the corner of her eye. "I'm sorry to put you in such a position, Telchide, but Veli told me you've already finished the music box."

Telchide turned a glare at Aveline. She waved his concern away.

"Greta was in trouble, Chide. Someone was spying on her and saw the dress. There wasn't anything we could do about it."

Telchide sighed. "I suppose that means I've no excuse to stay in my own workshop anymore. I'll be free to work on ... our other project."

Greta bit her tongue. There was no point in making him angrier by letting him know that she already knew about their secret project.

"Well then, let's finish this move so I can complete the dress without any more danger of spies."

Everyone got to work, picked up boxes and baskets and walking them through the Piazza.

\*\*\*

Greta stood alone in her new workshop. She'd sent the others ahead to find a table at Ristorante Zola where she would be treating them to dinner. Everyone's generosity had completely overwhelmed her. She couldn't believe that everything had been moved in a single day.

Her old workshop was completely empty now. Even her mannequins and all her workbenches had been brought over. There would never be a need to go back there again.

It felt odd, being back in Ranieri's workshop – *her* workshop. When she'd left it, years ago, it had felt like leaving home all over again. Now it was the reverse – she felt like she was coming home again. *This* was where she belonged. She'd always belonged here. Ranieri would have been happy for her to stay but knew she needed her independence from him.

She'd taken that independence and run with it. It amused her now, as it must have amused Ranieri, that she'd turned from his way of doing things when she'd left and then turned back to them when she'd realised they really were the best ways to do things. It had irked her at the time, but at least she could say she'd tried something different.

There was a scuffle at the step. Greta turned to see Domizio repositioning himself against the door. He'd insisted on waiting to escort her safely to the ristorante, even though it was only a few blocks away.

She turned back to the piles of boxes and baskets littering the workshop and sighed. There'd be time enough to deal with that in the coming days. She'd have to organise her staff so that there was always someone putting things in their rightful place so that the others could get on with their work in relative peace.

"Let's go," she told Domizio as she locked the door behind her. "You deserve that dinner."

"So do you," he replied with a nudge. "I know Pietro and I moved most of the bigger things, but you were the one organising where everything had to go. If it weren't for you, this workshop would be an even bigger mess than it is. At least this way we'll still be able to find the things we need without looking through every basket."

Greta took his arm and patted it gratefully. They'd all worked hard today. And tomorrow, there'd be no time to rest. She needed to get Signora Loyola's dress finished in time for her dinner party.

# Chapter 21 – Legaramedi 12 Inventrici 230 Years After Implosion

Greta woke in her old bed, with the same old crack in the shutters letting in the morning light. How she'd begged Ranieri to have it fixed! She smiled sadly in remembrance of his constant reply, "If the sun doesn't wake you, how in Caldera's smoke will I get you out of bed?"

This morning she was finally grateful for the cracked shutter. The ray of sun irritated her to the point of forcing her out of bed, even though she didn't want to get up. Domizio had offered to stay the night, to help her get used to her new home, but she'd refused. Now, she regretted that decision.

Finally out of bed, Greta wrapped her warmest shawl around her shoulders and slid her feet into wool lined slippers. She walked down the hallway towards the kitchen where the girls were opening and closing cupboards, talking in such loud whispers they needn't have bothered trying to be quiet at all.

"What are you doing?" she asked, leaning sleepily against the doorway.

Sofia turned from her precarious stance on a chair, both hands opening the highest cupboards. Annika was in a corner, opening cupboards under the bench top. Marta was the only one doing anything productive – at least she'd managed to light the stove and place a kettle on it.

"We wanted to make you breakfast, Maestra," Marta replied. "But there isn't anything to eat, and we can't find your tea. We were hoping Ranieri might have some tucked away somewhere."

Greta looked around the kitchen. "Didn't any of the baskets make it into the kitchen?"

Sofia and Marta looked guiltily at each other. Greta frowned, put her hands on hips and stared at them.

"They were too busy being distracted by boys," Annika teased. "We really don't know where the kitchen baskets are. And besides, I think with everyone helping us, we ate all our food yesterday. At the most, we might be able to make you a cup of tea, but that's all."

Greta closed her eyes and took a deep, calming breath.

"Sofia, come with me downstairs to find that basket of tea. Annika, Marta, go to Delfina's Pasticceria and buy us some breakfast and see if you can't buy a loaf of bread and whatever food we'll need for the next few days. We've a full workshop now and everyone will need a decent lunch."

"Yes Maestra," Annika and Marta said in unison, running to make themselves presentable for their early morning jaunt.

Greta fetched some silvers from the coin pouch in her room and descended to the downstairs kitchenette to begin searching through the baskets for her precious store of teas. Sofia joined her soon after and they eventually located the correct basket. It took longer than she'd thought it would and her tea was not quite as warm as she'd have liked it, but at least there was tea.

Annika and Marta rejoined them back in the kitchen with their hair brushed and kept neat with carefully selected lenzas to match their work dresses. Annika's was a pale blue, while Marta's was sunset orange. They'd taken great pains to make themselves more presentable than usual this morning. Greta wondered if the move to a larger property where they weren't stepping on each other's toes made them feel like they should take more care with their appearances. Perhaps it was partly due to the fact that she was finally paying them the proper attention they deserved as her apprentices and they were proud to be a part of the Sarti Guild.

"Don't take too long," Greta instructed them. "We have a lot of work to do and a new workshop to set up."

She handed them the silver coins with a stern look. They nodded, midway between excited and dutiful. Greta couldn't begrudge them their happiness. She'd have been excited if this weren't such a strange situation to be in. She tried not to think of it as she drank her tea.

\*\*\*

By eight o'clock, Greta was attired in her favourite work dress and seated at the only clear workbench in the entire shop. The shutters were wide open, allowing in the weak winter light. When a knock sounded at the door, Sofia opened it and let in the three Copper Sarti, with Annika and Marta close on their heels.

"Breakfast is served!" Annika called out from the kitchenette when she'd prepared everything.

Greta didn't move from her workbench. She'd worked up a good rhythm of stitching for the hem and didn't want to be disturbed.

"Maestra, it's time to eat," Sofia told her.

Greta shook her head, but Sofia lay a hand on her arm, forcing her to stop.

"Maestra, *please*. You only have the hem left to do. That will only take you half a day, but you won't last that long if you don't eat something."

"Sofia, I'll be fine." Greta attempted to ameliorate her concerns.

Sofia drew away only to be replaced by Nicolina.

"Signora Sarta, I must insist that you eat something. I've seen what happens when you don't." She carefully took the needle and skirt out of Greta's hands. "Come now and eat something while we figure out how to do anything in this mess of a workshop."

Greta paused and looked around. She hadn't really cared how disordered the rest of the room was once she had her own workspace clear for her dress. Before she could say anything in reply, Sofia took her by the elbow and gently ushered her into the cluttered kitchenette.

Annika had managed to move enough of the baskets for three people to sit down. She was eating her own pastry, standing up against the wall. It no longer surprised Greta that Annika hadn't selfishly taken one of the free seats herself.

"Marta and I were talking about it on the way to Delfina's Pasticceria and we think one person should be put on un-packing duties each day, that way things get put away but work still gets done. I'm happy to do it today if you'd like me to," Annika volunteered.

Greta paused, mouth full of cinnamon and pastry, and looked between Annika and Marta. Both girls were smiling and waggling their eyebrows in anticipation of her answer. She swallowed her mouthful and nodded.

"That sounds like a well thought out plan," Greta agreed, having thought the exact same thing the night before.

Nicolina clapped her hands. "Then it's settled, Annika will start packing things away. Mizi, Pietro and I will clear some space in the workshop and sort out the standing orders so we can get to work, and Sofia can continue on her dress."

Greta barely had a chance to nod before her Copper Sarti removed themselves into the workshop to begin their task. Marta finished her breakfast first and went to help them. Annika slowly chewed her pastry and looked around the kitchenette.

"Do you mind if I start here, Maestra?" Annika asked. "That way we can eat lunch in peace?"

Greta looked around. There were so many baskets and kitchen items spread out all over the place.

"It's going to take longer than you think but, yes, start here." She stood and washed her hands carefully. "I'm going back to work. Sofia, I don't want you worrying about other orders right now. Work on your dress until it's done. Annika, are you happy for Marta to begin one pair of the matching sleeves you took the orders for on Mercatodi?"

Annika nodded without looking up from her task. Greta dried her hands and returned to the workshop where her staff were jovially clearing space for everyone else to work.

Greta sat down and resumed working on the hem at the bottom of the skirt. The stitching needed to be as fine as she could make it, or it would show through the dress. It was the worst sign of poor workmanship for the hemline to show in a satin or silk dress. Sofia wouldn't have so much trouble with her material – cotton was much more forgiving.

By the time Greta was finished, all six workbenches were clear and being worked at. Her new staff had arranged everything so that Greta's own project was hidden from view. The two shop windows had a mannequin each standing in them, dressed in Ranieri's patterns from last season. She'd need to do something about that.

Four of the workbenches were arranged around the room in pairs, which would be convenient if more than one person were working on a project. Greta's own workbench was hidden from view with the dressing room curtain on one side and three mannequins arranged carefully in front of it. These mannequins were only partially dressed in the unfinished projects her hired Sarti were working on.

The final workbench was set behind Greta's own, so she had only to turn around to help her apprentice. Sofia was busily working on her own skirt and turned when she heard Greta move behind her.

"Are you finished Maestra?"

Greta nodded. "I just need to press it and then you can help me place it on the mannequin, Fia."

Sofia readily discarded her own dress in favour of helping. She warmed the iron for Greta and waited until the pressing was done. Together, they dressed Greta's favourite adjustable mannequin. Greta fussed with the skirt until it sat perfectly, then hooked the loop thread over the large bead cluster at the back of the neck.

When she stood back to admire it, the entire workshop went silent. Greta turned slowly to see them all staring at the dress. Nicolina was the first to go up and study every aspect of it, with Pietro not far behind. Domizio hung back and kissed Greta on the cheek before she'd even realised he was there. Her cheeks burned hotly at his openly affectionate attention.

"May I stay tonight?" he whispered, tickling her ear with his warm breath.

Greta moved away from him with a smile and a small nod. Domizio glowed and stepped forward to add his exclamations of admiration for the dress before Greta covered it with a large white cloth and sent everyone back to work.

# Chapter 22 – Orodi 13 Inventrici 230 Years After Implosion

The day had finally arrived. Greta muffled a laugh as Domizio mumbled a curse at the sun. She kissed the side of his neck before getting up and wrapping a dressing gown around herself.

"It's still early," he mumbled. "She won't be expecting you until later."

"Mizi, my dear, you know how important her patronage is. I don't want anything to go wrong with this order. Well, anything *else* to go wrong."

Domizio hastily pulled on his pants and walked to Greta's side as she tied the belt of her gown.

"*My dear*," he said, moving aside a stray curl to kiss her cheek. "I like the sound of that. My dear, you know Signora Loyola adores your work. She'll not reprimand you when you bring her the most amazing dress in all of Tor'Esint. Her friends will be knocking down your door tomorrow morning, mark my words."

Greta laughed and pushed him gently away so she could tie her hair in a tight braid, keeping all her curls under control.

"Tomorrow is Mercatodi, Mizi," Greta reminded him. "Fashionable signore like her friends do not visit workshops on Mercatodi. They send their servants out to buy the latest gadgets and the best quality food for their elegant dinners."

Domizio shook his head at her. "I think you underestimate yourself. I'm willing to wager at least *two* of her friends visit you tomorrow to be the first to place their order with you."

"A wager, is it?" Greta asked, cocking an eyebrow. "And what do I get if I win?"

"A date for the Guild Ball," Domizio said with a low bow.

Greta's breath caught in her throat. The Guild Ball was still months away. The idea they'd still be together then was quite presumptuous.

"And if *you* win?" she asked, her voice barely louder than a whisper.

"I take you out for dinner, at the finest restaurant I can afford," he answered, taking her hand in his and not taking his eyes off her.

A crushing weight fell on Greta's chest. She withdrew her hand and smoothed her hair, giving herself time to speak through the pain. "That's not exactly a fair wager. You win both ways."

"Don't you win both ways too?" he asked, genuinely confused.

Greta shook her head and rose. "I have to finish getting ready. I don't want to be late."

Without giving him a chance to respond, Greta rose, selected her clothes for the day and walked out of her room, straight into the large water closet. This was what she'd missed the most after moving into her small workshop

— the claw-footed bathtub, large enough to lie down in and soak her worries away. Of course, this morning, all she had time for was to quickly shower herself instead, but that was still a more comforting experience here than in her old, small water closet.

Dressed in her finest work dress, Greta joined the girls in the upstairs kitchen. *They*, at least, were happy, chatting carelessly over their bowls of honeyed porridge.

"Maestra, we made enough for you and Domizio too," Marta said, ladling out a bowl for her and sprinkling cinnamon on it.

"Thank you, Marta," Greta said, trying to sound happier than she felt. "Sofia, you'll need your best work dress and tidy hair today. Signora Loyola specifically requested that you accompany me."

Sofia grinned broadly, her dimples deepening in her cheeks. She quickly finished her porridge and ran to their bedroom. Greta began to eat her porridge as Marta poured her a cup of tea. Domizio came in soon after, helped himself to a bowl of porridge and stood by the stove to eat it. Greta said nothing to him – she didn't even look at him. She couldn't bear to. With a final spoon of porridge and a lengthy sip of tea, Greta fled the kitchen.

Downstairs, she took a large white box from Ranieri's stores and carefully laid the commissioned dress into it, skirt first, so that the beaded bodice would be the first thing Signora Loyola saw. She closed the box gently and tied a thick navy ribbon around it, securing it for the walk ahead of them. As she waited for Sofia, she filled her work corset with the Sarta tools she might need to make minor alterations.

Once Sofia was ready, Greta gave instructions to Annika to begin work on her set of sleeves for the matching order. Today was Marta's turn to unpack baskets.

"Start with your room," Greta told her. "Unpack everything so you don't spend so long getting ready every morning. If Sofia and I aren't back by lunch, don't wait for us."

She handed the box to Sofia, and they left the workshop. It was a slightly tiring, but pleasant walk up the hill to Signora Loyola's house. When they reached the enormous villa, Greta turned to admire the view.

From here, she could see the outline of Sentigura Caldera. It was surrounded by mist, as it almost always was. Greta wondered if it was smoke from the caldera or because of the jungle humidity. She was still amazed that Aveline, Telchide and Lucrezia had travelled there. She didn't think she'd have had the courage herself.

"Are you ready, Maestra?" Sofia asked, shuffling her hold on the large box.

Greta turned back and rang the doorbell. A maid opened the door and escorted them upstairs without ceremony.

Greta had never been inside a house so fine. True, many of her clients were well off, but they often sent their maids to pick up their clothes at her workshop or took their order from her at their front door, without asking her in.

Signora Loyola was the first to invite her into her dressing room. Greta marvelled at the splendour. The floors were a polished black marble veined with gold, only found on the mainland of Azzurrina, north of Beltigura. It would have been terrifically expensive to cut and ship so much marble to Tor'Esint.

They followed the maid up the marble stairs, down a long corridor and into a large dressing room. Mirrors lined one wall and shelves full of boxes just like the one Sofia held lined another. There were at least ten hat boxes that Greta could see and just as many shoe boxes. Greta wondered if Signora Loyola already had shoes to wear with this dress.

"Signora Loyola, will be with you shortly," the maid said before leaving them alone.

"It looks like she has a different dress for every day of the week!" Sofia whispered loudly.

Greta smoothed down her dress but didn't reply. People like Signora Loyola often had enough combinations of skirts, shirts, sleeves, and dresses that they needn't wear the same outfit for months at a time. It was a wonder they remembered what they owned with so many items in their dressing rooms.

"Signora Sarta! How lovely to see you. Is my dress ready?"

Greta turned to see Signora Loyola in such a simple pale-yellow dress that she was lost for words. It was the type of dress a poor non-Guild member would buy for their daughter – not something one of the wealthiest women in Tor'Esint would be wearing. But here she was.

Sofia nimbly stepped forward and placed the box on a small table to the side of the dressing room. Greta recovered herself and walked over to the table.

"It's ready for you. If you don't mind, I'd like you to try it on to make absolutely certain everything is perfect for tonight. Has Telchide Inventore finished the music box?"

"He has indeed," she answered, untying the satin bow. "I picked it up yesterday evening. Let me try on the dress and I'll show you on the way out."

She opened the lid and froze. Greta leaned forward anxiously.

"Is something wrong, Signora?"

Signora Loyola gripped her arm tightly. Greta stiffened. "Greta, it's more magnificent than I remember. I'm almost too scared to touch it."

Releasing her breath, Greta patted Signora Loyola's hand. Slowly, the grip loosened to the point where she could move away.

"If you'll allow us, we'll help you dress," she offered.

The stunned signora only nodded in response. Greta motioned to Sofia and together they helped Signora Loyola out of her plain yellow dress and into the spectacular blue gown.

"Young signora, be a dear and open that shoe box in the corner down there."

Sofia looked startled to be addressed but went to do her bidding. Inside were heeled slippers covered in a smooth silver satin. She held them up with such reverence that Greta almost laughed, though they were extraordinarily pretty.

The slippers were placed delicately on the marble floor and Greta held Signora Loyola steady as she stepped into them. The overall effect was marvellous.

"However did you manage to find such perfect shoes for the dress?" Greta asked.

"I knew I wouldn't be able to find a Calzolaio who could match this shade of blue, so I went for the next best thing colour – silver goes with almost everything." Signora Loyola admired her reflection in the mirror turning this way and that, still holding Greta's hand for balance. "Oh Greta, I cannot thank you enough. My friends will simply swoon over this gown."

"Your custom and recommendation are thanks enough," Greta said modestly, "though I'd like to point out that it was, in fact, Sofia who worked painstakingly on the beading."

Signora Loyola paused and looked closely at the blushing Sofia. "I had no idea you'd had such an important role in this dress. That makes me even happier to give you the gift I bought you."

"A gift? For *me*?" Sofia asked guilelessly. "But ... I'm just an apprentice."

"Never say "just", child," Signora Loyola reprimanded her. "You're not *just* anything. You're a talented Sarta apprentice with a keen eye and dedication to your work and your Maestra. Now, help me out of this gown so I can show you the music box and give you your dues."

\*\*\*

"Sophia, for Caldera's sake, stop touching it!"

Sofia quickly pulled her hand away from the new jewelled trinzale Signora Loyola had gifted her. Signora Loyola had handed her the gift in her dressing room so Sofia could position it properly in the mirror.

"I'm sorry, Maestra," she said in an injured tone. "It's like the necklace you gave me. I've never had such nice things before. If I touch them, it helps me believe they're really mine."

Greta pulled Sofia close and kissed the top of her head.

"They're really yours and you deserve them. Now, stop touching them or you'll gain the attention of a thieving ash-sucker."

Sofia looked up at her and laughed. It was such an infectious sound, Greta couldn't help but join in. They quickly made their way back to their new workshop.

Nicolina, Pietro and Domizio were working on orders at separate workbenches – each using the same one they'd used the day before. Annika was bent over the same patterns Marta had used the day before for their sleeve orders.

"My, Sofia, don't you look lovely today," Nicolina said, eyeing her new headdress.

Sofia touched the trinzale again and blushed, explaining Signora Loyola had given it to her. Greta wished they wouldn't make such a fuss over it – gifts from clients were not very common and she didn't want her other apprentices to be put out. Annika glanced over and raised her eyebrows slightly at the sight but said nothing.

Greta walked past everyone to her secluded section of the workshop and sat down to begin sorting through the remainder of Ranieri's orders. Domizio came around and stood a consciously appropriate distance away from her. Greta inwardly cringed at the sight.

"I've finished working on the first of Ranieri's orders. Shall I begin on another? Or would you like me to do some of the mending, Signora?"

Greta looked up sharply. *Signora*. This would not do.

"Actually, could you help me organise some tea for everyone?"

She rose and led the way to the kitchenette without giving him a chance to reply. Only once they were behind closed doors and the kettle was on the stove did she dare speak.

"This can't continue," she said quietly.

"Yes, you made that clear this morning. *This* is finished," he replied emotionlessly, gesturing between the two of them. "I am no more to you than a hired Sarto."

Greta shook her head and took a step towards him. He did not move, nor would he meet her eye.

"Mizi, that's *not* what I meant." She bit her lip and reached out her hand to caress his face. He moved ever so slightly away from her, but she reached further until she felt the stubble of his beard against her fingers. "I meant the formality, the discord over a wager that should never have been proposed."

Domizio leaned into her hand and closed his eyes briefly. "I don't understand what I did wrong. I thought you were happy with me, or at least satisfied."

"I am. More than happy. But that doesn't mean I want all Tor'Esint to know my business. What happens behind closed doors is a different matter. I don't want to throw that away, but I don't want to parade it for all to see either."

"Who would care?" he asked in an injured tone. "Your girls clearly don't mind and if you think Nicolina, and probably Pietro, haven't guessed by now, then you're blind. Who cares if anyone else knows?"

"*I* care," Greta replied. "I don't want to be tied down. I don't want anyone expecting that of me. If we're seen together in that light, people will assume things I don't want them to."

Domizio leaned down, his face so close to hers. Greta's stomach tightened. "I'm not trying to tie you down. I know you don't want that. But I don't want to hide either. We have nothing to be ashamed of."

The kettle whistled noisily. Greta's heart beat wildly as Domizio slid his arm around her waist and pulled her in for a delicate and tender kiss. She still had her eyes closed when he let go of her and took the kettle off the stove.

She touched her fingers to her lips and turned to watch him prepare two tea trays for everyone. When he was done, he passed one tray to her and took the other himself, but paused before leaving the kitchen.

"Do we have a wager then?"

Greta took a deep breath and nodded. "I take you to the Guild Ball if I win, you take me out to dinner if you win. But you won't win."

Domizio winked as he pushed the door open with his back. "We'll see."

As they took the tea trays out, Greta saw the quick glances and small smiles, not only from her apprentices. There was no malice in those faces. The judgements were in her mind alone.

# Chapter 23 – Mercatodi 14 Inventrici 230 Years After Implosion

Greta moved around the workshop, ordering things exactly to her liking. Sofia had offered to unpack that day, but Greta had insisted she finish working on her dress. Her education was more important. Greta was reluctant to admit aloud that if anyone else had tried to order the workshop itself, she would have been constantly watching and providing direction.

When the bell tinkled, she barely paid attention until she was called to the front of the shop.

An older signore waited patiently for her, hat perched precariously on his walking stick. Greta watched from behind the mannequins as Nicolina tried showing him to one of the comfortable armchairs by the window – the man refused to sit, in the politest way. When Greta walked over to him, he offered his hand in greeting. Greta shook it firmly.

"Signora Sarta, I would like to commission a dress for my companion and a suit for myself." He hesitated at this point. "You *do* make suits, don't you?"

Greta hid a grin. "Indeed, Signore. My Maestro, Ranieri Sarto, was one of the most renowned Sarti in Tor'Esint. My work differs only slightly from his own style."

She gestured to the suited mannequin in the shop front. The man turned to look and nodded to himself.

"Very good then." He fumbled in his pocket and produced a sheet of paper. "Here are my companion's measurements. I apologise for not allowing you to take her measurements yourself, but this is to be a surprise. Will one month be adequate time?"

Greta took the measurements from him and wrote them in her order book.

"It depends on what type of dress and suit you desire. What's the occasion?"

"No occasion," he said, tapping his walking stick on the floor. "Only that she so admired Loyola's dress last night. I know she longs for a beautiful gown for herself. Not the same one, of course, but something beautiful, nonetheless. Her favourite colour is green, if that helps."

"A green gown then," Greta replied. "Allow my apprentice to take your measurements while I think of something for your companion. Please, come this way, Signore...?"

"Excuse me. Emilio di Paulo," he said with a short bow of his head.

"Signore Emilio, this way."

Greta gestured to Annika who'd been watching the entire time. Annika quickly left her sleeve project to join them in the dressing room. She deftly took the situation in hand.

"Signore Emilio, if you'll step up on this platform, I'll take your measurements."

Greta left the two of them, sat down at her workbench and opened her pattern book. A dozen ideas floated through her mind, but she finally settled on two of them. One had a wide hoop skirt covered over with a layer of chiffon and a sleeveless bodice and sweetheart neckline with a long chiffon shawl that acted almost as a cape. The other had a narrower skirt with long sleeves and embroidery all along the bodice and at the edges of the décolletage and sleeves.

"All done, signore," Annika said loudly enough to get Greta's attention.

Greta almost laughed at how well her apprentices knew her. She walked over to them with her pattern book.

"Signore Emilio, I've drawn two dresses for you to choose from. I'm not certain what style would suit Signora..."

"Forgive me, Signora Sarta, I am not used to doing this. My companion is Luisa Musicista."

Greta froze.

"Luisa Musicista?" she repeated in a whisper. "You ... want me to make a dress for *Luisa Musicista*?"

"You've heard of my companion then?"

"*Heard* of her? My papà used to take my sister and I to listen to her play," Greta gushed. "I had her violin melodies in my head for weeks afterwards."

Signore Emilio beamed. "Ah yes, her music filled the Teatro Esinta for many years. Now then, show me these dresses."

Greta pulled her pattern book up to her chest. "I can't make a dress for Luisa Musicista. These aren't good enough for her."

Her heart fractured as Emilio's face fell. "*Please*, Signora."

Greta shook her head resolutely, but Annika walked up and prised the pattern book out of her hand. Before Greta could stop her, she'd opened it to the newest designs and showed them to Emilio. Greta heard Annika's explanations in a daze, her vision closing in.

"See the lightness here, this means it would be chiffon. If you'll follow me to this wall of material, I can show you which one it is so you can make your decision."

Firm hands gripped Greta's waist and arm as Domizio led her carefully to her workbench. He sat her down and held a glass of water to her lips. Greta took small sips. Her vision slowly cleared. Domizio was sitting by her side, obscuring her view of Signore Emilio.

"Greta, Luisa Musicista is your customer's companion. All he wants is a lovely dress to surprise her. You're the best Sarta in Tor'Esint. Would you really rather someone else have the honour of creating something for her?"

Fighting down her nerves, Greta smoothed her skirt over her knees and shook her head.

"That's what I thought," he said confidently. "Now, go over there and make sure Annika helps him select the right materials for the right dress."

Greta squeezed his hand tightly. "Thank you, Mizi."

She stood slowly, letting her nerves settle. Once she felt secure, Greta walked over and took her pattern book from Annika with a short nod of thanks. Annika handed it over easily.

"Signore Emilio thinks the full ball gown is too ostentatious for his companion," Annika told her.

"Yes, lovely as it is, Signora Sarta," he hastened to reassure her. "I think she'll feel uncomfortable wearing something quite so ... grand. This other one, however, is perfect for her. But I wonder if you could make it less shiny?"

Greta glanced at the satin material behind him and nodded in understanding.

"I think I have the perfect thing. Does Signora Musicista like the feel of velvet? It's a softer material, not suited to the sort of embroidery on this pattern but it would look lovely with some black lace instead. Allow me to show you."

She quickly amended the sketch and brought Signore Emilio over to the velvet section of the wall. Ranieri could have opened a haberdashery himself with all the material he had on hand. Greta held out a length of a dark forest green velvet for Signore Emilio to feel.

Instead of just feeling it with his hand, he rubbed it against his cheek. He sighed happily and nodded.

"Yes, this is just the thing for her. She'll love it. Thank you, Signora Sarta."

"And now for your suit. Is there anything in particular you'd like?"

Signore Emilio reddened at the question. "I've always been partial to those short jackets with long back tails down to the knees. Do you think I might have one of those? With lovely shiny buttons?"

Greta grinned. "Of course, Signore Emilio. Let me take a final measurement for the length of the tails, and we'll be done."

She took out her retractable measuring tape, took the measurement from his shoulder to his knee and wrote it down in her order book. With practised ease, she quickly sketched the coat tail exactly as described and showed Signore Emilio. He took the pattern book and ran his finger along the pencil lines.

"Magnificent," he said softly, then looked up at Greta hesitantly. "Do you think it will be suitable for a vecchietto like me?"

"Signore Emilio, it will be so becoming that everyone will wonder how you ever managed to dress without it. I promise."

He closed the book, patting the cover, and handed it back to her.

"Now you *will* tell me if one month is not enough time, won't you?"

"Signore, one month will be plenty of time," Greta reassured him. "However, you *do* understand your companion will need to have at least one fitting before the dress is complete."

"Yes, yes, she'll come for as many fittings as you need. But if the dress has already been started, she can't stop me from ordering it. She never wants me to buy anything special for her and I almost always listen. But the way she looked at Loyola's dress last night." He shook his head. "I want her to be *happy* and I know this dress will make her happy."

Greta took his hand in hers. "I promise, both you and your companion will be more than happy when your new clothes are ready."

Signore Emilio looked at her, almost teary at the promise of their new, beautiful clothing. With his free hand, he patted her hand. "I believe we will be. Now, my dear, you tell me the price and I will pay you now so Luisa cannot make me undo the order when she finds out about it."

Greta made a quick calculation. The material alone would cost at least a gold, perhaps more. Then there was the time involved in making them. She should really charge at least four gold coins in total but couldn't bring herself to do that when Emilio was such a lovely man, and his companion was Greta's favourite musician in Tor'Esint.

"I think two gold coins is fair," she said firmly.

Emilio nodded easily and opened his coin pouch. He placed four gold coins in Greta's hand.

"No, that's not what I meant," she quickly told him.

"I know what you meant," he told her. "But I also know what's fair. You're a Gold Sarta after all, and even if Signora Loyola herself wouldn't tell us the price she paid for her dress, her maids were not so discreet."

Greta was at a loss for words. She'd never had a customer pay her more than she'd asked. Before she could recover, Signore Emilio had donned his hat and left her shop.

"Does that happen often?" Nicolina asked, loudly enough for everyone to hear.

Greta didn't answer. She was still looking at the retreating figure of Signore Emilio.

"Never," Annika and Marta answered in unison.

Domizio came up beside Greta. "Now that's two orders in one. Have I won the wager?"

"Absolutely not!" Greta replied, snapping out of her stupor. "The wager was two of her friends. Technically, this wasn't even one of her friends."

"Oh no," Domizio said, shaking his head firmly. "If he overheard the indiscreet maid, he was at the dinner party. That makes him a friend. Now, if just *one* more comes in, I'll win the wager."

Greta didn't have a chance to answer before another two customers walked through the door. She gently pushed Domizio towards them and went back to begin work on the new patterns.

\*\*\*

It had been so busy that day, Greta had been forced to adopt Nicolina's suggestion of lunching in shifts to ensure the shopfront was never unattended. By the end of the day, they'd received five new orders, four as a direct result of Signora Loyola's recommendation.

Greta handed her hired Sarti their wages for the week as they prepared to finish up for the day.

"I wonder if I might have a word with the three of you before you leave." Six heads turned her way. Greta sighed. "Girls, could you please make preparations for dinner, *upstairs*."

They groaned audibly but left to do her bidding. Greta waited until she heard their footsteps in the rooms above before she addressed her hired Sarti.

"Is something the matter, Signora?" Pietro asked, watching her closely.

Greta shook her head. "In fact, quite the opposite. I'm not certain if it's because we now hold the patronage of two Sarti workshops or if it's all due to Signora Loyola, but I've never had a Mercatodi quite so busy as this one. I wonder if the three of you might agree to continue working with me."

"Signora, you don't need to ask again. We've already agreed to stay an entire month with you," Nicolina reminded her.

Greta smoothed down her skirt before answering. "Yes, but I was hoping you might agree to stay a little longer."

"Of course, Signora. How long would you like us to work with you?" Pietro asked.

"Indefinitely."

Nicolina dropped her thimble. It rolled unhindered across the workshop floor.

"Indefinitely?" she asked. "You mean ... *two* months?"

Greta shook her head. "I mean as long as I have more work than I can cope with alone, as long as you're willing to stay."

"So, until the Guild Ball?" Pietro suggested.

Greta shrugged. "Or longer."

"Greta, don't forget Annika will be finished her apprenticeship next year and may even earn her Copper Guild Mark then," Domizio said quietly. "You may not need us indefinitely, especially if you hire her as well".

"Domizio, I know what I'm doing," she replied firmly. "I have plans for the future and they require hired Sarti who I can count on not to leave me at the drop of a hat. Now, are you with me, or not?"

"I'm with you," Pietro answered immediately.

"Me too," Nicolina added.

Domizio looked between them and Greta.

"Well, Mizi, what's it to be?" she pressed him.

He walked up and kissed her on the cheek. "Of course, you can count on me."

"Pietro, you can walk me home," Nicolina said. "See you two on Gildadi."

Nicolina took Pietro's arm without ceremony and escorted him out of the workshop, turning the sign to "closed" behind her.

"About this wager," Domizio said, putting his arm around Greta's waist and pulling her close. "I do believe I won. So may I have the honour of taking you out to dinner tomorrow night?"

Greta bit her lip, hesitating.

"Come now, Reta, a wager is a wager."

"Very well then." Greta ran a hand through his hair, giving in to the luxury of his adoration for her. "You may take me out tomorrow night, but only if you stay in with me tonight."

As he leant forward to kiss her, Greta moved teasingly away and held out her hand. Domizio took her outstretched fingers and followed her upstairs.